GIVE THE SIGNAL. WE GO *NOW!*

Shining Eyes lifted his feather-decorated bow and waved it from side to side. From the far side of the draw, Follows Quickly and two other warriors fired their muskets. Shining Eyes nocked an arrow, but the order had already been given to gallop. The column of troopers from Fort Canby bent low in their saddles and raced down the ravine to avoid all combat.

"They run like rabbits!" shouted Shining Eyes. He loosed the arrow at the riders, then ran with the others down to meet the soldiers, his moccasins slapping against the sun-baked sand. He launched himself at a mounted bluecoat like a mountain lion.

Shining Eyes slashed savagely with his knife, but the trooper was stronger, older, more experienced. He swung a rifle butt around and knocked the boy back, to lie flat. The soldier fumbled to draw his pistol.

Shining Eyes's heart almost exploded with fear as he realized death stalked him. Flat on his back, he saw the soldier draw his pistol, cock it, and aim. He pushed himself up, but his muscles had turned to rubber and the world spun past him. He could not move and the muzzle of the pistol was centered on him. A shot rang out.

THE LONG WALK

KARL LASSITER

PINNACLE BOOKS
KENSINGTON PUBLISHING CORP.

PINNACLE BOOKS are published by

Kensington Publishing Corp.
850 Third Avenue
New York, NY 10022

Pinnacle and the P logo Reg. U.S. Pat. & TM Off.

First Printing: September, 1996

Printed in the United States of America
10 9 8 7 6 5 4 3 2 1

May "flights of angels sing thee to thy rest."

For Patty. Always.

While it is based on actual events, this book is a work of fiction.

"One of two things will have to be done with them (the Navajos)—a total breaking up of the nation, verging on extermination, or placing them in a reserve."

James F. Collins, Superintendent of Indian Affairs October 8, 1861, *Annual Report of the Commissioner of Indian Affairs*

Prologue to War

"Too many Dinéh are being taken for slaves," Manuelito said angrily, his dark eyes fixed on the distant north holy peak of Dibénitsaa, the Big Sheep Mountain. First Man had taught that a different sort of people lived there and in the other three holy peaks, and that they were intelligent people who performed magic. They were swift of foot and far-ranging, riding the rays of the sun and following the path of the rainbow. These Holy People, the Haaschch'ééh dine'é, were to be emulated. To do so meant walking in beauty.

But for all his desire to do so, Manuelito never could be like them because his turmoil forced him from the ways of inner harmony. The Holy People were immutable and felt no pain. Pain burned in Manuelito's breast and tore at him because of *los ricos,* because of the Ute and the Zuñi and the Biligáana, those ubiquitous whites pouring over the land like the incessant autumn rainstorms. All those enemies of the Dinéh stole his people for slaves, selling them in distant Mexico or keeping them for scut work as close by as Santa Fé.

Manuelito continued staring at the cloud-capped holy mountain, considering his words carefully to influence the other headmen gathered around the guttering fire of fragrant piñon. How he wished he had the special powers of speech to sway others as had his revered father-in-law, Narbona of the Red-earth

Streaked Clan, dead these twelve years after Colonel Washington murdered him in a dispute over a stolen horse. Narbona's victory at Copper Pass, Bééschlichíii Bigiizh, had not been as effective as his fine, persuasive words. Manuelito remembered well being taken into Santa Fé with his father-in-law to speak with the Mexicans, and how he had become bored quickly with the endless dark adobe corridors and honeyed words without meaning. Manuelito had enjoyed more sitting on the street and making the little Mexicans jump at the sight of a silent, six-foot-tall, powerful sixteen-year-old warrior of the Dinéh suddenly rising in front of them. They had yelped and run like rabbits, secretly pleasing him, though his solemn expression had never changed.

Narbona had not been amused by this harmless pastime, chiding him for not learning the ways of peace as well as the thrill of combat. The Holy People, Narbona had said, gave the Dinéh their lifeways. They gave the Beauty Way to nurture inner spirit, allowing everyone to walk the world in harmony, in *hozho*. But for all those fine words passed down from a man he respected above all others, Manuelito yearned for a Blessing Way chant to protect warriors against their enemies in battle, an Enemy Way sing to infect their foes with ghosts. He wanted death brought to the enemies tearing at the corners of his world and stealing the lovely women and small children.

So much passion boiled inside him that Manuelito felt powerless to convey fully what he felt. He was pulled between diplomatic, persuasive *naat'aani*, wanting peace, and his personal desire for war. The world spun about Manuelito and confused him, tearing him away from any hope of harmony.

He forced himself to remember his upbringing, even as his fingers danced on the hilt of the horn-handled knife sheathed at his belt. Words of a chantway prayer rose in Manuelito's mind to give him strength.

My feet for me restore.
My legs for me restore.
My body for me restore.

My mind for me restore.
My voice for me restore.

The convincing words would come to his lips. The words *must* come, or the Dinéh, the People, would be driven from their traditional lands of Dinetah.

"We are warriors," Manuelito went on, after being silent for several minutes, drinking in the distant beauty of mountains and mesa and knowing holy Dinetah could never be lost. To lose it meant losing more than life. It meant losing the soul of his people. "These others must never imprison us. They enslave our women and children. The Biligáana do not honor their treaties. We sign their endless, tedious pieces of paper and suffer. We become like the deer, prey for our enemies who ignore the Biligáana and their strutting bluecoat soldiers. We respect the white man's settlements and find our own lands stolen as if we were invisible. They trespass and nothing is done. We ride through Dinetah and are hunted like animals. How can this continue?" Manuelito settled next to the fire, staring at the embers glowing from once blazing logs. The heat rising in his breast warmed him more than the dying campfire. If only the words set the other Dinéh headmen afire, too. War was serious, but survival depended on it.

Wind howled along the sheer red rock cliffs of Cañon de Chelly, finding eroded holes through which to whistle and whine like a tormented animal. In the distance a coyote howled mournfully, mocking Manuelito. He poked the fire back to life with a charred stick, but the flare quickly died again. His own fury burned all the hotter.

After several more minutes, a sturdy older headman lifted his face, his chin pointing to the four holy peaks in turn, east, south, west, and finally north, gently reminding Manuelito of the power they derived simply living in Dinetah. Only when he had finished this slow circuit did the headman speak.

"You are young and angry," countered Barboncito, Hastiin Dághá, Man with Whiskers of the Ma'iideeshgiizhnii Clan, the

Coyote Pass People. "You strike out blindly because you are youthful and impatient and see no other course of action."

Manuelito held back a furious retort, his face impassive, refusing to be disrespectful. Barboncito was a wise leader, and Manuelito owed him the courtesy of listening, even if everything within his breast and across Dinetah screamed against the words. There was a time for soft words and a time for the slashing knife. Manuelito knew council must give way to war party.

Soon.

"When have the Dinéh ever walked without opposition?" Barboncito went on. "We are warriors, and warriors have enemies. We *must* have enemies, because through them our own greatness is found. The Dinéh endure great hardship, and yet we conquer. It is our way. I question only the need to fight the Biligáana with their rifles and cannon. They are like the coyote howling in the night and break treaties, and they are not like us. Each of their headmen speaks with a different voice. Can it be that we must fight with some and parley with others?"

Manuelito straightened, his mind racing. These were not the words he expected from Barboncito. Manuelito waited while others around the fire weighed what they had heard. After a respectful time for reflection on Barboncito's carefully chosen words, Manuelito spoke, shaping his argument more for the benefit of Barboncito than for the others around the fire. He saw how they perched on rocks like so many crows, unsure whether to fly or roost. If Barboncito followed him, the others would, also.

"What honor is there in dying like a rabbit, a *gah* refusing to come from its burrow? How can we abide knowing our women and children toil in the Mexican fields along the Rio Puerco? Is there beauty in the Biligáana seizing our land? Can we trust those who believe words on paper are to be obeyed while their tongues pour out lies? Fort Defiance is a festering sore on our body, keeping us from living in harmony with our land."

Manuelito saw the subtle shift of Barboncito's feet, the way the other headman reached to touch the hilt of the knife sheathed at his belt, unconsciously duplicating Manuelito's gesture. Manuelito had so much more to say but held back from voicing those fiery words. Barboncito's thoughts traveled the path Manuelito desired. Too much argument now might cause the older headman to reconsider.

Barboncito cleared his throat and asked in a firm voice that rang along the cañon walls and far into the night, "When can the Enemy Way sing begin?"

Cool breeze blew across Manuelito's back from the direction of the Chuska Mountains and a coyote spoke mournfully, warning of danger. Manuelito cocked his head to one side and listened as the Little Wind whispered encouragement in his ear. The coyote brought danger not to the Dinéh warriors this night but to the indolent Biligáana. He shook his head slightly to settle the mountain lion skin battle helmet adorned with carefully gathered eagle and owl feathers. He glanced around to assure himself all was ready for the attack. It was four hours until dawn and through the night's obscurity moved shadows within darker shadows. He lifted his bow and motioned toward the somber hulk of Fort Defiance, still slumbering like an unsuspecting cow. Straining to detect any mistake that might betray the onslaught of Dinéh power against the interlopers, Manuelito paused for long minutes. Even his keen ears failed to hear the sound of moccasins moving swiftly across the sun-baked earth, but Manuelito knew all around him a thousand Dinéh warriors converged on the hated fort.

Running lightly, he kept the dark adobe section of waist-high wall in sight. If a Biligáana soldier appeared above the wall, Manuelito would loose an arrow. Manuelito sneered when no one stirred; their sentries were neglectful. Probably asleep, he thought. Their discipline was as lax as their ways were devious.

Too many times the treaty of 1858 had been broken—and Bonneville's Treaty had allowed the Biligáana to steal much precious land. But the end of patience had come when those in the fort had tried to kill headman Agua Chiquito in January. Chiquito's cleverness alone had allowed his escape. Now Manuelito would see the bluecoated soldiers pushed back to Santa Fé, out of Dinetah. Dropping to the ground and sitting with his back against the cold adobe, Manuelito waited for others to join him.

"Do you have the rope?" he asked in a low voice. A young warrior, José Gordo, thrust horsehair rope into his hand. It took several minutes for a fire to be struck and the frayed end of the rope to be ignited. It smoldered sluggishly to a bright coal in the night, signaling the others all was well.

Coming to his feet and peering over the wall intended to keep small animals inside rather than warriors out, he selected his target. Manuelito stepped back, judged the distance, and tossed the flaring rope with a heavy rock attached directly onto a wagon bed. For a moment, nothing happened. Then the wagon exploded into twenty-foot-high flames that lit the parade ground like day.

Manuelito threw himself over the adobe wall, joined quickly by José Gordo and then the others. Distant murmurs of alarm rose from the sleepy soldiers. Those muffled sounds were drowned out by Manuelito's war whoop. He jumped past the blazing wagon and shot an arrow, the shaft flying straight and true into the chest of a Biligáana soldier blundering from a barracks.

Behind Manuelito crowded dozens of Dinéh warriors, spreading out through the expansive interior of Fort Defiance, firing arrows into anyone daring to stir. The few sleepy sentries making their rounds were the first to die. Manuelito knew there would be others. Soon. He wanted them all to die within their strange hogans, infecting them with *chindi,* the spirits of the dead. The entire fort would have to be abandoned then, or the bluecoats would risk ghost sickness.

The first ragged volley from Biligáana muskets prompted Manuelito to signal Barboncito, still outside Fort Defiance. Those warriors within the fort now crept along close to the ground, under the shelter of flying arrows, seeking safety from the gathering wrath of the bluecoat soldiers. Manuelito directed his warriors in the direction of the fort's woodpiles and low fences, using them as barriers against the increasingly deadly rifle fire. Manuelito ducked low and spun about, seeing a sentry behind him. The man—hardly more than a boy—stood clutching his musket, shaking so hard he could not properly tamp in the charge. In the dancing ghost light of the fire, now spreading to nearby structures, Manuelito saw fear and shock on the youth's pimply face.

Manuelito also saw the suffering of his own people and the perfidy of the whites. He lifted his bow and let fly an arrow that sent the young soldier to the ground with the feathered shaft embedded in his leg. The boy's cries of pain vanished quickly as an unblooded Dinéh warrior rushed over and drew a knife across the screaming stripling's throat. In the fierce light, the blood leaked out black, thick, sluggish.

Manuelito whooped in glee at the newly tested warrior. He remembered his own blooding so many years earlier against a Pueblo fighter. After that battle he had known he was no weak creature and had been called Haskéh Naabaah, Angry Warrior. That feeling of his first kill returned to Manuelito as he whirled, loosing one arrow after another. The fearful force of a thousand warriors drove the Biligáana soldiers from their barracks and back to their small kitchen and laundry. For an hour they fought, slowly crowding the surviving soldiers into smaller and smaller areas. One brave soldier succeeded in firing the cannon next to the flagpole, but in his rush he had forgotten to load the cannonball. A huge gout of flame licked out. As it set fire to dry grass it did more damage to the parade ground than to the attackers. The soldier died quickly as he turned to flee.

Resistance stiffened and many of the Dinéh began to shrink from the attack. They had reduced Fort Defiance to a burned-out husk that would wither and blow away with the approaching dawn. Many soldiers had died; few Dinéh had given their lives in the overwhelming attack.

But this was not enough for Manuelito. Prowling like the cougar whose skin helmet he wore, he hunted for any man not huddling within the two buildings. He flushed one from the ruins of the stables. The soldier rose up, his face dark with smoke and dirt. A thrown pitchfork caused Manuelito to swerve from his vengeance, giving the man the chance to bolt and run like a rabbit.

Recovering, Manuelito rushed after him, overtaking the half-clad fleeing soldier a dozen paces from the safety of the laundry. All around there cracked rifle shot after rifle shot, but the Dinéh war chief paid no heed. Manuelito tackled him, forcing him to the ground. His hand closed easily on the horn handle of his knife, but the trooper proved no easy adversary.

"You heathen!" the soldier grated from between clenched teeth, as he heaved and twisted. For a moment Manuelito was unseated. He rolled to one side and came to his knees, still clutching his knife.

The soldier kicked out, but Manuelito slapped the booted feet to one side and dived forward. His knife rose high, caught a hint of dawn, then plunged downward. The blade glanced off the soldier's upraised arm and then sank into exposed chest. Blood exploded from the wound, and Manuelito knew one less bluecoat would steal their land.

He pushed the body away and grabbed hair. He took a scalp and held the sandy thatch high in the air as he vented a heartfelt cry that combined hurt for his people and victory over his enemy. Sharp pain along his chest staggered him. Manuelito turned and faced the laundry where from the windows a dozen musket muzzles protruded—all aimed at him. A slug had opened a narrow channel on his chest, causing blood to flow slowly.

The pain focused Manuelito's attention on the battle. His anger must not overshadow the need to direct his clan. Others of his clan, the Folded Arms People, surged around him.

"Fire!" Manuelito called, waving to José Gordo. "Give them fire!"

José Gordo immediately broke off his attack and faded back,

taking several warriors with him. Scrambling away, Manuelito stood in the center of the fort's parade ground, firing arrow after arrow into the laundry. The adobe walls were too thick to penetrate, but he frightened those within. More than one rifle barrel vanished from its loophole never to be replaced.

Then came the real assault. José Gordo fired the first arrow. After that, Manuelito could not say who of his clan fired. Arrows carrying rags dipped in pitch arched upward and landed on the rooftops of the remaining buildings. Manuelito saw that Barboncito entered the fray with all the fervor of a brave warrior. Arrow after arrow left the older headman's bow. Each arrow sent its deadly message. Fear the Dinéh!

They would never be forced from their holy lands!

Soon the raging fire challenged the rising sun in brilliance, but the Biligáana soldiers did not surrender. They fought like wounded bears even as their fort burned around them. Manuelito had hoped for a total victory but saw this was denied him. Even against a thousand warriors and surprise, the blue-coated soldiers fought well.

He knew it was time to leave. The battle had lasted over three hours. The soldiers crowded into only two buildings, seemingly impervious even to the fire arrows. Before long the officers would take command of nearby cannon. The Dinéh could never stand against such firepower; pitting bow against musket proved increasingly treacherous. But if complete victory eluded Manuelito now, the Biligáana would never recover from the destruction of Fort Defiance. They had no stomach for real battle. Manuelito signaled for the warriors to slip away, to return to the vastness of Cañon de Chelly.

"Bucket brigades!" came a shout from the direction of the officers' quarters. Manuelito hesitated at this cry for action, nocking another arrow. No flashing gold-braided officer showed, and none of the men hiding in the laundry foolishly obeyed the order to put out the fires while their enemies remained inside their fort. Manuelito lowered his bow and vaulted the low adobe wall surrounding Fort Defiance.

A thousand voices lifted to the morning sun, voices chanting victory even as the thunder of their horses echoed across a revitalized nation. Manuelito smiled grimly. These were the sounds of his people, the sounds of the People. From within the fort came angry cries and the deafening crackle of fire spreading and men dying in flaming agony. He tipped his head to one side and smiled with real anticipation when he heard the confused, contradictory commands shouted by Biligáana officers. The time for the final coup neared.

"North," Manuelito urged his warriors. "North to our homes!" Manuelito had to chevy reluctant warriors to keep them moving away. They smelled the fear and defeat in the bluecoats, but Manuelito knew it was folly to remain any longer. His warriors would begin dying in larger numbers when the officers regained control of their troops. Manuelito had no fear of the bluecoat soldiers, but he did not want them to use their muskets and cannon—especially the cannon.

Manuelito could not forget how Colonel Washington had used cannon to kill Narbona. The soldiers and their rifles Manuelito would willingly face, but the cannon . . .

"Barboncito," Manuelito called, riding hard to catch up with the older headman. He got Barboncito's attention and motioned him to the north and east, toward Chuska Valley. Barboncito nodded, knowing their carefully devised plan would work. Soldiers would follow carelessly—into a new trap.

Manuelito and Barboncito rode slowly, then separated their forces, one going east toward the sun and the other west, each finding a position along opposite walls in the gentle, low-walled cañon. Their dust clouds had barely died when the bluecoated soldiers rode hard to overtake their attackers.

Two companies gave reckless pursuit, and the ambush went better than Manuelito could have hoped. When the commanding officer saw the arrows coming from his left, he ordered the men right, into Barboncito's warriors. Finding no shelter, the Biligáana officer led his men in full retreat. His company was cut to bloody ribbons by their own men, the second company trailing at a distance and not knowing who shouted and raced toward them.

Blood ran in thick rivers, and the thirsty land drank deeply.

It was a good day for the Dinéh, the first of many throughout the summer.

Raiding

Joseph Treadwell shifted his muscular five-foot-eight body, stamping frostbitten feet on the frozen riverbank, his pale blue eyes staring intently into the San Juan's clear depths. It had been well nigh an hour since he'd seen a trout, and his belly grumbled something fierce. What gnawed at him even worse, he knew his nine-year-old son was close to starvation. And his wife, Gray Feather, was three months pregnant. She never said much about the hardships she endured, but Treadwell felt her suffering more acutely than his own. The deer had vanished, and even scrawny rabbits were few and far between because of the intense cold and heavy snows that blew constantly off the Sangre de Cristo Mountains. Treadwell scratched a nit gnawing at his groin and stood, groaning as his aching joints protested the movement.

"Ain't gettin' no younger," he grumbled aloud, no longer caring if he frightened off the wary fish. He shook himself like a wet dog and sent sparkling snowflakes every which way into the air. Tiny rainbows shone in the wan winter sunlight, but Treadwell paid this minor glory no heed. His hunger was getting too powerful for any appreciation of nature. He wasn't much of a fish tickler, patiently waiting for an incautious trout to poke up its ruby-throated head before grabbing it with a single deft motion. Gray Feather was expert at it. He had seen her grab an entire day's meal in less than twenty minutes. But this wasn't for him.

He was a mountain man. He ought to be hunting bear or setting traps for otter and beaver, but trapping just wasn't as profitable as it had once been, what with all the fur animals being killed off and nobody back East much caring about beaver hats anymore. He shook his head in wonder. Fashion. Why had they liked beaver hats, anyway? Nobody could give Treadwell an answer to that. Almost in desperate refusal to acknowledge their declining markets, the mountain men's last rendezvous up at Green River had been a corker of a celebration, or so he'd been told by the old-timers he had run across. Some of them remembered—or lied about remembering—William Ashley and his first rendezvous back in '25. The later shindigs, at Pierre's Hole in the Bitteroot Valley or those at Ham's Fork along the Green River, weren't much less memorable.

Treadwell sighed. Memories stalked him as he had once stalked cougar and bear. There had been meat and fur galore for any man willing to work to get it then. No more. This winter was too cold and the snow too deep, and there were too many settlers pushing in from the East.

Treadwell pulled a plug of carefully hoarded tobacco from his pouch and bit off a healthy chew. He owed himself the moment's pleasure brought by the ropy tobacco. He was always missing out just by inches, it seemed to him. He was too young to have been a part of the summer rendezvous when they had been rip-snorting, whiskey swilling events that kept the mountains buzzing for a full year till the next one. A few years back Treadwell had met Jim Bridger—leastwise, he almost had, when he had worked his way through Wyoming's South Pass hunting for bear. Bridger hadn't been at his trading post, but Treadwell had a hint of what the man's remarkable life must have been from all the trophies on display for God and everyone to see.

Spitting, Treadwell left a steaming brown hole in a snowbank. He hefted his Hawken rifle and put its cold barrel over his shoulder, ready for the long hike back to the Tabeguache Ute encampment. Teaming up with the Ute had been the best thing ever to happen to him. Treadwell owed them much, beyond finding among them a good woman to bear him children and to provide for. In a way, Treadwell realized how unlike many of the real mountain men he was. They didn't just enjoy the long, lonely months spent in the wildness; they *needed* the solitude. The rendezvous were a chance to blow off some steam, but having to deal with other men—or the civilization inching in from all sides—wasn't possible for most of them.

Treadwell enjoyed the hunting parties with Gray Feather's brother, Long Tooth, sitting around the campfire spinning wild yarns, joking and envying them their clannish community. He had been with the tribe going on ten years, and still he felt an outsider. Treadwell spat again and moved the rifle to his other shoulder, rubbing the spot where it had rested. Arthritis had set in and not even the Ute medicine man could do anything about it with his chants and herbal potions.

Tramping along at a brisk pace, he found himself wallowing in memories that were even less comforting. The Ute were polite, more because of Gray Feather than anything else, but they would never accept him as one of their own. He would never belong fully—anywhere. Treadwell wasn't sure what had happened to his parents. Dead, that much he knew. He had spent his childhood drifting from one distant relative to another until he ran out of kin and patience. Nobody in Saint Louis had much missed him when he had lit out at fourteen to find that bumblebee Frémont had written about so movingly on Frémont Peak, maybe the highest mountain in the Rockies.

Treadwell smiled crookedly and rubbed crystalline snow out of his beard. That was another way he was different from other mountain men: he had learned to read and cipher. The tales of Frémont's expeditions scouted by men such as Kit Carson and Basil Lajeunesse had pulled him out to the Wind River as sure as a compass points north. He snorted in disgust at the little he had done since arriving on the frontier, sending silvery plumes exploding from his nostrils. For all the good his dreams had done him, he might as well have stayed in Saint Louis, pawing through garbage to stay alive. Still, Treadwell reflected, times would get better come spring. And there was Shining Eyes, and Gray Feather, big with another child.

"Wouldn't be so bad havin' a daughter what looked like Gray Feather," Treadwell decided, although another son would add to his prestige among the Tabeguache and do its share of building his own spirits. Life was hard this winter, but it'd get better. Having another son would make it that way.

Trudging up a steep slope, every step breaking through icy crust on the snowbanks, Treadwell quickly gasped for breath. Even living in the mountains did nothing to improve his stamina. He was like Frémont in this way. Altitude sickness got to him, giving him a light head and alternating bouts of euphoria and depression.

"No food," he decided, spitting again. That was what made him weak in the knees and dizzy in the head. He could keep up with the best of them. Even Long Tooth said so, and he was the unequaled hunter and fighter in their small company. Treadwell dropped the butt of his long rifle to the ground and leaned on it, fighting for breath. Freezing tendrils gusted from his nose and mouth and caught on his damp beard, turning it to feathery ice. He batted away the icicles, knowing the penalty of not doing so. His chin had been frostbitten more than once this winter.

Over his stentorian breathing came faint cries that made Treadwell stiffen.

"Now, who'd be makin' such a fuss?" he asked aloud. Only the echo of his own words answered. This sudden stillness was more ominous than if he had heard the shouting continue. Treadwell swung his rifle up once more, continuing his trek to the top of the hill to get a better view of the valley beyond. New sounds drove him forward at a pace that left him gasping by the time he had crested the ridge.

Treadwell went as cold as the arctic northern wind when he spied the Navajo raiding party making its way along the snow-packed cañon floor. The Navajo had ambushed a Tabeguache foraging party and massacred the lot of them. Treadwell saw how the white landscape had turned red—and that none of the Ute had survived the attack. How could they? They had been hunting for roots, not plunderage. Treadwell doubted any of them had been armed with more than the knives sheathed at their waists.

He pulled up the Hawken and sighted down the long octagonal barrel. Sunlight glinted off the front sight, making accuracy difficult. The range was too great, even if he had been the finest shot in the world, and the wind! The accursed wind was blowing down from the upper slopes with its teeth of ice and steel. But Treadwell didn't intend to inflict any damage. He wanted only to frighten off the Navajo raiders and warn other Ute of the danger stalking their peaceful valley.

The rifle kicked back and almost knocked him off his feet. He sloughed in the frozen mud and regained his balance. Treadwell squinted a little to see where his bullet had flown. He cursed, seeing how he had missed by a country mile. Although he hadn't reckoned on hitting any of the conniving bastards, he had hoped luck would be with him.

The Navajo pointed upslope toward him, then moved together into a tight knot to discuss his unexpected appearance. Treadwell let them talk while he reloaded. Just winging one of the warriors would do for him. The heavy .60-caliber slug would bring down a grizzly. Treadwell had heard tales of a bullet merely passing by a man's head and killing him. He wasn't sure if they were true but he hoped he could find out. If the next round narrowly missed—but still killed—it might continue on its deadly way and find another raider's body.

Two with one shot. Treadwell could only dream.

Before he had finished the chore of reloading, the raiders hurried off and mounted their horses. They galloped deeper into the cañon, and Treadwell cursed even more.

"Come back here, you murderin' savages! You piss your own pants, damn you, you—" Treadwell found himself caught between firing into the empty distance or going after the marauders. The Ute encampment lay in the direction the Navajo had ridden, and Gray Feather was there.

"Shining Eyes," he groaned, starting for the site of the massacre. His boy had ventured out hunting for something to throw into the family stew pot. Every step he took caused Treadwell's anguish to rise even more. His son might lay on the frigid ground with his throat slit by a Navajo knife.

Slipping and sliding down the hillside, Treadwell got to the cañon floor and rushed to the ambush site. The ground had turned muddy, not from melting snow but from hot blood. Gelid droplets splashed onto his knee-high moccasins until he thought he was in a slaughterhouse. He reached the first fallen Ute and saw the man's head had been nearly decapitated by a single savage cut going from ear to ear. Blood had spattered in a wide fan-shaped pattern and melted down into the snow. How could one human body hold so much blood? But Treadwell's eyes drifted to another corpse, drawn inexorably. He stared, wanting to look away, but paralyzed and refusing to believe the evidence before him.

"Long Tooth," he croaked out from a mouth turned to cotton wool. "Dear God, how am I going to tell Gray Feather you died like this?"

Long Tooth hadn't been given the chance to defend himself. His knife remained sheathed at his left hip. Treadwell's brother-in-law had perished without any struggle, taken from behind.

"They fell on you from the cottonwoods," Treadwell said, noting that the only tracks leading away were Navajo. To this spot he had seen only the familiar imprint of Ute moccasins. The raiders had lain along the thick overhanging branches long enough for a light snowfall to remove evidence of their approach.

Treadwell took a step toward Long Tooth, then spun and ran from the battleground, the slaughter ground where six fine men had met their deaths. They deserved a proper burial, but it would have to wait. His pale eyes fixed on the far end of the U-shaped valley, and his legs pumped hard to get him into a ground-de-vouring stride. The altitude wore on him and caused his heart to pound like a war drum, but Treadwell wasn't going to stop. Better to die than to let the Navajo raiders capture Gray Feather and his son.

Better for them to die, he thought. Treadwell couldn't bear the notion of his wife and son being captured and turned into slaves serving Navajo masters. He had heard the stories spun by the Capote Ute, always at war with the Navajo, and Treadwell believed them. The Lords of New Mexico, they called the Navajo.

"Arrogant bastards," Treadwell grunted, as he struggled along. "Why are you raiding the Tabeguache? We don't raid south."

The run seemed unending, but the rise outside the Ute camp came upon him with unexpected suddenness. Treadwell halted, his rifle lifting to find a good target, a good *Navajo* target. Only smoldering ruins and dead bodies showed beyond the muzzle of his Hawken. Treadwell lowered the rifle and walked down the slope, alert for any movement that might betray an attacker. He remembered how the Navajo had murdered Long Tooth and the others. Joseph Treadwell wasn't going to fall victim to another such perfidious trap.

The dull crackle of fire eating away at hide tents was the only sound other than the growing whine of wind through a nearby stand of tall ponderosa pines. Treadwell entered the camp cautiously, his stomach churning at the sight of so much death. Like the foraging party, those in the camp had not fought back. They had been taken by surprise. This told Treadwell that the small band of Navajo he had seen made up only a part of the raiding party.

"You swine," he hissed. The people who had taken him in and accepted him as one of their own lay dead all around him. And Gray Feather . . . where was she?

"Gray Feather!" he shouted, spinning in a full circle, eyes going wide with renewed fear. "Shining Eyes! Where are you?"

"Help," came a weak voice. "Help me. Pagowitch. Pago-witch!"

Treadwell rushed to the edge of the camp and found an old woman, Many Skirts, huddled over and clutching her belly. The thin trickle of blood told Treadwell she had been severely wounded. As Many Skirts looked up at him, he saw that she had been gutted and held herself in only by sheer will and shak-ing hands.

"Where's Gray Feather?" he demanded. Many Skirts was a goner. There was nothing he could do for her, but his wife and son . . .

He had to find them.

"Pagowitch," Many Skirts repeated, as if telling him some-thing he didn't know. Treadwell nodded brusquely. The raiders were Navajo. He had seen them. "They came upon us and stole away our young boys. And women. They took the young women, too."

"What happened to Gray Feather?" Treadwell forced himself not to grab the old woman and shake her. She had watched her people die and was dying herself, but if she didn't tell Treadwell what had become of his wife and son, he might finish the job the Navajo had begun.

"So many of them, riding down on us. They stole our horses, our boys, killed the men. There was no chance, no hope." Her face turned sallow with shock from blood loss. Treadwell stood and stared at her, knowing there was nothing he could do to make her talk. She had paid with her life already.

"What of Taiwi?" he asked, steering her in a different direc-tion. She would tell him of her son.

"Dead. They chopped him down like a tall pine. But your son, Shining Eyes, fought like a man. He fought, oh, how he fought the Pagowitch." Many Skirts rolled onto her side and shivered once before dying.

Treadwell reached down and closed the eyes that had seen too much abomination today. In a way, he envied Many Skirts. Her fight was over, even if the Navajo had won. She would find a better land to walk than this freezing cemetery. Treadwell rushed back to where his tent had stood. Even the seasoned poles had burned to charcoal. Poking carefully, Treadwell sought the body of his wife and son.

After ten minutes of sifting through the ashes, he hadn't found them. He wasn't sure if he was glad or not. Many Skirts had said Shining Eyes had fought like a man. That made Treadwell proud. How he wished he hadn't been down at the river, tickling fish like an old woman! He should have been here to defend his family, to show Shining Eyes how to fight the damned Navajo!

A quick tour through the encampment convinced Treadwell that Many Skirts was the only survivor, albeit an accidental one. The raiders had been efficient in their butchery. From the way the ground was cut up by dozens of horses, Treadwell guessed that the Navajo had numbered forty or more. Such a major foray meant they were after more than a small band of Tabeguache Ute.

Treadwell hunkered down and studied the tracks, looking up slowly to the peaks in the distance. The Navajo rode north, deeper into Ute territory. Treadwell had heard the rumors of Moache Ute raiding south into Navajo territory. Ute and Navajo had been mortal enemies since the dawn of creation, and since the assault on Fort Defiance had forced the Army to retreat the Navajos had become bolder than ever. Treadwell knew he ought to turn south and find Taos to report this to Carson, since that erstwhile scout was the Indian agent for the Moache and Tabeguache Ute, but he knew his destiny lay in another direction.

If he didn't find out what had happened to Shining Eyes and Gray Feather, he would go crazy. His resolve hardening, Treadwell scrounged through the debris and put together a pack to keep him on the trail for a week or longer. He cursed the Navajo anew when he saw how efficiently they had looted the camp. And as he searched, he kept a tally of the dead.

"Eight," he said with feeling, repeating the number of the missing women and children over and over. His wife and son were among them, kidnapped by the war party. They had to be. Treadwell wouldn't believe they had been killed—and he would never allow them to be taken so far that he didn't try rescuing them. His pack in place, he began the long hike after the Navajo.

Just past midnight, tired to the bone, Treadwell found the Navajo camp.

Their cooking fires guttered low, but the fragrance of burning piñon carried a long way on the cold wind. He dropped his pack and reluctantly placed his rifle on top of it. The work he had to do would be hindered by the long musket, not helped.

Fingers lightly touching the knife at his belt, he dug in his pack for a second blade. Treadwell drew it and held it high. Its silvered length would be bloody before he finished—and he would be reunited with his family.

"No revenge, no killin' just because they're bastards," he reminded himself. Getting back Gray Feather and Shining Eyes was all that mattered. Then they could figure out how to free the other prisoners and bring the raiders to justice. Treadwell knew Kit Carson wouldn't cotton to such forays into Ute country. As Indian agent, it was his duty to prevent such occurrences. Although the cavalry had pulled back from Fort Defiance and Fort Fauntleroy, there were enough troopers left to punish the Navajo, no matter that war brewed back East.

Such thoughts vanished as Treadwell crept closer to the enemy encampment. The aroma of roasting meat made his mouth water and his belly grumble. His forced march hadn't allowed him time to do more than chew on a piece of jerky that had tasted more like rawhide than edible meat. Treadwell pressed his face into the cold ground when a sentry drifted past, a war-painted ghost floating on the night wind. The Navajo warrior paused for a moment, sniffing the air. The cooking odors masked Treadwell's scent and the guard walked on, never knowing he had been within a few yards of a new mortal enemy.

Treadwell, his face covered with mud, slithered forward to

get a better look at the camp. He had approached from the far side, away from the remuda of stolen horses. For that he thanked his lucky stars. The horses would have betrayed his presence in an instant.

The Navajo strutted about, boasting of the day's victory. Treadwell was startled at one warrior, a six-foot-tall, well-built Navajo carrying himself with the regal authority of a king. The man stood and spoke loudly to gain the attention of the others in camp.

Seeing an opportunity to find the prisoners, Treadwell moved away and circled, wary of other sentries.

"You have fought well this day," boomed the tall Navajo headman. "Particularly José Gordo and my brother Cayatanita. Each killed four Nota-a warriors in combat."

Treadwell paused in his slow creep around the camp. Those two bastards had killed eight of his friends and relatives? His hand tightened on the knife until his knuckles turned white.

"And you, my brother Manuelito, you have fought even better." The one named Cayatanita lifted his chin and pointed in the direction of the makeshift corral. "Nine horses you stole today. And a woman with her son."

Treadwell almost reared up and shrieked in rage when he saw Gray Feather and Shining Eyes just beyond Manuelito. They were securely tied and staked to the ground near a small guttering campfire. From the remains of the meal, Treadwell saw the Navajo weren't starving their captives, but Manuelito's tone left no doubt about the fate of Shining Eyes and Gray Feather.

Slaves. The headman had claimed them as his personal slaves.

Treadwell's stare moved to Gray Feather and was held there by her beauty. She sat impassively, her face expressionless, and her eyes staring into the darkness. She betrayed nothing, as was fitting for a brave Ute woman. But Shining Eyes spat at anyone nearing him. Two warriors tormented the boy as they would a chained dog, poking him with their bows and drawing back as he tried to kick and bite.

Sinking back down into a shadow, Treadwell tried to deter-mine the best way of freeing his family. It wouldn't be done easily. The Navajo celebrated their victory and boasted of new and bigger conquests in the coming days. Manuelito spoke of atrocities committed against his people by the Ute, but they paled in comparison to what the Navajo had done to a small band this day.

He couldn't succeed if he attacked directly. Treadwell settled down, half sleeping and half passing out, waiting for his opportunity. It had to come when the fires died and the raiders went to sleep. Just before dawn would be the best time to creep closer and free Gray Feather and Shining Eyes. Then they would escape . . . somehow.

Treadwell jerked awake, aware that he had slept for hours. Too many hours. It was almost dawn, and the camp would be stirring. He cursed his exhaustion even as he rejoiced that the lookouts had missed him repeatedly as they'd made their circuit around the camp. Rubbing the sleep from his bleary eyes, he hefted the knife and worked closer to Gray Feather. She sat with her arms around drawn-up knees, belly pressed into her thighs to protect her unborn child from the cold. Shining Eyes slept fitfully on a Navajo blanket, his own distinctive Ute patterned blanket covering him, but his wife maintained her vigil.

"Gray Feather," he whispered. She did not respond. "Gray Feather!"

This caused her to turn. Her eyes went wide with recognition and her lips silently said, "Joseph!"

He scuttled forward and lifted the knife to cut the rawhide straps binding her. But Gray Feather cried out, and Treadwell saw the reason.

In his haste to free her, he had become careless. The one Manuelito had named José Gordo reared up from where he had slept only a few feet away.

"Nota-a!" the Navajo cried, thinking Treadwell was a Ute.

Before José Gordo could give another warning cry, Treadwell swarmed over him, knife slashing. The Navajo recoiled and stumbled—and this saved his life. Treadwell's blade missed

opening the warrior's belly by a fraction of an inch. A thin line
of blood appeared, showing how close Treadwell had come to
gutting José Gordo as the Navajo had done to Many Skirts.

"Joseph, run for your life! There are too many of them. They
come for you!" Gray Feather's warning fell on deaf ears. Treadwell would die rescuing her before he allowed Manuelito and
his followers to have her and Shining Eyes.

A strong hand clamped on his wrist, forcing his knife away
from vital organs. José Gordo gritted his teeth with the effort.
Treadwell rolled on top of the man, pinning him with his knees.
He stared into dark eyes and saw the tombstones there, the grave
markers for Many Skirts and Long Tooth and Taiwi and all the
others.

José Gordo was strong. Treadwell was stronger. He drove his
knife down into the Navajo's throat. A spurt of blood marked
the end of a murderous ambusher and woman killer.

"Here," Treadwell called to Gray Feather. He threw her the
bloody knife to free herself as he reached for the other knife at
his waist. The blade landed just beyond her reach—but not too
far for Shining Eyes to grab. The boy saw his father and the
knife.

The nine-year-old seized the knife and clumsily turned it
around to saw at his bonds.

This was the last sight filling Joseph Treadwell's vision. He
never saw the arrow that spitted him from behind. He toppled
forward and lay facedown in the snow, pink froth bubbling from
his mouth. The last Joseph Treadwell remembered was the world
swirling away into deep, impenetrable shadow.

Prologue to Defeat

February 15, 1861
Fort Fauntleroy, New Mexico Territory

"So many," grumbled Manuelito. "They swarm like ants. Everywhere we look, the Biligáana are there creeping about, nipping our flesh and stealing our food. They are worse than the Ute and the Zuñi *and* the Apache all taken together."

"But the Ute and Apache eat dogs," Barboncito said in a quiet voice. His dark eyes studied the array of gold braid and swords dangling at the officers' sides. "The Biligáana . . . who knows what they eat? Perhaps they eat their own young. It would explain much of their behavior."

Manuelito laughed without humor at the other headman's joke. He stood on the rocky rim of a deep, parched arroyo where water would flow in a few short months. But now the land was as dry as his spirit. Manuelito stared into the wintry distance but saw nothing of the fierce storms bringing a new white blanket to the mountains of Dinetah or the sharp lightning bolts that occasionally etched new paths through the slate sky. Manuelito saw only suffering. He raged uselessly, wanting to call the thunder's name even if it caused the lightning to come after him.

For a full year he had fought the whites, but they were too many, far too many when other enemies of the Dinéh entered the battle. The Ute had begun their unceasing depredations when

Fort Defiance was abandoned after Manuelito's attack. He could not reckon the number of slaves the Ute had stolen from the Dinéh, nor did he want to try. He had avenged some of those kidnappings and had killed many Ute, but they were now like thistles on the wind before his might, drifting away when he grabbed for them but returning to stick maliciously in his blanket if his vigilance lulled.

How could he fight the Ute when the Zuñi were always snapping at his ankles like a mad dog? Even the Comanche dared to raid from farther east. And the Nakai! The Mexicans had declared endless war on the Dinéh, taking many women and children for slaves.

Manuelito tried to remember when last he had pitched a camp to play with his nephews or make love with his wife, Juanita, and not been disturbed by Ute or Zuñi raiding parties. The Dinéh were strong and proud warriors, and these were their traditional enemies. But his resounding words and hot temper had unleashed a force beyond any he had expected when he had led the attack on Fort Defiance.

The Biligáana had been nothing. Any Dinéh warrior was more than a match for even a squad of the smelly, anxious bluecoated soldiers who tempted the gods by pointing this way and that with their stabbing fingers. Manuelito laughed as he remembered the times he had led entire companies of flustered soldiers in circles, confusing them and getting them lost in the Chuska Mountains or along Chinle Wash. They were their own worst enemies.

And yet they won, as a continual drip of water cuts a hole through even the hardest stone. The Dinéh fought on all sides. Not only did they fight Ute and Zuñi and Apache, they fought the bluecoats. Any casualty, by honorable death either in battle or capture, diminished their rank. But always there were more soldiers, new bluecoats come from the east to fight. They were inept warriors, but they returned with more of their muskets and accursed cannon. Easier to catch the wind and hold it in his hands than to continue fighting the Biligáana.

"We must do this thing, even if it burns our pride," Barboncito said behind him. Manuelito nodded in abject agreement.
The other headman spoke to the point, answering his unspoken
misgivings. Sometimes, Manuelito thought Barboncito read
minds. He had seen the man hunting the deer, following paths
too faint for a dog to find. When the chase began, Barboncito
kept up a steady pace, as if he knew every move the deer might
make, left, right, ahead. In the hunt, Barboncito always won.

So it was now that Manuelito listened to Barboncito's words
of peace.

"We beat them," Manuelito said sadly. "We beat them in
battle, and there was nothing they could do. We outstripped
them in every skirmish, and yet they won this war." He fell
silent as he stared in the four directions, finally settling his gaze
on the purpled shapes of the Lukachukai Mountains. He drew
no power from the wind blowing in his face. It was always so
with Yellow Wind from the treacherous north. The airy messengers of the gods living in the Holy Mountains sent him no encouragement now, no words of advice whispered in his ear by
a Little Wind. There was only a towering dust devil in the distance, a wind turning sunwise to bring misfortune down on his
head.

"Every day there are fewer in our clans," Barboncito said.
"Relief from war is the only way we will recover our strength.
They steal our cattle and destroy our food. There is no way we
can be strong with an empty belly."

"The Biligáana have never honored their treaties," Manuelito
protested. "We went to war because of their faithlessness. Why
will this time be different?"

"Canby speaks of a different world," Barboncito said, "but
it is a world where there are Dinéh—and Dinetah."

If true, Manuelito would listen to the bluecoat officer's words
of peace. Preservation of their holy land was foremost. Without
it, what use was life itself? The Dinéh drew power from the
land, from the holy mountains, from sky and earth and the gods

around them. Had not Changing Woman given them the Blessing Way and the means to walk in beauty?

Manuelito worried that he still received no soft sigh from a Little Wind in his ear to satisfy him that a treaty with the Biligáana was the proper road to travel. He looked at the ground and saw a lizard moving northward—not a good omen. In the north lay only darkness and the entrance to the underworld, with all its dangers.

"The Biligáana must force our enemies to obey their treaty, also," Manuelito said, his decision made. Barboncito was right. They had no choice but to sue for peace with the whites. Only in this way would the Dinéh successfully fight the Zuñi and Ute and Apache, holding them in their place. It was too big a burden fighting them and the bluecoats together, even with the whites' diminishing presence in Dinetah.

A rattling of swords and the rhythmic sound of marching bluecoats brought Manuelito about. How the Biligáana loved their pomp, with trumpets and angry drums and men walking in step, doing everything simultaneously and in a rush. Better to do things in harmony than in bustling conformity, thought Manuelito. But these were not his people or his ways.

"Canby is more than he appears, Manuelito," Barboncito said softly. The strutting officer thrust out his chest filled with colorful ribbons and glittering medals and motioned for a table to be set in front of him. Then a squad of soldiers marched up behind the assembled headmen, each bluecoat carrying a chair. The uncomfortable chairs were placed in a wide semicircle facing the table where Canby stood at rigid attention.

Manuelito did not require Barboncito's words to know the depth of this Biligáana officer. Canby fought like a true warrior, warring even in winter, something the whites had not done before. Manuelito glanced both left and right. Arrayed in front of Canby's table were twenty-four Dinéh headmen, the most powerful within the boundaries of their realm. They seemed as confused as Manuelito about the chairs immediately behind them.

"I see you have gathered all your great chiefs for this peace conference," Canby said without preamble, without the words that showed veneration for tradition. Where was *hozho?* Manuelito held back angry words. Canby stared at them boldly, not giving them the respect they were due, yet he did not go blind. Not only Barboncito but Herrero, Delgadito, Armijo, and Ganado Mucho were present to pledge their support for peace. The bluecoat officer might be a gallant fighter, but compared to the Dinéh headmen, he was an insect. Less! Canby said something more that Manuelito did not hear.

Barboncito whispered, "He acknowledges the two thousand Dinéh camped outside his fort." This was said with a chuckle and put Manuelito more at ease with the colonel. The man *did* recognize Dinéh power, after all, even if his ways were discourteous. Canby tried to lock eyes with each of the twenty-four headmen but had no patience to pursue this impertinence, and yet he was the best of the bluecoats. All the headmen agreed on that.

Manuelito fought to understand the strange ways of the Biligáana. How was it Canby cut his hair so short and yet thought clearly and well?

"Please, chiefs, be seated and we will begin negotiations." Canby made a sweeping gesture indicating the headmen should sit. Manuelito lowered himself hesitantly. The chair was as uncomfortable as he had thought it would be, but only when they were seated did Canby pull his sword to one side and seat himself. In this he showed manners befitting a man of his rank. But as quickly as those thoughts crossed Manuelito's mind, Canby worked to eradicate the silent honor given him by brusquely launching into terms of the treaty.

"You will stop all acts of aggression against the Pueblos and New Mexicans," Canby said, reading from a long paper in front of him. The cold wind caught the edges, and Canby lowered one elbow to hold the fluttering pages in place. "You will accept the authority of the government of the United States."

"We—" Manuelito was silenced by Ganado Mucho and Barboncito. He bit his lip and fought to control his anger. *He* would never allow his clan to be put under the white man's heel!

"Further, you will make war on other chiefs who continue to raid. You will not permit these *ladrones* to live in your country. Finally, all Navajo desiring peace will assemble west of this fort and live there until the entire territory is again at peace. Are these terms acceptable?"

"What of the Ute and Zuñi? They steal our women and children. What of the Nakai?" Manuelito could not keep from blurting out the things foremost on his mind. "Can we not fight them?"

Canby cleared his throat, and his hot eyes bored directly into Manuelito's. The Dinéh headman averted his glance politely, caught himself, and insolently locked eyes in challenge with the cavalry officer. For some reason, this arrogance on Manuelito's part softened Canby's response.

"The government of the United States is aware of your problems," Canby said, his delicate words dancing about the real issue. "We will render you such assistance as necessary for all tribes to enjoy true peace."

"What of our homeland?" Manuelito continued to stare arrogantly at the colonel. Canby smiled a bit now, perplexing the headman. Why did he accept such an insult without responding angrily? Truly, there was much to be learned about the Biligáana.

"We will begin withdrawing troops after the treaty is signed. Dinetah, as you call it, remains yours. Your homeland is safe from incursion by others."

Manuelito averted his eyes again and waited for the others to question Canby about the details of the policy. He was eager to leave and return to his wife and clan. There was considerable work to be done, now that the Biligáana agreed to no longer fight. The talk went on endlessly, but Manuelito waited until Canby shot to his feet and briskly saluted the gathered headmen. Manuelito stood and stared at the gold-braided officer with a mixture of wonder and contempt. This was the man who had brought the Dinéh to their knees?

Canby did a smart about-face and marched off, amid drum-rolls and the blare of shining trumpets. Manuelito heard the others muttering among themselves about the details of the treaty. He had little time for such talk now. He quickly walked from the fort and mounted his horse, riding west. He had heard enough to know he could again graze his sheep on the land around Fort Defiance. And he would. That irony was not lost on the other headmen, though Canby had not seemed to know the architect of Fort Defiance's destruction.

Manuelito rode toward the large encampment of his people, threading his way through the cooking fires and ignoring the chatter from the children and women, all demanding word of the treaty. He saw only the cooking fires of his family. Several of Cayatanita's sons rushed out to greet him, but he quickly pushed his nephews aside and looked for his wife and children.

"Are we at peace?" Juanita asked sarcastically. Narbona's daughter had inherited much of her mother's fire—and sarcasm. She, like her mother, had often asked for complete eradication of the Biligáana. If only it were so simple, Manuelito thought. If all he had to do was wave an arm and the whites would vanish from Dinetah forever!

"We will never be at peace," Manuelito said, listening to the uncontrolled sobbing coming from inside the small hogan set up for the duration of the peace conference. "Does she still cry for her lost husband and brother?"

Juanita turned from him disdainfully, not answering. She chased their children back to tend the sheep they had brought with them from Cañon de Chelly. It was Manuelito's duty to tend to those captured in battle. Manuelito could do with Gray Feather as he saw fit—and her boy child. They had been taken prisoner fairly and ought to do as he ordered. He went to the hogan door and hesitated.

Dealing with Canby seemed easier.

Entering the low-ceilinged dwelling, he knelt beside Gray

Feather. On the other side of the woman, hidden in a fine blanket, lay her son, Shining Eyes. The boy lived up to his name. His eyes were bright as the moon on a cloudless night and dry, filled only with anger.

Manuelito sat and waited a moment before speaking. "It has always been so," he said carefully. "Women tend the home fires, weave blankets, cook the food. Men go to war. Some die in battle, others are triumphant."

"You killed them!" blurted Gray Feather. "You killed my husband and brother!" She bit her lower lip, then fell silent, as if refusing to show any more emotion. The tears continued to well in her dark eyes, as they had for over a month since the raid on the Ute encampment. Manuelito had never been sure who had shot her husband, that Biligáana mountain man, nor did it matter. He had lived with the Ute, who had constantly raided into Dinetah. That made him as guilty as any of the other Ute with their Dinéh slaves.

"You are a beautiful woman," Manuelito said after some thought, "and you show great bravery. Both you and your son are worthy of inclusion in my clan, the Bit'ahni, the Folded Arms People."

This took Gray Feather by surprise. Her eyes widened and she shook her head. "No, I am Tabeguache Ute."

"You are my prisoner. Would you be sold to the Nakai? Or to the Pueblos? You know how they treat *their* captives." Manuelito saw that Gray Feather did know. Few who'd been sold into the service of the Nakai lived longer than a year. They died in the fields from exhaustion—or in filthy brothels from unspeakable diseases and mistreatment.

"The Dinéh are not cruel."

"The whites call you the Lords of New Mexico," Gray Feather said, some of her sorrow gone. "Many times my husband has called you that."

Manuelito frowned. He was unsure how to take this. An insult? Or recognition of the power of the Dinéh?

"I am *naat'aani,* headman of my clan and responsible to no

one, but I am no Lord of New Mexico." Manuelito frowned more deeply. The conversation took an odd turn he had not anticipated. "As headman, I do what is best for those I lead. It is my duty. I perform it well and am respected by other headmen."

"Let us go free," Gray Feather begged. "Let us go back to our people."

Her condition told Manuelito any travel for Gray Feather would be dangerous. She was beginning to show. The winter months were always the worst for the women, pregnant or not. This season had proved a great hardship on everyone because of Canby's destruction of so many cattle, sheep, and grain reserves.

"There is no one to greet you. Your band is gone, eradicated." Manuelito felt a swell of pride. He was sure the Tabeguache Ute had been responsible for the deaths of an uncle and several nieces, not to mention the taking of prisoners. The Ute were cruel taskmasters. All those they had kidnapped as slaves were dead, but Manuelito bore this woman and her son no ill will.

"I would have you as my wife and your son as my own," he said. "This is a great honor—and without my protection, you cannot survive until spring."

Gray Feather did not answer, nor did her son. Manuelito saw the fear and apprehension in their stern resolve beginning to crack. Gray Feather was an intelligent woman, and beautiful. Only through the marriage he proposed would she and her children be guaranteed a secure future. And only through the treaty with the Biligáana could Manuelito be assured of wealth enough to provide for a second wife and family.

Gray Feather nodded slightly, and she stopped sobbing. Manuelito rose and left the hogan, one problem solved satisfactorily. He greeted Barboncito and the others as they rode into camp. The headmen had much to discuss concerning Canby's treaty.

First Shots of a New Battle

April 23, 1861
Taos, New Mexico Territory

Christopher Carson sat on the porch of his home, surrounded by adobe walls in the Spanish courtyard style, carefully cleaning his rifle. He pulled out the cleaning rod and sighted down the smooth bore to be sure the last traces of corroding black powder grains were removed. He would need the trusty musket soon and didn't want anything to interfere with its accuracy.

"Kit," called his wife, Josepha, "there is another Indian knocking on the back door. Are you going to let him in?" The apprehension in her voice mixed with annoyance. Josepha cared little for the Ute coming in a continual stream to their home. And he shared a little of her exasperation, though there was nothing he could rightly do about it. He had complained to the superintendent about Indians entering the white settlements, but policy dictated there would be no agency buildings in Indian country. As the Indian agent, Carson had to tend to his wards' needs somehow. Traveling about the territory seemed a better solution to him, although it took him away from his family for long months. He could visit the Mohuache Ute encampments and see firsthand the problems they faced over the bitter winter without having evidence dragged to his back door. Kit wished he could simply call this fine adobe house his home and not burden his wife with business—and those who tramped to see him.

He put away the ramrod and patches for his musket, then fastened a pouch of musket balls, powder, and caps onto his belt. The rifle would see use before sunset, Kit feared—and it had nothing to do with the unrest stirring among the Indians. Without realizing it, he strained to see the flagpole flying Old Glory in the plaza to the west. The high adobe wall blocked his view.

"I'll see to him 'fore I go on over to the fort," he called to his wife. "Have you done as I ast?"

"Is it necessary to take such precautions?" Josepha came to the door, frowning hard. Her attractive face reflected concern for more than her family. It took in all her neighbors in Taos. "Disturbing the children . . ."

"It's downright necessary, Chipita," Kit said, using his pet name for her to soothe ruffled feathers. "Trouble's brewin' bad, and there ain't a whole lot I kin do about it 'cept run out and meet it head-on."

Josepha half turned, then stopped. She was undecided about his appraisal of the mood in Taos. President Lincoln had declared on the fifteenth that insurrection existed in the United States and had asked for 75,000 three-month Army volunteers. The news had spread like wildfire, reaching New Mexico Territory quickly, especially since the Butterfield Southern Express stagecoach schedule had been disrupted. Gossip always traveled faster than any mail. The line had been drawn in the sand, and Josepha Carson knew her husband too well. He had scouted for Frémont and listened to that worthy's opinion as if God Himself spoke. Not that it took any officer back East to tell Christopher Carson that he owed allegiance to the United States of America and its duly elected officials.

"Will it be as bad as before? When Governor Bent was killed?"

Kit knew the terror his wife had experienced during the revolt in 1847, when the territorial governor had been scalped and murdered in his own hacienda. Josepha had been there with the governor and his family and had helped Mrs. Bent and her children escape by digging through an adobe wall with fireplace tools.

"Might be," Kit allowed, swinging his musket around and leaning it against the wall just inside the door. "Folks got their dander up over the Texans movin' on Mesilla like they done. Can't rightly tolerate incursions like that, and folks here are up in arms over it. Leastwise, some are. Too many support the rebels, fer my likin'."

Kit scratched his stubbled chin, then smoothed his bushy mustache. He leaned past his wife and peered into a looking glass to be sure he was presentable enough. Blue-gray eyes stared level and sure, and his shoulder-length auburn hair, done in what he called "à la Franklin mode," looked to be clean enough and free of tangles. Tending the Indians was a chore at times, but he had found easier success dealing with their woes if he showed a well-composed face to them.

"If it wasn't for them being Texans moving up the Rio Grande, do you think the Territory would stay neutral?"

"Not if I have anything to do with it," Kit said firmly. He settled the buckskin shirt on his broad shoulders. He might be only five-foot-four, but he seemed larger because of his confidence. People noticed him when he entered a room, even if he never had much to say. His old friend John Frémont had commented on it, and Frémont's lovely wife, Jessie, had delighted in showing him around Washington, D.C. Kit missed those days, but not as much as he did the times he had scouted for Frémont on that worthy explorer's expeditions across America.

He would give his life for his good friend John Charles Frémont. And he would die fighting to preserve the country he loved.

Kit swung open the rear door and saw a scraggly Ute looking half past starving to death.

"You poor man!" cried Kit. "Come on in. I'll see that you git fed. What's happened to you?"

The brave stumbled in and sank to the floor beside the table, sitting cross-legged on the floor. He turned bright, feverish eyes up to Kit and said in Ute, "He's hurt real bad. Needs more help. I did all I could but—"

"My wife will see that you're tended to," Carson replied fluently in the man's tongue, his mind already turning to the meeting with the Taos garrison commander. The captain had sent a message the night before warning of possible Confederate rebel activity in the town.

"Please, Red Clothes, please," the Ute begged, calling Carson by a name used by Indians who had seen his woolly red underwear and been fascinated by them. "Not for me. My friend needs help. He can't walk much."

"You eat, then we'll see to yer friend. Is he far away?" Kit asked. Seeing his wife enter, Kit switched to Spanish and said, "Let him take the wagon out back, if that would help get his friend back here."

Josepha silently handed over a large hunk of coarse, stale bread and a bowl of thin soup. The Indian savagely attacked the food, as if he had gone without for the entire winter.

"I tole him—"

"I heard, Kit. I'll send Paco with him to fetch his friend. We can set up a small infirmary at the far end of the house." Josepha sighed. This was not the first time her husband had taken in strays. With war threatening, it wouldn't be the last, either.

"You get a'movin' on the other chore I set for you," Kit said, unwilling to air dirty laundry in front of a red man. He was always aware of the narrow road he walked as Indian agent. He pitied the poor wights, even as he tried to help them. It would never do letting them get too involved in civilized concerns.

Especially one as far-reaching as civil war.

Kit returned to the door leading to the inner courtyard and hefted his musket. It took almost a minute—thirteen careful steps—to load the weapon. Only then did he feel a mite better. With his rifle resting comfortably in the crook of his left arm, Kit set off to find the commander of the Taos garrison.

As he walked slowly from his house toward the plaza, Kit noted tiny knots of men gathered in doorways. They fell silent as he walked past, then resumed muttering among themselves. The hair on the back of his neck began to rise, as it always did before he got into a fight. He turned and walked north, toward the garrison. The few men greeting him did so with less than their usual bonhomie. They were guarded and as nervous as a long-tailed cat lying next to a rocking chair. Carson understood the dilemma facing them.

New Mexico Territory was part of the United States and had been since the Mexican War. The Gadsden Purchase gave clear title, no matter how much the Texans disputed it. Kit snorted in disgust. To listen to the Texicans, as they called themselves, coming through Taos, Texas owned all the land north to Canada. And maybe their squaw talk had them claiming everything all the way to the Yukon.

More to the issue, Carson sympathized with his neighbors who wanted to stay neutral. Let the fight back East pass them by. Don't choose and maybe no one'd get hurt.

He understood their stand, but it wasn't his. The Union had to be preserved. His hand tightened on the musket even as his resolve turned to steel. Carson stopped in front of the garrison gate, noting how the guards peered down at him—along their rifle barrels.

"I'm here to see yer cap'n!" His words echoed along the street, toward the plaza. Kit saw men scuttling back and forth, some vanishing inside buildings. Such behavior was unusual this early in the morning. Something was brewing, and Kit surely did not approve of it.

"Come on in, Kit," called a lieutenant, tugging open the squeaking garrison gate a few inches. "The captain's waiting for you in his quarters."

Kit nodded, squeezed past and heard the heavy door slam behind him. His hometown was becoming an armed camp, and he didn't like that. Struggle as he might, Kit couldn't remember the last time that garrison gate had been closed and barred while the sun was up over the Sangre de Cristos. Not since the 1847 revolt, at least.

He hurried up the steps to the post commander's office. He knocked and heard a faint "Come!" from inside. Kit lowered his rifle and placed it just inside the door before going to the commander's desk.

A tired man looked up, staring at the Indian agent with hot bloodshot eyes. Kit had never seen the officer looking so haggard. If he hadn't known better, he'd have thought the captain had been on a week-long bender, swilling potent Taos Lightning. In the time he had known him, though, Kit had never seen him take more than a polite sip of hard liquor.

"I'm glad you got my message, Mr. Carson. Thanks for coming by. Things are getting desperate."

"How many in Taos want to throw in with them rebels?" Carson wasn't one to mince words, and long speeches tired him out something fierce. He pulled up a chair and perched on the edge, his back ramrod straight. "I ast around and nobody'd own up to Southern leanings. But then, they know my persuasion."

"Might be as many as one out of every four wanting to secede, but they're a loud bunch and make out like they're more. Can't rightly say if they're just Texans or if their sympathies run deeper." The captain rose and began pacing. "I've got St. Vrain on his way. I sent him out to recall a patrol the instant I heard of possible . . . trouble."

"You reckon they'll try takin' control of town?" asked Carson. "That's mighty bold of 'em, if true."

Gunfire from outside brought both men around. The officer rushed to the door, threw it open, and shouted, "Lieutenant, what's going on?"

"Sir, St. Vrain's back, and he's been shot at! The troopers with him returned fire!"

Kit Carson grabbed his musket and rushed out. "What are we goin' do, Cap'n?" he asked.

"Don't know. Might be best to secure the garrison and then

decide." The officer came to a halt when his scout rode into the parade ground at the head of a ragged column of cavalry.

"What went on? How many fired at you, St. Vrain?" The captain's face was flushed and his hands shook. Carson didn't like that. The officer might do something rash and let the matter get away from him if he didn't calm down a mite.

"It was an accident, Captain" Ceran St. Vrain said, dismounting. The mountain man shook himself and sent a cloud of dust into the air from his battered buckskins. "One of your men's rifles discharged accidentally. There might have been another shot, or it might have been just an echo from the discharge."

"What did you see along the way?" Kit asked the old scout. He knew St. Vrain and the man's loyalties. Back during the revolt, St. Vrain had stood steadfast beside Kit to maintain order. "Any sign of rebellion?"

"There's a small group of men down the street, near the plaza. My good friend Smith Simpson's watchin' 'em real close. I didn't see what drew them, though I thought I saw—" St. Vrain bit off his words, as if not sure he ought to relate his experience.

"Go on, man!" cried the captain. "What did you see?"

"They was takin' a flag to the plaza. I reckon they want to lower Old Glory and put up their own flag." St. Vrain scratched himself and added, "Can't say that's what they were headin' over there to do, but it looked it to me."

"They will not!" raged Kit. He pushed past the scout, storming toward the gate. "Open up! Nobody's goin' to strike the flag of the United States while there's breath in my body!"

"Lieutenant," called the post commander. "Prepare to defend the garrison. You, Sergeant, form a squad of men into double columns. We're marching to the plaza!"

Kit was glad to have the commander moving to back him up, but he was already hurrying for the plaza, St. Vrain matching his short, quick strides beside him. The other mountain man coughed and wiped his nose on a buckskin sleeve.

"You up for a scrap?" Kit asked his friend.

"Kit, I'm *always* ready to dance. I don't have much love for most of them Texicans. Don't reckon I'd go out of my way to waste a bullet on 'em, leastwise without good reason. But I'm not lettin' them get away with anything!"

Kit had good reason. He pulled back the hammer on his musket, glad he had brought it with him. He and St. Vrain couldn't hold off much of a crowd, but the captain was bringing up his troops real quick.

"Kit! Ceran!" called Smith H. Simpson from a doorway. "They're gathered around the flagpole. I think they're fixin' to tear down the flag."

Kit exchanged a quick glance with St. Vrain. They were of a mind.

"Not gonna happen, Smith. Not if we have a say."

"Count me on your side, Kit," Simpson said, hefting his musket and resting it on his shoulder so he could march along beside the other two mountain men.

Kit Carson swung around the corner and stopped at the edge of the plaza. The cottonwood flagpole flying Old Glory was being pulled down and two men held a hurriedly sewn flag with what looked to be bars studded with stars, in the fashion of a St. Andrew's cross. They moved to put it up in place of the U.S. banner.

"Wait," Kit said, pushing down St. Vrain's rifle. The older mountain man would have plugged the man dragging the U.S. flag off the flagpole. "We don't want to start a riot, just knock some sense into their hollow heads."

In a louder voice, Kit said, "Don't go doin' anything you fellows can't back up." He lifted his rifle and aimed it squarely at the Texan leading the group.

"Kit, don't go getting yourself involved. We voted, and we want to stand with the South!" The man took a step forward. Carson's finger drew back slowly and his musket kicked hard. The man's hat went spinning into the air.

"Git that flag of yours off the *United States of America's* flagpole," called St. Vrain. He wasn't aiming to miss with his round, and the Texan knew it. The man held up his hands, as if this would stop the .50-caliber ball from ripping through his body.

"You three boys ain't gonna stop us. We outnumber you—" The man bit off his words when the captain arrived with his dual columns of troopers, in a formation intended to give the impression of more men than he really commanded. The tide had changed from favoring the Southern sympathizers to favoring the Federals.

"Our flag will not be struck," Simpson called. His short legs pumped hard to get to the flagpole.

"I don't ever want to see it pulled down off that pole," Carson said, pointing with the muzzle of his rifle. "Cap'n, you think your men could stand guard to be sure Old Glory continues to fly where it belongs?"

"It shall be done. Lieutenant," snapped the commander, "see to it. I want a squad standing honor guard in the plaza twenty-four hours a day. The flag of our great nation will *not* be lowered."

Kit started reloading, but those trying to put up the Southern flag were already slipping away, sneaking off through the far corners of the plaza. The danger had passed—for the moment.

"That showed 'em," boasted St. Vrain.

"It'll be a cold day in hell 'fore they think to drag *our* flag in the dust," chimed in Smith Simpson. "Think we'll see any more of those dogs?"

"For now they'll go lick their wounds," Kit replied. "We got to keep watchin' or they'll creep up on us when we least expect it."

"You thinkin' on joinin' up, Kit?" asked St. Vrain. "The President ast for a volunteer company. You'd make one fine officer, one I'd be honored to serve under."

"Military life's not for me," Kit said, puffing with pride at his friend's trust in him. He was even happier when Smith Simpson echoed similar sentiment.

"I've got my job as Indian agent to tend to," Kit said, noticing the wagon rattling along the street. His servant Paco held the reins, and the Ute fed in his kitchen crouched in the rear, tending someone. "And I see my good offices are needed."

Carson waited until Simpson had pushed the flagpole erect again, and the soft morning breeze whipped the red, white and blue flag out in its full magnificence. He hurried the few yards east to his house and went inside, running through the courtyard to the rear, where Paco and the Ute pulled a white man from the wagon bed.

Kit Carson had seen his share of dead men and this one looked to be deader than most. The front of his shirt had been soaked with more blood than any man ought to have in his body, and a crude, dirty bandage had been wrapped about his barrel chest. The square face was pale and drawn, pinched from shock, but the eyelids fluttered open to reveal pale blue eyes and the man spoke in a strong, clear voice. "Glad to meet you, Mr. Carson. What can you do to get my wife and boy back from them kidnappin' Navajo Indians?"

Before Carson could reply, Joseph Treadwell had passed out.

Sea of Enemies

May 8, 1861
Near Cañon de Chelly

Manuelito stretched mightily, trying to work the soreness from his broad shoulders. He had been too long astride his pony, and the war party had found too many enemies. Everywhere he looked, he saw only those willing to fire their muskets or drive their knives into his belly.

"We are being followed," Follows Quickly said. The young warrior glanced over his shoulder, scanning the rugged terrain behind. Here and there a few patches of snow remained from the harsh winter, but it was not the cold that made Manuelito shiver.

"Dinéh Ana'aii," he said softly, "those of our own blood who betray us to our enemies follow."

Follows Quickly blinked in surprise. He had thought his headman rode along the trail oblivious to all that went on around him.

"Who leads them?" demanded the young brave.

Manuelito shrugged. Who led the band of Enemy Navajo mattered little to him. He wished they were wiped from the world, not even their blood remaining to soak into the thirsty desert sands or to stain the rocks red. His hand moved to the knife at his belt when he heard a coyote howling. This was not a good omen—but for whom? Who rode across the coyote's path?

He shivered again. All Dinéh might so travel.

"We can fight them. They would kill us all, given the chance."

"Never! We are too strong!" roared Follows Quickly. He lifted a captured musket high above his head and shook it defiantly. Manuelito wished the fiery young warrior had ammunition for the weapon. Many muskets had been taken from Fort Defiance but no bullets or black powder.

Manuelito shuddered at the thought of the fort's cannon firing on them. It had taken long hours for the bluecoats to swallow enough of their fear to organize and swing their cannon about, but when they had there was no way any Dinéh warrior could stand against it. He hoped the treaty with Canby would put to rest such worries.

"We are Dinéh," Manuelito muttered to himself. "We must walk in beauty again. Honor must be served." He swung about on his horse and saw the faint traces of the Dinéh Ana'aii behind them. Manuelito was no fool, no young buck stalking his first kill. If he saw traces of the Enemy Navajo behind, then they were like the wind, blowing transparently in other directions. He lifted his chin, closed his eyes and took a deep breath. Like the needle of a compass, he turned slowly, listening, catching spoor on the sharp spring breeze, using senses other than sight to find those who stalked them.

"That way lies danger," Manuelito said, pointing out a small cañon meandering away to the east. They rode for the sanctuary of Cañon de Chelly but dared not enter and allow the Dinéh Ana'aii to find their clan's main encampment. He turned his pony's face and trotted in the direction he had indicated. Confused, Follows Quickly let out a yelp.

Manuelito never slowed his pace, nor did he urge his horse to more speed. Eyes fixed on a point directly ahead, he rode until he came to the lip of an arroyo. Dirt crunched beneath his pony's hooves, causing small slides to the rock-strewn dry gully below. Only weeks ago it had flowed with runoff from the mountains. But now it carried the last traces of harsh winter snows.

A harsh winter and a harsh foe.

"I would talk," Manuelito said in a level voice. From the tangled roots of a greasewood emerged a stocky Dinéh Ana'aii. The warrior wore dirt on his face to protect himself against wind and spring sun. He stepped away from his hiding place, war lance in his left hand. He lifted it and shook it in Manuelito's direction.

"I would kill you!" the warrior shouted.

"Is this how Sandoval's followers act?" Manuelito arrogantly stared at the warrior, further infuriating him. "I had thought better of those of the Totsohnii Clan, the People of the Big Water."

"Sandoval was born near Tsoodzil, what the Biligáana call Mount Taylor. Is that our land any longer?" demanded the warrior.

"We would make it so. What do the Dinéh Ana'aii seek? Your land back? Or to be the slaves of the bluecoats? Is that what they promise you to hunt down those of your own blood? Will you always act as if you have no relatives?"

"No!" The warrior shook his lance in Manuelito's direction. "We seek peace. You make war. We would honor the treaty, as Sandoval decreed before his death. You wage war against the Ute, range onto the eastern plains fighting the Biligáana, make trouble among the Pueblo. Is it wrong for us to oppose such hostility? You violate the treaty with Canby."

"You fight your own people," Manuelito said simply. He had nothing further to say to this traitor. The Biligáana used the Dinéh Ana'aii as scouts—and worse.

"We have no quarrel with you," the warrior said. "But we will if you continue your aggression. Leave the Biligáana alone. Do not fight *los ricos*. Let the Zuñi and Acoma harvest in peace. Abandon your fight against the Nakai."

"Peace," sighed Manuelito. Such a fine sounding word and one that always slipped away as water through the fingers or sunlight across the face. "We would live in peace, if *they* would leave us alone. We seek only to raise our sheep and watch the peaches grow in our orchards. The Biligáana will not let us remain on our land. You, of all people, should know that."

"We will again live on the slopes of Mount Taylor. They have promised us this in return for our loyalty."

"May it be so," Manuelito said carefully. "But consider the price you pay for the return of your clan lands."

Follows Quickly and the others riding with Manuelito spread out along the banks of the arroyo. The hot-headed warrior leveled his useless musket and drew back the hammer. The cocking sound echoed along the ravine with ominous warning. The result caused Manuelito to sigh again.

A dozen Dinéh Ana'aii rose from their hiding places in the arroyo, arrows nocked and pointed. Manuelito saw that this battle would be over quickly; the Dinéh Ana'aii would remain on this land forever if any of them loosed even a single arrow. All Manuelito's clan were still keyed up from their battles over the past ten days. These Dinéh Ana'aii had fat around their middles, from too much easy dining at the feet of the Biligáana.

"Wait!" The warrior Manuelito faced held up his lance and stayed the flight of arrows that would start bloodshed that neither side truly sought. "We will deal with them later," he called.

"You may pass through Dinetah," Manuelito said. "You will always be welcome—as Dinéh, not as spies for the Biligáana or as traitors. Let this be your choice. But remember—if you follow in Biligáana footsteps, you will become crippled!"

"Superstitions don't sway us!" The Dinéh Ana'aii spat, then moved away. The others went with him.

Manuelito stayed on the arroyo bank until he heard the thunder of hooves. Only then did he slump a little. The Dinéh fought their enemies. It drained him to know he now had to fight his own people. Sandoval had been a great leader, deserving of the title *hastiin* more than many who had trod the holy ground of Dinetah, but his sympathies had lain more with peace at any price than with walking in beauty. Or so Manuelito thought.

"We could have killed them. Why do you let them escape?"

Manuelito did not turn to Follows Quickly. Brashness made

the young warrior invincible in battle. Time would temper this fearlessness with wisdom. Manuelito hoped time and circumstance would allow this great transformation.

"Dinéh bloods flows through their veins, whether they ride for the Biligáana or tend their flocks in Cañon de Chelly. We will not kill our own people."

"They are traitors! They are no better than—"

"We can be with our families before sundown if we ride hard," Manuelito said, rudely cutting off the tirade. He had no desire to discuss the matter further. He might have fought the Dinéh Ana'aii and won, but every casualty in that fight would have been one of the People. A strong wind from the south kicked up as he turned into a red-rock cañon with tall steep sides. Here and there on the sheer sides grew tenacious plants, but Manuelito's eyes were straight ahead, along the floor of the deep cañon.

Branching valleys went in both directions. Many were box cañons, perfect for trapping anyone foolish enough to venture into Cañon de Chelly with evil in his heart. Red sandstone spires rose two hundred feet tall, blunt daggers aimed not at the sky but at any who entered Tseyi' uninvited. Manuelito kept on the main floor for more than an hour, his war party slowly drifting away as they passed hogans and orchards. Sheep began bleating, announcing Manuelito's arrival. From a large hogan, its door facing east so that bad luck would never be able to enter, came a trim woman, followed by a youthful warrior. Sight of the young man brought a smile to Manuelito's lips."

His son, Manuelito Segundo, looked more like him every day.

But to his heart came real joy when he dismounted and walked to his wife, Juanita.

"You are not pleased," she said, seeing his dour expression.

"I am pleased to be home," he said, meaning it. "War wears on me when I ought to be home. How goes the hunting?"

"Well," answered Manuelito Segundo, "only this morning I ran down a deer. We will eat well all week. I left the antlers and hooves for good luck."

"You did not feed the deer meat to your dog?" Manuelito accused.

"No, I want to get more meat!" Manuelito Segundo seemed offended that his father thought he would risk bad luck by feeding the mangy dog that followed him everywhere.

"Good," Manuelito said, the burden of leading his war party slipping from him now that he had returned home. He walked about, listening to Manuelito Segundo tell of the hunt, taking pride in how well his son had learned. Manuelito's brother, Cayatanita, had done well in his instruction. On the next war party, Manuelito Segundo would accompany him. Learning to hunt was important. Manuelito feared that learning the ways of war would prove even more valuable for the Dinéh.

Turning from his son, Manuelito walked along the hogan wall, obliquely coming up on the door. He pushed aside the hanging skin and ducked low, entering the cool interior. A cook fire heated a pot filled with savory venison stew. Manuelito took a wooden spoon and scooped up some, sampling it. Then he tossed another small piece of wood on the fire—never eat without feeding the fire, he had always been told. If nothing else, it kept the food hot.

He sank down to a blanket and waited for Juanita to speak. She finally did, and the relief at being home faded.

"They are outside, in the small hogan." She said nothing more, and Manuelito knew there had been trouble with his captives. Gray Feather was a fine-looking woman, but Juanita had nothing to fear from her. Manuelito tried to soothe his wife and failed. Part of the reason he loved her was the fire she'd inherited from her father, Narbona, but at times it wore on him. This was such a moment.

"The burdens grow, never slip away," he said. Manuelito left the hogan and walked around to the rear, where Gray Feather and her son were kept. He paused when he heard hushed voices inside the small hut. It was wrong to eavesdrop. Yet he could not keep from hearing Shining Eyes and his ardor, his anger.

"I will *kill* him!"

"No, Shining Eyes, no!" protested the boy's mother. Manuelito closed his eyes and knelt down. Had he been wrong in bringing them into his clan?

"They kill our family and keep us as slaves."

"Manuelito has been good to us."

"We are slaves," Shining Eyes insisted. "We must escape. Come, this night as they sleep. We can—"

"No, no," Gray Feather said. "I cannot. The baby kicks now." Manuelito imagined her putting hands to her belly.

"We *can* get away," her son said.

"You go. It is only right. If your father lived! Joseph would rescue me—us."

The argument raged. Manuelito rose and walked away slowly. Shining Eyes would be watched. He must never be allowed to escape, but his mother sounded resigned to her fate. Manuelito would see that they were fed especially well this night. Perhaps a belly filled to bursting would slow the boy's flight.

If not, tracking him down would prove easy. He was only a child. Manuelito had even seen him cross a snake's path without shuffling his feet. Such ignorance would be sure to draw lightning to strike him dead.

"Soon enough you will be a man and will catch a female coyote on foot," Manuelito said to himself. In that potential he saw a mighty warrior and the future of the Dinéh.

The First New Mexico Volunteers

May 24, 1861
Santa Fé

He missed his wife already. Kit Carson sat in the hard wooden chair, his back ramrod-straight, surrounded by the noise of wagons in the street and men practicing their marching in the plaza a few yards away, his blue eyes focused on the horizon past the Sangre de Cristo Mountains about where Taos and Josepha would be. It was late spring, but the wind blowing through his long hair felt cool, even cold with a tinge of the bitter winter lingering. He didn't want to be here under the porch of the adobe house where Canby made his headquarters. Kit knew his six children would be growing up without him, just as they had been born without him beside his wife.

Before, he had wandered the mountains trapping and hunting, scouting for General Frémont, exploring new parts of this great country. The thought of his good friend back in Saint Louis put even more steel into his spine. Kit missed his old friend and his elegant wife, Jessie, but events were twisting away from his grip, no matter how tight he tried to hold to it. Resigning his post as Indian agent had been as hard as anything he had ever done. His wards needed him more than ever with the war talk boiling like some unholy stew. Left to their own devices, the Navajo would come swooping across the territory, murdering as they came, and no Ute would be safe, not that Kit thought any less of the Lords of New Mexico for their actions. He, better than most, knew how the white man had dealt off the bottom of the deck in treaty after treaty, but that still did not make their behavior acceptable.

"Kit!" came a hearty greeting. He left his distant thoughts, shot to his feet, and turned to greet Edward Sprague Canby as the officer bustled from the adobe building. The brevet general thrust out his hand for Kit. The mountain man shook it and received a bone-crushing grip in reply. "So good of you to drop by our offices." Canby disengaged his hand and made a sweeping gesture of the structure, pointing through the narrow door at the small office just beyond, bare of furniture save for a desk at the far side. It amazed him how Canby ran the military of an entire territory out of such Spartan quarters. This caused Canby's star to rise just a little more in Kit's firmament. Canby had a reputation of being a commander more involved with his troops than with his own bivouac.

"Reckon you've a'heard of why I came to Santa Fé," Kit replied, never much for small talk. "I want to join up."

Canby nodded solemnly, ushering Kit Carson into his office. Kit's shoulders brushed the sides of the narrow door, but he did not need to bend low to keep from bumping his head on the sagging pine lintel as did Canby. Inside he got a better look at the quarters. The only real ornamentation in the room was nailed to the adobe wall and looked half past ready to pop its nail and fall to the floor.

Canby saw Kit eyeing the picture frame surrounding the fancy certificate inside.

"That's my diploma from West Point." Canby sank into a chair that barely held his weight. He rubbed his clean-shaven chin and shook his head slowly. Somehow, this small action caused his hair to fly into even wilder disarray than it was before. Kit touched his long, bushy reddish mustache and wondered if he ought to shave it off, following Canby's taste in grooming.

"Seems a hundred years ago when I tossed my cap into the air at the graduation ceremony," Canby said, his voice distant in reminiscence. "Hard to believe, it is, that it was only 1839."

Kit Carson shifted his weight uneasily. Rumination didn't set well with him, especially when it was a world so alien facing him. He had always been uncomfortable when Frémont talked of universities and books and how he had orbited in literary circles. The trips to Washington sponsored by Jessie Frémont had been enjoyable for Kit, even as they'd scared him a mite. Being surrounded by so many learned men and lovely, cultured women in fine dresses brought it home to him how different his life was from theirs. That Jessie's father was one of the most powerful senators in Washington had awed Kit more than he cared to admit. He had always turned up tongue-tied in Thomas Hart Benton's presence. The politician must think him a complete fool, no matter what his daughter said in Kit's behalf, though the man had always been unfailingly polite and attentive to Kit's wild yarns and simple tales of the West.

"Reckon it's even harder fer you to tolerate what your brother-in-law done to you," Kit said. The pain that flashed across Canby's face caused Kit immediately to regret having mentioned Sibley. "Didn't mean to sound so cruel, General. What I mean is, your brother-in-law is part of the reason I come to Santa Fé."

"I heard that your resignation as agent has been accepted," Canby said, eyes fixed on Kit. "It sparked my curiosity some when I learned you were abandoning your post, then I got to thinking about your reasons. Truth to tell, I hoped you'd see fit to come by and see me. I can use new perspective on the difficulty facing me."

"I've never made a secret of where my loyalties lay," Kit said, puffing with pride that a man as important as General Canby sought his counsel. "I'm foursquare fer the Union."

"I wish Henry shared your loyalty," Canby said, with a tinge of bitterness in his voice. "It is a great disappointment that a man of his ability chose to fight for the rebels."

"Rumor has it he's plannin' on makin' his way up the Rio Grande and seizin' the whole danged territory fer the South."

Canby inclined his head to one side, then tented his fingers under his chin. "Fort Fillmore at Mesilla," he said, as if conferring on Kit the wisdom of the ages. "That's where Henry— the rebels made him a general—plans on beginning his campaign. Needless to say, we cannot allow New Mexico Territory to fall into rebel control, even if Henry would be a benign despot."

"He was under your command when you laid out the treaty with the Navajo."

"A good strong field commander, he was," Canby declared. He reached into a leather case and drew forth a map. Canby spread it on his desk, using a rock to hold one curling corner so Kit could better see it. "That's why Henry is likely to come straight up the river."

"The *Jornado del Muerto*," Kit said. "You intend to make it a real journey of death for him."

"He has to come fast, before the summer heat works against him. Sumter fell a little over a month ago, so Henry has had only a few weeks to gather his forces."

"Been a sizable amount of hootin' and hollerin' on the rebels' part after Major Anderson surrendered," Kit said in disgust. "Be another month 'fore they sober up enough to start marchin' on us."

Canby shook his head. "Henry isn't going to do that. Coming north in the middle of the hottest part of the year and trying to fight after such a march would put him at a disadvantage. He needs to recruit men, train them, be sure of how they will respond in the face of real combat. Take my word on this, Kit, Henry Hopkins Sibley might be a rebel but he is no fool." Canby laughed without humor. "After all, my sister saw fit to marry him."

"You sayin' he might wait till fall to come north?"

Canby nodded. "Henry will expect a quick victory, since so

many of our troops are being pulled out of New Mexico Territory and being stationed farther east."

"That withdrawal poses somethin' of a problem, General," said Kit, fingers stroking over his bushy mustache. "The Navajo are complainin' that their traditional enemies are preyin' on 'em, now that the troopers are leavin' the western parts of the territory. Might behoove you to leave some troopers out there to keep the peace."

"Can't do that, just cannot. Orders," Canby said. "The Navajo can take care of themselves as they always have, and I discount the problem of others preying on them. The troops are needed back East if we are to score an early victory."

"Be foolish to use all the best-trained troops to fight battles along the Potomac when your men know these parts best," Kit allowed.

"That's why I am pleased you came by. You must have heard we are forming the First New Mexico Volunteers. We need men from the area who know New Mexico's mountains and valleys, the rivers and deserts; we need men like you, Kit, who can defend our proud sovereignty and hold the rebels at bay."

"That's why I came to see you, General. Swear me in so I kin git on to trainin'." Kit waited for Canby to administer the oath of fealty right away.

"You're not asking for a commission?" Canby's eyebrows rose in surprise.

"I'll serve in any capacity that suits you best, General. Preservin' the Union is my aim, not being some highfalutin officer. No offense." Kit wished he wouldn't trip over his own tongue so often.

Canby took no umbrage. He laughed heartily. "Kit, with a hundred more like you, we could turn Henry and his entire rebel force back in an instant. You want to serve the Union best?"

"Whatever chore you think I should take on, I will. I only hope it's somethin' interestin'."

"Then I am giving you one of the hardest assignments any man can ever receive," Canby said in his solemn tone.

Kit Carson drew himself up to his full five-foot-four-inch height, braced at attention as he had seen men under Frémont do, and waited to hear what the general had in store for him. He went cold inside long before Canby finished his passionate explanation of Kit's duties in the Volunteers.

Marriage

June 25, 1861
Cañon de Chelly

"Our son grows tall," Manuelito said proudly to Gray Feather. The woman kept her eyes on the ground, but Manuelito saw a shy smile dance on her lips. It pleased her that he considered Shining Eyes his son as well as hers. "Instead of a wedding ceremony for us, there ought to have been a Flint Way sing."

Gray Feather straightened as if she were unsure of his intent. Manuelito tried to allay her suspicions that he meant her—their—son any harm.

"It is a way of cautioning our children against unwise sex," Manuelito said.

"Is sex now unwise between us?" she asked. Again the small smile danced on her lips. Manuelito knew true beauty when he gazed on her. And there was something more. A peaceful quality, in spite of her obvious nervousness, settled on her shoulders like a Two Gray Hills blanket. She was no virgin. The bulge at her belly told him this, but it mattered little to Manuelito.

"The sing lasts into the night," he told her, moving to sit beside her. He felt the heat from her body, and it warmed him. For the moment, he could forget the troubles building throughout Dinetah. For the moment, only the promise of the future mattered to him. "This gives our people a chance to celebrate and feast."

"Why can I not see the sand painting?"

"Only men are allowed in the lodge to see this forecasting," Manuelito said, irritated now that Gray Feather challenged the old ways. "Perhaps, in addition to a Flint Way sing for Shining Eyes, we ought to have a Blessing Way for you."

"No," she said in a low voice. "So many ceremonials will impoverish you. You are a headman and a great provider, but the flocks are dwindling this summer."

Manuelito nodded, aware of this. The sheep usually thrived in the rugged terrain, along the mesas, up and down the stark sides of the cañon.

"We must move on and get the sheep to good grassland before their bones stick out like handles for us to carry them," Manuelito said.

When he married Gray Feather, he brought many of his sheep to this hogan for her. It would take some time for her to build the wealth necessary to survive. Blankets needed to be woven, corn grown, the peaches from the orchards picked—and enemies to be driven away.

Always those coming down from the Bear's Ears and over from Santa Fé and up from the pueblos.

"We are to live in this hogan? By ourselves?"

"There will be others to assist you when the time comes," Manuelito said, his hand resting on Gray Feather's belly. "But this is your hogan now."

"Away from . . . hers?"

Manuelito knew there had been no friendship between Juanita and this Ute woman. If he had followed tradition, his second wife ought to have been one of Juanita's sisters, but they were all married. Narbona's daughters were considered eligible, as Narbona was one of the greatest headmen in all Dinetah. Or he could have chosen any of a dozen others scattered around Cañon de Chelly.

He had chosen Gray Feather because of her beauty, and perhaps, though Manuelito felt uneasy treading these byways, because he felt sorry for her. Her entire clan had been slain. The Ute had caused this, Manuelito knew, but Gray Feather was too easygoing for her own good. She needed a strong protector.

Manuelito swung about when the blanket dangling across the doorway jerked away. Standing there, Shining Eyes glared at his mother and her new husband.

"Do you want me to tend your horses?" Shining Eyes's arrogance blazed forth and caused Manuelito some anger. Still, the boy adapted well to a new and better way of life.

"I do," Manuelito said. "You may ride one to the top of the mesa. Remember not to tire the horse. The horses must be rested for the races in two days."

"A chicken pull," Shining Eyes spat out, but Manuelito saw a hint of anticipation. Everyone enjoyed the chicken pulls. And the races. Many horses changed ownership after the races. It was a time of excitement and friendship that helped bind together the far-flung clans. Some of this exhilaration had to fire Shining Eyes's imagination and competitive spirit. Manuelito had seen the boy vying with others. He already used a bow and arrow better than most of the Dinéh, but he lacked the stamina required to run long miles and then use the weapon without a quiver in his hand or a blink in his eye.

Shining Eyes would learn Dinéh ways.

Manuelito said nothing. Shining Eyes stared at him with great impudence, then let the blanket fall back across the doorway. A few minutes later, Manuelito heard the *clop-clop* of a horse leaving. And then he turned to his bride.

Dawn poked through the blanket hanging over the door. Manuelito turned and pulled his arm out from under Gray Feather. The limb tingled as circulation returned to it; he stretched and flexed until the arm returned to normal. He swung around and sat cross-legged, simply watching the slow rise and fall of the woman's breast. He reached out and gently touched it. The warm flesh pulsed with life under his fingertips. Manuelito pulled back and just looked at her, savoring her beauty and thinking of their life together.

As Manuelito sat and thought, he frowned. He reached over and took his deerskin breeches and moccasins. Slipping outside, he stood in the warm light of the new sun and felt energized by its rays. Climbing into his clothing, he finally settled the knife at his hip and then went to find his son.

Manuelito saw that one horse was gone—still gone, he decided. Shining Eyes had ridden off the night before and had not returned. Manuelito might have suspected a joke being played on him, as he'd played jokes on so many others in his clan. But Shining Eyes had shown no tendency toward appreciating a good practical joke. There had been little more than smoldering anger.

Walking around, he verified that one horse was missing and with it Shining Eyes. Manuelito found his favorite pony and jumped onto its back. He patted its neck, then turned the horse's face toward the trail leading to the top of the mesa. While Shining Eyes could have camped out on the mesa in deference to his new father, Manuelito doubted this. He remembered the overheard conversation when Gray Feather had urged her son to escape, to return to their people.

The pony maintained a steady, slow gait as Manuelito guided it to the trail up the steep cañon wall. The horse strained as the trail turned steeper, and Manuelito jumped off. He had not come this way in many years and had forgotten how difficult the climb was. A few hundred yards along the switchback trail, Manuelito paused and stared down at the newly built hogan where Gray Feather slept so quietly. Leaving her tugged at him, pulled him back, but other considerations pushed him up the trail.

Here and there Manuelito saw traces of Shining Eyes's passage. Fresh horse dung. Broken bushes. Fresh scratches along the sandstone cañon wall. Scuffled dirt on the trail. His belly growled from lack of breakfast, but his stride never shortened and not once did he think of returning. More than an hour passed before he reached the crest and stared across the mesa top.

A quick glance down three hundred feet to the cañon floor and along it brought a pride to his breast. This was a part of Dinetah, *his* part, his clan's part. He lifted his gaze to the four holy mountains but found only Mount Taylor to the southeast uncloaked by haze.

"A sign? A reminder of the Dinéh Ana'aii?" Manuelito tried to figure out what this meant, other than that the weather kept him from seeing the other peaks. Nature played strange tricks at times, and this could mean nothing. Or it might be like the *Yei* speaking their indecipherable words. He saw no storms, no lightning or rainbows or snakes slithering along the mesa top to give him clues. He did see the track left by a fleeing Shining Eyes.

Manuelito had let his pony dine on the lush grass long enough. He swung onto the horse's back and started off following the path left by his new son. Less than an hour of tracking brought a slow smile to his lips. Manuelito knew Dinetah intimately. Shining Eyes did not. He pulled his horse's reins away from the trail as he cut off, going down a sandy arroyo and toward the north. Another hour of travel, Manuelito impassively riding, brought him to a narrow ravine.

His belly growling more now, Manuelito foraged and found enough to make a sparse meal. Hunkered down, not bothering to start a fire, he sat with a blanket around his shoulders and watched ants go about their business. His eyes snapped into focus when he heard horse's hooves pounding along the rocky rise leading down into the ravine. Pushing back his blanket, Manuelito stood and waited.

Shining Eyes let out a cry of anguish when he saw Manuelito waiting for him in the draw.

"Hunting is not good here," Manuelito said, his eyes fixed on the wayward boy. "There—there the hunting is better. I will show you." Manuelito mounted and rode off, never looking back to see if Shining Eyes followed.

Scout

June 25, 1861
Taos

Cold. So cold. Or was he hot? Joseph Treadwell could not tell. One moment he shivered, and the next he sweltered. Hands groping, he found the edge of a thick blanket and pulled it over him until his toes poked out from under it, only to shove the covering away seconds later as sweat poured down his face.

Blinking hard, he struggled to focus his eyes. Nothing was as it ought to be. He had vague recollection of the arrow he had taken in his back a few nights ago. Lying in the snow, he had well nigh frozen to death, but there was something more. He remembered the soft thudding of horses approaching.

His fingers clenched as if around the hilt of a knife. The mountain man remembered the riders and had wanted to kill them, thinking they were more Navajo come to work their mischief. The paint smeared on their expressionless faces. The way they sat astride their horses. The feathers thrust into their braided hair. Fragments of memory returned.

"Ute," he muttered. "They're Ute. I don't have to kill them. They'll help me!" Treadwell shot bolt upright in bed. Giddiness hit him like a twelve-pound sledge and made him wobble. He clutched the wooden sides of the bed and pushed the blanket onto the brick floor.

Words came to him from afar. The buzzing in his ears died

slowly as the dizziness vanished and his eyes finally focused in the dim light of the . . . kitchen.

"What is this place?" he demanded. He tried to shout the question but felt the words grating like sand in his throat. He knew it sounded like a coarse whisper instead of a forceful question. And then all strength left Treadwell's body. He flopped down like a fish out of water. Like the fish he had tried to tickle yesterday.

"Taos," came the soft reply. A stream of Spanish gushed forth and then switched to English when he obviously did not understand. "You are a trapper?"

"Who are you?"

"Josepha Carson," came the surprising reply. Treadwell tried to remember where he had heard the name. He was in the mountains, in the middle of winter, yet he lay naked to the waist and felt the waves of heat working into the house from beyond the distant doorway. Outside, the sunlight shone summer-bright, without a hint of snow anywhere.

"The Navajo Indians killed my brother-in-law," Treadwell said. "Slaughtered a foraging party. And they kidnapped my wife and son. Gray Feather. She's pregnant. I—" Weakness forced him to stop his outpouring. The woman knelt beside him and put a cool compress on his forehead.

"Rest, do not excite yourself. You have been feverish and so near death for such a long time. Rest, rest," she soothed. And Joseph Treadwell did.

"I can't believe I lost half a year laid up with that arrow in me." Treadwell thought this a cruel joke being played on him, but he saw no purpose—or perpetrator. Josepha Carson was a pleasant woman, and he had finally remembered that her husband was Indian agent. He had intended to appeal to Christopher Carson for aid against the Navajo before he took it upon himself to rescue Shining Eyes and Gray Feather from the raiding party.

"The wound was deep. A Ute medicine man kept you alive

until the spring thaw permitted travel. They brought you here, unable to do more for you," Josepha said in her quiet way. In the courtyard three noisy children played. Treadwell had seen an older girl and boy in another room, poring over books, struggling to do their school lessons.

"Our doctor, the one from the fort, dug out pieces of broken arrowhead and only then did you begin to improve."

"You cared for me? How long?"

"Almost two months." Josepha let out a tiny sigh that masked more than Treadwell wanted to explore. It was both exasperation with the world and resignation to fate the woman could not control.

Treadwell was at a loss to decide if the wound or the revelation of so much lost time weakened him most. One sapped his body; the other stole away his will.

"Your husband, Mr. Carson. I need to talk with him."

"He is due back from Santa Fé at any time," Josepha said, hands folded in her lap. "But he cannot help you any longer. He went to the capital to resign his position as agent."

"What? He can't do that. He has to help me fetch back my wife and son!" Treadwell calmed himself and then said in a lower voice, "If he can't give me succor, who is the new agent?"

"I don't rightly know. There might not be one, not with the war and all."

"War?" he asked, confused. Too much swirled around him that Treadwell could not fathom. "Against them thieving Navajo Indians?"

Josepha shook her head and stared through the low doorway at her children, still working diligently on their book learning.

"No, not them. The South. The Confederacy."

"I don't understand." Treadwell shook as if all strength had been ripped from him. He had a thousand demands to make, and Shining Eyes and Gray Feather to recover. They had been in the clutches of a Navajo raider for five months. By now they might be dead—or worse. The trail would be impossible to find. Spring runoff after such a cold winter had a way of wiping out any trace of where they might have been taken.

Treadwell gritted his teeth. It didn't matter. If he had to go all the way down the throat of Cañon de Chelly to retrieve them, he would. They would not remain slaves of the Navajo one second longer than necessary.

"Sip on this. You've been living on little more than soup and water for so long that you are gaunt. I don't know how you have fared as well as you have," the woman said, spooning broth into his mouth.

Treadwell choked on the hot soup, then found himself greedily drinking and wanting more. The liquid vanished and was replaced with tortillas and crushed corn mixed into a spicy chili stew. He gobbled down all he could until his belly began to ache something fierce. Only then did Treadwell stop eating, afraid of puking up all he had eaten.

"Such an appetite," Josepha said, "but you have been so sick with bouts of fever. It is time for you to regain your strength."

For the first time as he lay back on the bed, Treadwell noticed the itching in the center of his back. He knew, after all this time, he had to be imagining the spot where the Navajo arrow had entered him. But he could not be certain.

"It is healed," Josepha said, as if knowing what he thought. For a moment, Treadwell forced back tears. How like his Gray Feather this woman was, knowing what he needed and what flashed through his mind. Somewhere, as memories of his wife and son danced in his head, Joseph Treadwell fell back into heavy sleep.

"No, Kit, no!" Josepha protested.

Treadwell came immediately awake. He gripped the edge of the bed and heaved himself to a sitting position, feet on the cool bricks and head ready to pop off his shoulders. When he could keep his balance, he stood and walked on weak legs, his knees giving out under him. He caught himself against the edge of the heavy kitchen table and spun around to prop himself against it. His legs refused to move; Treadwell had to rest.

"I'm afraid it's true, my dearest Chipita," Christopher Carson said. "This is a burden I surely did not seek. Might be more 'n I can do."

"What do you know of such things, Kit? You've served with John, but not as a soldier. Not really." Treadwell saw Josepha pass across the narrow door leading to the sitting room and hug a short man with drooping mustache and shoulder-length hair.

"General Canby has confidence in me. That's why he made me a lieutenant colonel. I'll be in command of the First New Mexico Volunteers." Kit Carson hugged his wife, then gently disengaged. "Won't be much different than bein' agent."

"It's not the same at all!" flared Josepha. "You weren't responsible for the life and death of hundreds of men. Not like this!"

"I was responsible for the Ute," Kit said. "The only difference is figurin' out where to go and how to fight. Reckon I can do that. All I need is to keep my wits about me. I listened hard when St. Vrain talked about tactics and strategy." He crossed the room out of Treadwell's sight, but the words came through strong and sure. "Besides, all I got to do is what the general tells me."

"General Canby might not always be here, Kit. There is talk that he will be sent back East, where the fighting is."

"What fighting?" asked Treadwell, making his way to the door. He clung to the wall to save himself the indignity of collapsing. "Against the Navajo?"

"The Confederacy," Kit Carson said, turning. "You must be the man brought in by the Ute. A mountain man, from the looks of you."

Treadwell glanced down at his emaciated body and had to laugh ruefully. Before the raid, he had not been in the best condition, starving and not finding enough for his own family to eat. The past months of coma and fever had taken even more of a toll on him. He sat down heavily, his legs tiring quickly.

What of Gray Feather and Shining Eyes?

"Don't know nothing of the Confederacy," Treadwell said. "I need you to authorize a company of soldiers to go find my wife and son."

"Josepha must have told you I went to Santa Fé to resign. I got a commission to fight them rebels."

Treadwell swung around and collapsed into a chair at the side of the room. His hot eyes fixed on Carson, as if he could bend the short man to his will. The effort did nothing but give Treadwell a headache and new weakness.

"The country's changin', and it ain't for the better," Kit Carson said. "I know how you must feel. I have to leave my wife and children to go fight men who were neighbors a couple months back. There's no way we kin go traipsin' off into Navajoland after a couple prisoners."

"Then I'll go alone."

"Can't rightly blame you. If I was in your boots, I'd do the same. But you're in no condition to fight."

Treadwell saw cunning come into the sharp blue-gray eyes fixed on him.

"You'll need months to recover. How you plannin' to do that?"

"If I start walking, I can be back in my wife's tribal land before autumn. I can find other Ute Indians to help."

"Months, long months, and you're bein' real optimistic about your condition. I seen men better off who never got stronger with all the care in the world. My dear Josepha's a good nurse, but she ain't a miracle worker."

The woman snorted and muttered something about how often she had performed such a chore.

"Right good. I know from experience," Kit went on. "But you can't stay here, and your chances of ever findin' your wife and boy are passin' small. Unless . . ."

"Unless what?" Treadwell demanded. He knew when he was being rooked. He felt the ropes of argument tightening around him, holding him down, making him agree to something he did not want to do.

"I need scouts. Good ones. The quicker we make them rebels turn tail and run, the sooner we kin git to the real chores at hand, the ones what matter most to me and you." Kit let the words hang in the air for a moment. Then he added, "The Navajo matter. There'll never be real peace in the territory till we come to some accommodation with them. I kin put the full might of the First New Mexico Volunteers behind your hunt for your family."

"What's the price?"

"As I said, I need a scout. A good one, one the equal to St. Vrain over at the fort. You're a mountain man, just like us. I cain't go runnin' off if I have to command a passel of troopers. That don't mean I cain't use decent, accurate scoutin' reports. I will, I do. Help me whup the rebels, then I swear I'll do all I kin to find your wife and boy for you."

Treadwell shook his head, but before he could utter the words denying Kit Carson a scout, Josepha spoke up.

"You need to regain your strength. That will be a month or longer. Kit, how long will you be recruiting and training?"

"General Canby figures Sibley will march up the river come winter and attack then. A man would have three, four months to regain his vigor 'fore he had to go scoutin' for the regiment."

"You promise you'll help me find them?"

"I do," Kit Carson said. "I'm a man of my word. Help me crush them rebels and I swear I'll do all I can to get back your kith and kin."

Treadwell found himself holding out a frail, quaking hand for the newly commissioned lieutenant colonel to shake, sealing their agreement.

Raiders

Shining Eyes edged closer to the horse, hesitantly reaching out to touch its neck. Manuelito stood impassively, not looking directly at the boy but knowing his every movement. Since his attempted escape, Shining Eyes had been sullen but not aggressive against Manuelito or any other in the Folded Arms Clan. The only thing drawing him from his self-imposed silence and solitude crow-hopped beside the boy.

Screwing up his courage, Shining Eyes went to the horse and gentled the stallion. The large bay snorted but Shining Eyes gripped the bridle and kept the horse from rearing. Manuelito remained impassive but approved of the boy's technique dealing with the high-strung animal. Manuelito had taken the bay from a Ute raider. If he hadn't been content with his own pony, this is the horse he would have ridden into battle. That Shining Eyes saw the horse's potential pleased him.

"He has a strong heart," Manuelito said finally. "Like an eagle, he wants to soar."

Shining Eyes said nothing, but a tentative smile crept across his lips.

"The races begin soon," Manuelito went on. The clan had gathered for races and a day of gambling. A dozen warriors crouched nearby, throwing marked sticks and gambling on the lay. As the afternoon wore on, Manuelito knew the games would change to more combative ones, games of strength and ability with bow and musket—and at sundown would come the races.

"In a few hours," Shining Eyes blurted, as if the words slid of their own volition from his lips. He clamped his mouth shut at this self-betrayal. But the bay needed his attention and took some of the sting from his lapse.

Manuelito studied the other horses corraled nearby. Many were as good as the bay but none was better. Follows Quickly would give anyone in the race the greatest challenge. The young warrior showed recklessness that bordered on insanity in all that he did—and his mount matched him perfectly. The mare he rode was strong and surefooted on all terrain, especially on the shale-covered slopes and trails throughout Cañon de Chelly.

Settling down and staring into the distance, Manuelito used the quiet time to consider all that had happened over the past six weeks. He and Gray Feather had gotten along well, better than he did with Juanita. Narbona's daughter had a sharp tongue and used it to slice the flesh from his bones whenever he visited her hogan. Splitting time between the two women had been difficult. Every time Manuelito rode back from a scout, he passed by Juanita's hogan but felt guilty about allowing Gray Feather to endure her pregnancy alone, especially now that the time of her delivery grew closer.

So much to consider, and it all jumbled unless he took each issue individually. The press of the world forced him from harmony and left Manuelito feeling unclean, confused at times, and even angry. He accepted what must be, no matter how difficult it seemed.

Manuelito blinked and turned when a handful of warriors came over, led by Follows Quickly. They were joking and jostling, obviously ready for something more involving than gambling on the throw of a few marked sticks.

"We race! You and I will race, Manuelito," Follows Quickly cried loudly. He looked left and right to see the effect this had on the others. It was no challenge to Manuelito's right to be headman; it was a call to race, betting the horse each rode.

"I do not feel up to riding this afternoon," Manuelito said carefully. For a moment, Follows Quickly stared, stunned. Never had their leader refused to race—and seldom had Manuelito ever failed to win, no matter how good his opposition.

Follows Quickly stood and gaped, then burst out laughing. "You are joking. You think I will believe you."

"I do not race this afternoon," Manuelito repeated. "However, my son will race in my stead."

"Manuelito Segundo? Has he returned from the scout against the *gah yahzi,* the little rabbit Hopi?"

"My son," Manuelito repeated, "will race, riding the bay. Your horse against the bay."

Shining Eyes jerked erect, startled. He looked to the horse and then at Manuelito as if he was being tricked.

"My horse against that nag?" demanded Follows Quickly, beginning to dicker over the terms of the bet. "How far can we expect to race before such a spindly animal collapses? That would make it of no use after I win."

"If you win," corrected Manuelito. "Do you want a head start against Shining Eyes?" Manuelito knew the young warrior could never accept such a condition.

"We race to the end of Runs Wide Wash and back, across this line!" Follows Quickly toed a line into the dirt. He went to fetch his horse from the corral as the others gathered and made their own bets.

Shining Eyes came over to Manuelito. "You want me to race Follows Quickly? I cannot win."

"If you beat him, the bay is yours," Manuelito said. He considered the matter a moment longer, then added, *"When* you beat him."

Shining Eyes grinned widely and then went to the right side of the bay and jumped onto its back. The powerful horse snorted and reared a little, but the boy quickly regained control and guided the bay to the line drawn by Follows Quickly. The warrior let out a whoop and wheeled his horse about, darting from the corral.

Shining Eyes was not caught unawares. He saw that Follows Quickly would have a running start and put his heels to the bay's sides. The horse exploded like a cannon, leaping forward at the same instant Follows Quickly reached the line. Follows Quickly led for a few yards, but the bay inexorably closed the gap amid cheers from the onlookers. Manuelito allowed himself a smile when he saw how well Shining Eyes rode.

"A close race," spoke up Orejo Pequeño, a warrior of the Red House Clan who happened to be traveling by when he saw the chicken pull start and was invited to take part. "I will bet even more on your son."

This, more than anything else, swelled Manuelito with pride. Shining Eyes was not going to cede the race to Follows Quickly, and others saw how strong his heart was.

"The wash. They are neck-and-neck at the wash!"

Manuelito watched as the two racers returned, their horses' hooves hammering hard against the sun-baked ground. Bits of sagebrush kicked up as they turned a corner and started back uphill to the finish line. Shining Eyes whipped the horse using the reins, and Follows Quickly shouted at his mount.

The use of the goad served Shining Eyes better. He won by a nose amid cheers from the onlookers. Follows Quickly slid silently from his lathered horse and thrust the reins out to Manuelito. Manuelito shook his head and pointed to Shining Eyes.

"His," he said. "Both horses are now his."

The expression on the boy's face filled him with pride. Triumph was written there, and something more subtle. Manuelito read growing acceptance of his condition on Shining Eyes's face. He might never be Dinéh, but he would not be apart any longer.

"Manuelito, up on the mesa!" Follows Quickly pointed.

"It's Manuelito Segundo," Orejo Pequeño said. "I recognize his war helmet."

"He is summoning us." Jumbled thoughts flashed through Manuelito's mind. "Bring your weapons." Manuelito ran to the corral and grabbed his pony. He saw Follows Quickly going to another horse and mounting, useless musket in his hand. Manuelito wished the young warrior would carry a bow and arrow and leave the empty musket behind.

The band made their way up a steep trail to the top of the mesa, taking almost an hour to reach the summit. And when they did, they saw tragedy swirling like water down an arroyo. Manuelito Segundo and his small party crouched behind a tumble of rock, their horses slaughtered by the Zuñi war party following them. It took only a moment for Manuelito to realize his son had blundered across a war party invading Cañon de Chelly, intent on slaving and plundering.

Manuelito pointed to his left and Follows Quickly rode off with two others. Waiting a moment, Manuelito let the young warrior get into position, then let out a whoop and charged, his lance low and deadly as he galloped forward. His pony had tired from the climb to the mesa top but responded because it had great heart.

The headman swelled with pride when he saw Shining Eyes barely a horse's length behind. The boy struggled to fire his arrow from a running horse, but his aim was not far off target. A Zuñi warrior swung about in surprise at the nearness of the attack. Manuelito's brother had taught the boy well.

All thought of Shining Eyes's training vanished as Manuelito lost himself in the heat of battle to the death. He thrust with his lance and caught the shoulder of a war-painted Zuñi. The tip slashed to the bone, and before he realized it, Manuelito was sailing through the air.

He hit the ground hard, the air knocked from his lungs. Struggling, he found himself paralyzed, unable to move, although he saw a Zuñi rearing above him, knife drawn for the kill. From nowhere came Manuelito Segundo to grapple with the Zuñi. Manuelito gasped for breath, and it came too slowly.

As his son fought, a second Zuñi raider came up behind. The

Zuñi drew back the bowstring that would send death into Manuelito Segundo's back. Manuelito could do nothing about it. He tried to shout, and his voice failed. He attempted to throw his knife and his arms turned to lead. His legs quivered and betrayed him. All he could do was watch and fear.

The arrow sang its deadly song and a man died—the Zuñi died, an arrow fletched with a wild turkey feather in his back. Past the dying raider Manuelito saw Shining Eyes, still astride his newly won horse and a look of dismay on his young face. Manuelito doubted the boy had ever killed in battle, but he was now blooded—and had saved his brother.

The iron bands loosened on Manuelito's chest. He regained his voice before his limbs. He shouted, "Drive them back. Get them, kill them all. Scalp them!"

The Zuñi fighters began melting away like icy patches in the spring sun. By the time Manuelito slashed with his knife and kicked with his feet in real battle, the Zuñi had ridden away.

"We must go after them. Not a one must return to his pueblo to brag about this battle. Only in this way can we stop their raids," Manuelito declared. He paused when he saw Manuelito Segundo standing near Shining Eyes. Neither said a word, but Manuelito Segundo thrust out his hand. Shining Eyes hesitantly took it and then Manuelito Segundo clapped his brother on the back. More than death walked this field, and this sight gladdened Manuelito.

Horses were rounded up and the chase began. It took four days to ride down the Zuñi war party and kill them.

"Why are so many horses in the corral?" asked Shining Eyes. "Something is wrong!" He tried to get more speed from his bay, but the horse knew better than to hurry down the treacherously steep path leading from the cañon wall. For all his youthful worry and impatience, Shining Eyes kept remarkably calm.

Manuelito, too, worried what the gathered horses meant. He recognized one as belonging to a *natali,* a singer. Gray Feather must have required ceremonial cleansing—and possibly more. That the people were still within the hogan meant she had not died. If she had, her *chindi* would haunt the hogan and it would have already been burned down or closed up.

As Manuelito slipped from horseback, his brother, Cayatanita, pushed aside the blanket hanging over the door and emerged, a solemn expression on his face.

"My brother," Cayatanita said. "It is Gray Feather."

"My mother!" shrieked Shining Eyes, trying to rush past. Cayatanita reached out and held the boy easily with one hand, letting him struggle for a moment.

"Your mother, my brother's wife, is well," he said. "And you now have another son, a healthy son I have named Goes to War."

Manuelito sucked in a deep breath. Gray Feather had given him another son, one who would one day ride beside his other sons, Manuelito Segundo and Shining Eyes.

"If I have many more celebrations, I will find myself in poverty," Manuelito said, the smile on his face refusing to go away. "I would see my son, and my son would see his new brother."

Idle

January 3, 1862
Fort Craig

"You worry too much, Joe," a lanky trooper lectured Treadwell as he lounged back, feet hiked up on the end of his bunk. "I been in this here man's army for well nigh three years. Take it from me, the less action you see, the more likely you are to brag to your young'uns how heroic you was."

The mention of children caused Treadwell to stand and pace nervously in the small cabin he'd helped construct weeks earlier. Cold wind whipped through the poorly caulked walls, wind that came off the distant Navajo territory to the northwest. Treadwell sniffed hard, wiped his nose on his wool sleeve, and wished he could again catch scent of his wife and son. Wife and *sons,* he mentally corrected, sure that Gray Feather had given birth to a boy. Deep in his bones he felt it, just as he felt his family was still alive somewhere in Navajoland.

The need to rush out and find them was tempered constantly by his promise to Kit Carson to scout against the Confederacy. Since Kit had been transferred to this miserable, freezing table-land on the east side of the Rio Grande as it flowed past Socorro, nothing had happened. Treadwell had spent months recovering his strength as he'd helped Kit both recruit and get the First New Mexico Volunteers whipped into shape. Now he felt like a horse ready to race. Sleeping all day wasn't his way of fighting, not like most of the soldiers stationed here. Too many were like the one sprawled on his bunk, wanting only three squares and plenty of time to sleep.

War and killing would happen eventually, Treadwell knew, but he wanted it to happen *quick* so he could get on with finding his family. He leaned against the wall and felt the wind hammering hard in gusts that promised to strip the flesh from his face should he venture outside.

It had been a full year since Navajo raiders had completely turned his life inside out. Fulfilling his various obligations to Colonel Carson took his mind off that, but only a little and never for very long. Recruiting had been easier than Treadwell would have thought, the men of the territory willing to fight to keep their freedom. Many bunking alongside him spoke only of fighting the damned Texans and not of the Confederacy and slavery. Treadwell paid them little heed. Their reasons for making their mark on the bottom of the enlistment papers mattered nothing to him. The more recruits he signed up, the more that would fight the Confederacy, and the sooner the war would end, so he could hold Carson to his promise to find Gray Feather, even if it meant using the full force of the Union Army.

Treadwell touched his canvas shirt pocket where a wad of greenbacks rode thick and sassy. He had been paid well, getting a dollar for every man he'd signed to a one-year tour of duty. Being able to read and write helped in this chore, especially when he came to realize Kit Carson could sign his name and little more.

"Didn't mean to put a burr under your saddle," the trooper called insincerely, shifting so he could fold his hands under his head. "I figgered out real quick the best you can do is sleep when you can, eat what's set in front of you, then fight like bloody hell so you can be bored all over again."

"No offense taken," Treadwell said, his mind ranging far from Fort Craig and the pitiful walls surrounding it. Where they had found enough timber, they had used wood posts, but most of the defense came from high adobe walls. Treadwell knew they were mostly useless against Apache and Navajo raiders. He had seen a patient Indian toss over such a wall a long horsehair rope with heavy rocks tied to the end. Sawing back and forth cut through the sun-baked mud bricks and offered a huge doorway into even the best designed fort.

And Fort Craig was far from that sitting on the tableland east of the Rio Grande and nine miles to the north. It had been nothing more than a replacement for Fort Conrad, at the foot of Valverde Mesa. "Hay Camp" they called that abandoned fort now, giving them forage for their animals. Boredom Camp was all Treadwell could name it.

"We ought to go to them, not let them Johnny Rebs come up the river to us," he grumbled.

"I'd say it's purty smart of the colonel to let Sibley and his boys hike all the way up here. We can whup 'em after they've worn blisters onto their feet."

"Feet?" scoffed another soldier. "They're mostly Texas Rangers. They ride. You wouldn't expect them to ever touch earth with their fancy boots."

"Rangers and outlaws used to stealin' everything, includin' horses. Renegades, killers, road agents, the whole danged lot, I say," piped up another.

The men began arguing about the force Sibley commanded, the Fourth, Fifth, and Seventh Texas Cavalry, and Treadwell's mind drifted even more. He had heard all the rumors and wild speculation about the imminent attack. From his scouting trip a month earlier, he doubted Sibley would venture north in the cold for at least a month. If the lock winter held on the desert didn't ease, it could be a full two months.

"Hey, Joe, the colonel wants to see you," shouted a corporal poking his head in the door. Cruel wind whipped past and turned the frail warmth inside to brittle cold. "Make it quick. You're supposed to forage and get some firewood with the detail formin' up right now."

Treadwell nodded, not even minding the ice that formed in

his beard when he stepped outside. He was no bunkhouse law-yer satisfied with jawing, and he was no soldier content to repeat endless rumors and consider each of them to be the gospel truth. Head down against the gale, he made his way through the com-pound to Kit Carson's office.

He knocked but doubted anyone inside could hear over the tumult of the storm. Treadwell pushed on in, slamming the door behind him as an especially cold wind gusted after him.

"Treadwell, glad you got my message," Kit said, looking up from a map spread on the desk in front of him. The coal-oil lamp sputtered, its wick requiring severe trimming. Treadwell saw this was only one of the chores needing doing that Carson had neglected.

"I'm supposed to help find wood. In this weather, it'll be pure hell."

"Try across the river and south a ways," Kit suggested, his eyes fixed again on the map of the area. "I've got a message from Santa Fé."

"About?" Treadwell's heart raced. He knew Carson had sent out inquiries throughout the territory concerning Shining Eyes and Gray Feather. Nothing had come of the queries for months and months, and Treadwell hardly expected news in the middle of winter, but what else could the colonel call him over to say?

"About General Canby and his expedition south," Kit said. He sank into his chair and rubbed his blue-gray eyes. Treadwell saw they were bloodshot. Kit had put in long hours studying the map and Treadwell's scouting reports. Something was in the wind—other than snow and cutting cold.

Treadwell stayed quiet, preferring to let the colonel ramble on in his own vague way, as much as he cursed the slowness. Whatever Kit had to say, it did not involve Gray Feather.

"General Canby sent these defense plans for us to follow when Sibley rumbles up the Rio Grande and comes smack at us." Kit leaned forward, hands on the edge of the map covered with scribbled lines and notations too small for Treadwell to read. He wondered who had made them, since Carson could not write.

"Planning ahead too much can back us into a corner. Might be better to stay flexible."

"We're settin' at the northern end of the *Jornada del Muerto.* Canby wants us to stop his brother-in-law here and on no account let him press past Santa Fé. If Sibley gits that far, he might rip into Colorado and cut the country into pieces."

"Sibley will be tuckered out from his jaunt up the river," Treadwell said, staring at the upside-down plans. "He won't have the wherewithal to lay siege to us."

"Valverde," Kit said, not hearing Treadwell. "The general thinks Sibley'll cross the Rio Grande six miles south of the fort, circle 'round, and try to git back across the river at Mesa de la Contedera draggin' all their mountain howitzers with 'em." A stubby finger stabbed down at a spot to the north of Fort Craig.

"Canby will be here in person?"

"Reckon so, reckon so," Kit said, chewing on his lower lip. "He went south to engage them at Fort Fillmore in Mesilla and found Sibley had been reinforced. We'll be facin' upward of twenty-five hundred men, most of 'em battle veterans." Kit let out a sigh. The cold air carried a few silvery plumes before being erased by the feeble warmth in the room.

"Canby thinks they'll be here soon?"

"Within the month," Kit said. "Sibley is emboldened by turnin' back the general at Mesilla and thinks he kin push straight on through to Fort Union and seize all our supplies."

"Whatever became of your letter to Frémont?"

Kit shook his head. "I wrote Major General Frémont at his Saint Louis headquarters before St. Vrain resigned his commission. There's nothin' he can do, though he complimented me on my good judgment wantin' to keep raw recruits out of battle with them fire-hardened Texas rebels."

Treadwell knew how badly Carson had taken it when his old friend Ceran St. Vrain had resigned in September for health reasons, even if it had paved the way for promotion to full colonel in October. Treadwell didn't think Kit wielded the power of command too well, not since the piss-poor training he had given his troops in Albuquerque last fall. Carson had spent more time with his wife and newborn son, Charles, than he had drilling his men. Nothing much improved until Kit sent his wife and family back to Taos. Worst of all, in Treadwell's mind, was the way Carson depended so on other officers for the day-to-day running of the command.

Treadwell had nothing but contempt for Mac, the company drillmaster. He was everything Carson was not, and the pair of them hardly evened out to be one good soldier. Too much of the independent mountain man remained in Treadwell to approve of doing everything by the book. Still, Treadwell had to admit that Carson substituted common sense for military knowledge and held the command together. And something about Kit Carson's earnest good nature and obvious rectitude earned his respect, no matter how lacking Kit was in other quarters.

"Rumors are flying about how Canby will be gone soon, replaced by a general from out yonder in California." Treadwell trusted Canby as much as he did any military man but knew nothing of his replacement.

"We'll see battle 'fore General Carleton takes command," Kit said softly. "I know Carleton from way back and how he takes his time movin' troops. And I know Sibley. Oh, yes, we shall see battle. I want you to scout this here area real close right away."

Treadwell saw his commander pointed to Valverde, spitting distance to the north of their fort.

Meeting of the Clans

February 1, 1862
Cañon de Chelly

"We must kill them all!" raged Follows Quickly. The young warrior hesitated when he realized how loudly he had spoken. Still, even knowing he had shouted at the others gathered for the *nachiid,* he showed no contrition. And Manuelito did not blame him.

The thought of all-out war galled him. The winter had been hard and the sheep had grown thin until bony ribs poked through their woolly coats. Barely enough corn had been stored against this harsh weather and the precious peaches had been mostly destroyed by a hungry boring worm. Manuelito snorted as he thought that the worm afforded them more nutrition than the peach in which it resided.

War was not an easy measure to consider—or take. Yet he had counseled the others to go to war against the Biligáana and had driven them from Fort Defiance. That victory burned brightly in his breast, though he realized the Biligáana resolve had weakened as war gnawed at them from the east. Manuelito had tried to understand why the white man fought and had failed.

They wanted to prohibit slavery—or so they said. The very same bluecoats fighting to prevent slavery condoned it when the Hopi and Ute and Comanche and Nakai stole Dinéh women and children. How many of his clan had been stolen away and taken to the southern part of the territory, to be worked to death in Mexico? Or worse.

Manuelito had lost track of those who'd died. His proud clan had dwindled, even with the addition of Gray Feather and her two sons. *His* two sons. Only men were allowed in the circle of the *nachiid,* where the headmen and other wise men exchanged their thoughts on weighty matters affecting all Dinéh. Manuelito saw Shining Eyes just outside the circle of light cast by the blazing fire and saw the boy's rapt attention. He was ten years old and would soon sit within the gentle fingers of warmth, sharing his innermost thoughts and deliberating with his elders.

"Follows Quickly speaks bluntly," Manuelito said, after some time had passed. "He also speaks the truth. We are like a wounded fawn. A coyote nibbles on one leg. An ant bites another. The crow flies down to peck our eyes. And from behind, from behind come the Zuñi and Ute to poke at us!" This brought smiles to the faces of the headmen.

Manuelito wanted more than smiles. He needed their cooperation, and getting it would be difficult. The Folded Arms People had been hurt more than other clans living deeper in Cañon de Chelly, their beloved Tseyi'. Crops had not been good, but they'd lost fewer relatives to the war parties constantly scouting the fringes of the cañon.

"The Biligáana fight among themselves. Word reaches my ears that the graycoats move up from Comanche lands. Carson and the others who once spoke so eloquently for the Ute are fighting for their very lives. That is good. That the bluecoats are gone from our land is good, also."

"This frees the Zuñi to kill us! The Biligáana headman Carleton refuses to believe we honor their treaty, but the Pueblos do not!" Follows Quickly almost shouted his accusation, interrupting Manuelito. The others turned and stared at him until his anger had subsided. Follows Quickly settled down next to Manuelito Segundo, but the smoldering wrath remained.

"Again, Follows Quickly is blunt—and speaks to the heart of our problem. My clan shrinks daily because of the Pueblos' depredations. We fight, they run away. Only a few times have we fought them successfully." Manuelito turned to his son. "Manuelito Segundo killed more than a dozen of them before the first snow, before the Nightway Chant, before the Biligáana withdrew completely from Dinetah. That was the only time we have killed so many in one battle."

Manuelito settled down, poking at the fire with a long stick. The end began to char. He felt the same way. Most of him was whole; some was burned black and broke off, lost forever. With a sudden thrust, he tossed the entire stick into the fire where it blazed.

"We must *all* fight the Pueblos. Take the war to their doors. Kill them and steal their food and horses."

"You are always the Angry Warrior." Barboncito straightened and stared into the flames. Manuelito wondered what the old warrior saw. He hoped the spirits showed Barboncito the truth and warned him against always seeking the peaceful road.

"I am that," Manuelito declared. "I am also Hastiin Chilhajin, Man of the Black Weed. And others call me by many names." He hesitated to speak his other names, fearing his ears might shrivel.

"Holy Boy," whispered Manuelito Segundo.

"I am known by many names," Manuelito said, "because it is impossible to travel this world without showing different faces."

"A name is sacred," agreed Barboncito. "So is the declaration of war against the Pueblos. Many of us have empty bellies this winter. Is it wise to begin a fight that might last for years?"

"Yes," Manuelito answered without hesitation, so great was his desire. "The Biligáana will not attack us, even if we break their treaty. We *must* defend ourselves. Are our women and children destined to work as slaves? Do the Biligáana not claim they seek an end to such slavery?"

"They speak of many things," Barboncito said, shrugging. "Who can say what they really mean?"

"Consider the treaty. We have honored it. Do they? Do the Pueblos? We must either fight or die."

"All has been said that must," decided Barboncito. "We will weigh the dangers and the benefits of what Manuelito and the others suggest." Barboncito stood and walked off, leaving a hole in the ring. One by one, headmen from other clans left until only those of the Folded Arms People remained.

"We do not need them," Follows Quickly cried angrily. "They are old women. They seek nothing but a warm fire and a full belly. Give them that and they would see the rest of us in chains!"

"Not so," Manuelito said. "Barboncito is a wise man and knows the perils of war. Few others gathered tonight have shown his great courage in battle." Manuelito lifted his chin and indicated Follows Quickly, putting the impetuous warrior in his place. He heard the soft crunch of moccasins on the sand behind him and knew Shining Eyes hesitantly joined them. Manuelito made no effort to shoo the boy away. He had proved himself in battle by saving Manuelito Segundo.

"We fight?" asked Follows Quickly. "With or without the others?"

"We do," Manuelito said. "We do because we must. If we fail, the Zuñi and the Ute will destroy us all."

Manuelito turned to Shining Eyes and saw the boy looking frightened, but with a hint of anticipation, also.

"What is it, my son?"

"The others are wrestling, betting on their skills," Shining Eyes said. "May I bet, also?"

"What do you have to put up as a wager?" Manuelito asked, knowing the answer. All Shining Eyes owned were the two horses he had won so many months ago in the race against Follows Quickly.

"My blanket," Shining Eyes suggested, but Manuelito heard the undercurrent.

"Or one of your horses?" he suggested to the boy. "Are you so sure of the outcome that you would risk so much?"

"I am," Shining Eyes said.

Manuelito shrugged. Let Shining Eyes interpret the motion as he saw fit. The headman found it absorbing as he wondered what the boy would do. Caution, as Barboncito counseled? Or action?

"Thank you!" Shining Eyes turned and raced off. Manuelito stood, but Follows Quickly put a hand on his shoulder.

"You did not ask the true nature of the bet," Follows Quickly pointed out.

"What is he up to?" Again, the petty intrigue amused him and took away some of the edge he felt about the future of the Dinéh that rode so heavily on his shoulders. Manuelito took great pleasure in his sons, Shining Eyes and Goes to War, especially now that Manuelito Segundo had proved himself as a man and had gone off on his own.

"He has been tormented by Oso Negro for months."

"Oso Negro is twice his size, a warrior bringing great honor to any clan. Shining Eyes isn't thinking of challenging him!" The audacity—the stupidity—of such a match outraged Manuelito.

"You told him to follow his own star," Manuelito Segundo pointed out, "as you always encouraged me to do."

"You are born to the Dinéh, you—" Manuelito stopped. Shining Eyes was no less worthy because he had been born a Ute. He might be slow to adopt the ways of his new people, but he *had* learned. And he had shown great courage in battle. But to challenge Oso Negro?

The other, from the Coyote Pass People, lived up to his name. He had fought a black bear with nothing more than a knife and had won. The pelt hung in Oso Negro's hogan as a trophy, and he wore the head as a helmet when he went into battle. The six feathers decorating the bear head showed his ferocity as a warrior.

Manuelito walked to the ring drawn in the sand and saw the

heavy betting against Shining Eyes. The boy appeared scrawny compared to the burly Oso Negro. The Coyote Pass clansmen whooped and hollered, showing their support. And how they wagered! They offered impossible odds when few would bet on Shining Eyes.

"I bet my bay that I can win," Shining Eyes loudly proclaimed. Manuelito cringed. Better to make a lesser bet. Shining Eyes might stand against the heavier, better-trained warrior for a minute. He might not be pinned or thrown from the ring in that time. A better bet, but one that Manuelito could not take.

"I bet two ponies on Shining Eyes," he called.

"I also bet two horses," chimed in Follows Quickly. This startled Manuelito. He bet as a matter of pride in his son. But Follows Quickly's impulsive bet carried the ring of something more than support for a relative, a cousin's son.

Betting became more hectic as these wagers were taken and others made.

"We will have a fine string of horses," Follows Quickly predicted, grinning wickedly. "It is only fitting, because we must ride to war soon."

"We ride to war if the others agree," said Manuelito, "and we might walk if Shining Eyes does not fight fiercely."

"He can do that," Follows Quickly said. "He will do more." He tapped the side of his head. "He will fight with his head as well as his arms. Cayatanita has taught him well—but *I* have taught him even better!"

Before Manuelito could ask when Follows Quickly had given this instruction, the match began. Oso Negro moved forward, light on his feet for such a heavy man. Shining Eyes stood his ground, heels on the line, beyond which he dared not step. If he left the ring, he lost. If Oso Negro pinned his shoulders, he lost. Or if the other forced him to surrender.

"You walk as if your balls hurt you," Shining Eyes said. "But how is that possible when Lost Knife has them in her hogan?"

"What?" Oso Negro bellowed. "What do you know of Lost Knife?"

"What everyone else knows," Shining Eyes said, circling slowly. "Many sniff after a female coyote."

"Dangerous," Manuelito said softly to Follows Quickly, "to insult a man's sister. And how does he know so much of Lost Knife?" Manuelito frowned. His son showed knowledge beyond his years. Or was it? Shining Eyes was ten and almost a man. And Follows Quickly had been coaching him.

Oso Negro surged forward, slipping slightly in the sand. Shining Eyes had chosen his insult well, infuriating the larger man and making him forget caution. Ducking under an arm as thick as a log, Shining Eyes reached up and grabbed an ear. He pulled hard as he kicked at the back of Oso Grande's leg. The warrior's knee yielded and sent him crashing to the ground. For a moment, Manuelito thought the match was at an end. The air had gusted from Oso Negro's chest, leaving him vulnerable.

But Shining Eyes was not strong enough to pin the man before he recovered sufficiently to rear up. Shining Eyes sailed through the air, twisting about agilely and coming to hands and knees just inside the ring.

The bout began in earnest, Shining Eyes whispering taunts that kept Oso Negro enraged and unable to fight dispassionately, as he might have done otherwise. If the larger man had once swallowed his pride and forgotten his anger, he could quickly have ended the match.

Instead, the tide of battle went again to Shining Eyes. Trying to catch up the smaller boy in a bear hug proved Oso Negro's undoing. He missed and staggered forward, off balance. Shining Eyes's legs shot out, entangling thicker ones. Twisting hard, he brought Oso Negro down to the ground with another hard thump. This time Shining Eyes knew better than to attempt a pin. He kept rolling, catching up the other man's ankles. Turning them together prevented Oso Negro from kicking out—and it rolled him from the ring.

Sweating hard, panting from the exertion, Shining Eyes stood for a moment alone in the ring. Then he realized he had won.

Manuelito came into the ring and clapped his son on the back.

"How many horses have you won this night?"

"Five, Father," Shining Eyes answered quickly, but the victory went beyond that and both knew it.

Distant Victory

Treadwell almost fell from the saddle as he drifted off to sleep. Only his horse crow-hopping brought him awake. Wildly grabbing for the reins, he caught himself and saw the trouble. Long shadows off a tree limb dropped across the snowy ground and formed a snakelike shape that spooked his mount.

"Whoa, careful," Treadwell soothed, patting the horse on the neck. The wind had died and the winter cold had temporarily left the countryside. Treadwell suspected it would get cold again soon, but the letter he carried from Albuquerque warmed him a mite.

On his back trail lay Valverde, where Canby had met his brother-in-law and the Confederate forces head-on a month back. Treadwell's nose wrinkled as he imagined the scent of gunpowder and blood still in the air. Canby had brought in artillery and set up waiting for the Confederate regiments, which had swung wide around avoiding Fort Craig, as Kit Carson had been warned. Although he held the ground, Canby had taken heavy casualties owing to the inexperience of his soldiers.

Treadwell tried to forget the feeling deep in his gut when Canby's courier had arrived at the fort, ordering Carson and his First New Mexico Volunteers directly north to reinforce from the west. They had crossed the Rio Grande and come up to support Canby from the rear. During the morning of February twenty-first they had listened to the heavy cannonade and sharp crack of rifles. Treadwell had been scared before in his life but never as scared as he had been when Canby'd ordered in his reserves that afternoon.

They had crossed the river and charged into a band of 400 Confederate riflemen. Carson's volunteers had been positioned between the rebel force and a twenty-four-pound artillery piece trying to destroy Sibley's flank. Eighty yards had separated Union from Confederate troopers and the exchange had been heavy.

Treadwell shuddered as ice broke off a dead limb of a nearby cottonwood. The sharp crack reminded him of the rifle fire he had endured until the artillerists had swung their piece around and dropped a twenty-four-pound shell in the middle of the rebel line. That had ended the fight, as far as the soldiers from Fort Craig were concerned. The rebels had not regrouped, and Canby had ordered Kit Carson to retreat.

Their part in the battle had been brief, fierce, and frightening. They had done all they could to defeat Sibley and had failed, the rebel general disengaging and moving his men farther north in his quest to capture Fort Union. He had chosen to leave Fort Craig at his rear in the hands of the enemy—and this suited Treadwell just fine. He'd tasted battle and didn't much cotton to it.

From all he had seen of the First New Mexico Volunteers, none of them had much stomach for renewed battle, either. For almost a month Canby had remained at the fort, readying his troops for orders to move out. It had come a week back, Treadwell traveling with the general as far as Albuquerque. Canby had left Carson in charge with the orders to hold the fort against all attack.

Now Treadwell carried a message from Canby that would bring a smile to every man's lips when Kit read it—or had it read to the garrison.

Treadwell gentled his horse again as new shadows danced on the trail to frighten the high-spirited horse, then urged it forward at a brisker pace to reach the fort before sundown. He did not want to be on the trail another night, not with a wind kicking up that threatened to freeze his bones.

The pathetic fort was bathed in deep shadows when Treadwell rode to the main gate and waved his hat at the solitary guard perched atop the adobe wall.

"Got good news for the colonel," Treadwell bellowed. "Let me in."

"You anxious to get poisoned by the cook again?" came the joking reply. "You got a cast-iron stomach, Joe. Or a hankerin' to die."

Treadwell impatiently waited for the gates to swing open. He ducked low and rode in, hitting the ground and running the last few yards when he saw Kit's office showed a precious kerosene lamp burning brightly. Mostly, candle lanterns were used by the enlisted men. Treadwell shook off the cold and some snow that had accumulated on his buckskins, then pushed right on in without knocking. Kit Carson wasn't a man who held much for needless ceremony, and when he heard the news he would be pleased.

The shaggy-haired ex-mountain man looked up from his desk, his eyes bleary. A strained, haggard expression told Treadwell that Colonel Carson had not slept much since the Battle of Valverde. Canby had kept the troops on alert until his departure, and Kit acutely felt the pressures of command.

"You got back sooner 'n I expected," Kit observed. "Is the news good? Or do we move on out to support the general?"

"The best news there can be," Treadwell said breathlessly. He pulled the official documents from his pouch and laid them in front of Kit. Kit reached out and touched the envelope with its fancy wax seal, then pushed it back in Treadwell's direction.

"My eyes are actin' up somethin' fierce. You read it to me, since you already seem to know what's bein' said."

"I do," Treadwell said. He tore open the envelope and pulled out Canby's thick letter. He scanned the first page and saw nothing contradicting what he already knew. "There's mention of a citation for you and for the First New Mexico Volunteers' bravery in battle."

"We hardly fought," Kit said, pale eyes fixed on Treadwell. "Still, it's good to know we're bein' noticed."

"All the way back to Washington, it seems," Treadwell went on. "The War Department will be sending medals and such later."

"A bit premature," Kit muttered, "what with—" His eyes turned to steel as they fixed on Treadwell's broadly smiling face. "What else? Out with it, you scoundrel!"

"Sibley was whupped March twenty-sixth up in Glorieta Pass. Colonel Chivington and his Colorado Volunteers took on the rebels and laid into them something fierce," Treadwell said with satisfaction. "A supply train was burned, eighty wagons in all, and forty men captured. Sibley might not have half his men left. They broke rank and fled the field, his men straggling off. Canby reports them heading back to Texas in disarray and doesn't think even one in three will return to Mesilla. He's going to follow them the whole way, just to be certain."

Kit Carson let out a huge sigh of relief and leaned back. "That means the threat is over, fer the time bein'."

"Nobody expects the Confederates to invade us again any time soon. The war is heating up back East and pulling more and more of the Texas troopers into Mississippi and Tennessee."

"Good, very good. We kin git back to livin' our lives," Kit said.

For a moment Treadwell said nothing more. This silence caught Kit's attention.

"There's more news? Good or bad?"

Treadwell was not sure how he would interpret the second page of the letter he had brought. Canby's lieutenant had not bothered telling him this part when he had been given the message back in Albuquerque. Treadwell read it twice, thinking hard about it. Now that the South had been defeated decisively at Glorieta, New Mexico Territory was safe for years to come—

and that meant Kit Carson could turn his attention to helping Treadwell find his family.

Except the last paragraph in the letter.

"Spit it out, Joe. What more is there?" Kit stood and leaned forward, a bulldog of a man. His instincts were sound, and he knew this was good for him if not for his messenger.

"General Canby is granting you immediate leave to go visit your family," Treadwell said in a choked voice.

Kit Carson let out a whoop that echoed throughout the fort. He caught up Treadwell in a bear hug that about crushed the other mountain man's ribs, then dropped him and ran from the office, shouting for his subordinates. Treadwell knew Carson would be gone with the dawn, heading north to his family and new son in Taos.

The Civil War had briefly visited him, and Treadwell had done his beholden duty. Now he expected Carson to live up to his promise, using the entire might of the Union Army, if necessary, to find Gray Feather, Shining Eyes, and a baby he had never seen, a child well nigh a year old now.

He just didn't see how that was going to happen soon enough to suit him.

Los Ricos

September 12, 1862
Outside Santa Fé

He drew back the arrow slowly, taking great care as he aimed. Manuelito let it fly. It drove squarely into the man's chest. His victim gasped, clutched at the feathered shaft that had driven halfway through his body, then collapsed.

Manuelito motioned for the others to move closer. Raiding this near Santa Fé proved dangerous but necessary. Oh, so necessary, he thought to himself. At his right moved Follows Quickly, and behind came Manuelito Segundo. The two men would protect him well as he moved into the settlement. The ranch house was a large adobe showing the wealth of *los ricos* who lived within. Manuelito's lip pulled back in a sneer. They had cattle and crops—and more than one servant stolen from Dinetah. What cattle weren't run off and what horses weren't stolen would be killed and left as a warning.

As would the rich ones inside.

Manuelito ignored a musket ball that sailed past his head. From the frightened cries, he doubted any within the adobe would shoot straight, though their firepower was far greater than that of the Dinéh attacking. Loosing another arrow caused great turmoil inside the house. The arrow had sailed through the narrow window and might have injured someone inside.

"Too bad you did not draw blood, as with this one," Follows Quickly said, kicking the man Manuelito had already skewered with his arrow. The young warrior dropped to one knee and quickly searched the body, finding few items worthy of taking. The real prize lay in a large leather pouch heavy with gunpowder. Follows Quickly held it high and let out a whoop of joy.

"My musket will again sing with this fine gift!" he crowed.

"You fire too slowly with the Biligáana weapon," complained Manuelito. He nocked and loosed arrow after arrow. He could fire a dozen times while Follows Quickly loaded his stolen musket but once. Finding the range again, he shot through a small window until someone inside blocked it with a large board, possibly a table turned on its side.

But Manuelito was satisfied. The more those within cowered, the less likely they were to injure any of their attackers. He motioned for his warriors to move toward the outbuildings where the livestock—and slaves—were kept.

Joyous crying reached his ears when one small child was rescued. Manuelito did not recognize the boy, but he might have been of the Coyote Pass People. If so, it would please Barboncito that one of his relatives had been freed. And it would further solidify the old headman's support of this foray against the Nakai and Biligáana.

"Horses," Manuelito Segundo called. "A dozen. More!"

The pounding of hooves told Manuelito his son had taken the animals as booty. This would be a fine day. They had already run off two dozen head of cattle, and now they had horses. Manuelito stepped over the fallen body of the Nakai and studied the imposingly obdurate adobe. The thick vigas protruding offered a clue to destroying the house.

"Loop ropes around the wooden ceiling beams," Manuelito ordered. His warriors rode to the house and did as he'd ordered. "Pull them free!"

Most of the ropes slid free and only one rider succeeded, but the edge of the adobe began to crumble as the support in the roof failed. Manuelito dropped to one knee and used a burning glass to set afire an arrow. This he shot high into the air, arching it onto the roof. Another and another followed as his warriors worried at the protruding vigas.

The consternation within became apparent. Manuelito barely called out in time, "Hold your fire!" as a half-dozen small children darted out. All were Dinéh.

Follows Quickly and Orejo Pequeño guided them from the doorway as others fired their arrows into the building. Manuelito knew this trick of *los ricos*. They thought they could curry favor by releasing their slaves. Or perhaps they wanted him to kill his own people. Whatever the motive, it played into his hand. With the hostages freed and on their way back to Dinetah, he could punish those inside the adobe.

"The cavalry is coming," someone inside shouted. "We sent a messenger for them when we saw your war party."

"Liars," Manuelito grumbled. He knew that Carleton still commanded an army in disarray. The bluecoats might have defeated the grays, with the help of the mad shaman from Colorado, but Carleton lacked the iron grip required to move against the Dinéh. He still feared he would lose his country to those from the south and could hardly spare troopers to protect a single rancher.

Flames began dancing on the roof, spreading quickly. Manuelito formed his ranks and waited. Like prairie dogs drowned in their burrows, *los ricos* would soon rush forth and become . . . *los muertos*.

"We found more horses. Do we go on to the next *rancheria?*" asked Manuelito Segundo. "We will be as rich as these who take our women and children for their menial tasks."

"We fight this battle. Then we decide," Manuelito said, though he had already concluded that this would end their raid. They were only a few miles from the heart of Santa Fé, their revenge as they rescued their own people would be taken as an insult. His lip curled back. That was good. Perhaps Carleton would find it impossible to maintain his hold, even in the midst of his Santa Fé garrison, and would retreat eastward.

"Let the Comanche eat his liver," Manuelito growled. More loudly, he shouted to his raiders, "Now, fire now!"

They did not need his command. Follows Quickly's musket belched white smoke and spat a piece of lead into the man trying to escape the burning house. Manuelito's first arrow killed a woman. His second killed a boy hardly older than Shining Eyes.

But he did not stop his attack, nor did any of the others. These were people who thought nothing of slitting a warrior's throat as he slept and stealing away his wife and children. *Los ricos* sold the young women into prostitution or abused them horribly. Manuelito did not want to think of the life ahead for a slave Dinéh.

They measured their wealth this day in human lives taken, not horses and blankets. He felt only blood lust as he shot until his quiver held no more arrows.

Manuelito sat straighter on his pony when he entered Tseyi'. The sandstone cañon walls surrounded him, cradled him, promised him life and safety from his enemies. He was eager to see Gray Feather, to show her all he had accomplished. Riding slowly, he went past the hogan where Juanita lived. There would be time later to see her. First, he wanted to visit his new son, Goes to War.

Dust settled off his blanket as Manuelito dropped to the ground. From the hogan came Gray Feather, hesitant, still not recovered from her delivery. This worried Manuelito, but not unduly. He did not expect her to have the strength of a Dinéh, yet she still walked with a halt in her step, as if great pain attended her every movement.

"You've returned," she said. He could never tell from her tone if gladness dwelt in her heart or if she wished him dead. Gray Feather had never opposed him in anything he'd asked, unlike Juanita, with her fast tongue and quicker anger.

"Twenty horses," he said proudly. "For you and Goes to

War." Manuelito looked past his wife to the doorway. Shining Eyes pushed aside the blanket, stormclouds of fury on his young face. He had not been allowed to go with the war party, but Manuelito would not hurry the boy. The boy's victory over Oso Negro had impressed him, but it had also given Shining Eyes a false sense of his own ability. Having another impetuous brave like Follows Quickly at his side—and his son, at that—would have prevented Manuelito from leading the raiders properly.

"And for you, my son," Manuelito said, "I bring you this present." He reached into his belt and drew forth a pistol. It lacked ammunition and powder, but he had taken it from the last man to rush from the blazing house, and as a trophy, it carried great luck.

Shining Eyes silently took it, but his eyes showed no gratitude. Manuelito knew the boy had resented being left behind to help with the corn, to pick peaches, to tend the sheep for his mother as she nursed Goes to War. He had done woman's work while his adoptive father had been raiding.

"You will use it against our enemies with great care . . . and bravery," Manuelito said. But Shining Eyes did not respond.

Manuelito shrugged this off and followed Gray Feather into her hogan. There was so much to tell and hear.

A Clue

Joseph Treadwell wrapped the wool Army blanket around his shoulders and turned slightly to keep his face shielded from the brisk north wind.

It was promising to be another cold winter, but he wouldn't be spending it at some hole-in-the-wall fort too far south this year. He twisted around on the dry, hard ground and looked over his shoulder, his eyes lifted and fixed on snow-capped Mount Taylor. It was sacred to the Navajo, one of their four holy mountains.

He spat, wiped his mouth, flipped spittle from his tangled beard and let his eyes drift lower, toward Fort Wingate being built by Lieutenant Colonel Francisco Chávez's troopers. The fort butted up against the Navajo domain, and Treadwell could feel the nearness of his wife and family, as if he might reach out and touch her cheek again, hold his son once more or even cradle the new baby. He spat again, remembering how Carson had sent only a single letter of recommendation to the new commander of forces in the territory.

"Only one damned letter, and one that didn't carry much weight," Treadwell groused. Still, Carson had done what he could as commander of the First New Mexico Volunteers, permanently posted at Fort Craig as a bulwark against any invasion of Texans. The threat from the South was a distant drum roll no one heard much these days, letting Carson peacefully collect his $110 a month pay, with generous allowances for food and horse forage. At least General Carleton understood the real danger in New Mexico and had moved quickly to meet the challenge of the insurrectionist tribes to the west.

Treadwell had petitioned a meeting with the new military commander but had not been much impressed when it was granted. Men with vision were one thing in his mind, but men with religious vision always troubled Treadwell, whether Indian shaman chanting and sprinkling corn pollen all around or white men spouting the gospel. Nobody said a word against Carleton as a military officer, but Treadwell saw a fervor burning in the man's wide, dark, piercing eyes that went beyond simple duty. His chin jutted aggressively, and his arrogance worried Treadwell like a rock in his boot. Some called him a humanitarian, but Carleton's talk of the "savages" and how he was going to "civilize them" bespoke of a vision different from Treadwell's. Carleton never talked but always struck a pose and lectured dramatically, sometimes in a thundering voice about his dream for peaceful settlements scattered around the territory.

Treadwell snorted in disgust at such maundering. New Carletonia, the officer called his proposed settlement. A paradise for the savages to learn religion and culture and live in splendid peace, Apache alongside Comanche and Navajo.

Still, Carleton had assigned him to scout for Chávez as the Union Army returned to Navajoland. The year spent running off the rebels had brought Navajo raids and constant protests from New Mexican ranchers and farmers, but that would change now. Treadwell felt it in his bones. Whatever Carleton's motives, he recognized the threat to peace in the territory and sent his best troops to retake the land Canby had given up so easily.

Let Carson while away his time with garrison duty at Valverde, Treadwell thought in disgust. Damn his soul to hell and halfway back again. Treadwell spat again, dark thoughts building like the storm clouds around the distant Chuska Mountains. A tinker had brought unsettling word to Treadwell weeks back that might go a ways toward explaining Carson's reluctance to bring more persuasive arguments to bear helping Treadwell regain his family. Treadwell knew Josepha Carson for a charitable woman, but she had bought a Navajo captive from a band of Ute for a single horse—and Kit Carson had adopted the boy into his family.

Taking one last chaw off the plug of tobacco before stuffing the stringy wad into his pouch, Treadwell sat and stared at nothing in particular. The mountains dimmed under a shelf of leaden clouds, and he saw nothing in the somber shimmer replacing them. Carson had adopted one of the thieving, wife-stealing Navajo into his own family. A final brown gob hit the ground and splashed against a rock marking Treadwell's opinion of such behavior.

Gray Feather and Shining Eyes were out there. He knew it. They had to be or he would have nothing left in the world—or in his breast. He had traded a year's service for this moment. Chávez would sally from Fort Wingate into the heart of the Navajo realm, and Joseph Treadwell would be at the front of the column.

Treadwell stood and stretched his aching muscles before making his way down the slope past the soldiers toiling to construct the fort to the commanding officer's specifications. As he weaved in and out of the workers, Treadwell nodded in approval. Chávez knew how to protect his men; Fort Wingate would hold off even the fiercest Navajo attack.

"Treadwell, a word with you, if you please," called the commander, looking up from a sheaf of papers clutched in his hand. Treadwell turned to where Chávez oversaw construction of the post hospital. "I'm sending out a hunting party. Will you go along? You're the best hunter in the command."

Treadwell was pleased at the compliment and at the chance to get in the saddle again. Spending time watching others work wasn't his style, especially when any foray into land held by the Navajo might give him a clue to Gray Feather's whereabouts.

"I don't miss too often with my trusty Hawken," Treadwell allowed. "That the bunch you're sending out?" He jerked his thumb in the direction of a squad of four men under command of the corporal.

Chávez nodded brusquely and turned back to answer a question about the flooring in the hospital. Treadwell saw that the colonel insisted on an airspace below the floor, telling him Fort Wingate would be around long into the hot summer. There would be no retreat this time.

Nodding in satisfaction at this, Treadwell went to the corral and cut out his mare. The horse whinnied and nuzzled him.

"No carrots today," he said. "Maybe when we get back, if the hunting is good." A big brown eye stared at him, begging him to reconsider. A day or two on the trail before a treat did not compare favorably to one immediately.

Treadwell laughed and tugged on the bridle, getting his horse out of the corral and saddling quickly. He forked his legs over the sloping back and put his heels into the horse's flanks, trotting to catch up with the corporal and his men.

"You scoutin' for us today, Joe?" asked the non-com, a boy somewhere between hay and grass. Treadwell wondered if the corporal might be as old as eighteen and doubted it. That didn't much affect the way he thought of him, though, since men younger than this had died at Valverde. It wasn't the years but the miles—and bullets—that counted.

"Reckon I am. I've been out a couple times this past week and think we might find some mule tail deer in that direction." Treadwell pointed due west. He found some spoor showing old passage of a party of Indians also but could not identify them. Zuñi and Hopi traveled these trails, as well as the Navajo. No matter who rode the path, it looked to be good hunting ground with plenty of watering holes to attract game.

"Venison would suit me jist fine," the corporal said, "after all that wormy food we been gettin'. Even peaches and tomatoes from the airtights are tastin' bitter."

Treadwell had sampled some of the peaches put up in the tin

cans and had been unable to eat a second helping. A few of the troopers had gotten the runs, maybe from the fruit or maybe from something else. It was hard to tell and nobody much cared if the sickness didn't spread.

Treadwell kept up his side of the talk as he rode along, his eyes working back and forth in front along the path as he sought spoor. The time for talking would be over when he saw some sign of a deer, but this part of the terrain didn't look too encouraging. An hour later proved different.

"Corporal!" Treadwell snapped, holding up his hand for silence. Even as he had thought there was nothing to be seen here, his sharp eye caught the lone feather caught on the low thorny bush. "Quiet."

"What's wrong?" The boy hiked one leg over his uncomfortable McClellan saddle as if to drop to the ground. Treadwell shot him a cold glare, freezing him in place. He didn't want anyone trampling the trail he hoped to find.

On hands and knees Treadwell worked across the trail to the feather, sniffing at it and finally plucked it from its berth. Navajo. He tucked the feather away in a side pocket and found an unshod hoofprint in the soft dirt. Another five minutes convinced him the rider was not alone—and that Navajo had passed by less than an hour earlier. A steaming, still-warm pile of horse dung a quarter mile down the trail confirmed his suspicion.

"It might be a war party," Treadwell said in a low voice, "or only a hunting party, like us."

"Not like us," the corporal said, his brown eyes wide. Treadwell couldn't tell if it was anticipation or fear that set the vein to throbbing in the corporal's neck. "We know they're ahead of us. We can overtake 'em and get us a prisoner or two to take back to the colonel."

"What about the deer? I'm gettin' hungry," complained another trooper, even younger than the corporal.

"Hush. No talking from now on. It might mean your life," warned Treadwell. The men sent on the hunting party lacked experience, that he saw as plain as the sun setting low in the west. For all his tough talk, the corporal was shaking just a mite at the prospect of fighting Navajo.

"How many, how far?" the non-com asked.

Treadwell shook his head, unable to give a good answer yet. He thought there might be as many as five—an equal number, but not in a fight. He did not doubt any warriors they found would be blooded, experienced, ready to kill. Chávez had good men in his command, veterans with Indian fighting experience. These five were not of that ilk.

"What do you want us to do?" The corporal had the good sense to know he was not in charge, should they fight the Indians.

"Stay together so they can't pick off stragglers one by one," Treadwell said. "But don't get so close together you'll get in each other's way when the fighting starts." He walked slowly, his horse trailing behind. Treadwell found it harder to find spoor as the sun slipped behind the horizon and cast long, spidery shadows behind him. A touch of winter returned with the wind to remind him they were in the mountains. Treadwell walked even more cautiously when he realized the wind was blowing in his face.

Nose working like a hunting dog, he tried to find any scent that might betray the Navajo. If he knew them, they would be working into the wind, too, so he and the soldiers might come up from behind. A surprise attack. Quick fight, over soon. Treadwell prayed such would be the case as heavier musk caused his nose to wrinkle.

"Not too far ahead," he warned. He put his finger to his lips when he heard the soft *thud-thud* of a horse's hooves. He stepped off the game trail, tugging gently at his horse to keep the mare from spooking. Treadwell swung the reins around a low branch, grabbed his musket and set off at a goodly pace to overtake the Navajo ahead of him.

He had not ordered the corporal to stand fast and immediately regretted it when he heard the squad blundering along close behind. Treadwell lengthened his stride in an attempt to outpace them and almost ran over the Navajo warrior sitting crouched by the side of the trail, patiently waiting for game that wouldn't come now.

The brave's eyes widened in surprise at seeing Treadwell loom up out of shadow. His hand jerked toward his bow and arrow, trying to draw back the string and skewer Treadwell. A whistling noise sounded, then stopped in a dull thud. Treadwell staggered, then regained his balance. He had buffaloed the warrior with the barrel of his rifle.

"Danged waste," he muttered to himself, worrying that he might have knocked the rifle sights out of kilter. Treadwell pressed his hand flat on the man's chest and felt the harsh beating of a heart he longed to rip out with his bare hands. He refrained, knowing the others would be farther along the trail.

"Joe, you there?" came the corporal's soft voice.

"Got me a prisoner. You boys look after 'im while I explore some more."

"Jonesy, you do the chore. Rest of you, come along," the corporal ordered. Treadwell started to countermand that order, then froze. Three Navajo stalked along the trail, rifles resting at the ready in the crooks of their arms.

"I know that one," Treadwell said. "Barboncito, one of their headmen. An important one, too."

"Then we got ourselves something better 'n venison," said the corporal, fingers nervously drumming on his musket. The tapping sound—or any of a dozen other signs—caused Barboncito to stop and cant his head to one side, listening hard. Treadwell knew they would lose the chance if they hesitated.

Letting out a whoop, he charged forward, trusting the soldiers to follow his lead. Treadwell got off a shot at a warrior behind Barboncito. The lead ball went wide but sent the brave diving for cover and giving Treadwell the chance to grapple with Barboncito.

Arms filled with wiggling, twisting muscular frame, Treadwell tried to force the Navajo leader to the ground where he might subdue him. Treadwell wasn't sure what the bearded Navajo did but he found himself trying to stand—with both legs kicked out from under him. Treadwell crashed to the ground, rolled and tried to scramble back to his feet.

"Fire!"

The soldiers cut loose with a barrage that deafened Treadwell. The air filled with choking white smoke and someone kicked him in the side of the head in their rush to capture the Navajo hunters. Stunned, the mountain man fell to hands and knees. The fight washed back and forth above his head, then slipped away into the twilight before he could push himself to his feet.

"Corporal! Where the hell are you?" Treadwell shouted. He heard boots pounding against the hard ground and cursed. Green troopers chasing a seasoned warrior like Barboncito on foot, in the dark, over unknown terrain, spelled nothing but disaster. Treadwell fumbled to reload his rifle, then cursed some more and gave up on it, drawing his knife.

He barely arrived in time to grab the arm drawn back to drive a knife into the corporal's belly. A warrior sat across the soldier's chest, knees pinning him down. The knife gleamed in the dark as Treadwell lashed out with his. Steel met steel and sent blue sparks flying. With a savage shout, the mountain man plunged forward and hugged the upturned arm to his chest, twisting hard as he ran into the man.

The warrior was dislodged, and his knife went flying. But Treadwell gained no advantage. Arm slippery with sweat, the Navajo jerked free and sprinted off before Treadwell could react.

"Thanks, Joe," the corporal gasped.

"The others, where are they?"

The corporal hesitated a moment, then put his fingers to his lips and let out a shrill whistle. It wasn't the more subtle summoning a Navajo might use—a quail call or hooty owl—but it worked. Summoned from their fight, the soldiers made their way back. To Treadwell's astonishment, they were none the worse for the fight.

"They got clean away. Sorry," apologized the youngest of the squad. "Shouldna let 'em get off like that, not when we had 'em."

"Found their camp, though," piped up another, his voice breaking in excitement. "Got their game, too!"

Treadwell had to laugh. They had gone hunting and found Navajo. In spite of letting them get away, they would still return to Fort Wingate with some decent fresh meat.

"The prisoner. The one I nabbed." Treadwell set off at a dead run, returning to the shadows in the forest where he had left the soldier standing guard over the fallen hunter. He let out a deep sigh of relief when he saw the soldier still alive and standing watch over his captive.

Treadwell slowed, then approached one step at a time to let his Navajo prisoner know he meant no harm. Inside, Treadwell churned like a young buck going into battle for the first time. At no time during the fight had he felt this agitated. He squatted down beside the Navajo, staring at the dirt in front of the man. Treadwell knew better than to insult his prisoner by staring directly at him even if he wanted to cut his throat a slow inch at a time.

After a short while of respectful silence, Treadwell began asking his questions in poor Navajo.

The prisoner sat stoically, saying nothing until Treadwell's patience began to wear thin.

"You hunted with Barboncito," he said. This produced a slight widening of the eyes. "Barboncito is a great warrior, by far the wisest in all Dinetah." Treadwell mulled over how he ought to approach the subject of his wife and children.

"What you goin' on about, Joe? We kin get him back and one of them Enemy Navajo fellas can interrogate him all properlike."

"I need some information, Corporal," Treadwell snapped, angered at being distracted. "I need it *now.*" The edge to his words caused the young man to step back.

"Barboncito is not the greatest warrior of the Dinéh," the prisoner finally allowed. "Manuelito is!"

"I have seen him," Treadwell said, holding down his rage. He had seen Manuelito—stealing a pregnant woman and a young boy. Again his captive showed signs of astonishment. "He is a great fighter, but not the greatest. Barboncito is wiser, a better fighter."

"No! You lie!"

"I have been to Manuelito's camp in the Chuska Mountains," Treadwell said, fishing for information he could use.

The captive laughed harshly at this. "He lives in Cañon de Chelly, under the double red cliffs." Even as the words escaped the man's lips, he realized he had said too much. He seemed to fold into himself, arms pulled in tightly and legs drawn up so his chin rested on his knees. Treadwell saw there was no reason to continue the questioning. He had gained as much as he was likely to from the prisoner.

Treadwell rocked back on his heels. The man who had stolen his wife and family camped under twin cliffs in the middle of Navajo country. It wasn't much, but it was more than he had known before.

Double red cliffs repeated in his head all the way back to Fort Wingate. Double red cliffs . . . and Cañon de Chelly.

Mescaleros, Carson, and Carleton

October 26, 1862
Fort Stanton

Kit Carson inhaled deeply, filling his barrel chest with the sharp fragrances of piñon, juniper, and fir carried on the air. A tiny nip of winter blew across his leathery face, but he worried more about the snow on the rugged Capitan Mountains outside Fort Stanton. Returning to active duty might have been a mistake, he reckoned. If snow came early as it promised, he would be cut off from traveling back to Taos and his family. Josepha and the children had left Los Lunas for Taos a few days after Canby was promoted and transferred back East and Carleton was put in charge of the territory. Kit had not seen them since.

He had arrived here less than an hour ago after the tiring trip from Fort Union and already he grew homesick. Kit felt no thrill of a new command or the challenging job assigned him. His dear Chipita had been left behind a month ago, and now he saw no end to his tour of duty. He had dictated a letter to her during his brief stay at Fort Union. Was little Julian in school now? How he missed Julian and all the others of his growing family!

Kit sighed and shook his shaggy head. To protect against the wind, he shoved his hands under the front flap of his blue wool officer's jacket. He ought never have let Carleton talk him into coming south to fight the Apache. Still, he owed a debt of gratitude to the man for his civility and decided manners in the past. Kit wasn't exactly sure where it had gotten to, but back in '55, Carleton had given him the "finest hat ever made in the state of New York" as reward for his scouting. The hat proved less than useful outdoors in New Mexico and was worn only twice that he could recollect at Washington receptions. Kit usually kept better track of such awards, treasuring them as a way of basking in the reflected glory of powerful, educated, and socially prominent friends, but not this time.

He owed Carleton for such courtesy then and his quick acceptance of a poorly educated frontiersman as a fellow officer now. More than that, Carleton overlooked his shortcomings as an officer and insisted he could turn Kit into the best officer in any command in the U.S. Army. Kit wished he could find it in his heart to oversee his men with the iron hand required of an Army officer. Such discipline did not come easily to a man used to tall mountains, vast emptiness, and freedom to do as he pleased.

If James Carleton had placed chains around him, he could not have bound him any tighter.

"Colonel, you got a minute?" Captain James Graydon stood rigidly at attention, awaiting his pleasure.

For "Paddy" Graydon, Kit had little time or good feelings. The captain's report on meeting with José Largo and other Mescalero Apache chiefs a few days before Kit arrived was filled with obvious lies, but Kit didn't know how to ferret out the truth. Fact was, Graydon might have had to fire on them as he reported. It might have been self-defense.

Two chiefs were dead with nine of their warriors and twenty more wounded. Getting the Apache to surrender might prove more difficult than Carleton had thought after such a slaughter. Kit shook his head, remembering Carleton's boundless trust in

him. He had to live up to it, and Graydon's quickness with the
musket had ruined an opportunity to parley.

"What kin I do for you, Cap'n?" Kit looked past Graydon,
reflecting on how the officer had lost control of his command
at Valverde, a full company supported by 500 mounted militia,
when rebel artillery opened fire on his position. As with the
massacre of the Apache chiefs, Kit tried not to jump to conclu-
sions. He had not been present on either occasion.

Still, doubts lingered as to Graydon's quality as an officer
and a gentleman.

"The fort is a shambles, Colonel," Graydon reported. "Being
abandoned for such a spell, it's fallen into disrepair. We waited
for you to arrive to see what you wanted. We camped down the
hill a ways, putting up in tents."

"What part of the fort is in worst repair?" Kit had not even
ridden over to inspect Fort Stanton before finding a spot to pitch
his own tent. That tumbledown pile of wood and rock named after
the Secretary of War had been built before the war and abandoned
quickly in the months before Sibley's incursion.

"Everything," Captain Graydon reported. "The roofs are falling in, windows are broken, it's not safe to tread the boardwalks.
The cook says the water is potable, but he's been known to
make hasty judgments. What should we do? Continue to camp
outside?"

"Tents," muttered Kit, staring at his pitched a dozen yards
away. He had lived in a tent so long. He preferred the open sky
to the canvas flapping in the night. He preferred his own home
in Taos. "No, have the men begin repairs right away. We need
a presence to show strength to the Mescaleros."

"Shall I strike your tent and move you inside what's left of the
stockade?" Graydon's voice carried a hint of sarcasm. Kit wasn't
sure what to do about such insubordination. What would General
Carleton do? The man's autocratic manner often grated on Kit's
sensibilities, but he could not gainsay Carleton's commanding
presence. People did as the general ordered.

"Do so. Has Major Morrison returned from patrol?"

"Morrison is still out," Graydon said, his eyes narrowing slightly. "He's not a man to trust, Colonel. He knows nothing of these savages. I overheard him saying that he—"

"I will not have one officer bad-mouthin' another," Kit said brusquely. "And has Doc Whitlock showed up yet?"

"Whitlock? That—" Graydon bit off his contempt for the surgeon. "Haven't seen hide nor hair of him, Colonel."

"See that the hospital is repaired quickly. Whitlock is a good man. He patched up some of the boys back at Valverde that I didn't reckon would ever see the light of day again. They's ridin' out there now." Kit's arm swept across the panorama of southern New Mexico.

As he motioned, he saw a rider galloping hard and fast from the north.

"Courier's comin'," Kit observed. His keen eyes caught sight of the courier's pouch dangling around the man's neck, even at this distance. "You git on with your repairs, Captain. I'll see what the general's got to say."

Kit waited for the courier to drop from the saddle, out of breath from his desperate ride.

"Your horse is sore in need of tendin'," Kit observed. "Must be powerful important for you to run a good horse into the ground like that."

"Sir," cried the courier, snapping to attention. Kit saw that sergeant's stripes had been pulled from the man's sleeve, replaced by bars on his collar. So many men worked their way up quickly through the ranks. So many were killed leaving those positions a'begging.

"Here are orders straight from General Carleton's hand. I was ordered to deliver them without delay."

Kit took the sealed envelope and looked around. His reading wasn't the best. Fact was, he could hardly make out Carleton's florid script when the general got down to scribbling real fast.

"Eyes are actin' up on me, Lieutenant. Could you read it to me?"

"Sir, why, yes, sir, of course." The man opened the sealed

envelope and scanned the sheet. "General Carleton sends his greetings and best wishes to you on your new command here at Fort Stanton." The courier cleared his throat and glanced over at Kit.

"Go on, son. Read what the general's got to say." Kit rubbed one eye, as if he had dust in it.

"Sir, he says about the Mescaleros, 'All Indian men of that tribe are to be killed whenever and wherever you find them: the women and children will not be harmed, but you will take them prisoners and feed them at Fort Stanton until you receive other instructions about them.' " The lieutenant coughed loudly to get Kit's attention. The mountain man was gazing at the Capitans, thinking how many Apache rode free and wild among their tall peaks.

"I reckon the orders is clear enough. He wants us to move 'em to the new reservation he's havin' built to the north. What's he call it?"

"Fort Sumner, sir. He named it after Edwin Sumner, or so I hear."

"Fort Sumner," mused Kit. "He wants us to move the Apache to this new fort, but I've heard it called somethin' else."

"The Indians have taken to calling it the round grove, for all the cottonwoods along the Pecos."

"Bosque Redondo," Kit said. "The Mescaleros will be sent to Bosque Redondo right away." Resolve set in. "That's what General Carleton orders, and that's what we will do." He took the papers from the courier and stuffed them in the front of his jacket. When Major Morrison returned, he could get him to read the rest of the letter.

"Bosque Redondo," he repeated, the name rolling over his tongue. "Bosque Redondo." Kit Carson shook his head and started walking toward his new command at Fort Stanton.

Duel

"These are mighty serious charges you're bringin' ag'in Captain Graydon," Kit Carson said. He ran his fingers over the well-read copy of the *Santa Fé Gazette*. Major Morrison had brought it in from his last patrol, giving him the worst of the charges.

Dr. Whitlock puffed up like a rain-drenched banty rooster. He leaned forward, hands against the far side of Kit's desk. Dust lay everywhere and the renovation of Fort Stanton was only partly complete.

"I believe these charges to be the gospel truth."

"No blasphemin', now, Doctor," Kit said softly. "You got proof that Graydon murdered them Apache?"

"He lured them into drinking heavily, then cold-bloodedly killed them. Kit, I came here to ask for a recommendation from you, not to be examined. If anyone ought to be held accountable for his crimes, it is Paddy Graydon."

"Well now, he ain't one of my favorite officers," Kit allowed. He pushed back and hiked his feet to his desk. Believing Dr. Whitlock was far easier than listening to the swill Graydon poured forth. "Still, he deserves a hearing."

"Everything I wrote in that piece in the *Gazette* is true,"

Whitlock declared. "Having a murderer masquerading as an officer will only harm your mission."

"We been gettin' a few Apache willin' to surrender. Fact of the matter is, some have already gone to Santa Fé to palaver with General Carleton."

"I know, I know," Whitlock said impatiently. "They have agreed to go to Fort Sumner."

"Bosque Redondo," Kit said, the words slipping from his tongue. It seemed a name intended to hide rather than reveal.

"That's one name for it. He calls it Fair Carletonia." The bitterness in the surgeon's voice caused Kit to drop his feet and lean forward.

"You're a good doctor. I seen you in action and I know. You want a recommendation from me, and you'll get it. I'll have my adjutant write it up all proper-like. And as to Captain Graydon, I'll start an inquiry."

"Thanks, Kit. I always counted you as a fair and honest man. The general's got a better man here than he realizes."

Kit beamed. Men with book learning were always saying things he didn't quite understand. But this compliment rang with sincerity.

"Don't go too far, Doc. I'll have that letter whipped up in nothin' flat."

Kit thought hard. The discipline at Fort Stanton had been lax since he had taken full command, but he saw nothing wrong in letting the boys kick up a little dust. He just wondered where they got the firewater. One thing he had to give Graydon—the men in his command were loyal to him. Maybe too loyal.

More than once they had ignored a direct order from other officers—himself included—and gone to their captain for confirmation. Kit didn't much cotton to having an army within an army. Officers were to be respected for their rank and obeyed. He would have to see about that. When Morrison came back from patrol, the two of them might talk about it some.

A shot rang out. Kit jumped to his feet, grabbed the musket beside the door, and rushed onto the parade ground. Most of the buildings had some repairs finished, but mostly Fort Stanton still looked like a ghost town. The activity in the center put the lie to any ghosts milling about.

"What's going on?" Kit yelled.

"That varmint Whitlock," complained Graydon, clutching his chest. "That lying, no-account Whitlock!"

"You're wounded. What's goin' on?" Kit repeated, befuddled by the way the soldiers stood about. If there had been an attack, they'd have repelled it immediately, taking posts at the walls.

"I challenged him to a duel!"

"Whitlock? Where is he?" The words had barely left Kit's lips when he heard a ragged volley outside the fort. A second volley sounded, and a third and a fourth.

"Get your muskets, men. We're under attack!" Kit ran to the gate and angled through it without breaking stride. Piles of stone placed along the road leading to the gate would provide cover to repel any Mescalero assault. But what Kit saw turned him cold inside. Thirty of Graydon's soldiers stood in a line along an arroyo, their rifles smoking. They worked to reload, but their single target was long dead.

Dr. J. W. Whitlock had been shot from the saddle and riddled with bullets. Kit couldn't begin to guess how many rounds had found the fleeing surgeon. A hundred? More, he decided, from the way the man's body had been turned into bloody pulp. Kit had seen men at Valverde blown apart by Minié balls that looked prettier.

He jerked around in surprise when a new volley from Graydon's men caused the corpse to jump and twitch about.

"Cease fire! Stop yer shootin'!" Kit yelled. He had to step in front of the men to get them to obey. "Who ordered this?"

"He was runnin' away after the duel," one sergeant in Graydon's command said coldly. "No coward gets away with shootin' our captain, then hightailin' it off."

"There's gonna be an inquiry into this. Soon," Kit said, his belly tumbling at the sight of Whitlock's carcass. "Get him buried right away. I don't want him left for the buzzards."

To a man, Graydon's troopers formed into a double column, and their sergeant marched them back into Fort Stanton. Kit Carson was left alone with Whitlock's body, fuming and vowing the doctor's killers would not escape punishment.

The Last of the Mescalero

April 1863
Santa Fé

Kit Carson stood uneasily in front of General Carleton's huge desk. Behind the general a small window opened onto the courtyard where a half dozen soldiers drilled in the bright midday sun. Tiny dust motes kicked up around their heels and the faint fragrance of new buds on carefully tended flowers came through the open window, mixing in a blend that caused Kit's nose to twitch just a mite.

But Kit wished he could be anywhere else. In spite of the general's fine words, he felt he was undeserving.

"You have done a good job, Colonel," Carleton said, beaming. He stroked his flowing mustache as he went over the reports.

"I'm still mighty upset over the matter of Captain Graydon," Kit said.

"Spilled milk, Colonel, nothing more. You did as you saw fit. You followed orders."

"I couldn't git enough officers together to try him, so I figgered the civil authorities would handle it."

"Rightly so, sir," said Carleton. "But spit it out, man. What's eating away at you so?"

"He died 'fore yer orders arrived. I'd asked him fer a resignation, and he plumb refused. And he up and died on me 'fore he could be brought to trial. He murdered Doctor Whitlock!"

"That is incidental to your job, sir."

"Discipline broke down somethin' fierce after that," Kit complained. "Your order to bring him to Santa Fé for trial helped me a bit, but he upped and died before he could go." Kit shifted uneasily under Carleton's cold stare.

"Colonel, you are a credit to the Army. Your skills as Indian fighter are unparalleled. You tend to worry too much over trivial concerns, however. I find this a flaw in your character."

"Well, General," Kit went on, wishing he could put his thoughts into more convincing words. "The men never really obeyed my orders. I told 'em not to murder the Apache when they came across 'em out on the trail."

"That presumption on your part ran counter to my order. If the Apache did not surrender, they were to be killed. As the Mescalero are surrendering and being relocated at Fort Sumner, I deem your mission a success with a minimum loss of life."

"The patrols killed hundreds of Apache," protested Kit. He was eaten up inside that so many men under his command had blatantly disobeyed him. Protests of the massacres still rang in his ears. The *Santa Fé Gazette* and the *Las Vegas Optic* both castigated him personally for the slaughter.

"Good. That was *my* intent and *your* mission." Carleton's tone indicated he considered this matter closed.

"I'm resignin' my commission, General. I didn't do the job you think. The officers did as they pleased."

"There were complaints of drunkenness on duty and other breaches of good conduct," Carleton admitted, "but results matter. Think of it, Kit." Carleton's face lit up as if the sun shone on it. "Those Apache were living as heathen. Now, at their fine reservation, they can become godfearing Christians. Their lives will be changed for the better. What matters, a few drops spilled, when all the others will be saved? Eternal salvation is theirs!"

Carleton had risen to his feet, striking a pose. Kit looked up at the taller officer, marveling at his passion and determination. Some of it rubbed off on him. He hated the bodies left behind, mostly Apache, during the campaign, but perhaps he had done a better job than he'd thought. The general thought so. The general had *said* so.

"You were too close to everyday duty to understand the greater story being written, Colonel," Carleton said, his enthusiasm still burning in his breast. "A medal will be given you for your fine work. Yes, sir, a medal. And any talk of resignation falls on deaf ears."

"Deaf," Kit mumbled. "I would like to see my family."

"You shall, Colonel. After the savages are finally subdued."

"You want me to return to Fort Stanton?"

"No!"

Kit was taken aback by the general's thundering voice.

"No, no, a hundred times, no! I need you, Colonel Carson, and I need you where your abilities will be put to their fullest use. You have shown great resourcefulness in bringing the Apache to their knees. Now you must do the same for the self-styled Lords of New Mexico."

"The Navajo," Kit said in resignation. "They won't be near as easy. The Mescalero were teeterin' on the edge of surrender when we moved into Fort Stanton. The Navajo are never gonna give up like that."

"They will live in peace and Christian abundance at Bosque Redondo," Carleton said. "They might be ignorant savages now and unwilling to see that their future lies along the Pecos River, but you are the man who can take the war to them, make them understand, bring them God's merciful bounty."

"Don't know much about me actin' for God," Kit said, "but if you're orderin' me to Navajoland, I'll do it." Kit felt a moment's qualm at the task, but there was no denying General Carleton's enthusiasm for the project—or his support. Kit had an obligation to live up to such praise from a man so educated and sure of his position.

"You will move your command from Los Lunas immediately to Fort Lyon, where you will establish control over the Navajo."

"Where's this Fort Lyon? Never heard tell of it."

"We have decided the best place to launch our assault is from the old Fort Fauntleroy. It requires considerable renovation, of the sort you did so admirably at Fort Stanton. You are a capable officer, Colonel. Not only I but those in Washington have taken note of your fine work."

"Kin I take along some of the Dinéh Ana'aii?" asked Kit. "They were mighty fine scouts against the Apache, and I don't reckon they have any love for their own kind."

"The Enemy Navajo?" Carleton stroked his chin a moment, then nodded. "Why not use those already aware of our beneficence to convince those who resist? Use these savages as you see fit. You are my expert in such matters."

Kit knew there was likely to be more slaughter as a result, but the Dinéh Ana'aii were the finest scouts he'd ever seen. The break with their own people lay hidden in history, but he wanted a swift end to any campaign against the Navajo. Using their own as scouts in country no white man had set foot in would speed the war.

"With your leave, General, I'll be gettin' my command ready to make the move."

Carleton returned the salute and returned to the piles of paper on his desk. As Kit went through the door, Carleton called, "A moment, Colonel."

"Sir?"

"I am not one to lavish needless praise. You have done well, and you are the only officer in my command likely to succeed against the Navajo. Let me repeat that. You are the *only* man with whom rides my complete confidence."

"Thank you, sir." Kit left the office glowing with pride at such a vote of confidence. By the time he reached Los Lunas and gathered his men for the trip to the new Fort Lyon, he had actually come to believe he was General Carleton's only hope for victory over the Navajo.

Fort Wingate

June 2, 1863
Near Coyote Wash

Manuelito sat and stared into the distance, his eyes unfocused and his mind working over all that faced his clan. As headman he carried a burden the others did not. What if he made the wrong decision? Many, including his wife Juanita, claimed he was too eager to go to war. He had always been hot-tempered when it came to the Biligáana and their treaty breaking.

Always he had fought the Pueblos. And with his last breath he would curse *los ricos* and their slave-taking ways. Why couldn't it be easy, as it had been before the Biligáana swept through Dinetah like a vile whirlwind kicking up nothing but death and treachery?

The sound of pounding hooves caused Manuelito to look up. He heaved a sigh when he saw Barboncito and Delgadito at the head of their peace party. From the set to their heads he knew what had happened in Santa Fé when they'd spoken with Carleton.

He stood and behind him he heard the others with him also rising. He welcomed Manuelito Segundo's presence, and that of Follows Quickly. A glance over his shoulder told him Shining Eyes also joined them. A new warmth mounted as he considered the boy's progress. At times Shining Eyes fit in well. At others, he was obviously the outsider and had no interest in belonging to a better clan than any offered by the tribe of his birth. But Manuelito knew Shining Eyes would soon accept his position among the Lords of New Mexico, as the Biligáana called the Dinéh.

"Lords of New Mexico," scoffed Manuelito.

"What did you say?" asked Follows Quickly.

"For such a powerful people, we are reduced to begging." Manuelito lifted his chin in the direction of the riders. "They go to beseech Carleton for our own land. We have no need to listen to their talk. We know what the bluecoats' leader told them."

Before anyone could respond, Barboncito reined in and sat astride his ancient horse. Delgadito did not wait for the other headman but dismounted immediately. The ill-concealed fury on his face told Manuelito of the rightness of his appraisal.

"They want us to abandon Dinetah," Delgadito growled. "This Carleton wants us to leave our homes and go to Bosque Redondo!"

"Where is this?" blurted Follows Quickly.

"It is on the eastern plain, in the land of the Comanche." Delgadito no longer tried to contain himself. He exploded, "Carleton calls us hostile if we do not go to this . . . this prison!"

Manuelito waited for Barboncito to respond. The older headman always cautioned against war with the Biligáana, citing their powerful rifles and cannon . . . and their incredible numbers. Manuelito did not consider their numbers a problem as long as they fought among themselves. Every musket ball killed another Biligáana, with no blood spilled by the Dinéh.

Finally Barboncito spoke. "They will not stop building their new fort, the one they call Fort Wingate. Worse, they steal all our grazing land around it, claiming it for their own use. Do they offer payment? No. Do they apologize? No. They order us to Bosque Redondo!"

Manuelito still did not speak. Barboncito and Delgadito

swayed the others. Of the eighteen headmen who had gone to Santa Fé, he saw nothing on any of their faces indicating disagreement with their elders. Carleton had outraged even the most deferential in the Dinéh.

Good.

"So?" he asked. "Do we move our herds and go to the plains? What will our lives be there?" Manuelito knew he threw fuel on their blazing anger. Only when they forged a strong force would they drive the Biligáana back across the plains and east of the mighty river they boasted of constantly.

"They offer us nothing but imprisonment among our enemies!" raged Delgadito. "This is an outrage!"

Manuelito settled down on his haunches and let the others take turns telling of Carleton's arrogance and disrespectful behavior. Canby had startled them with his actions, but he had proved honorable. Manuelito was sorry he had not raided into Santa Fé and put an end to Carleton after he had rescued the handful of slaves from *los ricos*.

"I told Carleton," Barboncito said, "that we would not go to this bosque and that we would remain near Fort Wingate. He told me that he could not tell a peaceful Navajo from a hostile one and would consider us all enemies of the Biligáana."

"So be it," grumbled Delgadito. "We must accept this and believe the same of them. There can be no peaceful Biligáana, only hostile ones."

Barboncito fell silent, as did Delgadito. Knowing their thoughts were deep, Manuelito did not disturb them. The new Fort Wingate stole lands and signaled a new incursion into Dinetah. He frowned when he considered this new information. Carleton might no longer require his soldiers to defend the Southern ways from his own kind. If true, he could send wave after wave of bluecoats against the Dinéh. Such a war would be long, Manuelito thought, but there could be no conclusion other than the Dinéh reigning supreme once again. The Biligáana could never win, not as long as the Dinéh fought for their homes, on their own holy land.

"Carleton has given us until July twentieth to deliberate and send him our decision," Barboncito said.

Manuelito drew his knife and drove it into the ground in front of him. Follows Quickly and Manuelito Segundo did the same. Of the eighteen who had ridden to Santa Fé, all responded with equal speed except Barboncito. Delgadito stood, put his foot on the handle of his knife, and placed his weight on it, driving it even deeper into the sun-baked ground.

With great reluctance, Barboncito stood, drew his knife, and threw it point-first into the ground, standing with the others.

The Navajo Campaign Begins

July 15, 1863
Fort Lyon

"Bear Springs is right over the hill, in that direction," Captain Asa Carey told his superior. Kit Carson nodded, staring at the long line of his troopers and their broken-down horses and mules. The trip from Los Lunas had been done fast, with little time for resting. To go on from here was impossible, especially to make war against the Navajo.

"Git patrols out and be sure it's safe to water there," Kit ordered. "The Dinéh Ana'aii scouted the area for us and moved on already. Shush Bito, they called it." He knew he had only repeated an order Carey had already issued. General Carleton had done well selecting subordinate officers for this campaign. Kit admired Carey above the others, Abreu, Sena, Berney, the wounded Pfeiffer.

"How long 'fore we kin expect Cap'n Pfeiffer?" Kit asked suddenly. His heart went out to his junior officer. The last skirmish with the Apache near Fort Stanton had left the man's wife dead and him injured grievously. Kit had seen the man in action only once but had been well disposed toward Pfeiffer.

Carey shrugged. "Can't say. I understand your concern. He's

about the most desperately courageous man you'll ever have the good fortune to command."

"I've seen his record," Kit said, remembering what had been read to him. "A man that good fightin' ag'in the Indians will be a real asset for us out here."

His hand touched the folded papers stuffed inside his uniform jacket. Orders from Carleton read as had those concerning the Mescalero: no quarter asked or given. The only acceptable response was surrender and transportation to Bosque Redondo. It had worked against the Apache and would work against the Navajo, or so Carleton predicted with his usual bravado.

"This campaign is a mighty big undertaking. I'm glad to hear General Carleton's taking it seriously," Carey went on.

"How's that?" Kit's mind had wandered.

"A force of more than seven hundred men is considerable against the Navajo."

" Chávez has another 325 at Fort Wingate we kin call on, if need be," Kit said, his mind focused again on the routine necessary to whip his men into fighting shape. "Don't know how many we're up ag'in, but I've heard guesses over six thousand."

"A considerable number of those are women and children," Carey pointed out in his cultured, level voice. Nothing seemed to flap the well-educated officer. "After their squabbling with the Pueblos and the Ute, there might not be a thousand Navajo warriors left. We'll be evenly matched."

"It won't be an easy fight," Kit cautioned. "You know how the general talks about 'em."

"I've heard," Carey said, smiling without humor. The twenty-seven-year-old officer wiped sweat from his forehead. "When he's not feeling too Christian, he's called them 'aggressive, perfidious, butchering savages.' They're standing in his way of civilizing all the barbarians in the territory."

"We're to never let up when we find 'em," Kit said. This part didn't set too well with him. Carleton had personally told him that the Navajo could no more be trusted than the wolves that ran through the mountains. Kit had a different view, but he knew he had to follow orders. The sooner the Navajo began moving to Bosque Redondo, the quicker he could put duty behind him and be with his family.

"Bosque Redondo," he muttered.

"How's that, Colonel?"

"Nothing, nothing, git the men on over to Bear Springs and water the animals. They need the moisture in their dry bellies after such a dusty trail." He stroked his stubbled chin as he considered ways to take the battle immediately to the Navajo. Years back, General Canby had had thoughts on quelling the Navajo that Kit now worked to recollect. At the time he had not been too occupied with strategy or tactics. Being a scout was a sight easier than running the whole shebang.

"Ute scouts tell us there are fields of wheat 'round here. All grown by the Navajo," Kit went on.

"Sir?"

"Use the grain as fodder for our animals."

"I see," Carey said slowly. "And leave nothing behind when we've taken our share?"

"That's the way we'll do it," Kit said. "We feed our own men and mounts, and then make sure they cain't do the same for theirs." He scratched himself, the long woolly red underwear causing him some discomfort in the afternoon heat. "I'll be overseein' the collection of the grain."

That afternoon Kit Carson rode with Carey and two other officers as the full troop made a long, wide sweep through the rolling hillside. When he had taken as much grain as his men could carry back to Fort Lyon, he ordered the rest destroyed by trampling and by fire.

Ten thousand pounds.

Solitary Scout

July 20, 1863
Cañon de Chelly

Shining Eyes watched as the headmen gathered in the protected branching cañon. Manuelito and Delgadito demanded immediate war to erase the affront to all Dinéh. Shining Eyes spat to the dry ground and wiped sweat from his face.

Shining Eyes spat again, hunkering down in the shade of the hogan. Manuelito had treated his mother well, Shining Eyes decided, but this was after killing the rest of her family. And Goes to War was not Navajo; he was Ute. Ute and white, Shining Eyes amended mentally.

He missed his father, yet he had not done so poorly among these uncouth killers. Now and then he even slipped and called Manuelito "Father," much to his horror and chagrin. He had expected abject slavery and had found himself being taught to shoot a bow and arrow by Cayatanita, and if Follows Quickly had not taught him how to wrestle he could never have fought Oso Negro so successfully. Memory of that fight brought a small smile to Shining Eyes's lips. Follows Quickly had also told him the things most likely to irritate the bigger man. That had been a good day, a very good one.

Shining Eyes looked to the corral where six horses swung their tails, swatting away flies and nudging one another to get to the grain in their trough. He needed to water them again. The hot sun beat down and cooked everything. Shining Eyes liked the red rock walls of the cañon around him all decorated with mystic writing; it was not too different from the cañons in Mesa Verde where his father had taken him as a very young boy. Those had been special days. He missed living among the high mountains where cool breezes shooed away buzzing insects and kept the sweat off his face. Instead, he crouched on the floor of a cañon where sandstone walls rose to hem him in like an animal in a trap.

Wiping away more sweat, Shining Eyes considered how easy it would be to leave. Manuelito argued with the others over the coming war with the Biligáana. Shining Eyes felt his heart beat faster. The whites were his people—through his father. The Navajo went to war against the people of his father. Shining Eyes repeated this over and over, trying to work up indignation or even anger. Somehow, it refused to come.

What Delgadito and Barboncito said about their visit to General Carleton rankled. Why should anyone leave these fine, if hot, lands and go to some distant forest in the middle of the plains? Shining Eyes spat, this time for the Comanche. The Comanche and the Ute shared no love. If a Comanche rode up and Shining Eyes had a bow and arrow in his hand, the Comanche would die.

The boy stood and watched as the assembled headmen slowly left, finding their horses and riding off, all angry. Manuelito stalked back. Shining Eyes cowered, thinking the Navajo might strike him, so great was his wrath.

"Shining Eyes!" barked Manuelito. "Have you watered your horses?"

"I am getting ready to do so. Do we go to war against the Biligáana?" How easily the Navajo name for the whites slipped off his tongue.

"They are responsible for much of our woe, this Carleton leading them. We will fight. Even Barboncito has agreed to rally his people."

Shining Eyes said nothing, strangely torn. In this moment he did not want to see Manuelito die in a war with the whites. Or was it simply that without the headman, Gray Feather and Goes to War would find themselves alone in a hostile land?

They must escape . . . all of them.

"Has Cayatanita shown you the trails through the cañon?"

The question took Shining Eyes by surprise. He nodded, not trusting himself to speak. Manuelito might send him on an errand. If so, he might escape from the cañon and return to his own people. He had tried to ride off once but had been caught easily after getting lost in the twisting maze that was Cañon de Chelly. Shining Eyes tried not to show his eagerness.

"Today is the last day given us by the Biligáana. They assemble their bluecoats at Fort Wingate, but I do not think they will do more than send out scouting parties. We must know if they try to do more than watch the mouth of Tseyi'. Go up the trail to the rim and keep watch. Report any sign of Biligáana coming toward us." Manuelito stretched and squinted into the sun. "They never fight in winter."

"This is *not* winter," Shining Eyes pointed out, wiping more sweat from his face. Manuelito laughed and nodded.

"Take food and water with you but do not linger longer than a week."

"A week? You want me to scout for a week?" Shining Eyes hardly believed this. He was being given enough food to reach his home, his real home.

"Have I told you the story of the monster called the Gambler?"

Shining Eyes blinked and shook his head. Many times Manuelito had gathered the children and told stories, but he had paid scant attention, lost in his own thoughts. He hoped that he was right and Manuelito had not told this tale of Navajo myths.

"The Gambler won away the possessions of the Dinéh, being cruel as he played out all nine of his games. But there came a day when he lost the foot race, the stick game, the basket game, the pole and ring game, the crooked stick and ball game. Each time Dinéh won, and soon the Gambler had nothing left."

Manuelito straightened to his full height, more than six feet. His broad shoulders gleamed in the bright sunlight and his hand rested on his knife.

"The Gambler might win a little, but if he continues too long he will always lose. So it is with war. We have lost a little, but the Biligáana gambles and loses this time. They have played too long."

Shining Eyes nodded, wondering why Manuelito told him this.

"Go, scout sign of the enemy—and do not gamble." Manuelito clapped him on the shoulder and went into the hogan, where Goes to War cried loudly. Shining Eyes heard Manuelito soothing the baby until he stopped wailing. Gray Feather spoke, but Shining Eyes could not hear her words. He edged away and began choosing what he would take on the trip home. His mother had urged him to escape, but he had been reluctant to leave her behind while she was pregnant. Shining Eyes's father had died trying to save her.

Shining Eyes ground his teeth together. If his father had been a better fighter, he would have killed all the raiders and they would still be at home and his mother wouldn't be raising Goes to War in the Navajo lifeway.

His anger growing against the unfairness of it, he put his provisions into a leather pouch and slung it over the bay's neck. Shining Eyes jumped up and savagely sawed at the reins, sure that he could be halfway back to the land of his people before the sun set. The bay protested such unusual treatment, and Shining Eyes's temper died a little.

The trip up the side of the cañon took until late afternoon. He had ridden this far before. He turned and looked down into the floor of the meandering cañon and the stark beauty there. Gray Feather's sheep grazed close to the small stream running by her hogan, and a half dozen head of cattle lowed mournfully, their cries reaching all the way to his ears. The grass shone verdant and lovely and the corn would give a good harvest this year, unlike last year's. It would take considerable effort harvesting it, but the bounty would carry Gray Feather and Goes to War through the winter.

He turned to ride away from the red cañon and paused again. Before, he had come this far intending to leave, but Manuelito had found him. The headman had said nothing, although he had known Shining Eyes's intent. The boy hesitated and let his eyes run over the soaring red needles of rock in Tseyi' to the scattered hogans of the Dinéh and beyond. All four of the holy peaks were visible today, through the heat, haze, and distance.

Sisnaajini to the east, "Sierra Blanca," Shining Eyes called it. Tsoodzil to the south, Mount Taylor, where Sandoval's band had lost their land before becoming Dinéh Ana'aii, enemies of all other Dinéh. Dook'o'oosliid to the west, Never Thawed on Top, shone whitely with its cap of snow, and San Francisco Peak, Dibe'nitsaa, was to the north—Big Mountain Sheep.

He knew their Dinéh names. *"Navajo* names," Shining Eyes quickly corrected himself. "They're not *the* people. They are killers, plunderers. They killed my family and enslaved my mother and me."

From the floor he saw someone waving to him. Shielding his eyes with his hand, Shining Eyes saw Follows Quickly waving to him. He raised his own hand before he realized he had done so, returning the greeting. Lowering his hand, Shining Eyes turned the bay's face. He could ride directly north into Bear Ears—into Utah. How easily the Dinéh ways became his. He denied all he had learned since his capture.

Astride his bay, Shining Eyes stared in the direction of Fort Wingate and wondered what stirred there. Carleton had given the Dinéh until this day to leave their land and go to Bosque Redondo. From all he had heard of the Biligáana general, Shining Eyes knew Carleton would never accept Manuelito's stubborn refusal to abandon Dinetah. Bluecoats would be moving in this direction . . . if not today, then soon. Very soon.

"Mother," Shining Eyes said softly. "How can I leave you to this fate?"

He rode east, watching for any sign of incursion into Navajoland. If Manuelito expected him to be gone a week, no pursuit would come should he decide to go north to Ute lands. But if he saw bluecoats, he ought to alert Manuelito—so he could protect Gray Feather and Goes to War. With this conflict settled in his mind, Shining Eyes began his patrol.

Paiute Captive

July 22, 1863
Cañon Bonito

Ka-ni-ache dropped to the ground and pressed his ear down hard. Joseph Treadwell stood behind the Ute scout and carefully scanned the horizon for a sign of the Navajo war party they followed. He had been scouting with Ka-ni-ache and eighteen others from Fort Wingate. Word had reached him Carson was bringing a troop to Fort Defiance and that Chávez wanted his men to look good for their new commander.

Treadwell spat, thinking of Carson. The man had done what he said, but he hadn't done enough. He was too easy on the Navajo. For over two years Treadwell had sought his family and now he finally came close to finding out their fate—and being able to avenge their deaths, if necessary.

Somewhere deep inside, though, burned a mote of hope that Gray Feather and Shining Eyes were still alive. And the child he had never even seen. Was it a boy? Treadwell wished that were so, but a little girl would look like Gray Feather. That was fine with him, too. The three of them would be with him again before this summer ended. He would see to it if he had to crawl on his belly all the way through Cañon de Chelly to find them.

"Not much sound ahead," Ka-ni-ache decided, rising. "No horses. Few people, but some."

"No warriors?" Treadwell frowned. They had fanned through the countryside for a week now hunting for Navajo raiders and it had been like trying to hold sand with open fingers. Traces. That's all he ever got.

Ka-ni-ache shook his head.

"Herders," Treadwell decided. "I saw goat and sheep droppings a while back. They must graze this entire area." He studied the grassy, rolling hills and knew this would be prime farm- and ranchland for the Navajo. The closer they came to Cañon Bonito the more sign of habitation he found.

"Others join us." Ka-ni-ache looked past Treadwell to point out a band of four Ute scouts riding slowly toward them.

"Against shepherds and farmers, the six of us ought to be able to raise a little hell." Treadwell spat, checked his musket, and then swung into the saddle. His mare protested the weight, but he ignored her and turned her face over the hill.

As he and the Ute crossed the ridge, they saw the Navajo village. As was their wont, the Navajo spread out over most of the valley, their hogans often miles apart. They were a solitary seminomadic people, grouping in tight family units. This suited Treadwell fine. He could have his way with one group and then the next without a warning being passed along to others.

He lifted his buckskin-clad arm and motioned for half of the Ute with him to circle, cutting off escape of anyone in the nearest hogan. He saw sheep cropping the sweet grass a few hundred yards from the hogan and knew the shepherd had to be nearby, possibly a young boy.

Ka-ni-ache and Treadwell rode for the sheep, the rest of their party going straight for the hogan. They were almost at the hogan when a loud cry of alarm rose. The woman in the door of the dwelling screeched like an owl.

One Ute lifted his musket and fired, winging her. Then the others let out whoops and rode hard and fast for the hogan.

"Come on," Treadwell called to Ka-ni-ache. "We don't want to let them know we're on our way down their little valley." Treadwell's prediction of a young boy tending the sheep proved accurate. He fired at the boy and missed, a momentary pang telling him this might have been Shining Eyes.

Ka-ni-ache let out a wild shout and rode down hard on the fleeing boy. Treadwell saw that even the wily Ute was not going to capture this rabbit. He knew the land too well and dodged easily. With a sudden burst of speed when Ka-ni-ache least expected it, the young boy vanished into a thicket and went deeper into the valley.

"Let 'im go," Treadwell ordered. "We got to see how the others fared."

"We do not leave the sheep. And I want slaves," Ka-ni-ache said forcefully. "We have been out too long without booty."

"I count upward of twenty sheep. Take 'em. They're yours." Treadwell thought on it, then smiled crookedly. "Those woollies might make a fine gift to the new commander over at Fort Defiance."

"Colonel Carson? Why do we care for him?"

"He's fighting the Navajo, too. Might get some more work out of him." Treadwell had no love for Carson after the colonel had done so little to help after a year of faithful service, but cooperation would keep them all on the same path. He trotted back to the hogan while Ka-ni-ache rounded up the sheep and slowly moved them from their pasture.

"What'd you get?" Treadwell dropped to the ground and began reloading his musket as the others reported.

"Not much," complained one scout. "The Pogawitch woman Short Finger shot escaped. We killed another, a man. And see?" The Ute pointed into the hogan where a shabbily dressed woman hunkered. Treadwell knew at a glance this was not a Navajo woman. The woman they had fired on had worn the traditional red baize skirt and doeskin jacket held with a bright silver concha belt. Tracking her might prove easy, but Treadwell was more interested in the captive.

"Paiute?" he asked. One scout nodded. Treadwell entered the low-ceilinged hogan, not caring if a man had been killed inside.

He didn't believe in the *chindi* nonsense. No ghost sickness would possess him, no damned Navajo spirit could dare vex him!

Treadwell said nothing as he sank down and watched the woman. She hardly knew what to do. Her eyes darted about as she tended the fire, slowly feeding it small twigs to keep a pot boiling.

"We can return you to your people," Treadwell said in passable Ute. A Paiute ought to understand him, but he had no idea how long she had been a slave of the Navajo. Some prisoners were so cowed they never spoke again.

"I have been theirs for a year," the Paiute woman said, sobbing softly. "Is it true? You will give me back to my people?"

"I give you my word," Treadwell said. "I have only hatred for the Pogawitch." Using the Ute term for Navajo caused her to perk up, as if believing for the first time. "They have stolen my family. My wife is Tabeguache Ute."

For over a minute the woman fed more twigs into the cooking fire, saying nothing. Then she let out an angry shout, jumped to her feet, and kicked over the pot.

"I will rip out their livers!" she cried.

"Gray Feather," Treadwell said. "What do you know of another slave named Gray Feather? She has a young boy with her. Shining Eyes. And a baby." He closed his eyes for a moment when he realized this infant would be walking and Shining Eyes would be eleven. Almost a man, if he lived.

He *does* live, Treadwell told himself. Otherwise, his long years spent trailing son and wife would amount to nothing.

"A raiding party," the Paiute woman said. "A party has a woman and boy with them. A small boy. They might be Ute."

"Where are they?" Treadwell forced himself to stay calm although his heart wanted to explode in his chest. He clung to his musket as if it was his only salvation.

"Deeper in the valley. They passed by yesterday morning, moving slowly. Their horses were broken down."

"We'll see you get back to Fort Defiance," Treadwell promised. He spun and raced out of the hogan. Ka-ni-ache had gathered the twenty sheep around and the other scouts were examining their booty.

"Ka-ni-ache, turn these woollies over to the others. Let 'em get the sheep and the Paiute woman back to Fort Defiance and report to Colonel Carson. We got some hard riding ahead of us."

Ka-ni-ache saw the expression on Treadwell's face and nodded once. He motioned to three other Ute scouts. They chose the strongest of the horses and mounted, tearing off after Treadwell on his mission to find Gray Feather and the rest of his family.

"She might have lied to please you," Ka-ni-ache pointed out, after they had ridden for more than an hour with no trace of the raiding party. "She sees you as her savior and would want to gladden your heart with news of your family."

"I don't think so," Treadwell said, his pale blue eyes like chips of ice in the hot summer sun. He rode toward the sunset and did not miss a broken twig or a shiny cut on a rock made by a horse's hoof. "See this trail? It cuts up toward the rim of the cañon. Might have been used recently."

"Or not," Ka-ni-ache said. "You see what you wish to see."

The shot that rang out chopped off one of the Ute's eagle feathers. Half fluttered to the ground while the half still attached followed Ka-ni-ache from horseback to cover behind a jumble of rocks. Treadwell hit the ground running, his musket leveled in the direction of the shot. He knew they were close to the raiders but did not realize they had come upon them.

Arrows followed, telling Treadwell the Navajo had little ammunition for their rifles. He wiggled like a snake, moving to the left along the faint trail. He found a piñon tree and secured his position behind it. The other Ute were whooping and shouting to keep the Navajo occupied.

Treadwell chanced a quick look. Two Navajo. And another, higher along the trail. They could not escape on their horses, not from the way their sides heaved. Treadwell had no reason to believe he had herded the raiders this far this fast. Rather he had simply come across a band already tuckered out from fighting elsewhere.

Spinning around, Treadwell leveled his musket. His aim was deadly. The musket kicked hard against his shoulder and a surge of elation passed into him as he knew the ball flew straight and true. A young Navajo slumped bonelessly, dead before he knew he had been shot.

Pulling back, Treadwell reloaded. When he swung up his rifle for another shot, he saw the skirmish end abruptly. One Ute crept close enough to gut a Navajo with his knife. And Ka-ni-ache shot accurately into the remaining warrior, leaving him gasping for air on the ground.

The slug had entered one side of his rib cage and emerged from the other. The pink froth on the brave's lips told Treadwell he had little time to find what he needed.

"Shining Eyes, Gray Feather," he demanded. "Ute Indians taken as slaves. Where are they?"

Dark eyes stared at him. Treadwell thought he read recognition and surprise when he called out the names of his family in those bottomless pools of hatred, then he was no longer sure. The Navajo died without uttering a word.

"Ka-ni-ache!" he shouted.

"We have found their camp," came the Ute scout's soft words. "They rode alone. No prisoners. None."

Treadwell sank down, his head low as he fought back tears. Then he got back to his feet and saw that the Navajo were thrown over the backs of their horses. He'd have his own present for Kit Carson back at the fort.

Red Clothes

July 24, 1863
Two Gray Hills

Why had he returned? Shining Eyes sat cross-legged, wondering. The fragrant smell of burning piñon made his nostrils
flare and the odor of venison cooked earlier still hung in the
summer air. His belly was full, but he could have been among
his own people. The ride would not have been difficult. But he
had not fled when the chance had presented itself. He craned
his neck and peered upward at the rough red walls that again
seemed to be his prison. He had ridden out intending to flee.
Why had he not kept riding?

"My mother," he said in a low voice. "She needs me. And
so does my brother. He's only a baby. They will be without
relatives if I abandon them." Even as he said the words, Shining
Eyes knew he gave voice to only part of the truth. The rest he
dared not face.

He looked past the small fire to the bonfire where the men
gathered, preparing for battle. He had seen signs of Dinéh
Ana'aii scouts and had reported this to Manuelito. Others, ranging farther east, near the new Fort Wingate, brought unsettling
tidings. More than a thousand bluecoats had been sent to drive
the Dinéh from Dinetah.

A *natalii* chanted low, preparing the men for their battles ahead. Shining Eyes knew many of the rituals, though he had heard them but once. It took years of practice to become a singer, memorizing every word in week-long chants. A single mistake required the singer to begin again, a costly and time-consuming error that might doom warriors to an undeserved death. The Ute had nothing as complex as the Enemy Way chant or the Night Way chant or even the Red Ant sing for healing wounds incurred in battle.

He shook himself and rested his forehead on his knees, now drawn up close to his chest. Why had he come back?

"Shining Eyes," came a low voice that made him jump guiltily. He had been thinking of killing the man who spoke to him now. Shining Eyes looked up to Manuelito, stripped to only a thin doeskin breechclout. In the dancing firelight his body already gleamed with sweat. "Come with me."

"Why? What's wrong?" Shining Eyes demanded. His heart pounded. How had Manuelito found out he had intended to run away when on the scout? How did the headman know the anger growing like a black, dark maggot in his heart?

"Strip off your clothing and join the other men in the sweat." Manuelito watched him, eyes hidden by shadows. Shining Eyes slowly obeyed, then worked more quickly when he realized the honor afforded him. He was not a man, yet Manuelito had asked him to join the others in the sweat bath to flush out the spirits from their bodies that would weaken them in battle.

Once in the low, domed sweat bath, he helped throw the green twigs onto the fire and occasionally dribbled water onto hot stones to create suffocating steam. Yet Shining Eyes felt not the sweat running down his body but the strength pouring in.

Shining Eyes's hands shook slightly. He had spent many hours in the sweat bath with Manuelito, Cayatanita, Manuelito Segundo, and his other relatives. Shining Eyes bit his lip and tried to change the way he thought. They were *not* his relatives. Gray Feather and Goes to War were the only ones of his blood.

But Follows Quickly and the others had accepted him in their rituals. He wished he had not been forced to leave the camp without eating, but this had been part of the ritual. His belly growling and his hands aquiver, he wished to find Biligáana soldiers so he could get the battle over and eat.

"Bi'éé Lichíí'i," Manuelito said, after listening to a scout's recounting of the movement of the bluecoats. "Red Clothes."

"Who is this?" Shining Eyes asked.

"He is named Christopher Carson, and he has treated fairly with us in the past. He and Canby were friends."

"He is now colonel, the one who wears eagles on his shoulders," said the scout. "I have seen him leading his troopers. He is a short man, much shorter than you, Holy Boy," the scout said, indicating Manuelito. "A full foot shorter!"

"Honor can reside in any size body," Manuelito replied. "We might walk in beauty again, if we can talk with Red Clothes and have him carry our demands to Carleton."

"Why do you call him this?" asked Shining Eyes. "If he is a soldier, why doesn't he wear their uniform?"

"He does," said Manuelito, laughing. "Beneath his outer clothing he wears a woolly red garment that hugs his skin."

"Long underwear," Shining Eyes said, also laughing. "Many of the white men wear it." He fell silent, remembering that his own father had, also. "It keeps them warm in the winter."

"But he wears it in the summer," Manuelito said. "Strange, these Biligáana. We can deal with Colonel Carson. He is a fair man." Manuelito spoke with the scout for another few minutes, then left him to find food. Shining Eyes wished he had a similar order from the headman. His belly grumbled and his hands shook.

"You and Follows Quickly will go toward Tsaile Creek," Manuelito said. It took Shining Eyes an instant to realize he spoke to him. Somehow, Shining Eyes had become accepted as a warrior, a man deserving of trust. He puffed his chest at this recognition.

"What do you wish from us?" Follows Quickly crowded

close, hand resting on his knife. His other hand clutched the musket, again without powder. Shining Eyes found himself sharing Manuelito's notion that the warrior ought to use a bow and arrow rather than carrying the useless musket, but he held his words. Follows Quickly was a proven warrior.

"Seek out Colonel Carson and bring back word of his bivouac. If we parley with him, we can bring about Barboncito's dream of peace."

"But Carleton is a general," Shining Eyes said, thinking he understood more of the white man's ways than even Manuelito. "If Carleton orders Carson, your Red Clothes will have no choice but to obey."

Manuelito shook his head. "Carson is an honorable man and will see how building Fort Wingate and stealing our land is wrong. Find where he camps, and I will speak with him. But avoid all others."

"You send only one warrior," cut in Oso Negro. The burly man pushed forward. "Is this wise?"

"They only scout, they do not fight," Manuelito said, "but you are to be commended for your foresight, Oso Negro. You and Orejo Pequeño shall go, also."

Shining Eyes appreciated the way Manuelito did not deny warrior status to him, yet soothed Oso Negro's outrage. Ever since he had lost the horses in the wrestling match, Oso Negro had been a thorn in Shining Eyes's side, continually making mocking comments about his size, his parents, everything.

"I beat him," Shining Eyes muttered, telling himself Oso Negro was only resentful at losing so many horses. The boy went to the remuda and cut out one horse he had won from Oso Negro and made great show of mounting. Shining Eyes didn't look directly at the older brave but knew what the effect was.

He rode off slowly, letting Follows Quickly catch up with him. When their knees touched, Follows Quickly said softly, "You make a dangerous enemy in Oso Negro."

Shining Eyes shrugged. They were all his enemies. Even Follows Quickly, though the Navajo warrior had been nothing but generous with his time and advice. Shining Eyes tried to work through the complex family relationships, but thought if he truly believed himself to be Manuelito's son, Follows Quickly would be a cousin.

They rode steadily, Shining Eyes's belly growling more and more. But he found that the hunger made him more alert, more on edge and ready for a fight. The weakness had passed and left his senses finely honed like the knife at his belt.

"Two Gray Hills," Follows Quickly said, lifting his chin in the direction of the double knobs poking up from the ground. "Many fine blankets come from the area. The sheep grow wool so fine—"

"You do not know what you are saying," Oso Negro said. "Only in Tseyi' do you find the best wool. My wife's blankets are far better than any made by the squaws *there*." He rudely stabbed his finger in the direction of the two hills.

Shining Eyes held his tongue, knowing Oso Negro only sought to draw him out in a verbal fight that might require blood to settle. Manuelito had sent them to find Colonel Carson's camp, not to murder each other over an old feud. Even as the thought came to him that he ought to ride a little faster and separate himself from the other three, Shining Eyes saw the glint of sunlight off brass.

"Wait," he called. "There's someone ahead." He looked around and saw the tall pines and lush grass under his horse's hooves. All seemed very quiet, yet he had seen the brief hint of others sharing this countryside.

"What do you know, youngling?" Oso Negro started to laugh, but a musket shot rang out and knocked him from his horse.

Shining Eyes crouched low and galloped ahead, hoping to get out of the crossfire as bullets whined past him. He had ridden only a few yards when his horse gasped. Front legs collapsing, the horse hit the ground face first and died amid a last gasp of frothy pink foam from its nostrils.

Shining Eyes struggled to get out from under the dead horse. Looking up, he saw a soldier advancing. The bluecoat had his musket leveled, but he had fired his one round and relied on the wicked silver bayonet fixed to the barrel. Poking with the long, sharp bayonet as if he already fought an enemy, the trooper advanced.

Shining Eyes simply collapsed on the ground, eyes closed. His fingers played across his knife and worked it free from its sheath. He moaned slightly and turned, freeing his leg from beneath the dead carcass, and when he judged the time right, he opened his eyes a crack. The soldier stood a few yards away, unsure if he ought to come closer and stab Shining Eyes.

His indecision proved fatal. Shining Eyes rolled quickly, fetching up hard against the side of his dead horse. Using the heavy animal as support, Shining Eyes blasted to his feet and dived forward. One hand knocked away the tentative thrust made by the bayonet. The other hand carried his knife directly for the bluecoat's belly.

Liquid warmth spewed over Shining Eyes's hand as he drew the honed knife upward and felt the tip meet slight resistance before entering the soldier's heart. The man's eyes were wide with surprise. Then he sank to the ground as if all the bones in his legs had turned to dust. Shining Eyes pulled away, losing his balance, and fell to one knee. His heart raced so fast he thought it would explode.

He wiped the blood from his hand on a heavy thatch of grass and just stared at the dead man. Boy, Shining Eyes corrected. The soldier was hardly older than he was. Fifteen? Perhaps not even that old. He had not yet begun to grow a mustache, as so many of the bluecoats did. But in death he looked young. Very young.

Shoving himself away, Shining Eyes started to call out for Follows Quickly and the others to help him. Then he saw their plight. Orejo Pequeño already lay dead on the ground. Of Follows Quickly he saw no trace. And Oso Negro fought three bluecoats. The warrior struggled in their grip but quickly weakened from a bloody wound opened on his thigh. The time it took Shining Eyes to see what went on was all it took for another soldier to grab him in a bear hug and lift him kicking from the ground.

"Lookee what I got here. This un's still wet behind the ears," called his captor.

Try as he might, Shining Eyes couldn't free his arms from the powerful hold. It felt as if steel bands had been dropped, but he refused to surrender his knife. But even with such determination, he could not bring it into position to use it.

"Might be a boy, but he done kilt Gutherie. The cap'n is goin' be fit to be tied over losin' him. I think the boy was a nephew." One of the men holding Oso Negro—a corporal, by his stripes—released his grip and let the other two secure the brave. The corporal frowned and went over to stare at Shining Eyes.

"What's wrong?" asked Shining Eyes's captor.

"I might be a blood-spittin' horny toad, but this kid matches up with what the colonel's scout is lookin' for." The corporal rubbed some of the dirt and blood from Shining Eyes's face. "He's the one. He's no Navajo. Boy, are you part Ute?"

Shining Eyes felt the man holding him loosen his grip slightly. "Tell him to let me go and I'll answer," Shining Eyes said in passable English.

"It's him! I knew it. He's the one Tr—" The corporal got no further. As Shining Eyes's arm slid free of the soldier's grip, he lashed out with the knife. A long, shallow cut opened on the corporal's chest, causing him to recoil. This gave Shining Eyes all the opening required to lock his foot behind the ankle of the soldier still holding him. Rearing back, driving his head into the man's chest as he kicked forward, caused the bluecoat to fall to the ground.

Shining Eyes slashed again at the corporal, forcing him to roll away rather than fight. The boy threw his knife accurately. The corporal died without uttering another word. And then Shining Eyes launched himself at the two soldiers holding Oso Negro. They made the mistake of reacting to him, instead of using their captive as a shield. Shining Eyes had come only a pace toward them when Oso Negro roared and broke free.

The two came back to back—and then it wasn't necessary. Whooping and hollering at the top of his lungs came Follows Quickly with two horses.

"Go on," urged Shining Eyes. "You're wounded."

Oso Negro caught the reins of one horse and painfully pulled himself up. His right leg still bled and seemed too weak, but the warrior wheeled about and reared his horse, knocking down a soldier intent on recapturing Shining Eyes.

The boy mounted the second horse and they raced off, the wind blowing in their faces as they galloped. Shining Eyes looked back and saw the bluecoats reloading their muskets. By the time he saw the flash of light and puff of white smoke, he was beyond range. Nowhere did he see horses.

"Foot soldiers," said Follows Quickly. "Their cavalry must be occupied elsewhere while these laid their trap."

"We didn't find Carson's camp," Shining Eyes said, beginning to tremble. "We killed them."

"You killed two. The others escaped," said Oso Negro. Shining Eyes could not tell if the warrior blamed him for their failure. He had tried to warn the others of the trap but had not succeeded. Orejo Pequeño had died. With head bowed, Shining Eyes rode into Manuelito's camp behind Follows Quickly and Oso Negro, who both urged their horses to top speed to get into camp first. He perked up when he heard Oso Negro's loud voice.

"He is a true warrior. He saved my life. He killed two bluecoats and would have killed more, but we thought it best to return and tell you of their treachery." Oso Negro lifted his chin and indicated Shining Eyes. "If any harms Shining Eyes, let him know he will be attacking Oso Negro's brother!"

Whoops went up in the camp. Shining Eyes blinked in surprise. Manuelito stood, his arms across his broad chest and the hint of a smile on his lips. Shining Eyes was being hailed as a hero, and all he could think of was that Orejo Pequeño was dead . . . and how hungry he was.

Carson and Treadwell

July 29, 1863
Fort Defiance

Ka-ni-ache and Treadwell stayed low as the Navajo raiders passed within a dozen feet. Treadwell knew better than to hold his breath. He often thought the Navajo could sense that tension in a body. He inhaled and exhaled slowly, keeping his heart from exploding and sounding only like soft breeze through the pines. Every warrior passing his gun sight caused him to want to squeeze the musket trigger. He held back. He wanted more than a dead enemy.

He wanted information.

Ka-ni-ache tugged at his sleeve to signal the last of the Navajo in the party. Treadwell slid noiselessly from his hiding place and watched as the Navajo rode on down the trail, unaware of the trap ahead of them. Treadwell wiped dirt from the front sight of his musket, then hiked the weapon to his shoulder.

He had barely hefted the rifle when gunshots rang out and the Navajo realized the trap they had fallen into. The other Ute had lined themselves along the trail. It would be only seconds before the Navajo tried to retreat.

"Now!" Treadwell shouted. He fired his musket, then cast it aside and pulled out a brace of pistols thrust into his broad leather belt. The Army Colt in his right hand fired. The one in his left jammed. He cursed the equipment Carson had brought with him from Los Lunas. He should never have trusted the colonel to maintain weapons or ammunition. Treadwell took better aim with the pistol in his right hand, cocked the single-action pistol, and fired slowly and methodically.

"Got him!" Treadwell shouted. Beside him Ka-ni-ache fired arrows with the speed of a machine. By the time Treadwell had accounted for one Navajo warrior, Ka-ni-ache had wounded two. And then the battle ended.

"Prisoners!" Treadwell fired into the air to signal the other Ute. "Take prisoners!" He wanted to interrogate the men about Manuelito's whereabouts. All he had gotten so far were hints and slips that might be true or intentional lies.

Joseph Treadwell wanted his family with a determination that kept his anger blazing even in his deepest dreams.

"Round them up and get the survivors over here," Treadwell ordered, shouting curses in Ute when he saw the scouts with him were more inclined to take scalps.

Ka-ni-ache slapped him on the shoulder and went to argue with his tribesmen. Treadwell quickly reloaded the good pistol and picked up the other one he had discarded in the heat of battle.

"Rust," he muttered. There had been scant time before leaving Fort Defiance to do more than load the weapons. He tucked it back into his belt and retrieved his trusty musket. If only he could find one of the Henry repeating rifles, he would have the accuracy of his musket with the firepower of the Colt.

Then he no longer worried about such killing measures. Treadwell saw that the excursion from Fort Defiance to the Rio de Pueblo Colorado had been worth the effort. Eight warriors captured, three dead, three more wounded.

"Where were you heading?" Treadwell asked in broken Navajo. He received only stony, defiant stares. "We can take you back to Colonel Carson and let him interrogate you. You've heard how he is with captives." Behind him Ka-ni-ache made silent but graphic gestures showing what Carson was likely to do. The Navajo Indians turned impassive, lost in their own thoughts and no longer amenable to threats.

"Red Clothes would never do such things," one tall, slender warrior said. He carried one of Ka-ni-ache's arrows in his upper arm. He reached over, broke the arrow, then pulled it out. Treadwell saw the pain flash momentarily on the man's face before he threw the arrow to the ground. He spat on it and muttered something about Ute squaws that drew the ire of a Ute scout.

"Hold on," Treadwell said, stopping the Ute from harming the prisoner.

"We need them as slaves," cut in Ka-ni-ache. "They will work well for us. It is only fair. They steal our boys and women. We should use them as they use us."

"Back to Fort Defiance," Treadwell decided. Questioning the prisoners would take days, and the lever needed to force out truth might be long in coming. But he would see to it.

Trotting along behind the prisoners, eyes sharp for any sign of rebellion, Treadwell herded the Navajo from the river back to Fort Defiance, arriving just before sundown.

"Hallo, Fort Defiance!" he called. "Scouts returning with prisoners. We want to talk with the colonel right away." Treadwell waited for the gates to pull open. The pitiful wood struts wouldn't hold back a dozen squaws with knives, much less an all-out Navajo attack. Still, the men seemed to sleep better, thinking they were safe.

Treadwell snorted. He had seen repeatedly how little protection any fort provided to a determined attacker. The best walls were those of completely killing your enemy and *then* sleeping peacefully.

"Good work, Mr. Treadwell," Carson greeted. "Did you suffer any casualties on yer part?" Carson puffed himself up to his full five-foot-four stature. It was everything Treadwell could do to keep from laughing. He dropped to the ground, towering four inches over the diminutive officer.

"Nothing worth mentioning, Colonel," he said. "I'd be

obliged if you could get the questioning over so I can get back out and act on what we find from these braves."

"There's no hurry," Carson said. "We got plenny of time."

"The Ute want them for slaves," Treadwell said. "It seems little enough pay for all they've done." The mountain man saw the emotions working on Carson's face.

"They have done for us, haven't they?" Carson mused. "I reckon they kin keep the Navajo."

"Sir, a moment," spoke up Captain Carey. "You know the general's orders on this point. He was most specific."

"He's back in Santa Fé," Treadwell said testily. He had no truck with Carleton's desire to Christianize the Navajo. "We're out here, and you're in charge, Colonel. What's your pleasure in this matter?"

"Captain Abreu, begin the interrogation. Find out what you can from these men." Carson watched his junior officer march off the Navajo. The colonel turned to Treadwell, shaking his head. Captain Asa Carey stood close behind.

"Mr. Treadwell, this is som'thin' I got no control over. I'd let the Ute keep 'em, I would. Every last one of them out there loose is a new way of dyin', but the general wants the captives taken straight away to Bosque Redondo."

"To live with the Apache?" scoffed Treadwell. "That's about as crackbrained an idea as I ever heard. If the Navajo don't kill the Apache, then the Apache will have at the Navajo. They've hated one another for hundreds of years."

"This is part of their civilizing," spoke up Carey. "They must learn Christian charity and how to worship God."

"So says General Carleton," Treadwell grumbled. "If the Ute aren't allowed to keep those prisoners as slaves, they're likely to go back north, and you won't have their services anymore."

"They are good trailers," Carson agreed. "But orders are orders. Captain Carey is right." He sighed deeply. "The Navajo must go to Fort Sumner and the reservation to begin new lives."

"You're bringing a heap of trouble down on your head,"

Treadwell warned. "The Ute hate the Navajo and will help us, if we go along with them."

"Our quarrel is with the Navajo," Carson finally said. "If we got to let our scouts go, then so be it. There's always the Dinéh Ana'aii."

"Always the Enemy Navajo," said Treadwell, wondering where their loyalties really lay. With his Ute brothers, he could ride safely and be secure at night.

"Come, Mr. Treadwell, join me for a bite of late supper," urged Carson. "It ain't much, but it's likely more 'n you've had for a day or two. It's good seein' you ag'in, now that Chávez has sent you over to my command."

"No offense, Colonel, I'll see how Abreu is doing with the prisoners." Treadwell turned and walked away without a backward glance. Breaking bread with Carson was nowhere as important as finding out if Gray Feather even lived.

Ambush

"We are scouts," Major Cummings said irritably, "but then he changes orders and turns us into wet nurses. How can we find and kill the savages if all we do is watch the rear end of a mule train?"

Joseph Treadwell shared the impatient major's concern. He had wanted to sink deep into Navajo territory in pursuit of the elusive Manuelito. They knew the war chief had to be in the area. For a pair of days they had chased after him, never quite finding him. Twice they had blundered onto old camps, the fires long since turned to ash and the spoor too cold to follow.

Then Carson had sent out a courier with new orders: guard a mule train bringing in supplies to the new Fort Canby. Treadwell wished he had simply faded away in the night the corporal had arrived. With all the cavalry troopers at his back, he could penetrate far into Cañon de Chelly for a real scout—to get real information.

Treadwell was never quite sure what caused him to sit straighter in the saddle. Cummings and his squad rode their broken down horses, every step bringing new neighs of protest. But the troopers slogging alongside the mules were footsore from walking all the way from Los Pinos.

All Treadwell knew was that something changed. He sniffed hard at the cool air but scented nothing unusual. Then he realized the distant squawk of quail had vanished.

"Major, we got trouble," he called. Even as the words left his lips, the arrows began to fly. One arrow took the courier who had brought the ill-fated orders directly between the shoulder blades. Behind the arrows came a ragged volley from either side of the ravine they rode down.

"It's a trap. They're ambushin' us!" came the frightened cry from ahead.

Treadwell yanked up his musket and got off a shot at a half-seen shape along the bank of the arroyo. Sand kicked up at his feet, but the Navajo warrior never moved. He was too intent on drawing a bead on another soldier, farther down the ravine. Treadwell cursed loudly and charged, putting his heels cruelly into the sides of his exhausted horse. Letting out a wild whoop, he hoped to startle the Navajo enough to make him miss.

The Navajo's musket bucked and white smoke rose from the muzzle. Treadwell didn't know if the scream of pain following seconds later came from the brave's target or another soldier fighting on a different front. Kicking his heels back, Treadwell got up in the stirrups, gauged distances, then launched himself. He smashed hard into the sun-baked side of the arroyo. He scrambled for purchase, then got to the top—and found himself locked in mortal combat with a Navajo hardly more than a child.

Treadwell was immensely stronger than the half-starved boy but had no time to recover his balance. A strong hand locked around his wrist and shoved him backward. Treadwell kicked and lost his balance. He fell heavily into the arroyo, the impact knocking the wind from him.

Through blurred eyes, Treadwell saw the warrior lift a war lance in preparation of casting it straight into his heaving chest. Distant shots rang out and the Navajo vanished, nothing more than a mirage in the afternoon sun.

"You still in one piece, Treadwell?" came Cummings's fussing words. "Then get your ass up and help us fight. They're driving off the mules with our supplies—the ones I was supposed to bring to the colonel personally!"

Treadwell rolled and came to his hands and knees, fighting to draw air into his lungs. By the time he regained his mount, the skirmish was over. Three troopers lay dead on the ground, two from arrows and the third with a musket ball smack in the middle of his face.

"After those thieves," raged Cummings. "They're getting away with our supplies! I was supposed to see them to the fort! Assemble and go after them!"

"You kin go to hell," grumbled a trooper near Treadwell. "I ain't gettin' my scalp lifted for no case of peaches and bags of flour."

Treadwell saw that Cummings had no chance to bring order into the frightened troopers. The major drew his saber and held the keen metal blade high above his head. Light flashed off the weapon and then Cummings ducked fast as an arrow sang toward him.

"We're still in the midst of their ambush!" Treadwell worked to get his musket reloaded, but doing it on horseback was difficult. The horse, frightened and tired from rapid marches, crowhopped and tried to throw Treadwell. He gave up and contented himself with not being thrown back to the ground.

"That's all right, Major," Treadwell shouted to the officer. "We can track them. Those mules will leave a trail wide enough for a blind man to follow."

Cummings turned red in the face in his vain effort to whip his command into a semblance of order. The soldiers were more inclined to save their own hides than the supplies. Treadwell realized the skirmish had cost Cummings more than the supplies and his temper. Half his command was now afoot, their horses either dead or run off. And the horses that had hightailed it into the high country were undoubtedly being roped by the Navajo for their own.

Having to hike back to Fort Canby in disgrace would put

Cummings's command into an even deeper rut. There would be no end to the ridicule heaped on their heads.

"You better make danged sure the Navajo aren't still out there close by," Treadwell said. "If they pick us off one by one, nobody will ever see the new fort."

Cummings swore volubly and ordered his men to pick up any dropped equipment and get it out of the sandy-bottomed arroyo.

"Up there, into that stand of loblolly pine," Cummings ordered. Treadwell followed behind, alert for any new treachery. Manuelito was a wily general in the field and had set more than a simple ambuscade in his day. In a way, Treadwell almost admired the man and the way he kept his warriors continually moving, just a day ahead of the cavalry's best attempts to capture him.

"This looks to be grazing land," Treadwell said, as he followed the officer to the spot chosen for tenting. "The Navajo need their sheep. Reckon we might do something to keep them off balance a mite?"

"What?" demanded Cummings. "I'm for anything that gets back at the bastards for what they've done."

"Think more about the campaign and less about your reputation, Major," snapped Treadwell. He had reached the limits of patience with the prideful officer. "Carson is out on patrol, 'less I miss my guess. General Carleton didn't send him out here for his health."

"You will address me with a civil tongue, or I swear, as God is my witness, I'll cleave it from your head!"

"Think, Major," Treadwell said, forcing himself to calm. "They had no trouble waylaying us. It's not your fault," Treadwell added hastily, seeing how red Cummings got in the face as his temper neared the breaking point. "What I'm saying is, we stumbled onto their land."

"They think this is *all* their land," Cummings said bitterly.

Treadwell held his counsel. It was their land. Carleton had sent Carson and almost a thousand troopers to move them from it. The hints of gold being found in these parts might have unearthed a venal streak in Carleton's soul, but Treadwell believed the general truly wanted to end the fighting and bring a touch of religion to the Navajo, as he was doing with the Apache.

That didn't make it right, and it didn't matter one whit to Treadwell. Carleton could convert every last man, woman, and child in the territory to his religion, and it still wouldn't restore Treadwell's family to him.

Cummings cooled off and turned in a full circle. "So this is all their grazing land."

"*Potrero,* the Mexicans call it," Treadwell said. "Pasture. You know what Carson has been doing when he goes out on a scout."

"The same as they're doing to us in turn," Cummings said, still not reaching the conclusion Treadwell already had. "We steal their food, they steal ours. The thieving . . ."

"They've taken to stealing our supplies because everywhere they turn, Colonel Carson has destroyed theirs." Treadwell kicked significantly at the grassy land rolling away past the stand of piñon pines. "We were to scout, then bring in the supply train. Nothing says we can't do like the colonel has been."

"Their sheep can't graze on burned grass," Cummings said carefully, finally reaching the point Treadwell had led him toward so persistently.

"Burn it. Burn it all while we head higher into the hills, away from here. That might even flush them out, if any stayed behind to bedevil us."

"Excellent, Treadwell, a very good idea." Cummings hurried off without another word to give the orders to put the torch to anything that might burn.

Treadwell patted his mare's neck and led her away from the trees. In less than an hour, the blaze stretched from horizon to horizon, but the soldiers cared little. They were upwind and secure in a camp for the night.

Treadwell lay back on his blanket staring at the stars above. Now and then thin wisps of smoke from the grass fire they had set obscured the bright points. He coughed and rolled to one side, assuring himself that Cummings had not failed to post sentries. After a fight like the one they had endured this day, the tendency was to let all the men sleep. In this country, after firing so much grassland, that would be sure death. Hairs rippled on the back of Treadwell's neck at the nearness of the Navajo. He closed his eyes for a moment to adjust them to still lower levels of light, then peered into the darkness.

He heard nothing. He saw nothing. But the feeling of eyes watching remained strong in him. He sat up, thinking to slip into the night and check the sentries for alertness. Losing even one or two men to a renegade brave now would do nothing to bolster Cummings's feelings of failure at losing the supply train.

"You gonna get any shut-eye, Treadwell?" A corporal sank down beside the bedroll. "The major's put me on duty tonight. Danged bother, if you ask me."

As he talked, the soldier oiled his leather, stroking slowly to ensure a supple play. Treadwell's eyes fixed on the mechanical motion, hypnotized.

"What's going on around the camp?" Treadwell asked. A large bonfire flared at the far end of their bivouac.

"Somebody stumbled over some Injun blankets. The major's told 'em to burn the lot."

Treadwell climbed to his feet, pulling his own blanket closer around his shoulders. The night seemed a little colder for some reason. He turned toward the bonfire fed by the blankets.

"Tell you, Treadwell, we ought to save these for the winter. It's gonna be a cold one, mark my words. I seen the woolly worms a'wigglin' along. They got thick coats already. That's a sure sign of a real cold winter. And the squirrels! Their tails are bushy, too." The corporal rose and followed the scout, who ignored his ramblings about the weather to come.

"You might be right," Treadwell answered at length, to stem the flow of words from the bored sentry. He stopped at the edge of warmth caused by the flaring wool. Such beauty in those blankets, such loving care, and all rising on thin fingers of smoke to mix with the fires from burning grass. The funeral pyre of an entire tribe.

Somehow, the notion of the Navajo tribe dying out affected him less than the loss of the blankets. The man turned so that the fire silhouetted his face. The sense of being watched came to him even stronger than before. He pushed it aside. Too many of Cummings's men stirred restlessly in the cold camp, unable to sleep. Of course people watched him, as he watched them.

As he gazed into the dancing flames, he saw the faces of his family flickering. Mesmerized, Treadwell tried to reach out to them, to urge them to join him. So close, they seemed so close, especially Shining Eyes. But a sudden puff of wind caught the fire and chased away the vision.

"May all those Navajo bastards burn in hell," Treadwell said, savagely kicking another blanket into the fire. He only wished it had been Manuelito, rather than the work of his squaws, that caught fire and turned into fiery motes.

"They will, they will, if the colonel's got anything to do with it," the corporal assured Treadwell. With that the soldier returned to his sentry duty. Treadwell watched until the coals formed from the blankets turned to dull red embers. He walked to the perimeter of the camp where two sentries paced endlessly. He stared into the darkness toward Cañon de Chelly. He knew where his destiny lay.

If only Gray Feather and Shining Eyes were there to see it when he killed Manuelito.

Guerrilla War

Shining Eyes hugged his pony's neck trying to keep from being shot. All around flew the lead fired by bluecoat muskets, but any bluecoat was as bad a shot as Follows Quickly. Shining Eyes had to smile when he thought of his cousin riding less than ten yards away. Nothing seemed to drive the cold spike of fear into Follows Quickly's breast. He waved his musket over his head, yelling and hooting as Manuelito had instructed him.

Shining Eyes proceeded more cautiously in luring the foot soldiers into the trap. For a week, since he and the others had been ambushed, they had worried the edges of Carson's force. A thousand men had been the report. Shining Eyes could scarcely imagine such a huge army, though he had seen evidence of it many times.

He was more concerned with keeping one single soldier from killing him. A new volley sang through the air as he used his knees to turn the horse down a dry ravine. Dust and rock kicked up under his pony's hooves, leaving behind a cloaking cloud that made it even more difficult for the bluecoats to shoot accurately. At the precise point Manuelito had shown him, Shining Eyes cut to the left and forced his struggling horse up the sandy embankment. Wheeling about, he sat straighter and reached for his bow.

On both sides of the arroyo were arrayed most of Manuelito's force. Shining Eyes quieted his heart as Follows Quickly waved from the far bank. Less than twenty warriors faced an entire company of Biligáana, but this bothered Shining Eyes less than the thought of going another day without food. They had traveled fast and far, seldom taking time to eat.

All thought of hunger vanished when the leading trooper marched into view. He plodded along after his horse-mounted foes. Shining Eyes felt a flash of pity for this one and the others immediately behind him. Then the brief motion passed when he saw the recognition of a trap bloom on one man's face.

Shining Eyes fired his arrow, barely missing the sergeant giving orders for his squad to retreat. But Shining Eyes knew it was too late for them. The rest of Manuelito's band would be attacking from the rear now. They had one squad trapped. He fired slowly but accurately, wounding two before he heard Oso Negro's spine-tingling ululation warning them to break off the fight and escape.

The rest of the company advanced. No matter how many men Manuelito had with him, they could never meet the main body of the Biligáana soldiers in open battle. It was their fight to shoot from ambush, then run away.

Shining Eyes found himself curiously slow in breaking off the attack. A hand on his arm tried to pull him back. He shook free, then saw it was Manuelito.

"Another day. We allow them to live so we can kill them another day," Manuelito said confidently. "Besides, we have what we wanted."

Shining Eyes saw a dozen mules being led away, all burdened with U.S. Army supplies. They had wanted foodstuffs, not death, in this raid. But why? His belly grumbled and he had to ask Manuelito, "What do we do with all the food we take?"

"I am hungry, also," Manuelito said, seeing the boy's expression. "We hide the food against a day when our need is real."

"My belly thinks my throat has been cut."

"Dinéh endure," Manuelito said. "When we return to Tseyi' we shall feast!" With that, he put his heels to the horse's side and raced away. Behind him came the dying echoes of musket fire and the occasional moans of men wounded in the brief but fierce fight. Riding to keep up with his adoptive father, Shining Eyes saw the others joining them from all sides.

He tried to see if they had lost any warriors during the skirmish. He did not think so. When Oso Negro rode up, he heard the stocky warrior's terse report.

"The bluecoats lost three men, one to Shining Eyes's arrow! And I killed another." Oso Negro brandished his still bloody knife. "Another was shot in the back by a comrade too scared to know better." The brave laughed harshly. "Manuelito, let your son and me take on their entire army. We have earned this honor with our death-giving this day. Shining Eyes and I can destroy them!"

"Your chance comes," Manuelito promised. "Are any following us?"

"On foot, they cannot walk a mile before we are over the horizon!" bragged Oso Negro.

Shining Eyes worried about this. They had fought the Biligáana soldiers for a week now and they never stopped. One or two might die, they might lose all their supplies and have their weapons stolen, but they always came on. And he worried at the way they burned everything around them. Colonel Carson fought the war as if he did not expect anyone ever to live off the land again.

"Shining Eyes, look for the main body of their troops. I need to know if their cavalry has joined the foot soldiers."

"Let me go with him," begged Oso Negro.

Manuelito shook his head. "Your leg troubles you. I need a quick report, one Shining Eyes is best able to give." The words made Shining Eyes glow with pride. After he, Follows Quickly, and Oso Negro had escaped the ambush, everyone had treated him as an equal. Oso Negro's loud proclamation of blood-bond had helped, but he had proved himself in battle repeatedly. It shocked him to realize he had slain more of the Biligáana than any other in the band during this foray. He was only eleven years old, though large for his age.

What shocked Shining Eyes even more was how he had come to think of himself as Dinéh.

"Cayatanita will go with you, if you like," Manuelito said.

"I can walk through their camp and never be seen," he bragged. "Oso Negro has shown me the way with his courage." The words were boastful, but they also cemented his friendship with the older warrior.

"Go, but return before this time tomorrow. We will continue riding past Ciénega Amarilla and turn west. If you take too long, return directly to Tseyi'. We will await you there. Come in by the southern entrance."

Shining Eyes nodded, although he did not know of the south way into Cañon de Chelly. But he could find it. He could do anything. Wasn't he riding with the Dinéh?

Without another word, Shining Eyes veered away from the line of travel and began a zigzag path back to where the short fight had occurred. He avoided the wash, keeping to the higher ground until he found shelter in a tumble of rock. Slipping to the ground, he led his horse to a hiding place and waited.

The smell of burning grass tweaked Shining Eyes's nose. He slowly stood and peered around the rock sheltering him. The line of fire walking across the horizon bothered him. Carson continued to burn everything in his path. No sheep would graze on the sparse terrain for a year, until after the fall storms brought moisture Even then only a thin regrowth would poke up before the snows came.

Through the haze of smoke and fire Shining Eyes saw the men setting the blaze. He mounted and circled cautiously, thinking to come upon them at nightfall. It took longer. The wheel of stars overhead showed it well past midnight by the time he wiggled like a snake into the heart of the Biligáana camp.

Oil and leather assailed his nostrils, making them flare. He closed his eyes and let his other senses guide him. He located their store of arms and ammunition. The pungent odor of gunpowder made him want to sneeze. Shining Eyes held back the betraying sound, as he kept from going to the weapons.

Oso Negro would think even more of him if he stole a musket. And if he returned with gunpowder and lead slugs, Follows Quickly would be able to fire wildly in battle for a month. But this was not the reason for his scout. Shining Eyes kept low and moved so that shadows cast by the guttering fires shielded him from view by the slowly pacing sentries. They occasionally looked in his direction, but their eyes were hooded with fatigue and no one saw him.

Shining Eyes moved deeper into the sleeping camp, counting the rows of men quietly snoring under their blankets. No one knew the enemy crept through their camp. On impulse, Shining Eyes reached out and touched one soldier. The man stirred and tugged harder at his blanket.

Smiling at his boldness, Shining Eyes slipped away again and kept counting. The smell of burning wood—and grass and blankets—drew him to the far edge of the camp.

A deep pit filled with firewood blazed merrily. Three men heaved blankets into the pit, where they smoldered. Shining Eyes wanted to cry out. These were fine Dinéh blankets, lovingly crafted. Where they had been captured by the Biligáana he didn't know, but Shining Eyes mourned the loss of such beauty. Great effort had gone into those blankets now so casually tossed into the fire.

"Tell you, Treadwell, we ought to save these for the winter. It's gonna be a cold one, mark my word."

"You might be right," answered another, who stood with his back to Shining Eyes. The boy hesitated. The voice sounded familiar and the soldier had called the man Treadwell.

Joseph Treadwell?

His father?

Shining Eyes rose up, forgetting caution now. He tried to get a better look at the man's face. If this wasn't his father, it might be some relative. His father had never spoken of a brother or uncle, but it might be.

The man turned so that the fire silhouetted his face. Shining Eyes's heart leaped in his breast. And then he sank back into shadow when a sentry noisily paced nearby. Indecision struck him. All he needed to do was walk over to this man he thought to be his father.

"May all those Navajo bastards burn in hell," Treadwell said, knocking another blanket into the fire with a savage kick.

Shining Eyes shrank back even more. He had seen what Manuelito needed to know. Silent as a ghost the boy left the Biligáana camp to return to his people.

Fort Defiance Troubles

August 4, 1863
Fort Defiance

"Burn it to the ground," Carson ordered in a bitter tone. "Danged if I see any reason to leave it standin' behind us. There's been nothin' but trouble, tryin' to stay here."

"Why bother?" asked Treadwell, irritated that Carson thought more of the fort and its establishment than pushing deeper into Navajo country. He knew the Army needed a secure base, but things were boiling over along the Rio Pueblo Colorado—and deeper up in Cañon Bonito. He had even heard Manuelito might have returned to Cañon de Chelly from his raids. Arguing over where to build a fort had little to do with the urgency he felt for action.

"The general wants a fort we kin rely on," Colonel Carson said. "And we got more officers a'comin' soon." He smiled broadly. "Major Morrison's on his way, 'long with a few others I knowed down in Fort Stanton. I need 'em for the scouts I'm plannin'."

"Always planning, never doing," snapped Treadwell. He had come to the end of his rope. Ka-ni-ache remained with a few of the Ute scouts, but many had returned north, denied Navajo slaves as reward for their work. Somehow, the hardtack, beans, and long hours on the trail hunting the threatening Navajo wasn't enough for them. Carleton's orders had been taken too much to heart by Carson, Treadwell thought.

"I understand the fire lit under your butt," Carson said. "I don't cotton much to spendin' time on garrison duty, but that's a soldier's life. It's my *duty*." His pale blue eyes locked with Treadwell's, daring the mountain man to argue further.

"The best place for your new fort is about five miles outside Window Rock," Treadwell said. "It might give you control of travel into Cañon Bonito, but I wouldn't count too much on that."

"I need a safe haven for my men," Carson said. "I trust your judgment." Carson smiled crookedly. "Besides that, Mr. Treadwell, I scouted the same area myself and agree. It's a good place for Fort Canby."

"You're not calling the new one Fort Defiance?"

"Seemed the thing to do," Carson said, his eyes distant. "I admired General Canby. A fine fella, truly fine. And we got other work to do ourselves."

Treadwell remained quiet. He had more than a fire lit under him. His feet itched. He had to be out where he might find Manuelito—and those he sought so ardently. Captain Carey had warned him this had turned into revenge, pure and simple, and hatred was a piss-poor lens to look through at the world. Treadwell wasn't so sure. Hope still burned in his breast, albeit weakly, that he might find his family again.

"Find Major Cummings, Mr. Treadwell," Carson said. "Go on a scout back toward the Pueblo Colorado and give me your best estimate of supply problems and travel times for a troop of four hundred."

"Four hundred?" Treadwell whistled. This would be an invasion of unparalleled proportion into the heart of Navajoland. "Reckon you need good intelligence for that big a move."

"All the way into Cañon de Chelly this time," Carson said. "But kindly don't go spreadin' that word around. Not yet. I—" Carson fell silent when he saw Lieutenant McAllister leading a small squad of men.

"Run about your duty, now, Mr. Treadwell. I see the lieutenant's found Major Morrison. I oughta greet them proper-like." Carson smoothed out his uniform jacket and walked toward the distant gate. Treadwell watched the little banty rooster of a man for a moment, then shook his head sadly.

Sometimes he pitied Kit Carson, other times he hated the man for being too soft on the Navajo. Right now, he wasn't sure what he felt. Carson was finally beginning the action he had not taken all summer, but he seemed trapped within the confines of a fort. Carson was no more a garrison soldier than Treadwell was.

From the way the lieutenant snorted smoke and fire, Treadwell knew Colonel Carson had his hands full. He went in search of Major Joe Cummings. It was past time to get on the trail again.

Kit Carson glanced at Captain Carey, then back at Lieutenant McAllister and Major Morrison. He was out of his league and didn't know what to do.

"I want to get this straight. Now, Lieutenant, you're tellin' me the major was drunk and disorderly on the way to the fort?"

"All the way from Los Pinos, sir," McAllister said. "It was disgusting, a spectacle. He was so drunk he could not even stand!"

Morrison stared hotly at his subordinate but held his tongue.

"While in uniform, he was drunk?" This was something Kit hardly understood. He took his duties seriously and had always thought Morrison did, also. Yet the officer had reported at Fort Defiance smelling of liquor and with eyes so bloodshot they looked like a scouting map.

"And vulgar, sir. He rode along shouting that he was the best 'damned pimp in the territory.' His words, sir. He offered to find us prostitutes as we rode."

Kit went cold inside when he saw the truth on Major Morrison's face. Almost in a panic, he glanced from the corner of his eye and saw Captain Carey also read the confession plainly. Kit felt boxed in, his subordinates in control.

"I ain't got officers to waste out here, Major. You proved yourself to be one of the best in my command at Fort Stanton, and I was countin' on your support here." Kit heaved a deep sigh. "You leave me no choice but to air our dirty laundry in public view with a full court martial."

Kit saw McAllister puff up at this. The young buck was happy that his superior was in hot water. Kit could only wonder why. Cutting Morrison down did nothing to build up McAllister's position.

"However, it is within my power to let you resign, if that be yer pleasure."

"Sir, it has been an honor serving under you. Please accept my resignation, effective immediately." Morrison dropped his saber onto Kit's desk, stepped back, saluted, and executed a slightly wobbly about-face before marching from the room.

"Dismissed," Kit said to McAllister. The lieutenant saluted and followed the disgraced major from the tiny office.

"What do you make of this, Asa?" asked Kit. He was in over his head. "Why'd young McAllister come out and press charges like that? You'd think he never heard of a man findin' women for his friends and comrades."

Carey snorted. "My advice, Colonel, is to keep an eye on McAllister. I've heard rumors that he doesn't much like women, if you understand my meaning."

Kit Carson closed his eyes and leaned back, knowing he had to leave garrison duty to others able to handle the problems.

Carson and Blakeney

August 12, 1863
Fort Canby

Kit Carson paced and finally stopped, staring out the unfinished window of his office. Fort Canby was more a dream than a reality, and he wanted nothing more than to be away from it. Weights held him to the ground while he remained in garrison. Only when he got into the mountains and tracking did he feel alive.

"Colonel," spoke up his clerk, Sergeant William Need. "We got another communique from General Carleton. Sergeant Campbell just arrived with it."

"More of the same?" Kit had come to dread the all-too-frequent orders from his superior as a hindrance to being free ever again of paperwork. Carleton demanded detailed reports, even when nothing was worth reporting.

"Afraid so, sir. He says that the Ute are *not* to take slaves, that any prisoners we take are to be sent directly to Fort Sumner." The sergeant shifted uneasily when he saw the distress on his commander's face. Kit had already bowed to pressure and let Ka-ni-ache and his scouts to take more than a dozen women and children north as their slaves. Their pay was little enough, and Carleton wanted results.

Results would come faster with the cooperation of the Ute—

and the Pueblos and Hopi and Zuñi and other tribes of sworn enmity to the Navajo.

"Take this down, Sergeant. Tell the general I'm preparin' for a big scout, a month-long one that'll go right to the heart of Cañon de Chelly." Kit's mind raced. Finally a smile wrinkled his lips and his mustache twitched a bit in delight. "Put in there that reports will come direct from Major Blakeney, as I've put him in command of the fort." Under his breath, Kit added, "Let the man do some of the work for a change."

"Sir, what of Lieutenant McAllister and his drunkenness?"

"Has the private chosen to press charges?"

"No, sir, but this is a powder keg waitin' to blow, if you ask me. And I know you did not, sir." Need fell silent, his fingers clenched around the pen recording all his colonel said.

Kit didn't know what to do with McAllister. Major Morrison was gone from the fort because of the lieutenant's charges, but McAllister was no prize. If the private pressed charges of sexual assault, Kit might have to relieve the lieutenant of his command. The drunkenness was hardly a charge he could make stick without being tarred with the same brush, since he had inadvertently approved a requisition for the whiskey, unable to read what he was signing.

"Blakeney kin handle that, also," Kit decided. "I want to get out onto the trail where I kin carry the campaign to the Navajo. Is the troop assembled?"

"Yes, sir. They await you at the head of the column." Need peered out the open window at the assembled men, 333 strong, with 16 officers keeping the large band in order.

"Get some message to the general that will keep him happy." Kit paused and smiled again. "Tell him his fair-haired boy Blakeney is to be in charge. Since Blakeney served with the general and considers the son of a buck his protégé, that oughta keep Carleton happy for a spell."

"Sir, you are leaving a man in charge who does not see himself as belonging to the New Mexico Volunteers. I've heard him say time 'n again that he was prouder of being with the California Volunteers than anything else."

"He was born in Californy," Kit allowed. "And he did serve reasonably well with the Seventy-first Pennsylvanians."

"Sir, Major Thomas Blakeney reporting as ordered." Blakeney appeared in the doorway, snapping a crisp salute. Kit jumped at the man's sudden appearance, then wondered if Blakeney had been spying on him as he dictated to Sergeant Need.

"I'm puttin' you in command of the fort while we're gone, Major. You're senior officer now that Morrison's gone. General Carleton recommends you highly."

"Sir!" Blakeney snapped to an even stiffer attention. Kit wondered if an iron rod had been shoved up his butthole. "This is a singular honor you bestow on me. It is my great pleasure to serve under such a distinguished frontiersman as yourself."

"Keep things from fallin' apart too much," Kit ordered. "We're gettin' camp followers all around swarmin' like flies on a hot summer day. Keep the men from them women, if you can. And threaten to horsewhip the fort sutler if he peddles any more of his tarantula juice. Order will be kept while I'm on scout."

"Of course, sir."

Kit paused at the major's tone. Sarcasm? Superiority? Kit winced a little at this. Blakeney had the advantage on him, as an officer in the Army with real training. And education. Blakeney's book learning was obvious in every word that came from his lips.

Kit threw the major a salute, motioned for Sergeant Need to get the report out to General Carleton immediately, and then heaved a sigh of relief as he mounted his horse, Apache, at the head of the long column. The gates opened for him and he gave the order to move out. The bugler sounded the advance and Kit rode from the prison that Fort Canby promised to become.

Somehow, the air felt fresher on his face when he fixed his eyes on the horizon—and Cañon de Chelly.

"A moment, Sergeant," Blakeney ordered.

"Sir?"

"Show me the report the colonel is sending to General Carleton."

"That isn't proper, sir."

"Do it, or I'll see you in the stocks for a month, Sergeant." Blakeney held out his hand. Sergeant Need hesitated for a moment, then silently passed over the report. Blakeney scanned it quickly, then crumpled it and tossed it aside. "I'll compose a report of my own. You are dismissed until I am ready for you to take it to the general."

Sergeant Need saluted and silently left. Blakeney walked about the small office, sniffed at the primitive conditions, then remembered how much worse it had been in the field, riding with Carson.

"The man is an animal," the major decided. "He lives like one and has no sense of how to maintain order among real soldiers." Blakeney fumbled inside his tunic and drew out a small silver flask. He quickly drank of the fiery contents. The liquor settled warmly in his belly and put iron into his resolve to run Fort Canby as it should be run.

Emissary

"It is not possible for me to attend the meeting of headmen, but Barboncito must be heard, and our concerns must be given to him," Manuelito said. He stretched his arm, injured in a recent fight with the Biligáana soldiers. "I must watch their scouts entering Tseyi' without the sunlight of false hopes shining in my eyes." He squarely faced his adoptive son, his demeanor somber.

"You want *me* to be your emissary?" Shining Eyes hardly believed his good fortune. Such a role was one not lightly given—or lightly agreed to. His words would be those of Manuelito. And he would sit among warriors as an equal. Manuelito was fifth chief; only four others were more honored among the Dinéh. Shining Eyes would be a headman, a *hastiin,* for this meeting.

"Manuelito Segundo is scouting near the east entrance to Tseyi', trying to find the forward base Carson uses. I must see how fast the Biligáana move north, if they unite with the Ute merely to skirmish or if they intend a major invasion of our lands. Follows Quickly brings reports that are far too heartening to be true." Manuelito lifted his gaze to the sky, to an eagle catching a hot updraft to float far above the sheer red rock cliffs.

Shining Eyes wanted to ask questions but saw Manuelito was not finished. He impatiently held his tongue, waiting for the headman to finish his thought before barraging him with questions.

"Cayatanita will accompany you, and you shall listen carefully to all he says." Manuelito paused and added unnecessarily, "And what he leaves unsaid."

"I will never disgrace you," Shining Eyes said. Of all those Manuelito might have chosen to be his tongue, his ears and eyes, Shining Eyes stood in awe of the choice. *He* would represent the Folded Arms People.

Shining Eyes turned when he heard bawling from his mother's hogan. Goes to War demanded food, and there was little. Red Clothes refused to parley, except when it benefited him. Manuelito still thought of the short Biligáana as a decent man, but Shining Eyes tried to tell his adoptive father that Carson spoke with another man's thoughts. Whatever Carleton in Santa Fé wanted, Colonel Carson did immediately and without question.

Shining Eyes's belly grumbled, but he knew Goes to War needed the crushed corn mash more than he did. He was a warrior of the Dinéh and could survive long weeks with only a handful of grain, a slice of venison jerky, a sip of water. He puffed out his chest in pride. He was accepted in men's circles.

He was to bring good wishes from Manuelito to Barboncito, Ganado Mucho, and the other headmen.

"Go to your uncle's hogan and leave immediately to speak with Barboncito. There is a chill in the wind that disturbs me greatly." Manuelito straightened to his full height, towering above Shining Eyes. The boy thought he had never seen a more powerful warrior, yet there was a sadness in Manuelito's face he could not deny. Did he fear the Biligáana so?

No, Shining Eyes knew instinctively. Manuelito feared nothing. His wound was minor and bothered him only a little. He was not turning into an old woman incapable of making decisions or going into battle with no fear.

"Manuelito," began the boy. He stopped when he realized what would have spilled from his mouth. He became like the Biligáana, speaking without putting careful thought behind his words. Manuelito did not fear Treadwell—he might not even know the man still lived.

"Go, find Cayatanita and ride," Manuelito said, giving him no chance to make a fool of himself. Of course, Manuelito did not fear Joseph Treadwell or Christopher Carson or any of the Biligáana.

Shining Eyes nodded brusquely and hurried into the hogan, first to see that Goes to War had food, then to gather his gear. It was a day's ride to Cayatanita's hogan and another two through the winding canyons of Tseyi' to the meeting.

Shining Eyes hunkered down on a fallen log, trying to pay attention to the slow ebb and flow of conversation around the piñon fire. Too many spoke endlessly without saying anything, but Shining Eyes perked up when Barboncito spoke of the latest scout against the Biligáana.

"They enter the easternmost end of the cañon," he said in measured tones. "Their scouts are good, one a Ute and the other a white man who has lived among the Ute. His sally from the outlying regions of Dinetah shows he has great skill."

"Treadwell," muttered Shining Eyes. He knew he had seen his father, but he had been burning Navajo blankets, blankets that could keep Goes to War warm. Shining Eyes pulled his closer around his thin frame, shivering in spite of it. He began to realize what Manuelito meant. It would be an early winter, no matter what the season. The tide of approaching soldiers would bring with them icy death.

His own father would bring that death. Shining Eyes tried not to let this thought consume him. He might have left the Dinéh that night at the soldiers' bivouac. He had heard the other troopers say someone sought one of his description. Seeing

Joseph Treadwell among the soldiers convinced Shining Eyes who sought him.

He could have stood and approached, no matter that Treadwell was so intent on destroying the lovely blankets needed to keep dozens of people warm through the approaching winter. Shining Eyes knew he would have been accepted by Treadwell and yet, and yet—

"What does Manuelito counsel on this?" Barboncito's question hung in the air like a sailing arrow. Shining Eyes jerked a bit straighter, the blanket slipping from his shoulders. Everyone listened intently, no one impolitely staring at him.

"Shining Eyes will speak for my brother," Cayatanita said, giving Shining Eyes a moment to corral his runaway thoughts, "but there is no doubt that Red Clothes seeks to lay waste to Dinetah as his soldiers travel. They burn grain—"

"And blankets," interrupted Shining Eyes, his anger rising. He stood, hands turning into tight fists as memory flooded him. "They burned blankets and set fire to the land, destroying all grass. Smoke stalked Dinetah like *chindi* as they seek to starve our sheep and cattle by burning grassland. I have seen this with my own eyes. If they enter Cañon de Chelly they will destroy our flocks, fields, and belongings."

"The winter already touches us," said Cayatanita. "Snow flutters on the higher mountains. Dibe'nitsaa, the Big Sheep Mountain, already carries newly fallen snow."

"We would seek Carson and parley," said Barboncito. "We would find peace amid all the bloodshed. They kill few of us compared to the number of them we slay, but what you have said is truth. I, too, have seen the Biligáana destroying all within their reach. It has always been so with them. They do not walk in beauty."

"They walk amid confusion and death," Shining Eyes said, bitterness in his voice. The sight of his father so angrily burning the blankets returned to haunt him. Then he knew it was not so. Treadwell was not his father.

"My father, Manuelito," the boy said proudly, "advises eve-

ryone to store as much food and supplies against the coming
invasion as possible. The Biligáana will enter Tseyi'. They must
never leave."

Barboncito petitioned for peace again with the bluecoats, but
even he saw the folly of this. There could be no truce when the
soldiers fought in such a cowardly fashion. Agreement with
Shining Eyes rumbled from the throats of those circling the wan
fire. Shining Eyes had told them what he had seen—and he had
brought Manuelito's message. His *father's* message.

The First Big Scout

August 23, 1863
Cañon de Chelly

The morning sun shone brightly as Kit Carson stared into the western entrance of Cañon de Chelly. The stillness seemed more befitting a cemetery than such a magnificent pile of rock. Fingers of red and brown layered sandstone rose like monuments he had seen in Washington, D.C. Soft, thick grasses cushioned his horses'—and his men's—every step and a quiet settled like an old familiar blanket around him.

"We go in this time," Kit said softly. "We passed 'er by the first time we swung by, but not this time. We been burnin' as we go and not findin' enough Navajo to scare a snake with."

"I reckon they're all in there," Joseph Treadwell spoke up. He had joined Carson's scout a week back when the troopers were still scudding along the edges of the Chuska Mountains hunting for a Navajo force to engage—any Navajo.

"We'll get some revenge for what they did to Major Cummings," Carson said. "He was a good officer. I shall miss him."

"He was a danged fool," snapped Treadwell, not mincing words. His nerves were on edge since riding this close to the Navajo stronghold. He had warned Cummings, and the officer had still been picked off during a skirmish five days earlier.

What remained of his command had joined Carson's for this push into the heart of Navajoland.

"No need chewin' on that piece of fat anymore, Joe," Carson said, eyes probing the cañon before rising to the two-hundred-foot-high rims. "We got more important matters to tend to."

Treadwell nodded curtly. He had sought Manuelito throughout the countryside and had always been a day late and a dollar short. Never quite engaging the wily headman's forces had been a real sore point with him. In a way, Cummings's death gave Treadwell more freedom to do as he saw fit in finding the war chief. The shavetail lieutenant left in charge of Cummings's patrol had been willing to agree to about anything Treadwell suggested.

When Treadwell had found Carson's trail, he knew returning to Fort Canby was a waste of time. This was where the real action would occur. Soon.

"Sandy approach to the cañon," Treadwell said, studying the two-hundred-yard approach to the tall red, brown and tan walls streaked with vertical black marks like rising smoke. Chinle Wash this was called. The mountain man tried to tell himself these weren't the jaws of a giant ready to bite down. His imagination must not get the better of him. Not now, not with such a large force behind him.

"Don't hold tracks long in this wind," allowed Carson, squinting in the bright light. "Always blowin', it seems to me." He sniffed hard and smiled. "A bit of smoke on that breeze. You catch it, too, Treadwell?"

Treadwell nodded brusquely. The cañon was beautiful, about the finest he had ever seen, but it wound around and vanished in the distance. A trap. A mantrap with its jaws open to snap down on him—as it might have already done on his family.

"We've got some work ahead of us, Colonel," Treadwell said. "You want me to see what's waiting for us?"

"A moment, Mr. Treadwell." Carson motioned for his officers to join them. He waited until they gathered and settled their mounts. Too many of his troopers were afoot, their mounts either dead or nonexistent. He saw no reason to make this a quick sally into the cañon, if he could take with him those troopers hiking along at a more leisurely pace.

"We need to go into the cañon with a show of force, gentlemen," Carson said. Treadwell kept looking over his shoulder in the direction of the entrance. Warriors on those walls could fire down at them with impunity. Worse, they did not even need rifles or bows and arrows. All they had to do was push a few rocks to the rim and wait for the feckless troopers to walk beneath them. An avalanche of stone would bury any command venturing too close to a cañon wall—and Cañon de Chelly narrowed rapidly, from what Treadwell could discern.

"Tell your men we're puttin' out a bounty for what we find in there," Carson went on. "No farm is to be left intact. Burn it. Everything on it. For every sheep or goat taken, a reward of a dollar is offered. And for a horse, twenty dollars." Carson waited as several of the officers exchanged glances, digesting this news. Two captured horses might match their salary for a month.

"And do not forget. We are to take prisoners, and they *will* be sent to Bosque Redondo."

"What if we find ourselves up ag'in it?" asked one captain whose name Treadwell could never remember. "We got only two ways to go once we get inside that cañon—forward or back."

"We will fight. We will fight fiercely and well," Carson said. "So far on this scout, we have done danged little fightin'. That's now to our benefit, as we have ample ammunition left us."

"From our dead we got plenty of ammunition," groused Treadwell, thinking of Cummings being shot from ambush, never seeing his attacker. The Navajo fought well, but they were like the very wind. By the time a soldier formed into a rank to fight properly, the guerrilla had slipped away.

"Mr. Treadwell will scout for us, warning us of any traps. We advance now, keepin' at the pace of our slowest foot soldier. Mr. Treadwell, do your duty, sir."

"Right, Colonel," Treadwell said, wheeling his horse around and starting alone into the cañon. He felt the eyes of the officers on his back, knowing they did not envy him this mission. For all the fear he felt at first, Treadwell found it quietly vanishing, replaced with anticipation.

Natural beauty unlike any he had ever witnessed surrounded him within minutes. Riding along the north wall of Cañon de Chelly, he kept a sharp eye out for the source of the fire he and Carson had smelled. Less than twenty minutes into the cañon he found the small cooking fire two women had built. Tucked away up Cottonwood Cañon stood a mud-walled hogan. A few sheep cropped at the sparse grass here, but Treadwell saw more promising land farther along the twists and turns of the maze of cañon.

He came within a hundred yards before a small boy let out a yelp of warning. The women, startled at their cooking, leaped to their feet and ran hard for the hogan. Treadwell considered following. The few sheep around would bring him as much as ten dollars in promised bounty, but Treadwell had no stomach for such booty.

He needed more than blood money. He needed information.

Hooves pounding, his horse quickly lost its wind as Treadwell tried to run down one of the women. The older woman he had chosen as his target dodged with the agility of a young doe. Treadwell's horse tried to follow but failed. This forced him to dismount and pursue on foot. He reached the door of the hogan as the woman grabbed a war lance.

She swung about, the iron point leveled at him. Treadwell held his musket, knowing he could easily kill her. Instead of leveling it, he placed it on the ground beside him and spread his hands in front of him to show he carried no weapons.

"Manuelito," he said, maneuvering the woman around to face him so he could study her expression. "Where do I find Manuelito?"

The headman's name brought a flash of recognition to the

woman's dark eyes, but her face remained impassive. She advanced, determined to stick him with the lance.

"Gray Feather. Shining Eyes," he said. He got no sign from the woman that she understood those names. Treadwell watched her closely as she tried to circle. He saw her ploy immediately. She had no desire to kill him. She wanted only to escape into the rocky tumble behind her hogan. Once there, a pack of hound dogs would have trouble locating her.

Treadwell rushed her, his hand batting away the lance. His other hand grabbed at her wrist and pulled her to him. She fought like a wildcat, but Treadwell was stronger. His arms crushed like steel bands around her shoulders as he wrestled her to the ground.

He landed heavily atop her, momentarily stunning her. Treadwell moved while the advantage lay with him. Binding her wrists with a rawhide strip, he stepped away when she began kicking and spitting at him.

"Lie still, now," he said in a low voice.

Treadwell shook his head slowly. "Still thinking like a Ute," he said. He tapped his chest and said, "Nota-a."

The woman spat at him when he named himself a Ute. He wished he spoke Navajo good enough to get the information he wanted from her. But she might not know, living here at the edge of the Navajo stronghold. Manuelito would have his domain deeper in the rocky fortress of Cañon de Chelly, where the valleys tangled together like string in a yarn ball.

After securing the now passive but sullen woman to a large log she could not drag off without alerting him, Treadwell poked about inside the hogan. Following orders, he piled anything that might burn in the center of the dwelling and then set fire to it.

Ducking outside as thick, choking smoke billowed from the hogan, he saw the stricken expression on the woman's face. He was burning her home. Treadwell knew the Navajo moved from one hogan to another, regularly following their sheep and cattle to new grazing pastures. It was not losing the hogan that bothered her, it was the lost contents that constituted her entire life's worth.

About an hour later Carson rode up with his troopers.

"Good work, Mr. Treadwell," Carson said, seeing the smoldering hogan. "We have captured about ten sheep from this flock."

"Been watching how things go in the cañon, Colonel," Treadwell said. "Don't see any trouble brewing. If we push along fast, we can capture even more. Might get ten miles into this rock fort before tenting for the night."

"Agreed." Carson gave the orders. Treadwell turned the woman over to the soldiers trailing behind to guard the prisoners, then put his spurs to his horse's flanks to get back into the vanguard.

That day they gathered more than a hundred goats and sheep, burned fourteen hogans, and captured eight women and two children. And not a one of the prisoners, upon interrogation, would speak of Manuelito—or showed any hint of knowing whether Gray Feather still lived.

Death of Two Emissaries

August 26, 1863
Fort Canby

"Major Blakeney, we got another of them savages wantin' to palaver." The sentry stood uneasily at the door of the freshly painted commander's office. A fine desk had been fashioned from pine and had been sanded properly before anything else had been done at Fort Canby to make it more livable. Blakeney insisted that his office be the equal of General Carleton's.

It lacked much in the way of quaint charm of the general's in his faroff Santa Fé quarters, but it was mightily improved from when Kit Carson had left.

"You want we should shoot 'em, like we did before?"

Blakeney frowned as he hiked his feet to the desktop and laced his fingers behind his head. His belly growled from need. Brown eyes drifted to the flask in the open top drawer. His thirst got the better of him and he reached for the whiskey. A quick nip and Blakeney replaced it, ignoring the obvious desire on the sentry's suntanned face for a taste of the liquor.

"What happened immediately after the colonel left on his scout was an accident, a tragic occurrence. You will not refer to it again," he said sternly. Blakeney wished the incident would die its own death. The bald Indian begging to surrender so he could talk with his white "brethren" had been an annoyance, nothing more. Perhaps it was best that he had tried to escape and the guards had cut the craven down.

"Brethren, indeed," Blakeney scoffed, as he recollected the old Navajo's words. He hardly could imagine the gall of the savage placing himself on a par with even the enlisted men, much less the commanding officer of Fort Canby.

"Sir?"

"I'll see what the trouble is, since the officer of the watch seems incapable of tending to it," the major said irritably. He tucked the flask into his tunic, buttoned the woolen front and stepped into the hot afternoon sun. He adjusted his hat, made sure the braid dangled jauntily, then settled his shining saber. As he marched across the parade ground, the men melted away from him, wary of his hair-trigger wrath. It was not his fault they were sloppy soldiers.

Soldiers! he thought. They were not soldiers. They were rough-clad volunteers from the lowest classes in New Mexico Territory. Not a one was fit to polish his boots. With any luck, Carson would stay out on his dusty patrol for another month and might return to find his post whipped into proper military shape.

"Sir," called a captain whom Blakeney tried to place but could not. "Four Navajo are approaching under a white flag. They're signaling for a truce, it seems."

"How astute of you, Captain," Blakeney said sarcastically. He took the officer's spyglass and adjusted it to focus on the four. The one waving the flag slowly remained at a safe distance as the other three approached.

"They are unarmed, sir. What are your orders?"

"Admit them to the fort, of course," Blakeney said. He handed the spyglass back to the captain, motioning for the gates to be swung open. The three Navajo stopped for a moment and exchanged looks. Blakeney strode forward, hand held out.

"Come in, do come into our web," he said. The captain stiffened at this expression. The three stepped forward.

"We come as friends," said one Navajo warrior with a long puckered scar running diagonally across his left cheek. "We want no more war. We hunger. Our people wait outside your fort to surrender."

"Indeed?" inquired Blakeney. "And how many would that be? Just the one with the dirty flag?"

"One hundred of the Tótsohnii, the Big Water Clan. We seek peace with Red Clothes. He burns our fields, kills our sheep. There is—"

"Seize them!" cried Blakeney. "Take them to the stockade."

"Sir, they—"

"I gave you an order, Captain!" raged the commanding officer. "Arrest them now, or I shall issue an order for the sentries to open fire on them!"

The three's eyes widened in surprise as the guards surrounded them, bayonets leveled and muskets ready to fire.

"To the stockade," Blakeney bellowed. "This will mean three less to bother us." He watched as the captain marched the new captives to the rude jailhouse at the side of the fort. Without taking his eyes off them, he asked the sentry, "What of the other one, the one wagging his flag?"

"Sir, he has vanished. When he saw the bayonets, he—"

"Never mind," Blakeney said. "This is a minor provocation on their part. They did not intend to surrender. They want only to sneak into our fort and do mischief."

Hands clasped behind his back, Blakeney thought for a moment. "Sentry, tell the captain to put those savages to work rather than allow them to lie about. Clean up the fort. The horse dung is beginning to stink. And that pile of dead dogs . . ." He pointed to the far side of Fort Canby. "Have the Navajo get to work burying both the offal and the smelly dogs. There is no reason even one of you New Mexicans ought to do such vile work."

The major returned to his office, humming "Lorena" as he went. He wondered if Carson had captured three warriors as easily this day. He doubted it.

* * *

Gunshots awoke Thomas Blakeney. He pushed up from his cot and rubbed sleep from his eyes. The sun had set and a faint alcoholic fog bedeviled his sight. Rubbing his eyes harder, he reached for his saber and pistol. By the time he had the weapons strapped around his waist, heavy bootfalls approached and he was ready to meet the challenge of commanding these ignorant frontiersmen.

"Sir," panted the sergeant of the guard. "The Injuns. They tried to escape. Two of 'em, at any rate. The guards shot 'em."

"What happened?" he asked, stretching and yawning widely.

"We put 'em to buryin' the dogs and shit as you ordered," the sergeant said. He didn't notice how Blakeney cringed at the crudity of his speech. "They got down to it real quick, jist as if they'd done it all their pitiful lives."

"Get on with it, Provost-Sergeant," snapped the major.

"Well, sir, they tried to make a break for it as they dragged some of the carcasses outside the fort walls."

"They are all three dead?"

"Only two, sir."

"Then get the remaining savage back to his job. You did not give them any potential weapons, did you?"

"I don't understand, Major."

"No shovels or picks. Make him use his bare hands for the work. I want the entire parade ground policed by morning."

"What of the two we shot?"

"Have him bury them."

"I think they were headmen of their clans, Major. There might be trouble from this."

"Did you not tell me they attempted escape? Provost-Sergeant, your men have done well. See that they continue to do so in the matter of the third prisoner. Now let me rest. Tomorrow will be another taxing day, I am certain."

The sergeant saluted and left, muttering under his breath. Blakeney bit back a command to stop the man in his tracks, then shook his head and wondered at the dimwitted men in this command. If Carleton would see fit to put him in command and return that bumpkin Carson to Taos, where he belonged, the Navajo would be subdued in lickety-split time—and the disorderly soldiers of this command would quickly be brought into full military demeanor.

Thomas Blakeney lay down again, took a long pull on his whiskey and slept peacefully throughout the night.

Increasing Resistance

August 30, 1863
Fort Canby

"There ought to have been more," Kit Carson said, looking back over his shoulder in the direction of the cañon they had just left along Whiskey Creek.

"Sir?" Captain Asa Carey pulled alongside his commanding officer. "What do you mean?"

"Navajo," Kit said, taking off his hat and wiping sweat from his face. The summer hung on, even in this high country, with claws and teeth this year. That meant a cold winter would follow. "We went the whole danged length of Cañon de Chelly and didn't find a handful of 'em. Think they was hidin', or was they watchin' us the whole while?"

"Mr. Treadwell found no trace of significant activity. What we found was . . . what we found," Carey finished slowly. "Most of the warriors might have been on the warpath and we missed them. But we did not miss their homes."

"No, Asa, no—that we did not," Kit said. They had burned more corn than he could shake a stick at. It was past wheat-growing season, but the corn crop would have been a good one for the Navajo farmers. And blankets and hogans and grassland to feed the sheep they had not captured, all burned to cinders.

"We musta put 350 acres of corn to the torch, but where were the people? We came chargin' in and . . . they were not there."

"They fear you, sir," Carey declared. "They know how powerful a force you took into their stronghold."

Kit snorted and shook his head. The stronghold he had feared so much was lovely, filled with grassy slopes and abundant water. An Eden on earth—until he passed through it. Behind him he left scorched land and slaughtered animals. With them came 1,100 sheep and goats and 25 horses, but only a handful of prisoners.

Where had the fighters been? That first day, immediately after entering the west end of the cañon at Rock Cañon—*Tsegi,* the Navajo called it—had they encountered any resistance. Treadwell had caught one woman, and the troopers had tracked down a half dozen more in subsequent days. But even Treadwell had trouble finding anyone in the paradise after the initial encounter. The Navajo had vanished like spires of smoke on the cool afternoon wind.

"We chopped down their peach trees, also," Carey said, trying to buck up his commander. "They will have no grain or fruit to see them through the winter."

"Did they watch us?" Kit repeated. "Did they see how we turned their world into desolate wasteland? Where were they the whole time we was workin' at burnin' their world down around their ears?"

"That means they fear us greatly and would rather run than fight."

Kit said nothing. He had heard the stories of Manuelito, Herrera Grande, and Barboncito at war and had seen the aftermath of their ferocious attacks. The Navajo were not cowards hiding from bullies. The war they fought was different, striking and fading into the darkness to deliver a new blow a hundred miles away the next day. They fought and ran faster than the U.S. Army could ever follow.

"They will surrender," Kit said after a spell. "They have no choice after this scout. They've got no food left in reserve, now, do they, Asa?"

"None, sir, none that we left them. They will have no choice but to come in, accept emigration to Bosque Redondo—or turn into birds and fly south."

"They won't go south," Kit predicted. "The Hopi and Zuñi will stop them 'fore they git too far. And they ain't the Apache, able to go into Mexico. They ain't nomads; they're farmers, and this is their land." He settled down in the uncomfortable saddle and studied the terrain ahead of him, the land outside the eastern end of Cañon de Chelly. He had feared entry into the Navajo citadel and had emerged after only brief days, his command intact and in possession of livestock.

He felt no triumph. He had brought destruction but had not completed his mission. Carleton had wanted thousands of Navajo sent to Bosque Redondo. In that Kit had failed miserably, and it gnawed at him. He didn't like disappointing the general.

"The land ahead surely is a sight for sore eyes," he told his assistant. "Let's turn north for a spell and find some of the water promised by those trees." Putting the towering red buttes to his left, Kit relayed the order to his foot-weary troopers. They groaned and protested but picked themselves up and began the trek northward.

"We'll keep a sharp eye out for any ambush," Carey promised. Kit only nodded, lost in thought.

Ahead lay Round Rock and Los Gigantes Buttes. The column reached the plateau near sundown and then turned away from the sandstone columns. Kit considered pushing on but called a halt when he saw Treadwell riding slowly toward him. He wondered about the taciturn mountain man and his hunt for his family. Something had made Treadwell bitter toward him, and Kit could never quite figure out what it had been.

He had done all he could for the man who had served so faithfully at Valverde. It was hardly his fault Carleton had plans for the Navajo that did not include Treadwell's family. Truth to tell, Kit doubted Treadwell would ever find his wife and son, but he had never tried to put a damper on the man's hunt. It never did to take away what kept a man alive and kicking.

Kit wiped his nose and watched Treadwell approach, studying the set to the scout's body and deciding the man had discovered something of interest. As Treadwell made his way up a winding trail from the east, Kit saw a long rope dangling down. The scout had caught himself a prisoner.

"Captain Carey, fetch a couple guards to help Mr. Treadwell," ordered Kit. He dismounted and waited for them to arrive. He stared past Treadwell and his prisoner to the long red fingers of rock stretching away from the plateau. The dust would prove a problem for the men unless they kept moving to the north before turning for Fort Canby.

"Colonel, got me a woman who's telling a fantastical tale."

"What might that be?" Kit settled down and motioned for the woman to join them. She shucked off the rope from her shoulders and sank down. Kit had Carey bring water and food for her. He sat, saying nothing for almost twenty minutes as she ate. He knew she recognized him from the way her dark eyes darted repeatedly to the bright red woollies poking out from under his uniform.

When a decent time had passed, Kit inquired of her clan.

"I am of Herrera Grande's clan," she said. Kit looked up at Treadwell, who impatiently shifted. He had eaten when the woman had, but the scout itched to be back on the trail. With the Ute gone north and so few captives taken, Kit needed Treadwell's skill more than ever.

"Mr. Treadwell, what can ya tell me of findin' her?"

"She tried to skedaddle, but I caught her. I caught her down near where the creek runs from the cañon, the *tsaile,* the Navajo call it."

Kit waited for the woman to say more. Herrera Grande was a powerful headman. To find his camp would be the victory he needed for this scout.

"He went to surrender," she said unexpectedly.

"What? Herrera Grande went to surrender? At Fort Canby?"

She nodded slowly, her eyes fixed on the ground in front of her. "He asked to surrender, but the bluecoat killed those sent to talk peace."

Slowly the story of Blakeney's treachery unfolded. Kit took off his hat and wiped at the sweat on his forehead.

"I declare, every time I think we got a leg up, somethin' snakes out from under a rock and bites me. The major killed two men sent by Herrera Grande to negotiate surrender."

"She might be lying, sir," suggested Carey, but Kit heard the officer's tone. Asa Carey was no fool. He knew the truth when he heard it, no matter if it came from a white man or Navajo woman.

"Why bother inventing such a story?" spoke up Treadwell. "She's caught fair and square. She's got no reason to lie, and there's plenty of evidence of a large band of Navajo moving around down there recently." Treadwell indicated the base of Tsaile Butte.

"As many as a hundred?" asked Kit.

"About that, I'd say," Treadwell agreed. "If that's Herrera Grande moving about there, and Blakeney had a chance to accept his surrender and didn't, the man's a damned fool."

"Yes, Mr. Treadwell, I fear that he is that and more." Kit dreaded returning to Fort Canby and facing General Carleton's protégé in this matter. Allowing a feared warrior with a hundred of his people to slip away when they had come peaceably to surrender was the height of arrogance—and stupidity.

"He's set Herrera Grande's heart in stone now. From what I hear of the headman, he's a fighter. Can't believe he wanted to give up, but if he did . . ." Treadwell closed his eyes and swayed slightly. Kit might as well have read the scout's mind. Herrera Grande would fight to the death now, along with Manuelito and the others, lengthening the campaign and making it even more difficult to find any trace of the mountain man's family.

"We'll take her with us in hope of finding Herrera Grande. He might still palaver," Kit said. He stood and looked out at the western slope of the Chuska Mountains. They would set out for them in the morning, then move southward. The creeks that ran into Cañon de Chelly below might be dammed, cutting off water to those remaining in the Navajo stronghold, but Kit had no temper for such an elaborate engineering project now. The water flowing into Cañon del Muerto from Tsaile Creek and the other—Whiskey Creek, it read on his map—would do little to bring the Navajo to Bosque Redondo.

Every little thing he did was countered by great stupidity such as exhibited by Blakeney. To be asked to accept the surrender of a powerful chief and to refuse!

"We head for the flats tomorrow," Kit decided. "As lovely as it is to camp in the pines, we will be facin' scrub brush from now on till we get back to the fort."

"Colonel," spoke up Treadwell, "you thinking on any real action against the Navajo?"

"If we find Herrera Grande," Kit said, "we'll do what we can to change his mind. Don't seem too likely, but we kin only try."

"It's straight on back to Fort Canby from here," Treadwell said. "A blind man could find it."

"We are hardly blind, Mr. Treadwell," Kit said. "If you are requestin' permission to stay in the field and poke about a mite, I'll grant that."

Relief spread over Treadwell's face. He nodded brusquely and left without a word. Kit watched the man leave, wondering what demons rode him so hard. Then he knew those would be *his* demons if he ever lost Josepha and his children.

"Go with God, Mr. Treadwell. I only hope your mission is more successful than ours has been thus far," Kit said softly to the man's back, then turned to be certain his troops were properly bedded down for the night. Getting back to Fort Canby by the following nightfall would require considerable effort.

Gray Feather!

September 1, 1863
Cañon del Muerto

Joseph Treadwell reentered Cañon de Chelly riding along Tsaile Creek, picking his way slowly through the crazy tumble of tan, dusty sandstone rock. Cañon of the Dead One, mused Treadwell, as he followed a faint trail back into the heart of the Navajo refuge. He had never heard how the valley got that name, but all the soldiers whispered it as they rode past with real relief. As with so much of the surrounding land, the Navajo had controlled it for so long that many of the Spanish names were little more than reflections of their long-ago difficulty in dealing with the Lords of New Mexico.

The stony walls rose sharply on either side and an itchy feeling developed between Treadwell's shoulder blades, as if some hidden warrior had aimed an arrow there. He pushed the notion away. The silence in the steep-walled narrow cañon wore heavily on him, nothing more. He had ridden along the main cañon days earlier with Carson and the rest of his soldiers trailing behind and emerged safe and sound. They had no reason to think this time would be any different.

The only troubling thing that wore at Treadwell's gut was the lack of resistance. The Navajo lived here, yet they slipped away and never defended themselves. Treadwell shrugged it off. The few times he had ridden near the steep cliff face, rocks had tumbled down on him. This might be the best resistance the Navajo could muster.

He had done all he could for Carson and the cause of peace in the territory. Moving the Navajo from this majestic land to Bosque Redondo struck Treadwell as ridiculous, but he had never taken much of a shine to Carleton or his intelligence in dealing with practical matters. Why Carson so blindly obeyed Carleton was a poser for Treadwell, but that was the way of the world, and he accepted it. Carson was a good enough mountain man—his reputation mattered a great deal to Treadwell—but he didn't have a lick of initiative. Treadwell spat. If Carleton yelled "frog!" Carson would jump straight up in the air and catch flies with his tongue.

"A pox on all their houses," grumbled Treadwell. He shifted in the saddle, trying to get more comfortable. So long astride his dependable horse, he seemed more a man with four legs than one with only a pair. But comfortable? He would never be easeful on horseback. He preferred his own long, sure stride over the ground to enduring continually aching hindquarters. If it hadn't been for the need to cover great distances through Cañon de Chelly, he might have staked the horse and gone ahead on foot.

From his earlier foray through the stronghold, Treadwell knew simply finding an Indian would be difficult. And there would be little chance he would stumble across many Navajo in the areas put to the torch by Carson's men. He needed to explore different terrain—and he knew there were hundreds of miles of it he had only a hint about.

Grass still smoldering made his nose wrinkle. A few miles down Cañon del Muerto brought him to a small branching valley. Treadwell dropped to the ground, rubbed his posterior, and then studied the dirt for any spoor telling him this side cañon might be occupied. The evidence came to him in small details. A bit of dried horse dung. A shining bead. Two broken quills, shaped for ornamentation and partly buried under a clump of sagebrush.

This caused him to examine the ground for signs of recent human passage. Treadwell finally decided the feathers had fallen some time ago, then dirt blown up around them as they fetched hard against the exposed roots of the sage. Still, it meant a Navajo warrior had ridden here some time back.

On foot, Treadwell entered the branching cañon, staying close to the sheer red rock walls. Any sentry above him would have difficulty spotting him at the base of the cliff while letting Treadwell spot any guard on the far rim incautious enough to expose himself against the bright blue sky. Occasional glances above convinced him no one spied on him as he worked his way deeper into the maze of cañons. For the first time in months, Treadwell rode without the support of the cavalry—and he felt a curious relief being on his own. If he was discovered by any Navajo, Treadwell knew his scalp would be hanging from a pole outside a hogan before sundown. In spite of this cold understanding of his position in the heartland of the enemy's power, his step was light and his spirits were buoyant.

He did not ride on Carson's mission. He did not hunt for warriors to fight. For the first time since Manuelito had left him for dead two and a half years ago, he felt close to finding his family. He could travel where he willed without asking permission of some meddling bureaucrat. Throwing in with Christopher Carson had proved a mistake, Treadwell now thought. The man had done little to aid his hunt, coldly using him at Valverde and after for his own purposes.

And there was Carson's attitude toward the Navajo. Carson had actually adopted one of the murdering bastards into his family.

Treadwell scratched himself and fixed his eagle-eyed gaze on the red-streaked cliffs as he thought seriously on the short colonel for the first time in months. Kit Carson was something of a mystery. Carson saw nothing wrong in taking in a stray Navajo to keep him from slavery among the Ute, yet Carson had without hesitation allowed Ka-ni-ache and his scouts to take a dozen captives back north as slaves, in direct opposition to Carleton's orders.

Treadwell decided Carson was a man torn by too many different forces. Carleton wanted his reservation at Bosque Redondo to be filled with both Apache and Navajo—a laughable if deadly mix, Treadwell knew. And turning the Indians into good Christians was even more of a chimera to chase. On the other hand, Carson had argued for Canby's solution to the Navajo problem: let them keep their precious land in return for the solemn promise not to raid other tribes or the New Mexican settlers.

That held no real solution, either. The Civil War unbalanced the power in New Mexico Territory forever, letting one faction prey on the other with impunity. Through it all, Carson had never found his own voice or done anything more than slavishly follow whoever sat on his fat rump behind the military commander's desk in Santa Fé.

Heat rose in the narrow cañon and sweat beaded on Treadwell's face. He moved deliberately, occasionally backtracking to be certain no warrior tracked him. He might have been transported to the moon, for all the humanity he saw. Twice he passed abandoned hogans. One had a skeleton inside. Treadwell knew fear of ghost sickness had forced the hogan owner away from the dwelling. Nothing the bluecoats could have done would have ensured more rapid desertion of the mud-and-log home. The other hogan had been abandoned for no reason he could find. All belongings inside had been removed, so death was not the problem.

"Just tired of the hogan and moving on to better pastures," he decided, taking in the evidence of a deliberate abandonment. He kept walking deeper into the cañon, stopping in mid-afternoon for a cold meal of jerky and beans. As he ate, his sense of being watched grew. The scrape of moccasins on rock alerted him long before he saw the woman.

With his hand resting on his knife, he turned and stared at her. Her wide-set black eyes bored into his. When he dropped his gaze politely and held out some of his food, he found himself with an immediate dining companion.

The scrawny woman came over in a rush, dropped down, and gobbled the food in complete silence. Only when every last drop of the peaches in the airtight had vanished did she stir.

"Your hogan?" Treadwell asked, indicating the nearby mud-and-log hut with his chin in Navajo fashion. He had learned much about them. Forcing the interrogation would gain him nothing.

A polite silence fell, then she said, "It was. I moved when the soldiers came down the cañon. When *you* and the soldiers came down the cañon," she accused.

"I returned to find my wife and son," Treadwell said. He silently pushed more food to the starving woman. In the midst of the green valley with its former luxury of abundant food, it did not surprise him to find a hungry woman. Carson and his troopers had done a good job destroying food reserves as they'd passed through. They might not have captured many of the Navajo, but they had removed important supplies.

It was hardly the edge of autumn and already the Navajo grew hungry enough to come down and deal with their enemy.

"I seek Manuelito. He has my wife and son."

"Manuelito is a great headman. Bit'ahni Clan." She gobbled more of the food. Treadwell silently opened another can of beans and passed these to her. Her eyes darted furtively to him, then dropped to the food. She began shoveling it into her mouth using two fingers.

"Your clan?"

"I am of the Coyote Pass People," the woman said.

"Barboncito is a great leader, also," Treadwell said, trying to keep the clans and their leaders straight in his mind. "A greater leader than Manuelito."

The woman's face remained impassive as she licked the last drops of sauce from the can. In spite of so much food, her ravenous expression remained, reminding Treadwell of a buzzard waiting for dinner to die in the hot noonday sun.

"I would parley with Manuelito," he said. "I would find my wife and son."

"Manuelito is a great leader with many wives and a large family," she said. From the hesitation that came, Treadwell knew he needed to prime the pump to get more information. He quietly drew out four more airtights of food, including an oilcloth holding hardtack. One at a time he placed them on the ground between them. The woman never stirred, as if raising his poker hand.

"My wife is a Ute captive," he said. This produced no spark of recognition. "She is named Gray Feather."

He forced himself to keep from leaping to his feet and grabbing the woman by the shoulders to shake the truth from her. The widening of her eyes told him she recognized the name.

"She is one of Manuelito's wives," she said. "Their sons are strong, good boys."

"Sons?" Treadwell almost lost his voice. "A boy about eleven years old and another? How old is he?" Treadwell prayed the answer would be two rather than younger.

"Shining Eyes is a brave warrior. He is eleven summers," the woman said, nodding slightly. Her eyes turned to the tall buttes around them. Treadwell followed her gaze and thought he caught sight of light glinting off silver. The flash passed too quickly for him to be certain. The sense of being observed returned with a vengeance.

"The other boy—what is his name?"

"Goes to War, I think," the woman said, gathering her barter and tucking it in the folds of her voluminous green baize skirt.

"Where are they? Near?" Treadwell's fingers went to his musket. He would cut the woman down if she did not reply. His heart threatened to explode in his chest and the world spun in wild, wide circles around his head.

"There. Down there. Two miles. A little more," the woman said, indicating a hidden branching cañon Treadwell had not noticed before. And then she hastened off, taking her newfound wealth with her up the valley and away.

Treadwell wasted no time packing what remained of his food supply. Once free of Cañon de Chelly he could hunt again. Or he could live off the very air! After more than two years, he had chanced upon a woman who knew of Gray Feather, Shining Eyes and . . . Goes to War.

If he found Gray Feather, he need never do anything but rejoice! Rejoice with his *two* sons.

Packing his gear quickly, Treadwell set off at a brisk trot, finding the narrow mouth of the cañon easily, now that it had been pointed out. As he rode, he watched the ground for spoor. More showed itself along this trail than he had found even in the larger valley. This trail had been used frequently—and recently. If Manuelito had brought his captives here, it might mean the headman's camp was ahead.

Treadwell did not slacken his pace. If necessary, he would ride into hell and face down Lucifer himself to regain his family.

The passage narrowed until Treadwell's shoulders gritted along the sandstone sides before widening to a small, lush box cañon. He slowed his pace and cast an eye about for hogans.

The tumble of a single small stone from above alerted Treadwell. He swung his face upward and saw the sentry drawing a bead on him. The long barrel of the Navajo's musket wavered slightly as he shifted to get into better position. Only this instant's hesitation allowed Treadwell to dive to one side in time to avoid the heavy lead ball trying to rob him of his life.

Treadwell hit the ground hard, rolled, and came to a sitting position. He hiked up his own musket, aiming and firing in one smooth motion. The heavy rifle bucked and Treadwell let out a yelp of delight. His slug flew straight and true. He saw the Navajo warrior jerk back, freeze for a moment, and then sink down.

Scampering to his feet, Treadwell ran down his spooked horse and savagely dragged it around by the bridle until it stopped trying to run.

"Stand still, durn your hide," Treadwell growled. He fumbled in his saddlebags for more gunpowder and ammunition. With practiced skill, he tamped, put in the patch and gunpowder, followed it with the ball and another patch, then primed the pan for a second shot.

He squeezed the trigger immediately when he saw the half dozen braves advancing on him from down in the cañon. Treadwell had walked open-eyed into a trap.

The shot drove the warriors to ground, giving him time to reload and pick his next target with care. Above him on the tall bluffs he saw constant movement. For the first time he was sorry not to have the full column of Carson's men trailing behind him. But Treadwell would not easily surrender, not now that he had learned that Gray Feather still lived. And his sons. *His sons.*

The musket flared a third time, and then Treadwell found himself occupied with fighting off a brave wielding a knife. Swinging the barrel of his emptied rifle, Treadwell caught the man on the side of the head and sent him spinning. A quick step forward put Treadwell in range. He drove the metal-sheathed butt of his heavy musket into the warrior's face. Then he worked to reload.

A few tiny puffs of dirt kicked up around him, followed by reports from rifles. Treadwell had no fear of such long-range shooting. If the Navajo with the firearms kept to the rim of the cañon, they might shoot all day and never do more than frighten his horse a mite. And those coming at him from the valley wielded nothing more deadly than their wicked knives.

Treadwell fired again and winged a brave almost on top of him. Treadwell stepped up and looped a brawny arm around the warrior's throat.

"Manuelito—where is he?"

The brave fought desperately, but Treadwell saw that the same starvation which had turned the woman in the outer valley so gaunt also afflicted this man. He weakened quickly. Treadwell shook him like a terrier would a rat.

"Manuelito. Where is he?"

"I am of the Coyote Pass People," the warrior grated out. "I fight for Barboncito!"

Treadwell dropped to one knee and used the warrior as a shield as a flight of arrows arched from the cañon rim. One struck his captive in the leg. The man shrieked and flopped about. Seeing that he would be unable to present any danger to him, Treadwell shoved him away.

"Where's Manuelito?" he repeated. He got only a cold glare in return. After only one day of hunting in Cañon de Chelly he had found more warriors than Carson's entire force had in three weeks of scouring the length of the Navajo stronghold. But it did Treadwell no good if he did not get away from the trap Barboncito had set—and which he had fallen into so easily.

Treadwell reloaded and swung into the saddle, turning his pony's face back into the narrow gap. He galloped away, hating to leave, but knowing he could return. Firing at a lone brave on the ground in front of him, Treadwell leaned forward and sent his horse into a long jump that cleared the wounded man's body. He raced away from the deadly box cañon.

And did he also leave behind Gray Feather? Treadwell knew she still lived, her and Shining Eyes and Goes to War.

"When I come back, it'll be with the entire New Mexico Volunteers," he vowed.

He burst into the larger cañon and headed back toward Carson, his mission almost accomplished. Almost.

Now that he knew they still lived, Joseph Treadwell would be back for his family. Soon.

Squaw Dance

September 2, 1863
Cañon de Chelly

Shining Eyes stumbled, his toe catching a rock, and caught himself. It wasn't dignified for a warrior blooded in battle to fall in front of so many people, especially those of other clans. He pulled himself up and used the horse walking slowly beside him for support. Of the string of ponies he had won and stolen only the bay given him by Manuelito remained in his possession. The others had been ridden into the ground during the escape from the bluecoats or had simply died.

Forage was becoming scarce.

He looked around the large gathering and wondered why he had allowed Follows Quickly and the others to goad him into coming. Everywhere bustled women dressed in finery and silver *heishi* necklaces and men swaggering, captured muskets hiked onto their shoulders and bows slung across their backs. The sings were important, he knew, if the Dinéh were to triumph in battle. But the long hikes between the sites chosen wore heavily on him. Each day required a new location some distance from the others. Missing two of the nights of the ceremony had put him at a disadvantage reaching this one. He had only recently returned from a week-long scout and had ridden the length of Tseyi'. For many of the warriors, such a trip would have been nothing.

Shining Eyes felt great pride as he knew how few other eleven-year-olds were included in that select group. Warrior! But his body lacked the muscle to keep up with Follows Quickly, Manuelito, and the now scattered Folded Arms People.

He missed his mother and brother but knew why they had remained miles and miles away in their hogan. Goes to War could not keep down the food given him. Goat milk came back up quickly, and mush of corn and squash caused him to choke. Travel with a sick child was not possible, even for a curing sing. Shining Eyes looked around to see if a hand-trembler was sitting alone and could be approached for advice.

While he had little to offer for a curing for Goes to War, Shining Eyes knew he must find a medicine man soon or his brother would die. If only Goes to War could have traveled! The excitement of more than five hundred people gathered in the dish-shaped valley communicated to Shining Eyes, giving him back some measure of his vitality. Goes to War would have regained his spirit simply being with so many people.

Shining Eyes walked and marveled at the assembly. He had never gone through the Night Way chant to formally initiate him into the Dinéh, but Shining Eyes felt no loss at this. He had so much to learn—and all while he sought out the movement of the Biligáana. His head spun constantly from the barrage of taboos, the *báhádzid,* the ways to work and fight and live that would permit him to walk in beauty.

Passing through the fringe of the camp preparing for the night's sing—the Squaw Dance—Shining Eyes felt the scrutiny of many who had never seen him before. He knew their thoughts as surely as if they had shouted them.

"Who is this? Why does he enter our camp? Is there no one to challenge him?"

Shining Eyes jerked about when he heard a horse trotting up to him. He leaned over the bay's back and saw his uncle. Shining

Eyes let out a sigh of relief. Cayatanita was a friendly face amid the tension he caused simply by entering the camp.

"Where have you been?" asked Cayatanita. "Manuelito sought you at your mother's hogan and was told you had left."

"It took me much longer than I had thought to come here," Shining Eyes said. He did not tell his uncle how he had fallen from horseback, dizzy from lack of food. The smell of cooking all around him caused his mouth to water, but he knew no one. Who would feed him when he brought no gifts?

"Everything takes longer now," opined the man. "A Squaw Dance this late in the year? This is a summer healing, not a fall chant." He shook his head. "The old ways blur before my eyes. Too much changes and we do nothing to stop it."

"I saw nothing on my scout," Shining Eyes said, knowing what his uncle needed to hear. "The troopers only skirted the southern entrance to Tseyi', but they burned everything in their wake." Shining Eyes snorted in disgust. "If an early snow falls, they will find themselves cut off, trapped in Dinetah without a retreat. Their horses will never find grass to keep them moving all the way back to Fort Defiance."

Cayatanita shook his head. "They have few horses. Most are afoot."

"We can attack their supply trains," Shining Eyes said, warming to the conversation. He felt no kinship with the others scattered around him, but this was his life, fighting the Biligáana.

"I must go," Cayatanita said abruptly.

"Wait, Uncle. Where—?" Shining Eyes's words fell on distant ears. Already Cayatanita trotted off to join a small band of riders heading directly across the campground. Shining Eyes had no idea where others from his clan might be. He had much to do and no easy way of accomplishing any of it. Goes to War needed a healing chant, but Shining Eyes did not know where to look to find a singer capable of such a cure.

He listened for sounds of a bull-roarer that might show him the way to a singer. Nothing. Walking slowly tired him. The boy found a rock out of the way of the traffic moving sluggishly through the camp and sat, glad to rest. His horse cropped at a few juicy clumps of grass growing in the shade of a large boulder.

From his vantage, Shining Eyes watched the others. How much apart from them he felt. But he did not belong with his white father. He had seen Joseph Treadwell and felt only revulsion, not kinship. But what of his mother's people? Bile rose as Shining Eyes thought of the death brought by the Ute to the Dinéh. He might be of Ute blood, but they were no longer his people. His clan had died under Manuelito's knife—and the headman had brought a young boy to a better life, the life of a Dinéh warrior.

Shining Eyes touched the blade sheathed at his side. He knew how to use it against his enemies, and this gave him definition. The socializing he saw everywhere seemed alien to him—and made him increasingly uneasy. The Dinéh led a solitary life herding sheep and farming. Only during the sings was the solitude broken.

He jerked around to see a young girl staring boldly at him. The instant she knew he had seen her, she averted her eyes and hurried off. Shining Eyes started to call out and challenge her. Why did she stare so impolitely at him? But he held his tongue. He had much to think about and wanted no interruption.

When the sun dipped behind the rim of the canyon, Shining Eyes lifted his gaze to the stars popping from azure into the blackness of night. Divination was possible to those who spoke to the gods. But for him there was no message save for coldness.

Shivering, Shining Eyes pulled his blanket closer to his body and hopped down from the rock. He tugged at his bay and led the horse into the camp. The ceremonial began soon, and he wanted to find his uncle. Cayatanita could introduce him to a singer. He slowed when he saw several headmen gathered near the large fire. Barboncito began, speaking slowly and clearly, exhorting everyone to the ways of righteousness before settling a dispute between a husband and wife in his clan.

The others took their turn, telling of the greatness of the

Dinéh and how the Biligáana could be met and defeated. Such posturing bored Shining Eyes, especially when he found a large stewpot and a woman serving any who came up with the simple request for food. He returned several times until his belly ceased its week-long growling. The simple fare suited him better than the finest meal might have because it was filling and nutritious.

Hunkered down by a large fire with a dozen others all intent on what their headmen said, Shining Eyes again grew uneasy. He cautiously looked around and again saw the girl who had so boldly stared at him earlier. She did not immediately see that Shining Eyes had exposed her interest in him and this gave him a chance to study her.

Tall, she was more than half a head taller than he. She wore a green baize jacket and doeskin skirt with blankets slung over both shoulders, shielding her from a cold wind whipping down the canyon. Her long black hair had been braided and interwoven with silver and turquoise. A simple squash blossom necklace dangled around her neck, but she wore intricately made bracelets and rings, showing she came from a rich clan.

A slow smile crept across Shining Eyes's lips: a rich clan. For all Manuelito's leadership in war, the Folded Arms People were not wealthy. The number of horses and sheep had decreased slowly over the summer months as the Biligáana had made hesitant intrusions into Tseyi'. The headman wore intricately wrought jewelry but made no pretense at its quantity. Rather, Manuelito concentrated on his relatives, his friends and people.

Shining Eyes never knew what happened. He might have stared too long, or the girl might have noticed his returned interest in her. She stiffened and hurried off amid a swish of her long skirts without even a backward look. Shining Eyes continued to eat slowly, using cornbread to soak up the last of his stew. He did not want to leave even a drop of the meal behind for the ants.

His attention swerved from the fire to the singers beginning this part of the Enemy Way chant. Those needing healing were called forth for their part in the ceremony to drive out the bad spirits accumulated from contact with the Biligáana. Shining Eyes's thoughts meandered back to his baby brother and what must be done to heal him. An Enemy Way would not work— Goes to War had never come into contact with the Biligáana. His sickness came from other sources—thunder, perhaps, or a snake. The baby walked constantly and knew nothing of the dangers of contamination by snakes or the winds or what treachery might be borne by a coyote. A Holy Way chant might be needed.

Shining Eyes found himself humming along with the beat from the Enemy Way. He jumped when a hand on his shoulder brought him out of his reverie. Turning, he saw the green baize jacket of the girl who had been so impudently examining him like some newfound bug.

"We dance, Shining Eyes," she said. She stepped back and pointed to the larger bonfire, where couples now danced with slow deliberation. The music would pick up tempo soon and catch them all in a more active gambol.

"No, no," he said, shaking his head. He could not believe this. She picked him out to dance with her. It was her right, but he would not do it.

"Then you must ransom yourself," she said. "What do you offer me in return for your freedom?"

"I . . . I have nothing," he said honestly. Such a revelation caused him to blush. How could he find a singer willing to heal Goes to War if he had no gift to offer? A long chant might require services for a week or more. With so many warriors returning wounded during their skirmishes with the Biligáana, healers were overworked.

"If you have nothing, then you *must* dance. I am Looking Arrow of the Tabaha Clan, the Water's Edge People. My uncle was Zarcillos Largos, who rode with Narbona."

Shining Eyes slowly related his lineage, ashamed that he knew so little of it. Still, mention that Manuelito was his father and Cayatanita his uncle brought a light to Looking Arrow's face that caused Shining Eyes to puff with pride. All knew of Manuelito and his bravery.

"We dance now," Looking Arrow insisted.

Shining Eyes shook his. head again but saw his uncle approaching.

"Why do you refuse her?" Cayatanita asked.

"I don't know how to—"

"If you don't pay her a big ransom, you have to go with her," Cayatanita said, a broad grin on his face. He bent closer and whispered in Shining Eyes's ear, "You are a man, Shining Eyes, also known to his clan by his war name as Angry Knife. Go, and do not disgrace your family."

Shining Eyes stared at his uncle. He had been given a war name, a secret name used only during the most holy of ceremonies. In the course of life he ought to have endured a sweat and an initiation ceremony before receiving the name, but he knew how customs were changing rapidly. The more the Dinéh tried to preserve the old way and to walk in beauty, the more chaos filled their lives.

"We dance," Looking Arrow repeated, tugging on the blanket thrown around his shoulders.

Shining Eyes—known as Angry Knife to the warriors of his clan—stood and followed her to the circle. She began to dance, slowly at first, then faster as the tempo increased. Shining Eyes stared at his own feet, moving clumsily. He learned the steps quickly enough watching other men as they danced and soon found himself enjoying the ceremony.

He even came to appreciate the girl's grace and beauty, though she must be two or three years older.

A Different War

September 1863
Fort Canby

Kit Carson's pale blue eyes went wide when he faced the array of soldiers vying for his attention. Then he screwed up his face as a dozen different thoughts crowded in, all trying to confuse him. He held up a hand, wondering if he might ever restore order to the fort.

"Quiet, dang it," he said. He heaved a deep sigh and looked sideways at Asa Carey. The young captain was as flustered as he was but fought to cover his bewilderment. They had hardly ridden into the fort from the month-long scout when one solider after another had come to him, begging to talk. Most all these troopers elbowed one another to get in front of the others to bring charges against Major Blakeney.

"Provost-Sergeant, you hold the highest rank here. You speak for the others. If they don't much cotton to what yer sayin', I'll let them say their piece." Kit settled down in the chair behind the fine desk he did not recognize. He ran his fingers over the smoothly sanded pine surface, marveling at it. General Carleton didn't have anything this elegant.

Too much had happened at the post during the last month while he was out on a scout and none of it looked to be good.

Thought of the summer scout turned Kit morose. There were

no real engagements to report to the general. Only a handful of prisoners, and these had already been spirited away to the north with the Ute as payment for their service. Kit knew he would have to answer for this if Carleton heard of it, since this flew in the face of the standing order that all Navajo prisoners be sent directly to Bosque Redondo.

Being called up on charges might improve his outlook, Kit decided, even if such a dishonor would reflect poorly on him and his family. It was certainly easier than trying to untangle the garbled stories being spouted out by his men.

Kit shucked off that crazy notion right away. Chipita might understand him enduring a court martial, but what of her family? He shook his head sadly. He had been given a job and would do it. Honor demanded nothing less than his best, even if it might not be the equal to that of a regular Army officer.

"Colonel," the Provost-Sergeant said in his deep bass voice. "Most all these men are willing to swear that Major Blakeney has spent most of the time, while on duty, falling down drunk."

Kit closed his eyes and wished the sutler had lost every last barrel of firewater. The whiskey had brought only trouble.

"Further, he has been catering to the camp followers, bringing them into his quarters."

"Sergeant," Kit interrupted, "are you sayin' the major's been seein' women in his quarters?"

"I am, sir, while he was on duty. And this is the least of his transgressions." The provost-sergeant cleared his throat, then rushed into the story of the three emissaries sent by Herrera Grande and how two were buried in shallow graves just outside the fort.

Kit leaned forward in the chair, his thick hands on the desktop. His nails dug into the soft pine surface as his anger mounted.

"Herrera Grande wanted to surrender and Blakeney did *that* to men comin' in under a white flag?"

"Sir, that is correct. It is our belief the major intended to murder those Indians from the outset." The sergeant swallowed hard, as if tasting bile. His eyes fixed on the wall somewhere behind Kit. "His orders were such that any man, much less a proud Navajo finding it difficult to arrange for surrender, would attempt escape."

"These are real serious charges," Kit said, hoping Carey would come to his aid. The captain stood impassively, his face now a mask. The more Kit tried to figure what his aide thought, the less sure he was that Carey had heard even one word of these damning indictments.

"We are aware of that, sir. While it might be said that the antagonism between us has been drawn along lines of New Mexico and California, we believe it goes deeper. Major Blakeney's drunkenness is only part of the problem."

"I'll look into this right away, Sergeant," Kit promised, wishing he could return to Cañon de Chelly as fast as a bird could fly. He might not have found a solitary Navajo warrior to fight, and he never did much like destroying food and property for the sheer orneriness of it all, but even that was better than dealing with his own officers.

"I'll fetch Major Blakeney, sir," offered Carey. The captain pushed past the tight knot of enlisted men. Kit stared at them, wondering if he ought to have them confront the major directly.

"Sergeant, what's happened with the third Navajo? The one that did not, uh, die?"

"Stockade, sir."

"Set him free right away. Let him go, and outfit him with enough food so he can return to Herrera Grande with my good wishes." Kit hardly knew what else to do. He had no desire to talk with the maligned Navajo. Blakeney's actions would harden Herrera Grande's resolve never to surrender. From all he had heard, Manuelito was the most stubborn of the headmen, but it would take only a little mistake to keep men like Herrera Grande in the field and fighting their guerrilla war.

If only the Navajo had a single war chief to dicker with. Each fought on his own, with his small clan behind him. That Manuelito swayed so many only added to the trouble getting them moved to Fort Sumner and General Carleton's reservation alongside the Apache. This disaster would not do much to convince the other headmen of the bluecoats' good intentions.

"You men are dismissed. I want to talk privately with the major," Kit said, seeing Captain Carey and Blakeney approaching. The major wobbled as he walked and his face was as white as bleached muslin. His bloodshot eyes told Kit all he needed to know about part of the provost-sergeant's accusations.

"Didn't know you'd got back, Colonel. Welcome to Fort Canby." Blakeney tried to salute and almost fell over. Carey caught the man and held him upright. The captain quickly stepped away. Kit still could not read what went on in his aide's head, approving or not.

"You're drunk. Sober yerself up and then we'll palaver," Kit decided. "Till then, I want to talk with the doctor."

"Peck? The son-of-a-bitch. Don't lissen to 'im, Colonel. Go ask Doc Prentiss what's happenin'. He'll give it to you straight."

All that the provost-sergeant had said came back to Kit. The division between those officers hailing from California and the First New Mexico Volunteers reared again. Allen Peck was Fort Canby's head surgeon and James Prentiss was an officer who had come to New Mexico Territory with Carleton and Blakeney.

"I assure you, sir, I'll git it right. Sleep off your drunk. And do it alone."

"Not even with one of those sweet l'il things from outside the camp? You don't know wha' yer askin' of me, Colonel. Need to keep my bed warm somehow."

"Dismissed, Major."

Blakeney saluted and somehow managed to walk through the door without banging into either side. Otherwise, the entire parade ground was hardly wide enough for the drunken major as he returned to his billet.

"Asa, what am I to do 'bout this muddle?" Kit pleaded.

"Sir, a full report to General Carleton is necessary, as distasteful as it will be to draft."

"I want you to take it all down. Don't know where Blakeney's sent my clerk. I am gettin' around to hate sendin' in so many reports." Kit felt lost amid the confusion of his command.

"Tell me all 'bout it, Doc," Kit asked his chief surgeon. Allen Peck wiped his nose on a filthy handkerchief, then tucked it into the front of his tunic.

"Come on out to the porch, Kit. We can talk there." The surgeon left the small infirmary and settled into a rickety chair. Kit sank down beside him in another chair so they could watch the officers drilling the troopers in an attempt to get some discipline back into the command.

"We been havin' a passel of trouble since you left. Blakeney thinks the whole danged fort is his to do with as he sees fit," Peck said. "Being saddled with Prentiss is wearing me down, too."

"I talked with Lieutenant Hodt. He tole me Prentiss was usin' the hospital stores of whiskey and wine for his own use."

Kit watched Peck closely. The sour expression on the man's face increased. Peck took a bite off a plug of tobacco, chewed a while, then spat accurately, hitting the post at the end of the porch. Only then did the doctor speak.

"Prentiss and Blakeney are drunks," Peck said. "Wouldn't trust either of 'em as far as I could toss 'em. But then again, I don't much cotton to young Hodt. He's as inclined to take a swig as either Prentiss or Blakeney."

Kit felt a tide of rising desolation. He had sent a letter to Carleton outlining the situation at Fort Canby and still awaited a reply. Blakeney was under arrest in his quarters and Prentiss was relieved of duty until matters could be sorted out properly. Other than making the drunken doctor pay for the supplies he had used, Kit was at a loss to conjure any punishment for a man whose skills he desperately needed at the fort.

"What of them two whores?" Kit asked, frowning as he spoke. This produced a chuckle from the doctor.

"You mean the little catfight between Mountain Cal and our

dear Mexican Heroine? Didn't amount to more than a few bruises when they got into a dustup over booze."

"I want all liquor placed under your control," Kit decided. "The whores, the firewater, it's all out of check."

"You need a strong hand runnin' things inside the fort," Peck said. "Blakeney was always lookin' out for hisself."

"I'm thinkin' Carey's the man for the job." Kit watched the young officer marching a ragtag company back and forth, bellowing at their sergeant and keeping all in line.

"Good thinkin', Kit," agreed Peck. "But you got other problems."

"What might they be?"

Peck did not answer directly. His eyes drifted easterly and he spat again.

"You ain't sayin' the general is a problem? Doc, he is an educated man and a regular Army officer with strong Christian convictions. He is a hero with the medals to prove it. General Carleton has a career that makes him the envy of other officers."

"Reckon all that is true," Peck said, spitting again. "Mark my words, Kit. You'll never bring Blakeney up for court martial."

"The general would never let him go free after murderin' two of Herrera Grande's men like he did. He might as well have pulled the trigger hisself."

"You might be right, Kit, you might be right." But Peck's tone said something different.

Four days later, Carleton's messenger arrived with a personal rebuke for Blakeney, an immediate transfer to Los Pinos and the dismissal of all charges.

The Fall Campaign

September-October 1863
Along the Little Colorado River

"I been cooling my heels for almost two weeks, Colonel. My wife and children are back there and I need to find them," Joseph Treadwell said. "If you're going to stay at the fort, I'll head back on my own, with your permission."

"There is a small delay in our scout, Mr. Treadwell," Carson said. He shuffled nervously, giving Treadwell the image of a racehorse waiting to begin its race. It might be that Carson was as antsy to get into the saddle as he was, but the colonel had been hanging back for more than a week on departure.

Treadwell had left Cañon de Chelly and ridden back to Fort Canby slowly, thinking hard how to convince the cavalry to get back into the field. The skirmish against Barboncito's clan had convinced Treadwell he could not take on all the Navajo singlehandedly. He needed Carson and the bluecoats riding behind him.

But returning to the fort had been a mistake. He knew the instant he fell into the dark, swirling waters of animus at Fort Canby he should have remained in Cañon de Chelly to find Gray Feather. Facing the Navajo would have been safer. Blakeney had been sent to Los Pinos and Lieutenant Hodt court martialed for drunkenness, but the undercurrents tugged at everyone, separating the camp into two factions. Those who thought Blakeney had been wrongly sent away tended to be those who had come from California and had little time for the yokels serving in the First New Mexico Volunteers.

Not too surprisingly, Treadwell found himself siding with Carson in his belief that Blakeney ought to have been hanged for his misconduct. The war had been lengthened by the death of the two envoys sent by Herrera Grande. Worse, the Navajo now had even less reason to believe anything a white man might say.

Worst of all were the orders coming like a never-ending freight train from Santa Fé, all signed by James Carleton.

"I been tryin' to figger how to get around this order," Carson revealed. He fumbled in his pocket and drew out a crumpled sheet of paper. He handed it to Treadwell. The mountain man scanned it quickly ignoring the florid style in favor of finding the kernel of information held in it.

"This is outrageous!" Treadwell cried.

"I agree. You can see how the general makes matters worse for us," Carson said, heaving a deep sigh.

"There's no reason to subdue the Zuñi pueblo," Treadwell protested. "They're not the enemy. It's Manuelito and Barboncito and—"

"No need to preach to the converted, Mr. Treadwell," Carson said. "I tried to explain to General Carleton, but he would have none of it. He considers the Zuñi to be harborin' the Navajo."

"But to seize six of the Zuñi headmen and hold them as hostages is an outrage! They have no love for the Navajo. They would dance a jig if we put the lot of them Navajo onto the reservation."

"We leave for Zuñi pueblo at dawn," Carson said. "I have my orders from General Carleton, but perhaps there's some palaverin' we can do to make the Zuñi chiefs see cooperatin' with us is better than bein' put into the stockade."

"They'll cooperate," Treadwell said, shaking his shaggy head. Carleton lived in a world far distant from the reality of western New Mexico Territory. To threaten the Zuñi as Carleton had done, to offer to "destroy their village as sure as the sun shines," only threw fuel on a fire that smoldered. Where the general had heard the Zuñi and Navajo were allied, Treadwell could not say.

"We need to retrieve stolen livestock and be certain the Navajo are not hidin' there," Carson said. A slow smile crossed his lips as he added, "And mayhap we can replace Ka-ni-ache and his scouts with some fine Zuñi trailers."

Treadwell cared little for that. He was adept at following any trail, white or red, and every path led back into Cañon de Chelly. If he was put on that track he would never flag.

"Navajo? Pah!" The Zuñi headman spat into the ground at Carson's feet. "We do not give them shelter. We *kill* them. For years they have stolen our horses and women."

"General Carleton has been sadly misinformed," Carson said carefully. For the first time since leaving Fort Canby, he seemed to enjoy his role as commander. Treadwell noted how the burden of garrison duty wore down the former mountain man and how Carson had blossomed when he had turned over full command to Captain Carey.

"We do not steal white men's cattle," the Zuñi said proudly. "We steal those of the Navajo!"

Treadwell listened with half an ear. They had left Fort Canby and gone to Ciénega Amarilla, where a hay camp had been established. The alfalfa for the 192 horses proved adequate to get the full company of 400 to the Zuñi pueblo to the southeast. But his scouting had shown movement to the west, a large group of mounted men moving.

As Carson dickered with the Zuñi, Treadwell slipped from the circle and walked to the edge of the village. He had seen no hint that Navajo had ever hidden here or that the Zuñi had allowed them to put stolen livestock in with their herds. Carson's first scout had been effective in reducing the amount of food available to the Navajo in Cañon de Chelly. The Zuñi were not likely to supplement any remaining food for their traditional enemies.

Shielding his eyes with his hand, Treadwell squinted at the horizon and the faint cloud of brown dust moving his way. He found his mare and swung into the saddle. If he wanted to give Carson a fair accounting for his money, he had better be sure these horsemen weren't Navajo warriors come to loot and pillage the Zuñi pueblo.

Riding out past the sentries Carson had posted, Treadwell quickly assured himself the approaching riders were not Navajo. He sat a'saddle and waited for the Indian scout to approach. The man wore an Army jacket with sergeant's stripes sewn on the sleeve. The flat-brimmed hat sported two eagle feathers and the single slash of white on the cheek told Treadwell the Indian belonged to some tribe he did not know.

As if understanding what went through his mind, the Indian called out, "Mojave! I scout for Captain Pishon."

"From California?" Treadwell wanted nothing to do with more uppity California officers, but if the Indian was telling the truth, a full company of them trotted behind their guidon.

"Fort Mojave. First Cavalry of California Volunteers come to help whup the Navajo."

At this Treadwell laughed.

"If you can find 'em, you can whup 'em all by yourself," he called. He rode to the scout and spent the better part of twenty minutes swapping lies—Ute tales for Mojave prevarications—until a youngish man with flowing dark hair rode up.

"Reckon you must be Captain Pishon," Treadwell greeted. "Colonel Carson's in the pueblo putting things right with the Zuñi."

"We're on our way to Santa Fé to report directly to General Carleton," the officer said in clipped tones. "If you're hunting for Navajo, we have come across no sign of them between here and the Little Colorado River."

"Too bad," Treadwell said. "They're proving real hard to

find. Just like grabbing a handful of smoke and trying to hang on tight."

"But they have not simply vanished from the face of the earth. The stories I heard coming from Fort Mojave . . ." The captain's voice trailed off. "They raid constantly. Perhaps it will be my good fortune to rejoin your command at some later time and deal with them properly."

"Luck with the general," Treadwell wished, adding a silent hope he never saw the captain again. The man struck him as being too much like Major Blakeney in his arrogance. Treadwell spent another five minutes talking with the Mojave scout, then touched the brim of his floppy black hat in silent salute to the Indian. He didn't envy the Mojave scout one bit reporting to Carleton in Santa Fé. The good general would have him patrolling Bosque Redondo for signs of unrest, a garrison duty no man in his right mind would eagerly accept.

Treadwell spent the next hour poking about the perimeter of the Zuñi village, satisfying himself that they had nothing to do with Navajo raiders. He finally heard the column moving from the Zuñi village and saw Carson astride his horse, Apache, at the head of the cavalry. Carson reined back and said to him, "We'll be joined by twenty Zuñi scouts. They have agreed to help in our hunt."

Treadwell nodded. "I reckon they would. I finally saw some sign of Navajo—in fresh graves not a mile from here. Seems the Zuñi don't cotton to them any more than we do."

"I dispatched an urgent message to General Carleton tellin' him he was wrong 'bout them," Carson said. "I sent it with Captain Pishon and his troopers."

"Might as well put the interloping Californicator to some use," Treadwell allowed. He wheeled his horse about before Carson could reply and started for Jacobs Springs, some thirty-five miles southwest of the Zuñi pueblo. The watering hole in the middle of the plains would make a good base of operation to hunt down the thieving Navajo.

And Manuelito.

* * *

"Not a trace, Colonel," Treadwell reported. "Me and the Zuñi scouts did all we could to spook any Navajo hiding to the south, but—" He shrugged. The past three days had been wasted chasing shadows. Still, Treadwell didn't count it as a complete loss. He had come to know the Zuñi trackers and his admiration of their skills had soared. The entire region to the west of Zuñi was unknown, and this afforded him a chance to learn the lay of the land while Carson watered his horses and mules at Jacobs Springs.

"Then we go immediately north," Carson decided. "They will think we are befuddled, we cannot find them, we have no plan. We will root them out from wherever they hide along the river and this time, by God, I shall engage them!"

"Fine words, but that's not the way they're likely to fight," pointed out the abrasive Captain Francis McCabe. The officer wasn't one to stand on formality when he saw someone going astray. For that Treadwell liked him.

"Captain McCabe, we *will* engage them this time," Carson said decisively. "I have had my fill of burnin' and lootin'. This time we shall *fight.* By God, we shall!"

"So we march straight up to their door and go in?" demanded McCabe.

"We did before," Treadwell cut in. "But there might be a band of raiders to the west, Colonel."

"Then Captain McCabe shall provide a diversion and you and I will find them, Mr. Treadwell!"

"By the light of the moon, Colonel?" Treadwell scratched himself. He had been on the trail more than the officer and his men and needed a bath. If Carson wanted to leave immediately, he wasn't likely to do more than graze his horse for a few hours before pushing on in search of the elusive Navajo.

"Think you are unable to track that way?" taunted Carson.

"I can follow a bug through a dust storm," Treadwell bragged.

"Prepare to leave immediately. I would see for myself where the Navajo hide."

Treadwell and Carson set out just after sundown. The moon rose and cast a silvery sheen across the barren land, turning it into quicksilver everywhere Treadwell looked. The occasional cold gust made him pull his jacket a trifle closer to his body. It was only early October but the wind promised a harsh winter, as had indications ever since midsummer.

"Been too long since I rode out like this. I feel like a prisoner of my own makin', Mr. Treadwell. Gettin' back to the countryside is what I need, away from the worries of command."

"McCabe can handle the troopers," Treadwell said. "He'll be waiting for us north along the Little Colorado. I've heard tell there are dozens of hogans in the area."

"I want to find Navajo. We chase and chase and only capture a few women and children. An engagement, a decisive fight. That's what I need."

"Finding my family is what I need, Colonel," said Treadwell.

"Do they still travel with Manuelito?" Carson asked softly. They made their way carefully down from a rim into a deep cañon cut by a tributary to the Little Colorado River. As they rode they sought any sign of Navajo raiders.

"I'm sure of it. That woman wasn't lying just to get food. It was my bad luck to run into Barboncito's band. And she named my son without me mentioning it first. Shining Eyes. She said he was a fine young man."

For a spell Carson said nothing, then finally: "He might fight with the Navajo. After such a spell separated from you and his people, his loyalties could lie with Manuelito now."

"Shining Eyes is a good boy. He would never leave his mother, and he would never betray his own people." Even as he spoke, Treadwell wondered how much of those words he believed, truly believed. Never would Gray Feather accept the Navajo—but Shining Eyes was only a child, a quarter of his life lived as a Navajo. And his other son, Goes to War, had been born among the Navajo.

They rode in silence for more than an hour, Carson occasionally dropping from his horse to study the ground. The bright moon gave them adequate light to track—if there had been anything to find.

"We are chasin' our own tails," Carson declared. "Have you seen any spoor?"

"Nothing to show that the Navajo rode here any time within the past month," admitted Treadwell. "Are they all hidden away somewhere else?"

Both men turned and gazed into the dark toward the north and the river. No matter how they sought the slippery Indians, nothing availed them. The Navajo always danced just beyond rifle shot, in the shadows and waiting for them to turn their backs.

"We've been this route before, Colonel," protested Treadwell. They had ridden through the high-walled, red rock cañon for almost a week without seeing a single living soul. Treadwell and the Zuñi scouts had forayed every side cañon they'd encountered, with no good result. Hogans abandoned by their occupants days or weeks earlier they burned. Some stores they captured and destroyed. A few stray sheep they rounded up and brought back to Carson. But of Navajo warriors they saw nothing, not even a fluttering eagle feather.

"If we get lost in the mazes, we might not return to Fort Canby before the first storm hits," Carson complained. The weather had turned colder night by night, although the days remained warm. Treadwell sniffed and caught the scent of heavy moisture in the air. The old mountain man was right about the cañons and getting snowed in.

They would be at the mercy of any Navajo—if there were any.

The frustration rose like bile to burn in Treadwell's throat. What good was it knowing his family lived if he could not find a solitary Navajo to question?

Worse for him, they prowled around outside Cañon de Chelly where Treadwell had the gut feeling Manuelito and the others hid. Poking into the pastures and cañons to the west of Chinle Wash and along the river had shown how extensive the Navajo presence was—or had been. Where had they all gone?

"We have already run through Cañon de Chelly," Carson pointed out. "We need to widen our search."

"Along the Little Colorado?" scoffed Treadwell. "They live here, I see that, but where have they gone?"

"We're burning everything as we go, Treadwell," spoke up McCabe. "What more can we do?"

"We're nothing but pirates plundering as we ride," Treadwell complained. "I'm with the colonel in this. We need to find a band of them to fight. Setting fire to grain and stealing goats and sheep is no fit way to wage a war."

Smoke rose from the latest burning. They had come upon two hogans in a peaceful, gently sloping valley five miles from the river. A few blankets and intricately decorated pottery jars filled with grain gave them their only success that day. Although Treadwell had the sense they were watched intently, neither he nor the Zuñi scouts found any trace of the Navajo inhabitants.

"We head back to the fort," Carson declared. "We've been on this scout long enough to know we ain't gonna find them, 'less they want to be found." Carson's jaw set with determination. "Captain McCabe, order that everything we pass is to be destroyed. Leave no blade of grass unbroken. Every plant is to be set afire, if possible. And keep drivin' those sheep ahead of us. We can slaughter them for mutton on the way home."

McCabe rode off to pass along the order to the other officers. Treadwell heaved a deep sigh. He had come along hoping to find Manuelito. The entire time in the field, he had seen not a single Navajo, man, woman or child.

"One last foray, Colonel. I can't go back without my family. That's all that's kept me with you this time, knowing they are here somewhere."

"Do what you must, Mr. Treadwell," Carson said, his sharp tone turning softer. "I know what you are goin' through."

"It would be hell to lose your adopted Navajo boy, wouldn't it?" Treadwell said, some of the old bitterness returning. Carson had done all he could to follow Carleton's orders. It wasn't his fault they had been unable to find the slippery raiders. Not once had Treadwell felt the colonel was holding back, but the futility of their search wore heavily on him.

"No man wants to lose any of his family, Mr. Treadwell." Carson put his heels to his mount's flanks and trotted off. Treadwell sucked in a deep breath and coughed, the smoke from their latest arson catching in his nostrils.

The day was slipping into dusk when Treadwell saw one of the younger officers, Captain Pfeiffer, talking with Carson. The young officer's agitation carried. Treadwell rode over.

"Definite tracks, Colonel," the excited Pfeiffer said. "A party of ten or more. Horses, at least that many."

"Treadwell, you accompany Captain Pfeiffer," snapped Carson. "Take a hundred men with you. Get me some prisoners to send back to Bosque Redondo. This scout is going to be a failure if we do not take *some* prisoners."

"Can't be much of a failure for everyone," Treadwell said dryly. "I saw the Zuñi scouts herding fifty or more sheep on their way back to their village."

"I told them we no longer needed them," Carson said. "If only we had discovered this spoor earlier!"

"We'll follow 'em to the ends of the earth, Colonel," Albert Pfeiffer promised. Treadwell had gone on wild goose chases before, but if the captain had seen fresh dung or other evidence of a horse, he could not doubt too severely the passage of Navajo. The Lords of New Mexico went nowhere without their mounts.

"Good work, Treadwell," congratulated Pfeiffer. The officer dropped to his belly alongside Treadwell on the hillside. He pulled out field glasses and studied the crossing on the Little Colorado where seven Navajo worked their small herd of horses. "Fifteen horses, as you predicted."

"No prediction, Captain," Treadwell said. "They left enough track for me to identify each horse." Treadwell glowed with a sense of accomplishment. He had worked harder than ever before tracking the raiders, using every skill he had accumulated in his years of tracking and hunting. There wasn't a great deal he didn't know about the men or horses below.

"They're driving them north, trying to find a ford, unless I miss my guess."

"There's a flat a mile farther," Treadwell said. "If they intend to cross the Little Colorado, that's where it would be."

"We have them! We'll have prisoners to send to Bosque Redondo for the general!"

Treadwell's ambitions were less exalted. He had no hankering to Christianize them. He wanted only the single thing he had ever since the cold January day almost three years earlier—to be reunited with his family.

"If we're going to overtake them, we have to get a'moving," Treadwell warned. "Our horses are winded from being rode so hard all day."

"You are right." Pfeiffer signaled to his sergeant that they were to mount and attack.

Treadwell did not wait for the bugle to sound or the cavalry to thunder down the hillside in the direction of the Navajo. He put his spurs into the sides of his horse and rode hellbent for leather to reach the tiny band. He saw no reason to sneak up on them. The way the cañon by the river twisted and turned, the Navajo could go in only one direction; sneaking up on them was not possible. If he ran them into the ground, Pfeiffer stood a better chance of capturing them.

The chase turned into an all-out race between him and the seven Navajo. They yelped and stampeded their horses ahead of them, racing northward. But Treadwell quickly discovered his mare lacked the last ounce of stamina needed to overtake his quarry. Every step caused the horse's strength to ebb further until the lathered, heaving-flanked horse was too winded to continue.

"Get 'em, Captain," Treadwell cried, as the officer and his column passed him. "My horse's too worn out to go on."

For all his good wishes, Treadwell saw that Pfeiffer's mounts were in no better condition. They might have tried capturing the Navajo in some other manner, but for his life, Treadwell didn't see what it might have been. They had no way to get in front of the rapidly moving Indians. And chasing them down now looked like a fantasy.

Disgusted, Treadwell hit the ground and walked his horse to the swiftly flowing river to let her drink. He heard the echoes of hooves pounding against rock farther to the north, knowing from the cadence that the Navajo with their fresher horses were likely to escape.

"Damnation," he muttered. "The only warriors we see get away from us." He hunkered down near a pool and stared into it. A sense of presence caused Treadwell to shift slightly, his hand going for his knife. A sudden flash in the pool set him in motion.

He whipped out his knife as he turned. A small body crashed into him, sending him staggering into the water. Whereas his attacker landed heavily in the water, Treadwell maintained his balance, knife ready to gut his foe.

Instead of driving his blade into the exposed back, Treadwell reached down and grabbed the boy by the scruff of the neck. He pulled the kicking, squalling boy of eight or nine from the water. Holding him at arm's length, Treadwell studied the youth.

"You're a skinny one, now aren't you?" he said in Navajo.

"You ride with the bluecoats," accused the boy. He stopped his struggle only to give a convulsive jerk in a vain attempt to slip free. Treadwell was prepared for that. He tossed the boy to the bank and sat beside him.

"I scout for Red Clothes," Treadwell said, choosing his words carefully. "And my family goes with Manuelito." He didn't know how else to put it.

"Manuelito? In his camp to the—" The boy bit off his unconscious betrayal.

"In Cañon de Chelly," finished Treadwell. His heart almost exploded when he saw he had been right. The boy knew where Manuelito camped—and it was in the rocky stronghold of the Navajo's most secure terrain.

By the time Captain Pfeiffer and his troopers returned empty-handed, Treadwell had a good idea where Manuelito camped in Tseyi'.

Duty—or Family?

October 18, 1863
Cañon de Chelly

Joseph Treadwell huddled against the wall of the cañon to keep from being blown over. He was lightheaded from not eating enough the past two days. His saddlebags rode light behind his saddle, the result of almost three weeks of his having been unable to live off the land. Treadwell had thought the winter three years earlier had been cold and barren. It was only October and game was nonexistent now. Never had he seen so little trace, even of small animals like rabbits and prairie dogs.

"Carson's got to be driving 'em into the hills," Treadwell grumbled. He had seen the results of Carson's earlier foray through Cañon de Chelly. The grass was still burnt, making it worthless for grazing. And with the cold winter winds whipping down from the north a month or more early, this drove off even the hardier animals.

"No deer, nothing," he complained to his horse, pulling his Army blanket closer around his shoulders. His mare nickered and protested the cold, but she was safe enough for the night. He had found a tiny crevice that opened into a small sheltered area. Even in here Carson's fires had blackened the grass. Treadwell found a few handfuls of dried grass along the trail, however, to keep the horse content. With tall red rock walls protecting them from the wind, neither of them was likely to freeze to death.

Treadwell's belly grumbled more, and he gnawed listlessly at a piece of jerky. He went over the directions in his head again. The boy he had captured and left with Colonel Carson had said Manuelito's camp lay in the center of the maze of tangled valleys that formed Cañon de Chelly. While the boy's directions had been succinct, Treadwell wondered if he might have missed something.

A mistaken left for right or a distance misjudged would send him in the wrong direction. But in his gut he felt he was getting close. He had been cautious making his way through the destruction of the Navajo country, alert for another ambush but even more vigilant for any hint that Manuelito was near.

"You stole her away, you bastard," Treadwell said, his anger warming him against renewed cold blasts. "I'll get her back. Her and Shining Eyes and . . . Goes to War." Treadwell almost choked on that name. It wasn't a Ute name. It had the ring of Navajo to it, and that rankled. He had not named his own son.

He had never even see the boy.

Somewhere in the night he slipped into a fitful sleep.

Treadwell awoke with a start, pressure against his side. Panicked, thinking a Navajo had sneaked up on him, he thrashed about. Snow flew everywhere. Treadwell calmed when he saw that no one had joined him in his private den. His mare swayed gently, asleep a few feet away. But it had been snow drifting against him that had finally awakened him.

He gazed at the leaden sky and shook his head. The snow had started fast and continued until almost three inches on the flat covered the small cul de sac. The drift had come up to his elbow, pinning him.

"Time to move," Treadwell told his horse. The mare shook herself, sending snow everywhere. The long tail swished about, and she tried to kick as Treadwell put on the saddle. He accepted no protest from the animal. He was hungry. So was the horse, but they had to push on. He neared Manuelito's camp. Deep in his bones he felt it.

Guiding the horse through the narrow crevice took him into a wonderland of white. The three inches of snow stretched from one red walled side of the cañon to the other, interrupted only by soaring needles of layered sandstone. The clean air razored at his nostrils and lungs as he breathed, but the gray clouds already broke apart in places to reveal the purest blue imaginable.

Treadwell wished he was hunting for bear or deer, not his family. He felt more alive than he had in years and wanted the sensation to last, if only for a few hours. But his keen eyes fixed on a trail already cut into the crisp snow. Edging along the cañon wall, he kept from sight of any Navajo sentry along the hundred-foot-high rim until he came to the trail.

"A dozen riders, maybe more," he told his horse, patting the mare's neck. "And all going in the direction of Manuelito's camp. Why else so many traveling in weather like this?"

He might be clutching at straws, but hope still flared in his breast. He rode directly to the center of the trail already cut by the earlier riders. His tracks vanished in the mix of mud and snow. Although exposed to any prying eyes turning in his direction, Treadwell took the risk. Waiting until darkness fell at the end of the day would have proved impossible. His heart pounded and he could taste victory.

To hell with caution, he decided. Better to press on and find Gray Feather. All the old rage flared anew. Long Tooth. Many Skirts. All the other Ute that Manuelito had killed rose to haunt Treadwell. They must be avenged.

Treadwell's fingers moved to the knife sheathed at his left side. Better to press on and drive the blade into Manuelito's belly.

By mid-afternoon he had crossed the cañon width and found a meandering trail that led into a branching valley. His lips curled back in triumph when he saw the hogan with a thin wisp of smoke rising from its chimney. Beyond, a mile farther, he spotted another hogan. Carson had driven the Navajo into this unsullied valley to survive.

Treadwell dropped to the ground and tethered his horse. Musket in hand, he advanced on foot. By the time he reached the first hogan, the sun had set. Small cook fires popped up around the valley, showing tiny knots of campers. His nose twitched at the odor of hot stew. These Navajo had some small amount of food left them. For the moment.

Left to his scorched earth policy, Carson would steal even these tidbits from their mouths.

Treadwell fell prone and began wiggling forward, thinking to spy on those in the hogan. To his disappointment, the dwelling was empty. A small blaze guttered in the fireplace and blankets showing at least four people slept in the hogan lay stretched nearby.

The chanting caught his attention. Treadwell worked his way to the roof of the hogan and peered toward the largest of the fires, almost a mile distant. He made out figures dancing around the bonfire and realized something big was in the wind. Clutching his musket, Treadwell set off, knowing providence had shown him the way. Locating his family in the vastness of the cañon might be well nigh impossible.

An important gathering would draw everyone, maybe including Navajo slaves to serve their masters. He stood a better chance of finding Gray Feather and his boys at the assemblage than going from one hogan to the other like a thief in the night.

Twice Treadwell took to earth, hiding behind fallen logs and in rocky, snow-filled ravines to avoid being discovered by prowling braves. The warriors were focused on something more than finding a spy in their midst, and this saved Treadwell. He managed to wiggle snakelike toward the fire until he saw a tall, slender man he remembered all too well.

Treadwell slid his musket forward and rested the barrel on a low rock. He pulled back the hammer and worked to get Manuelito in his sights. But good sense made him hold back. As satisfying as this shot would be for Treadwell, he needed more from Manuelito than his blood spilled onto the cold white snow.

Treadwell wanted his family back.

Forcing himself to look away from the magnetic Navajo leader, Treadwell studied the intent faces of those gathered around the huge fire. Men, all men. Was one of them Shining Eyes? He saw no child the age of Goes to War.

He hiked up the rifle again when he heard moccasins crunching through the snow. The brave passed within ten feet of Treadwell, never seeing him. The man dashed down the slope to the fire and went directly to Manuelito. The two spoke for several minutes. Manuelito finally nodded brusquely and held up his arms to pull attention to himself. Then the Navajo headman settled down beside the fire and waited for what seemed to Treadwell an interminable length of time. Finally, Manuelito spoke. His voice rang out clear as a bell in the crystal cold night air.

"Red Clothes has returned to his fort," Manuelito said. Treadwell had some difficulty following the rapid speech, but the effect this announcement had on the crowd was obvious. Many nodded slowly. Others ran their hands over their knives and rifles.

"Unlike other white men, he fights during the cold of winter. He has burned more rangeland and robbed us of five hundred sheep. He has stolen fifty horses and captured a boy."

Grumbles among the assembled warriors reminded Treadwell of the noises made by Carson's troops when they'd been told of Navajo depredations. His finger tightened on the cold metal of his musket trigger but did not squeeze off the shot. He found himself curiously drawn to what Manuelito said.

And there was no way of knowing where Gray Feather might be. Treadwell's mind raced. If he followed Manuelito after this meeting, the headman might lead him directly to his family. Treadwell's finger relaxed as he struggled to better interpret what Manuelito said.

"With his bluecoats at Fort Canby," Manuelito went on, "we

are presented an opportunity to strike at their heart. His warriors are exhausted from their destruction of our food and belongings. They will not expect us to drive our lances into them now!"

Treadwell blinked when Manuelito shot to his feet and hurled a war lance into the dark. A cheer rose from the gathering that chilled his blood. They planned an immediate attack on Fort Canby, when Carson would least expect it. Carson thought the campaign of attrition went well, that Manuelito and the other headmen would be crippled and disheartened by the loss of their land and herds.

A successful raid might kill Carson and drive the Army out of Navajoland altogether.

Treadwell blinked as smoke blew into his eyes. He hunkered down and tried to fade into the shadows. For the first time he realized the folly of his expedition. He was a single man against hundreds of bloodthirsty Navajo warriors.

The panic passed quickly and Treadwell pushed back to catch sight of Manuelito. He thought he saw the six-foot-tall headman on the other side of the fire, but he could not be sure. Knowing how difficult it would be to circle with the Navajo now more active as they whipped themselves into a killing frenzy, Treadwell found himself confronted with an agonizing decision.

He might follow Manuelito to his campsite, get his family back, and escape the cañon—or he could slip away to warn Carson of the raid.

Treadwell suddenly realized a third possibility was more likely. From behind he heard movement. Rolling to one side, he slipped free his knife and waited as a half dozen warriors passed him. With the additional activity, he would be spotted if he stayed much longer.

When he tried to locate Manuelito one last time and could not, Treadwell realized he had lost his chance. To blunder about in enemy territory now would mean his death. That would do nothing to save Gray Feather, and it might mean Carson's death. He had a grudging admiration for the short mountain man colonel, in spite of differences. Carson had given him more leeway than other officers might have, even if Carson had effectively hobbled him in the name of Carleton's insane campaign to put all the Navajo on the reservation at Fort Sumner.

Coming so close to Gray Feather, though, decided Treadwell. There were a thousand reasons to leave and warn Carson. He slipped into the night and returned to the hogan, hoping it might be Manuelito's. Four warriors huddled inside, warming themselves when he chanced a quick look inside. Where were the women and children?

Treadwell retreated further, finding his horse. The noise in the valley convinced him he would never find Manuelito before a prowling Navajo brave found him. That did not stop him from riding along one steep, rocky cliff to get deeper into the cañon. In that direction might lie the headman's camp.

Hours before dawn Treadwell thought he had found Manuelito. Again approaching on cat's feet, Treadwell kept a sharp eye out for any women. Frowning, he tried to make out the shape huddled under a blanket near a small campfire. A woman? Manuelito?

Treadwell reacted without thought. He swung about, his musket singing in the air. The barrel crunched loudly into a warrior's knee, forcing out a loud cry of pain. The warrior behind Treadwell instinctively bent to clutch his damaged knee, dropping his knife. This gave Treadwell precious instants to close on his attacker and wrap his arms around the man's shoulders. Crushing down hard, Treadwell heaved and threw the warrior to the ground. It took several more seconds to get his hands on the Navajo's windpipe and crush the life from his body.

Panting harshly, Treadwell pushed back from the dead man beneath him. Sudden pain exploded into his arm from the knife slash. He twisted away and kicked hard, one booted foot knocking the other warrior's leg from under him. The Navajo who had slept near the fire with his blanket around him now foundered on an icy patch. This moment of unbalance saved Treadwell from a second, more deadly cut.

Treadwell's fingers closed on his rifle. He pulled it toward him and pointed it in the Navajo's direction. Treadwell read only death in the man's dark eyes. As the warrior lifted his knife to plunge it into the mountain man's chest, Treadwell fired.

The explosion deafened him. And the leaden slug ripping through the Indian saved Treadwell. He was alive; two Navajo lay dead in the snow.

"Neither of you is Manuelito," Treadwell said dejectedly. He had blundered into the wrong camp. And he had not seen a single woman the entire time he had ridden through this cañon encampment.

Treadwell knew better than to remain at the site of a double killing. Any chance he had of finding Gray Feather had now evaporated. When the Navajo discovered their brothers dead, they would hunt him down and kill him. Scores of them would be on his trail—and from his death they would rally on and destroy Fort Canby.

Hating himself for abandoning his family when he was so close, Treadwell mounted and retraced his path out of the cañon. An emptiness filled him, an emptiness of *almost* finding his family. But he had to warn Carson of the impending attack on the fort or the Army might pull back from Navajoland for months or years.

If that happened, Treadwell would have to fight on alone to find Gray Feather. Success then in the face of such a retreat looked bleak, indeed.

Small Victories

October 21, 1863
Laguna Negra

"We have found them, Holy Boy," Follows Quickly whispered. He lifted his musket in the direction of the Biligáana encampment. Manuelito nodded and absently rubbed his injured shoulder. "We can strike now! They will die where they sleep!"

"It is a good plan," Shining Eyes spoke up, following his cousin's lead. "I saw no sentries over their flocks. Their leader, Major Sena, sleeps as if he died. It will be easy, Manuelito, very easy."

Shining Eyes watched his father closely. Something more than the coming raid danced behind his dark eyes, but the boy could not decide what it might be. He knew Manuelito was no coward. He had seen a few Dinéh turn tail and run as if they were coyotes, though most of those had died these past few months as the Biligáana increased their activity.

"Our women go hungry, our children starve," Shining Eyes said, thinking of Goes to War and their mother. The infant had survived, though barely, after a sing. Shining Eyes had given his precious bay to the singer and had gone afoot until winning another mount from a warrior in Looking Arrow's clan who was slower in a foot race by precious seconds. If Shining Eyes had lost, he would have been reduced to little more than a breechclout.

But he had won. And he remembered the expression on Looking Arrow's face when he took possession of the sorrel.

"We can use the sheep right away, not in the future," Follows Quickly finished for Shining Eyes. Follows Quickly moved closer to his headman and lowered his voice. Shining Eyes could barely hear as the warrior said, "Hastiin Chilhajin, we must carry the fight to the Biligáana. If we do not, they will bury us like a sandstorm hides the bleached bones of a dead cow."

"I refused the medallion carried by Zarcillas Largas because I am not the leader he was," Manuelito said slowly. "My ways are not his, and I have seen only death."

Shining Eyes saw the change in his father. Manuelito stood taller, towering above all the others with him. His jaw tensed and then he said, "Angry Knife, take their sheep. We will starve them as they starve us."

The use of his war name filled Shining Eyes with pride. He nodded once, then slipped into the night. Behind him came Follows Quickly and several others. They moved on foot rather than taking their horses to reduce the sound of approach.

Falling to the ground, Shining Eyes crawled a hundred yards on his belly until he could peer directly at a corral near the Army bivouac. It was as he remembered from his earlier scouting. Guards had not been posted.

"Can you hear them?" asked Follows Quickly.

Shining Eyes shook his head. He had been close enough before to listen to their commander's orders and learn the man's name. Major Sena was not a bluecoat to follow orders. Shining Eyes had seen other companies and how their officers behaved. Colonel Carson was no fool. He always posted sentries to protect his sleeping men and their supplies.

Shining Eyes motioned and the others moved silently to the corral. To be sure he did not lead the handful of warriors into a trap, Shining Eyes circled the corral, every sense straining. He smelled the remnants of the cook fire and the heavy meal

the Biligáana had devoured. But he also heard their snoring as
they slept off the effect of such a large meal. They might have
marched for long hours and thought they deserved such a ban-
quet, but Dinéh warriors rode farther, fought harder and survived on far less.

A sheep bleated, bringing Shining Eyes's attention back to
the pen. The woolly creatures stirred at the unusual activity near
them but did not protest unduly. Follows Quickly slit the leather
thong holding the corral gate shut and began leading the willing
sheep from the pen. Shining Eyes continued to watch for any
sign of alarm being raised.

The bluecoats slept peacefully, content in their bedrolls under
their tents. Shining Eyes's breath came quicker when he saw
those gray blankets. They were plain, no evidence of skill or
loving attention paid to them. He was not certain how they were
made, but they were no match for the blankets he had seen
being burned.

Those were Two Gray Hills blankets. Good, warm, carrying
the spirit of the Dinéh in them.

Shining Eyes longed to burn these blankets and the men
slumbering within them, but he had learned caution. Stealing
Major Sena's sheep would cause more trouble in the bluecoats'
rank than murdering them in their sleep. Shining Eyes smiled
broadly. Carson might replace Sena with someone who was
more clever and attentive to duty. This way, Red Clothes was
forced to suffer an incompetent in the field or waste time arguing with those in Santa Fé about replacing him.

Like a shadow, Shining Eyes faded into the night and caught
up with Follows Quickly and the others. He helped shoo along
the sheep until they reached the hollow where Manuelito waited.

"Eighty-nine sheep!" boasted Follows Quickly. "We have
enough to feed us for a month!"

"Get them back to Tseyi'," Manuelito ordered. "Divide them
according to the number in our band."

Shining Eyes always felt uneasy demanding a share of the
booty. He knew he was only eleven, but the others accepted

him as a blooded warrior. Still, he often thought of himself as an interloper no matter how the others boasted of his exploits or gambled with him.

Only Looking Arrow made him feel like one of the Dinéh.

He mounted and helped herd the flock they had stolen back into the cañons. Shining Eyes was asleep in the saddle by the time dawn broke and sent warm rays of light against the blanket draped over his back. He jerked awake and saw that the flock had already been driven down into the valley near a small stream where they drank deeply after the night-long travel.

"We have beaten them again," Manuelito cried, from his position deeper in the valley. Shining Eyes wondered at the headman's change. At Laguna Negra he had seemed unsure. Now he boasted of a small victory. Very small, even if it put mutton in many bellies and provided much-needed breeding stock. Come spring, these sheep would also provide wool for new blankets.

Looking around Shining Eyes was disturbed by the lack of blankets worn by the warriors. Many left their sole source of warmth on the trail in hogans for wives and children. Too many. He was lucky to have a good blanket without taking warmth from Goes to War or his mother.

"You, Shining Eyes," called Manuelito, "you deserve four of the sheep for your part in the raid."

"I claim five," the boy said, as startled as Manuelito at the impudent request. Shining Eyes slumped a little and worried what would be said about this disrespect. To his surprise, Manuelito spoke gently and quietly when he rode closer.

"Angry Knife, why do you question my division?"

"I need five," Shining Eyes repeated. "Looking Arrow's father was killed last week, and she has no one to provide for her."

"Looking Arrow?" Manuelito's eyebrows rose in a broad arch higher than any of the soaring rocks in the southern Bear Ears country. "So?"

Shining Eyes said nothing. Manuelito could decide without further information.

"Very well. My son is a fierce fighter and a clever scout. You may give one to Looking Arrow, if you realize what this might mean."

Shining Eyes flushed. A man providing for a woman meant he chose her.

"You are young, but who among us will live to an old age?" Manuelito shrugged and pointed to five sheep. "Take those as your due." With that, Manuelito rode off to continue the division of the flock.

Shining Eyes was dismayed at the ease the headman had acceded to his demand. And he wondered at Manuelito's parting words. Did he not believe the Dinéh would live forever in Dinetah and again walk in beauty after the Biligáana were driven back?

At times, Shining Eyes could not fathom the headman's thinking. He urged his sorrel to the sheep and got them moving in the direction of his mother's hogan. The four he allotted for her would be needed. The coldness in the wind promised a winter more frigid than anything Shining Eyes had ever seen. Snows already covered the upper slopes and occasionally drifted down along the valley in chilly gusts.

Shining Eyes inhaled deeply and sniffed the wood smoke on the wind, mixed with the earthy smells of horses, sheep, and cattle. Closing his eyes, he felt himself carried away to other places, but they were not home. He remembered the land in Colorado where his mother's family had been killed in Manuelito's raid, but the details were dimmer with every passing day.

One image that burned brightly was Joseph Treadwell kicking the bundles of blankets into the fire as he cursed the Dinéh.

"Shining Eyes! You're back!" Gray Feather came from her hogan, carrying Goes to War in her left arm. The infant kicked and cried noisily. Shining Eyes heaved a sigh of relief that the sing had brought back health to the child.

"I have four sheep," he announced, slipping from the sorrel's back. He took his baby brother and held the boy high. Shining Eyes felt as if he stared in a mirror distorted only by time. Goes to War had the same sharp pale blue eyes and curving nose as his brother—as his white father.

"There are five," Gray Feather said. "Did you miscount?"

"It . . . the other is for . . . it's not ours," Shining Eyes said, barely keeping from stuttering. Why did he behave this way? "It is for Looking Arrow."

"Her mother is ill," Gray Feather said. "We spoke a few days ago, after you left with the war party. This is a fine gift."

"We must all work together," Shining Eyes said lamely, "no matter what our clan."

Gray Feather said something he did not catch as she turned away. Shining Eyes continued to toss his brother into the air. The infant enjoyed it and used all the words he had learned in an attempt to make Shining Eyes continue, but it was to no avail. So much had to be done.

"There is a celebration tonight," Shining Eyes told his mother. "We can go and—" He bit off his words when he saw tears in his mother's eyes. "What is wrong? The sheep are healthy and will give good wool in the spring shearing."

"It's not that," she said, sitting just inside the hogan door. The wind took on a cruel edge as it whipped about. "It's us, you, the Pogawitch."

"Dinéh," Shining Eyes corrected, hardly aware that he did.

"I want to be with my own people. Manuelito treats me well, and he dotes on Goes to War. But I long for my familiar mountains, not these dusty red rocks towering on all sides. And how can I forget they killed my brother, Long Tooth, and my husband?"

Shining Eyes almost spoke, telling her he had seen Treadwell, but he did not. He could not say why he had neglected to tell his mother Treadwell was still alive. He knew her heart longed for other places, but it was needlessly cruel for her to pine away over a husband she thought dead and who now fought to kill her new clan.

"Manuelito is your husband," Shining Eyes said coldly.

"You are one of them, my son, and I don't want you to be. I want you to know your real people, the Tabeguache Ute."

"Your husband among them was Biligáana," Shining Eyes replied, his anger rising.

"Joseph was a good man. I am sorry you no longer think of him that way, but then there are rumors of your betrothal to Looking Arrow. What does Cayatanita think of this, since he must arrange the marriage?"

"There is no talk of marriage. I am too young," Shining Eyes said, even though he uneasily thought of Looking Arrow in a way unlike the way he thought of the other girls.

"You are a warrior among warriors. I hear how Follows Quickly and the others speak of you. Oso Negro praises you when all he has to say of warriors, even in his own clan, is contemptuous."

"I must prepare for the celebration. Tomorrow I ride out again." Shining Eyes paused when he saw the unashamed tears running down his mother's cheeks. He hesitated, then sat on his haunches, reaching out to brush away the tears. "What is wrong, Mother?"

"I had a premonition," she said. "It frightens me. I see no victory for the Navajo, only blood and death. Never is a vision of victory sent to me." She turned her tearstained face toward him. "I fear for you, my son, for you and your brother."

"Manuelito is a great leader. Our victories will grow," boasted Shining Eyes.

Gray Feather shook her head. "There will be no more victory. I see coldness and death, and I want you to return north. Go and find others of the Tabeguache. Or even find an Indian agent."

"Go to the Biligáana?" The words burned Shining Eyes's tongue. How dared his mother even suggest such treachery?

"You are half white. They cannot lose their fight. I saw it in my dream."

"I will die before I surrender to the Bilagáana," Shining Eyes said, astounded and angry with his mother.

"Such hatred in one so young—and it is misdirected. Manuelito killed your father and uncle and brought us here, not the whites."

"How *they* treat their slaves? How do the Nakai? And what of the Pueblos? Only in Dinetah can one captured in battle be treated as an equal. I am accepted—and you, my mother, *you* are the wife of a headman!"

"I want what is best for you," she said.

"I must prepare for the celebration." Shining Eyes got to his feet and pushed past her, wishing he were anywhere else now. Not even Looking Arrow's praise of his prowess at the gathering and ready acceptance of the gift sheep soothed his displeasure with his mother.

Ambush

"Their brass buttons make good targets," Shining Eyes said, his lips pulled back like a wolf's snarl. "We can kill them and they will never know."

"We must restrain our attack," Manuelito said uncharacteristically. "I have had a premonition. This will not go well, unless we show the cunning of the coyote with the striking speed of a snake."

Shining Eyes snorted derisively. Manuelito began to sound like Gray Feather. He had never experienced a dream so intense it controlled his life, though he knew the others placed great store in such visions. Once, when he had gone without food for almost a week, he had turned dizzy and thought he'd seen animals approaching. If those were visions, they'd fled when he'd lifted his bow and loosed an arrow. Never had he seen the future.

"They continue to bring supplies into their fort," Shining Eyes said. "If we can interrupt their supply line, they will be forced to draw troops from their attacks into Dinetah to protect themselves."

"True." Manuelito watched as the bluecoat major rode down the draw, two wagons laden with firewood rattling behind. They were only a few miles from Fort Canby with the needed supply of wood, having ranged as far as Fort Lyon the day before. Abreu was the man's name, and Manuelito had matched wits with him before. This was no easily frightened soldier, as Sena had been. Abreu rode straight-backed and proud in his saddle, eyes restlessly moving to scan the terrain. No fear dwelled within this man's breast, nor was there any nervous anxiety as Manuelito saw in his son.

"Stay with me," Manuelito ordered Shining Eyes. "Stay and learn."

"I am no coward!" Shining Eyes's temper flared, and he almost shot to his feet. Manuelito restrained him, making the boy even angrier. To alert the enemy now would ruin their ambush, and Shining Eyes hated to admit he had been responsible for the momentary lapse of good sense. He settled down, seething.

"Give the signal," Manuelito said in a low voice. "We go now. Now!"

Shining Eyes lifted his feather-decorated bow and waved it from side to side. An immediate reply came. Follows Quickly fired his musket, as did two other warriors on the far side of the draw. Shining Eyes rose and nocked an arrow, but Captain Abreu had already given the order to gallop. His column of troopers bent low in their saddles and raced down the ravine to avoid all combat. They had been sent to protect the wood gatherers, not to fight.

"They run like rabbits!" shouted Shining Eyes. He loosed his arrow, but it arched up and came down far behind the last rider in the column.

"They run to the rest of our warriors," Manuelito said. "Come, we must not allow them to retreat along this path." The headman slid down the sandy bank and trotted off briskly. Shining Eyes found himself hard-pressed to keep up with his father, but fuming anger kept him moving. Ahead came the sounds of a vicious fight, the bluecoats' muskets firing raggedly. Shining Eyes knew none of the Dinéh would fire a rifle now. The weapons were too hard to load and inaccurate. A bow gave more intense firepower, a dozen arrows shot in the time it took for the troopers to reload only once.

His moccasins slapping against the cold sand, Shining Eyes almost ran into one soldier trying to retrace his path. The boy's arrow went wide; he dropped his bow and whipped out his knife, launching himself at the mounted bluecoat like a mountain lion.

Shining Eyes slashed savagely but the trooper was stronger, older, more experienced. He swung a rifle butt around and knocked the boy back, to lie flat. The soldier fumbled to draw his pistol.

Shining Eyes's heart almost exploded with fear as he realized that death stalked him. He rolled to one side, then quickly reversed and tried to flee in the other to avoid the pistol. Flat on his back he saw the mustached soldier draw his pistol, cock it, and aim. He pushed up but his muscles turned to rubber and the world spun past him, beyond his control. The barrel moved with heart-stopping slowness, but Shining Eyes could not move. The front sight shone like a silver bead in the morning sun. The scratched muzzle of the pistol centered on him. A shot rang out and Shining Eyes fell back flat onto the ground, gasping. For a moment he could not move, then realized he had not been shot.

He opened eyes he had not known he had closed and saw the cavalry trooper clutching his right arm. The bluecoat had been shot in the forearm, forcing him to drop his weapon. Loud cries came from Major Abreu, but Shining Eyes heard nothing. It was as if he had been dropped into a bubble of silence that wrapped him securely. He moved in slow motion and heard nothing, nothing at all.

All he could do was sit and watch as the battle flowed like treacle about him. Then, magically, no one remained.

Through the unearthly quiet came a soft voice Shining Eyes knew well.

"Come, Angry Knife. We must go. We have won."

"Won?"

"They abandoned their wagons and ten mules. We will leave two."

"Why?" Shining Eyes felt his head spin. He hardly knew what had happened.

"Those mules are sick. We cannot go far with them."

"We won?"

"Yes," Manuelito said softly. "We won. The bluecoats had three wounded before they ran away, and none of our warriors was even scratched. We are setting fire to their wood and are taking the mules." Manuelito pushed the boy along, then stopped him. "Here, take this."

The headman held out a cavalry pistol.

"He would have shot me," Shining Eyes said, the picture of the mounted trooper vivid in his mind. He took the offered pistol with shaking hands. It was the one dropped by the soldier when he was shot.

"Follows Quickly is to be thanked. He captured another musket, one loaded and ready to fire. His aim improves. Now we must go quickly for Abreu races to Fort Canby. A larger party will come after us, and we number only eight."

Shining Eyes brushed off the dirt from his hide britches and started toward the small stand of cottonwood trees where they had left their horses. Behind him he heard Manuelito talking with Follows Quickly about the ambush and their quick victory.

Somehow, it seemed less impressive when all Shining Eyes could remember was the sight of the large pistol coming from the soldier's holster and the huge bore pointed directly at him.

The Raid

October 28, 1863
Fort Canby

Treadwell's horse had died two days back, first the legs freezing and then the rest of her valiant body succumbing to the cold. He heaved his saddlebags over his shoulder, wiped snow from his face, and kept trudging up the gradual slope leading to the fort. Getting free of Cañon de Chelly had proved more difficult than he had thought; to his eternal dismay, he'd gotten lost in the winding byways so thoroughly he'd hardly found his way free. A precious week had been lost. The only bright spot Treadwell could see in his going astray so badly lay in not having any Navajo warriors on his track.

Killing two of them in their own camp ought to have stirred the entire nation to come after him. And perhaps it had. The vastness of Cañon de Chelly might have swallowed up any pursuit, as it had swallowed the Navajo when Carson had made his scout through there earlier.

"The devastation," he said, repeating what had impressed him most. "The way there's no food left. That's why they didn't come for me. There's nothing for them to eat." His own belly complained about the lack of food. He had been scrabbling for roots and the occasional prairie dog the entire trip back to Fort

Canby, after what meat he could garner from his horse had been devoured.

The sight of the adobe and wood fort looming through the blowing snow strengthened him and caused his stride to quicken. It had not been destroyed. Not yet.

"Who goes there?" came the immediate challenge.

"Treadwell, to see the colonel. I got important news."

"Advance," ordered the sentry. The man held up an arm to keep snow from obscuring his vision. A crooked grin slipped across the soldier's face when he recognized Treadwell. "Good to see you again. We been needin' your money in the card game every Wednesday, Mr. Treadwell. You're the only one who can play whist like he means it."

"Glad I've been missed," Treadwell grumbled. His feet tingled, the first sign of frostbite.

"Only your money, Mr. Treadwell, nothin' more!"

He let the guard slap him on the shoulder, enduring the stab of pain from his unhealed arm. After the Navajo had cut him, Treadwell had tried bandaging the wound the best he could. It had hardly been enough. Staggering a bit, he made his way directly toward the commander's office. Treadwell wasn't too surprised to see that Fort Canby had changed considerably. With Asa Carey in command, it had been spruced up and discipline had been tightened.

Treadwell wasn't sure how long Carson had been back from his scout, but it had to be better than three weeks. Time had become something of a mystery to him as first he rode lost in Cañon de Chelly, then hiked on unfamiliar frozen ground to return.

"You're a sight," Carson greeted him. Seeing the bloody sleeve and the way Treadwell walked, the colonel barked, "Sergeant Need! Fetch Doctor Peck immediately. We got a casualty walkin' in on us."

"Good to see you, Colonel," Treadwell said, easing himself into the humid interior of the office. The heat bludgeoned him after he'd suffered the cold for so long. He sank into a chair, his eyes closed and heat seeping into his tired bones. "Get your officers together. There's going to be a raid on Fort Canby. I'm surprised Manuelito hasn't already struck."

"What do you know?" Carson asked, sitting close to Treadwell.

"I snuck into the heart of their camp, in Cañon de Chelly," Treadwell got out. He accepted a cup of coffee from Carson's aide and simply held it. His fingers refused to bend right for several minutes. By then the coffee was cool enough to drink. In the meantime, Treadwell spun his story.

"I spied on Manuelito," Treadwell said. "I didn't find Gray Feather, but I heard him planning a big attack on the fort. He wanted to level it, from the sound of his fury. Don't understand how I beat him here, but I'm glad I did. You might lay a trap for him when he and his hordes come thundering up."

Carson looked to Sergeant Need and then smiled a little. His pale eyes shone.

"We thank you for this bit of information," Carson said carefully, "but it wasn't much of a raid. We did not know it was Manuelito leading the skirmish—"

"Skirmish? I heard 'im planning a *big* assault. He had a hundred or more warriors around that fire."

"Captain Abreu was out on patrol yesterday morning. A few shots, an arrow or two—three of his men were injured. They weren't supposed to do more 'n guard the firewood gatherin' detail."

"There must be more," Treadwell said, shaking his head. He sipped at the coffee, letting it warm his gullet. "I heard 'em planning a major attack on the fort. They wanted to drive us out of the territory."

Carson chuckled. "We lost a few head of horses. They been hittin' real hard at the edges of our herds. More 'n twelve cattle have been stole these past weeks. An embarrassment to both Captain Carey 'n me, to be sure."

"They must be massing for an attack." Treadwell felt like a dog worrying a bone. He shook and shook, but nothing happened. He had to get Carson to understand Manuelito was coming on with most of his warriors to wipe out the fort.

"Not too likely, Joe," Carson said. "I sent Major Sena out with a patrol after they attacked the woodcutters. In the meantime, they made off with ninety sheep. A sergeant and two troopers followed till it was obvious to a blind man that the Navajo had hightailed it back into Cañon de Chelly with their booty. You musta crossed paths with them gettin' here."

"But I heard—" Treadwell stared at Carson in disbelief. A raid that brought Manuelito only ninety sheep and three injured bluecoats?

Was this the best assault the starved Navajo could mount?

The hollow feeling returned to haunt Treadwell. Gray Feather was a captive of a tribe unable to do more than pink their foes out of spite. And he had left her somewhere in Cañon de Chelly with two small boys.

The First Surrender

November 22, 1863
Fort Wingate

Shining Eyes sat astride his sorrel, shivering as the cold winds whipped down and worked their way under his blanket. He tried to think of these Little Winds as whispering to him, giving him information he could use. Manuelito claimed the Holy Winds worked for the Dinéh. All Shining Eyes had seen over the past few months told him it was not so. The winds—the Holy Winds, be they Black or Yellow, White or Blue—brought only suffering and death.

And now he shielded his eyes against dancing white motes of snow as he watched the gates of the fort pull open. From within rode four horsemen, warriors he had been told to escort into Tseyi'. Shining Eyes's belly grumbled but he had jerky. He gnawed a bit of dried venison as he watched the slow progress of the four. He knew Delgadito could hardly walk and that riding caused his old joints to hurt. Shining Eyes did not know the other three, nor did he care to.

"Traitors," he hissed, sending twin plumes of exhalation into the biting wind. The boy worked more on the tough meat and finally thrust it back into his pouch next to his fetish bag holding a bit of turquoise, small sticks and stones, and the pollen needed to keep his spirit alive. He had no time or energy to worry at the jerky now. He had only his anger to keep him warm and alert.

Twenty minutes after the gate had closed, the four riders came up the slippery slope where Shining Eyes waited silently. He hated this fort built halfway between Los Pinos and Fort Defiance as a symbol of Biligáana triumph. They expanded slowly and surely, with nothing stopping them. The more mules and supply trains Manuelito and Barboncito destroyed, the more that came.

"Ya-ta-hey," greeted Delgadito.

"I am to take you to the headman of the Dinéh," Shining Eyes said stiffly, insulting Delgadito and his position. "Manuelito grants you audience this afternoon, if we ride hard."

"Our message is important," Delgadito said slowly. The leathery face had cracked from exposure to harsh weather, leaving behind tiny crevices that seemed filled with his blood. Lips shattered like dropped glass formed the words Shining Eyes did not wish to hear.

The boy spun his horse about and started at a brisk pace he knew the others would be unable to maintain. From the way his own mount faltered quickly, he knew the sorrel would not go much farther in the icy wind. He slowed in spite of his conviction to keep separate and found Delgadito beside him.

"There is no reason to hate us," the headman said slowly. "We are not weak or cowards."

"You surrendered," Shining Eyes spat out.

"We had no choice. Our flocks are gone, our grain is destroyed. We are naked and freezing. Is it any better with Manuelito's clan?"

"We will never surrender, no matter how many troops they fling against us. Every time they enter Tseyi', they grope for us and find only wind. We slip through their fingers and leave behind no trace."

"Yes, we did the same. We shot at them from ambush, stole their horses, and tore small pieces from the fabric of their domain, only to find more bluecoats, better supplied and more willing to burn what we had to abandon as we escaped." Delgadito straightened his bent shoulders in memory of better days, days filled with honor and beauty, not death and starvation.

"It is warmer along the Pecos," Delgadito said at length. "I do not say Hwééldi can ever give us the beauty we find in Dinetah, but there are food and blankets."

"Biligáana food and blankets," snapped Shining Eyes.

"General Carleton calls the place Bosque Redondo, near Fort Sumner," Delgadito said, before a coughing fit silenced him. Shining Eyes politely refrained from speaking until Delgadito recovered and continued. "Carleton promises all our people warmth and food if we go to Hwééldi, and he also promises death and continued destruction of our lands if we do not."

"You surrendered," Shining Eyes said, nothing worse in the way of insult possible for him. "Better to die."

"Our women and children die faster than our warriors, and who can deny that the Biligáana kill our warriors by the score?"

"They have not killed a single fighter from our clan," Shining Eyes shot back.

"How many have died of lack of food or of this bitter cold? It is only two months into winter. The worst months lie ahead." Delgadito pulled the thick wool Army blanket closer around his thin body, but this did not stop the nervous shiver.

"I might freeze, but it will be under a Dinéh blanket," Shining Eyes said caustically, as he stared at Delgadito's protection against the cold. He turned his eyes to the snow-packed trail and settled into the trip through the eastern entrance of Tseyi'.

The tall walls of red rock soon rose around Shining Eyes and he guided the small band through the maze of cañons to Manuelito's new camp. The soldiers had driven them off their usual range, burning hogans and stores of grain and any wool blankets left behind. Shining Eyes stiffened as he remembered how the Biligáana had killed old women and young children unable to flee before them.

The ability to fade into shadow and let the enemy pass had its drawbacks, he knew. The oldest and youngest of the Dinéh were not able to follow this path to safety, even given ample warning of the incursions made by the savage bluecoats.

As he rode, Shining Eyes could not help but glance left and right to the burned areas where once the peach trees had grown in fine orchards. The fields of grain were blanketed with gentle white now, but the bare limbs and burned stumps of the trees poked up as ugly reminders of lost livelihood.

"I see that others have gathered for our *nachiid*," Delgadito said, noting the corral with a dozen horses in it. Shining Eyes had missed this detail. It had been weeks since Manuelito had had such a remuda, but Delgadito had known right away that other headmen had come to talk. The obvious loss of wealth on his father's part filled Shining Eyes with new resentment toward Delgadito and those who'd betrayed the Dinéh. All should fight and not give in to the wind of Biligáana blowing over their precious holy homeland.

Shining Eyes dropped from the back of his sorrel and put the horse into the corral, where it might fight with the others over the small amounts of hay there. A captured supply wagon a week earlier had yielded several bales of hay and two of alfalfa. The fodder quickly vanished into the mouths of the remaining stock.

Shining Eyes ducked as he pushed through the blanket covering the door of the hogan. He saw his mother sitting at the rear, cradling Goes to War. The boy did not cry out, but mewed like a small kitten. Shining Eyes knew his brother suffered the pangs of hunger again. He went to them and crouched down, reaching into his pouch and handing Gray Feather the partially eaten slab of jerky.

"For you," he said. "If you chew it until it is soft, perhaps Goes to War might be able to swallow it."

"This is yours," Gray Feather said. "You need it to keep up your strength. You ride with warriors but are only a child yet."

Shining Eyes had heard this before, and it infuriated him. "I sit with chiefs. Manuelito is my father, and I am accepted as a man. I am your son, but I am no child. Tend to Goes to War."

Shining Eyes swung away and went to the other end of the hogan, where Manuelito and Delgadito exchanged greetings. From the set to his father's face, Shining Eyes knew Manuelito did not suffer Delgadito easily.

But the glow from the small fire reflected in Barboncito's old eyes told a story different from that in Manuelito's. Hastiin Dághá, the Man with the Whiskers, wanted to hear Delgadito's fine words of a land along the Pecos. He wanted to believe—and he would. For that, Shining Eyes cursed both Delgadito and his message, and Barboncito, with his need to surrender.

"We did not expect to see you again in Tseyi'," Manuelito said, choosing his words carefully but still implying more than a hint of insult.

"Going to Fort Wingate and submitting to the Biligáana was not an easy decision," Delgadito said. "When they hurried us to Hwééldi on the Pecos River, what General Carleton calls Bosque Redondo, it was with heaviness in my heart. The grass-lands there are different from Dinetah," Delgadito said. "But in that difference lies our survival."

"They gather us in Hwééldi with the Apache so we may all die at the same time," Manuelito said angrily.

"Is this not better than dying by slow measure, from hunger and disease and exposure to the fierce winter clutching at our throats?" Delgadito countered. "Hwééldi is no paradise. It is no Tseyi'," he said, longing in his voice. "But Carleton offers us sanctuary and peace."

"They would not hunt us like animals at Hwééldi," Barboncito said.

"In Dinetah the Biligáana hunt free men. In Hwééldi they find only slaves," Shining Eyes shot back. Manuelito motioned for him to subside. It was not his place to speak as an equal with headmen, but the fire within him could not be banked. He had to allow Manuelito to speak for him until the others voiced their opinions. It might take a long time, but he would get his say.

Shining Eyes settled down and eyed the men who had ridden

from Fort Wingate with Delgadito. They were warriors of renown, yet they had given themselves up as prisoners. Where was the honor in such a surrender, not even in battle? Delgadito and the others had voluntarily gone to Red Clothes and surrendered.

"Make no mistake," Delgadito said. "Tseyi' is my homeland. When I was only a small child, I sat on a cliff and watched a sandy wash carefully. From above came a loud caw. A crow wheeled, its black wings shining in the summer sun. How fragile it looked," Delgadito said in remembrance, "and so vital. Its wings snapped back suddenly and it dived for the sandy wash. Swooping down, it investigated a bright object, a silver bead dropped by some unknown warrior passing by."

Delgadito coughed harshly and wiped his mouth, but his eyes were clear and his back had straightened more than at any time on the ride into the cañon. His memories were more vivid than the reality of his abdication to the Biligáana.

"The crow hopped along and left tracks in the smooth sand. I knew that when the autumn rains came and filled the arroyo with water, those tracks would vanish completely.

"How like the flood we Dinéh could be, washing away the tracks left by the Biligáana," Delgadito said. He sighed, faint tendrils of breath cooling in the hogan, in spite of the fire burning fitfully in front of the old warrior. "We have washed away the tracks for as long as we could. Now flocks of them blacken our skies—and our lands. Often I have performed the Beauty Way and done so proudly. Our ways fall to theirs, and we can no longer erase them from our lives. We must understand them, come to a peace, and go on with our lives if we are to survive even one more month."

Delgadito lapsed into silence and did not speak again. Barboncito poked at the fire, deep in thought, and Manuelito glared hotly, his gaze fixed beyond Delgadito on the blanket flapping fitfully in the doorway. The wind had died but left behind the occasional gust that proved worse than any constant breeze. Just as Shining Eyes expected only respite from the cold, there came a brief blast that robbed him of sense and all thought save for regaining warmth.

So it was with Delgadito's speech. He made a good case for weakness. Who could deny desiring warmth and a full belly?

"At what price?" Manuelito asked, as if completing Shining Eyes's thoughts with his heated words. "What price do we pay for loss of freedom to roam as we choose? We walk in beauty when we follow our flocks and herds through Dinetah. Changing Woman gave us these lands. The War Twins fought the Monsters so we could live here in harmony. We are a solitary people, not one accustomed to living elbow to elbow on a reservation. But we could live with our own people. But with the Apache? They are our traditional enemy. How do we find beauty surrounded by those who bear us only malice? But I believe you, Delgadito, if you say the Biligáana promise us peace and food there."

These words startled Shining Eyes. He had not expected Manuelito to accede to Delgadito's plea for migrating halfway across New Mexico Territory to Fort Sumner. Then came the words he had thought Manuelito incapable of uttering.

"I grant you that Carleton might even keep his promises. But there is something you have not considered. This Hwééldi will kill our spirit, if not our bodies."

Manuelito sat as if a steel rod had been driven down his spine. He had spoken. It was time for the others to say their piece as he listened and considered.

Shining Eyes heard Barboncito begin bravely enough, but the old man's words turned to smoke and he came around to urging the others to accept the conditions Delgadito had brought from General Carleton. They were to abandon their homes and leave Dinetah, going to faroff Hwééldi. In exchange for this peaceful withdrawal, all warfare would cease and they would be taken care of, growing their food along the Pecos River and hunting on the eastern plains. Any remaining in Dinetah would be hunted like deer and slaughtered.

Waves of argument flowed through the hogan, some supporting Delgadito and Barboncito, others hinting that the Biligáana had broken treaties with impunity before and there was no cause to believe Carleton's words were more honorable than Canby's or Sumner's so many years earlier.

"How did Carson greet you?" Manuelito asked suddenly.

"Red Clothes?" Delgadito frowned and picked up a twig at the edge of the firepit. He poked the embers to life. The surge of warmth faded quickly. "He was abrupt and did not deal with us directly. We were taken to Carleton in Santa Fé, then to Hwééldi. Only after a week there did Carleton commission us to return and urge you to return with us."

"Hwééldi or death?" suggested Manuelito.

"Yes," Delgadito said, his voice so soft Shining Eyes could hardly hear it. "Those are the only two choices."

Shining Eyes was pleased to see that Manuelito knew a third. They would fight. They would fight and win against the Biligáana!

Slow Death

December 8, 1863
Cañon Bonito

The storm never stopped. No matter what shelter Shining
Eyes sought, the winter wind and the snow it carried so wetly
on its tongue always licked at him. He huddled down in the
rock crevice, his threadbare Ute blanket pulled around him. This
was a holy spot, a place where a warrior might come to find
tranquility and purpose.

All he could think of was staying alive.

He scooped a portion of the snow into his trembling hands
and moved it to his lips. For a moment it seemed as if his body
heat would not melt the snow. Then the moisture touched his
mouth and drifted down the back of his throat. It was small
enough, but it allowed him to go back to the jerky he gnawed.
The maggots were the first things he had eaten. They were soft
and his teeth moved in his head whenever he tried to chew.

But the jerky was still good. It filled the spot in his belly that
had not known food in too long. Shining Eyes stared into the
white sheets of blowing snow and tried to remember the last good
meal he had eaten. It was with Looking Arrow, he thought. Yes,
definitely, with her and her brother. He tried to remember when
they had slaughtered the sheep he had given her. He had hoped she
would use the sheep's wool to make new blankets come spring, but

their need had been too great for food. The mutton stew had been sparse, with only a few carefully hoarded vegetables tossed into the stewpot. Looking Arrow, her mother, and her younger brother, hardly a summer younger than Shining Eyes but a much smaller child, perhaps owing to malnutrition, had feasted that night with Gray Feather and Goes to War.

Shining Eyes tried to remember where Manuelito had been but could not. So many memories slipped through his mental grasp these days. It took all his concentration simply to remember what cañon led where in Tseyi'. More than once he had been followed by the bluecoats. Always he had eluded them, but never had he fired even a single arrow in their direction.

To have done so would have meant his death. There were never more than a dozen in each squad, but other squads burned, pillaged, and raped nearby. Hundreds of the Biligáana flooded into the red rock cañons, even in the throes of winter. Manuelito had said this was unusual. The Biligáana did not like winter scouts, yet Carson flung his men repeatedly into the heart of Dinetah.

And it worked. How it worked!

What few supplies that had been cached were gone, either through use or lost to the soldiers. Shining Eyes drifted into a feverish sleep, visions of plentiful food and warm summer meadows in his head.

"Don't sleep. Wake up, wake up, Angry Knife," came distant words barely penetrating the warm, muzzy fog surrounding him. Shining Eyes pushed away—or tried to. His arms refused to move, and his cramped legs had gone numb. "You will freeze to death. There are no more Biligáana. We can return to our hogans."

"Manuelito?" Shining Eyes thought he had gone blind until he realized his eyelashes had again frozen. A trembling hand broke the ice and allowed his sight to clear.

"Walk, move, do not sleep. It is the great killer now, this horrible coldness." The headman's teeth chattered but he held himself proudly, though he was bare to the waist. The sight of his father's flesh turning blue and the man never giving in to such weakness spurred Shining Eyes to action more than the words.

"How far?" Shining Eyes could not remember.

"Not far, though it would be better if we had a horse."

"My sorrel? What happened to her?" Shining Eyes could not remember.

"Angry Knife, walk. We will speak of this when we reach your mother's hogan. Looking Arrow is there, too. Walk!" A hard shove sent Shining Eyes stumbling. He caught himself and forced his legs turned to lead into movement. As he blundered along, the blood flowed faster in his veins and warmed him. Finally mustering enough strength to shiver, Shining Eyes knew he would reach the hogan he saw through the dancing motes of snow.

"There it is," he said, his lips puffy with frostbite. "Gray Feather, my brother."

"Yes, both are there," said Manuelito. He shoved Shining Eyes again, but this time the boy fell to his knees. Through the blizzard Shining Eyes saw another figure, a short, stolid man dressed in buckskins and carrying a long musket over one shoulder.

"Father, look, there. That's . . ." Words left his lips. Who was it? He fought to remember. Then it rushed into his head like spring runoff water in a dry arroyo. The force of the sight made Shining Eyes gasp. "Joseph Treadwell, my father. That's my father. Where?" Shining Eyes looked around and saw only whiteness around him.

"Treadwell!" he shouted. "You burned our blankets. You were dead and then alive, and you left us! You left us for the Navajo raiders!" Raging against the injustice of it, Shining Eyes whipped out his knife and slashed wildly at the man half seen through the snow. Somehow, Treadwell managed to slip away, cleverly avoiding the knife's tip just as the Biligáana soldiers always managed to evade the Dinéh arrows.

"Come back. Fight me. Don't run away again and leave me. Show me your blood!" Shining Eyes stood and went for the dimly seen figure. "Manuelito, my father, help me." Shining Eyes's head spun in crazy circles but he continued to slash with his knife. Always, Treadwell kept beyond his reach, taunting him, speaking to him in soft words he could not understand.

With a last desperate cut Shining Eyes was carried forward, only to smash hard into a wall. He slid down the dirt and rock wall, realizing he had found his way back to a hogan. The blanket across the doorway had long since been taken down, rocks stacked instead, forming a pitiful doorway. Scrambling clumsily over the sharp-edged rock, Shining Eyes tumbled into the hogan's cold interior.

For several seconds the darkness defeated him. His head spun in circles bigger than even Sierra Blanca. Shining Eyes giggled when he thought of his head filled with rocks like that sacred mountain, and snow atop it. He reached up and brushed a thin coating away with a numbed hand. His eyes adjusted to the darkness and he saw Follows Quickly sitting at the rear of the hogan, crouched in front of a cold fire. Only blackened, charred twigs remained.

"You are lazy, Follows Quickly," the boy chided his cousin. "There is wood to be gathered. Out there." Shining Eyes pointed and broke into giggles that refused to die. How could they gather firewood when it lay under a thick blanket of new fallen snow? As if there were any wood beneath the soft, wet blanket. Red Clothes and his soldiers had destroyed everything in their path.

Shining Eyes had even considered chopping down the stumps of the peach trees to use as firewood, but he could not find the orchards in the blizzard. They had moved often, sometimes only minutes ahead of the troopers and their blazing muskets. Manuelito knew the rocky ways of Tseyi', but Shining Eyes had not been born here. He became dazed easily by the rapidity of their forced marches, the distance covered and the work required to build new hogans. He had helped his mother build new dwellings twice in the past month, each less able to hold back the cold thrusts of winter than the one before.

"No wood, even for hogans," Shining Eyes muttered. He turned to Follows Quickly. "What was that, my friend?"

The huddled figure nodded slightly and Shining Eyes had to agree. "It is very cold. So cold I can barely keep awake. Mustn't stay long. Gray Feather and Goes to War are ill. Looking Arrow needs me—Looking Arrow and her little brother. Too little food, too much ice." Shining Eyes shivered and tried to find where Follows Quickly had his stack of blankets. He saw none. Resigning himself to sitting beside his cousin, Shining Eyes drifted off to a fitful sleep, only to jerk awake many times.

The slackening of the storm woke him. He shielded his eyes against the brilliance of sunlight reflected off pure driven snow coming through the hogan's open doorway. Shining Eyes sneezed and pulled his threadbare blanket closer around him. He wished he still had the vest he had won after the last *nachiid,* but he had quickly bet and lost it on the throw of sticks. Shining Eyes could not even remember who had taken the precious warm vest from him—or who had lost it originally.

His mind seemed dipped in molasses and moving slowly, ever so slowly.

"Storm's over," he declared, coughing to clear his scratchy throat. The boy tried to stretch his arms and found it impossible. His joints had frozen, and his flesh lay blue against the bone. Exposure exacted a dreadful payment from him. He couldn't even remember what he had been doing out in the storm.

"Hunting," he said suddenly. "I was out hunting. Have you found any game, Follows Quickly?" Shining Eyes turned to his cousin and shook him gently. The body toppled over and lay still.

"No, no!" Shining Eyes shot to his feet, ignoring the pain and the way he stumbled on frozen toes. He reached out to touch his cousin, then stopped. "Ghost sickness. I have slept in a hogan where Follows Quickly died. I will have his *chindi* haunting my body." Dread gripped at Shining Eyes's throat and choked him. He backed away.

When had Follows Quickly died? During the night? Shining

Eyes thought he had heard his cousin talking all night long. Or
was that his ghost? Shining Eyes saw now that Follows Quickly
did not have a blanket tossed over his shoulders. Rather, the flesh
had turned black with exposure. All food and belongings inside
the hogan were gone. Follows Quickly's relatives had taken what
they could and moved on, leaving his body and hogan behind,
as was fitting. But they should have sealed it to prevent another
from blundering inside.

Another like Shining Eyes, now cursed with ghost sickness.
He sobbed painfully and lurched for the door and burst into the
eye-dazzling radiance that was now Tseyi'. The red rocks were
cloaked in streamers of white, fresh snow having fallen during
the night. Tendrils of fog drifted along the lowest sections of
the cañon floor, hiding juts of red and tan and mysteriously
revealing valleys running off in a wild tangle of rock and death.

Shining Eyes plowed through the knee-deep snow, oblivious
to the sharp pain in his feet and limbs. Not once did he look
back at Follows Quickly's hogan. He feared what lay there as
much as he did what lay ahead.

"Mother, Goes to War," he muttered, as he fought to run.
Tears froze on his cheeks and his heart threatened to explode.
"Be alive, please . . . please, don't be dead!"

The Winter Campaign

Joseph Treadwell stretched his tired muscles under the double layer of jackets he wore. The winter proved worse than he had thought even two months earlier, making excursions toward Cañon de Chelly difficult. But for all the trouble he had venturing out again, the weather worked to hold the Navajo in check. After the pitiful raid against the sheep at Fort Canby the Navajo had faded away, not to be seen again.

This gave Treadwell hope that his wife was in one place and not being moved about. He felt he had been so close to her in October, only to have her slip away. But then he'd thought Manuelito had planned a major attack on Fort Canby designed to destroy the U.S. Army control of their homeland. The massive attack had proved to be a feeble raid by no more than ten warriors. He rubbed his cheeks and cleared the snow from his eyelashes as he stared into the crisp, clear distance. The imposing red buttes of Cañon de Chelly rose majestically, a day's ride off.

The vast tide of Navajo fighters had come from there—or so Manuelito had led him to believe. If Treadwell had known it was only a penny ante raid, he'd have remained in Cañon de Chelly to find Gray Feather. If only . . .

"You find the trail?" The sharp words brought Treadwell

around and stopped his useless rumination. He pulled his vision away from the eastern entrance to Cañon de Chelly to face Major Sena. The officer's temper had been poor since he had chased Manuelito's band and lost them. Treadwell couldn't blame Sena too much since Carson had chewed on the man more than any of the others, and he couldn't see it was any fault of the major's. Manuelito was wily and the raid had been small, quick, and well executed.

But if he thought Sena blameless, that did not excuse the man's bellicose nature.

"It goes that way," Treadwell said, showing the footsteps in the fresh snow. The bright sun had melted the edges of the tracks, rounding them. "Maybe a day at most. I make it to be a party of a half dozen."

"Braves?"

Treadwell shook his head slowly. "Can't say, but I doubt it. From the size of the footprints, women and children. They have a few sheep with them, but no horses."

"We can overtake them before sundown?"

"Reckon so," Treadwell told the major. Sena lifted his arm and motioned his company forward.

"You planning on taking them prisoner?"

"If possible. General Carleton is disappointed by how few Navajo are being moved to Bosque Redondo. Not enough to suit him, not enough," grumbled Sena. "We have our orders."

"About the orders, Major," Treadwell said. "We've been on the trail three days now, and you haven't told me what we're supposed to do. Finding these tracks didn't seem to be what you'd expected. I heard rumors that the colonel was leaving the fort, too."

"You have no reason to know where we are going. You follow orders, Treadwell. Nothing more."

"Major, I'm not in your army. I'm not some buck private afraid of getting put on report. Tell me what's going on, or I'll just hightail it north. There's no reason for me to stay in the dark like this. The Army's not paying me near enough, much less enough to take your arrogant guff."

"Sergeant!" Sena twisted and barked again at his sergeant. "Put this man under arrest."

"Sir?" The sergeant's eyes widened. "He's our only scout. We need him if—"

"Do it!"

"Go on, Sergeant," urged Treadwell. "Take me on back to Fort Canby. I'll have this out with Colonel Carson."

"The two of them go back to Valverde, sir," objected the sergeant. "Treadwell's been into the cañon. He knows all the routes. Everyone says he's about the best there is when it comes to scouting."

"So we're heading to Cañon de Chelly?" Treadwell glanced over his shoulder at the towering cliffs. Gray Feather was there by the double red cliffs. And he would be there, too, with or without Major Sena and his company at his back.

"There is so little time. We have not traveled fast enough," complained Sena.

"Time is important? That sounds as if the colonel is launching an attack into the cañon again." This surprised Treadwell a little. The Army wasn't noted for mounting winter campaigns. He remembered Manuelito commenting on this before the October raid but thought little more about it. If Kit Carson planned a major incursion into the heart of Navajo power now, he might crush them entirely.

For all their supply problems, Sena and the others were well outfitted. Treadwell knew Carleton had sent considerable amounts of matériel to the scattered forts but had no idea it had been in support of a winter foray.

"We are to join the colonel's troops in less than twenty-four hours. Time is of great importance, Treadwell. And you shall get us to the eastern entrance of the cañon by noon tomorrow."

"Can't do that, Major," Treadwell said, relishing the moment of power over the blustering officer. "You put me under arrest. No way can I scout while the sergeant is guarding me."

Sena's face darkened with rage. Treadwell wondered if the officer's anger might reach the point where he had a fit of apoplexy. If that happened, a shavetail lieutenant would be in charge. Treadwell wasn't sure if that might not improve their chances in the field.

"You are toying with me, Treadwell. I do not appreciate that."

"Don't much like being threatened, Major. That makes us about even. I can get you to the mouth of the cañon by noon tomorrow, but it will take some hard riding."

"Do it," Sena snapped. "Show us the trail."

Treadwell smiled grimly. The verbal victory carried only the taste of ash with it. When they joined Carson's horse soldiers, Treadwell vowed to remove himself from Sena's command. The major had the air of a man whom destiny had chosen for nasty outcomes.

Starting on the trail, following the tracks left by the earlier— possibly Navajo—party, Treadwell set a fast pace. Those soldiers on foot found themselves hard-pressed to keep up, but Sena refused to allow more than a few minutes of rest every hour. Even when Treadwell returned to report he had stumbled over the small party ahead of them, Sena showed little interest in resting.

"You can please the general by capturing them, Major," Treadwell pointed out. "How many Navajo have *you* sent to Bosque Redondo?"

"None," came the surly answer. "They always dance away, refusing to fight."

"These won't fight. Looks to be an old woman with four young children. They're butchering their sheep, and they're heading back into Cañon de Chelly."

"Troop, forward!" cried Sena. The mounted soldiers charged downhill, horses' hooves kicking up a shower of mud and snow. Treadwell frowned. He had not expected Sena to launch a full frontal assault on an old woman and a few children. The officer had not even asked if the small band was armed.

Treadwell followed and found that the thunderous approach

had allowed the four children to escape. They had taken to the ravines and had vanished like fog in the wan morning sun. The old woman limped and had been caught less than twenty feet from her camp.

"Destroy their property," ordered Sena. "Leave nothing for them to recover."

Treadwell dismounted and went to the old woman. She might have been fifty, or she might have been a hundred. Treadwell found it impossible to guess. She glared at him with impolite arrogance. Treadwell chose not to play the game. He politely averted his eyes in the Navajo style and settled down beside her. He waited a decent interval before saying, "We mean you no harm, Grandmother. You will be sent to Bosque Redondo, where you can live in peace and plenty."

"I go home to Tseyi'," she countered angrily. "There is no food here. I will die surrounded by beauty."

"Get her on her feet. We're moving out right away," came Sena's sharp words.

"What do you mean? You're sending her back to Fort Canby, aren't you?"

"We have to rendezvous with Colonel Carson in just hours," Sena said. "She comes with us."

Treadwell glanced around, wondering how close the four children were who had run off.

"She can't keep up, Major. She's gimpy."

"That is not my concern. Tell her to keep up." With that Sena put his spurs to his horse's heaving flanks and raced off. The troopers struggled to keep up with the quick pace set by their commander. Treadwell stayed with the woman until the foot soldiers marched up.

"We're to keep her with us, Joe," a corporal said. "Don't know how this is going to work out. She don't step high like we do, or quick, for all that."

"Take care of her," Treadwell said. He started to give the woman a few words of comfort, then bit back the words when he saw the anger on her face. She knew she was a prisoner of war and nothing more. The only bright spot for her lay in heading toward Cañon de Chelly rather than being sent immediately to Fort Canby for later transport to Fort Sumner.

He mounted and edged his horse down a rocky slope into a snow-filled ravine. Keeping his eye peeled, he sought any sign of the tracks left by the four children. Treadwell had to admit their skill in covering their tracks exceeded his ability to find them. Pitying them, Treadwell knew the night would be harsh and the day worse without any of their provisions. And as Sena's patrol had crossed the countryside between Fort Canby and the mouth of Cañon de Chelly, they had destroyed anything that might have been used to support the Navajo.

Angling out and returning to Sena's line of travel allowed Treadwell to sweep through the terrain and rejoin the main body of troopers just before twilight fell. He shook off some of the dampness from his coat and walked toward the bonfire that was warming most of the troopers.

"Where's Sena?" he asked a sergeant.

The man shook his head. "Him and the lieutenant rode off to look for something up on yonder hill. Don't know what they want to find."

"Sign of the colonel," guessed Treadwell. He rubbed his hands together and moved closer to the fire. "Where's the old woman?"

"The one we caught out on the trail?"

"How many have you seen today?"

The sergeant bit his lower lip and started to speak, then thought better of it.

Seeing he wasn't going to get an immediate answer, Treadwell reached out and grabbed the sergeant's shoulder. "What happened to her?"

"She couldn't keep up. The major was setting a furious pace. He wanted to outdistance you, Joe."

"The old woman," he pressed. "I don't care how the major sees fit to run you bluebellies into the ground. What happened to the old woman?"

"She tried real hard to keep up. When she couldn't, Sena ordered her left behind."

Treadwell simply stared. They had destroyed the woman's food and belongings. With only a single blanket draped over her shoulders, she had no chance of surviving the freezing night.

"How far back?"

"Not fifteen minutes after you rode off to scout," the sergeant said.

Treadwell sank down. Even if he rode like the wind, he could never get back in time to save the woman. She would have frozen to death hours before he could hope to locate her.

"We didn't want to do it, Joe—honest. But the major he said we had to. Joining up with the colonel was more important."

"More important," Treadwell repeated dully. If they had left the woman with her gear and the children to aid her, she might have survived long enough to return to her home.

To die.

Treadwell stalked off, wanting to be left alone for a spell. Killing Manuelito was something he dreamed about. Letting an old woman freeze to death on the trail home was another matter.

"Capture every last one you find," Kit Carson ordered. The short colonel stood beside the map, spread on the cold ground, held down with large rocks at the four corners. "We'll sweep in and find them. They won't expect us this time of year."

"Weather might go against us, Colonel," Treadwell pointed out. "It's been clear and cold for a week, but the storms are building again." He pointed at the flat gray clouds slipping down from the north.

"All the more reason not to waste time jawin' 'bout this," Carson said. "They won't expect us to attack in the winter. We swoop in like hawks, scoop up as many prisoners as we kin, then git out."

Treadwell held his tongue. He almost told Carson he could have had one more prisoner to send to General Carleton and

Bosque Redondo if Sena had not let the old woman die on the trail. Such recrimination did nothing to bring the woman back to life. If she hadn't died on the trail, she might have died at Bosque Redondo. At least she had died near her precious holy land.

"Why worry about prisoners?" asked Sena.

"We will take as many as possible, Major," Carson said firmly. "The success of the reservation rides with us."

Carson spoke the words Treadwell had heard before, but underneath he heard something more, something new. He fell silent and let the colonel finish his briefing about the winter campaign. Only when the others had drifted away to shape up their troops and be sure they were bedded down for the night did Treadwell approach Carson.

"A word with you, Colonel," Treadwell said. "I know the Navajo won't expect us knocking on their door right now. That's good. Take 'em by surprise."

"I'm sure you are hankerin' to return to find your wife. There's a chance we might catch her as we cast our net."

"Why are we here? They aren't going to pose any problem till spring. If the big attack Manuelito bragged on turned out only ten warriors, there's nothing any of the other headmen can muster that threatens us."

"True. Delgadito, Cha-hay, Tsee-e, and Chiquito saw how hopeless their plight was in September. It's only a matter of time before empty bellies convince Manuelito and the others that they have made a bad mistake."

"Why are we chasing them into the cañon?" repeated Treadwell. "There's something more you're not telling me. They're no threat. Their bravest fighters are starting to surrender. There's nothing to eat in Cañon de Chelly. The earlier scout destroyed danged near everything. I saw that a couple of months back, and it surely has not improved any."

"That's 'bout the longest I've heard you speak, Mr. Treadwell," Carson said.

"That's because I want the truth, not the pap you're dishing out to your officers. What's the real reason for this campaign?"

Carson heaved a deep sigh. Twin gusts of breath shot forth from his nostrils. He stood with his hands clasped behind his back. For a moment he looked almost wistful. Then his face hardened.

"I asked General Carleton for leave to git on back to Taos to be with my family for Christmas. It means the world to Josepha and the children."

"The general's not granting you leave, is he? Not till you send him a quota of new residents for Bosque Redondo."

"Bein' an officer ain't always easy, Mr. Treadwell. I look for one hunnerd captives from this campaign. Now, git yerself on over to yer bedroll. We've a hefty amount of preparation ahead of us if we are goin' into Cañon de Chelly within the week."

Delays

"A hunnerd," muttered Kit Carson.

"How's that, Colonel?" Joseph Treadwell sat up and stared at the short man. He swore he saw tears in Carson's eyes, but as fast as he thought he saw them trickling down cheeks red from the bitter cold, the officer turned from him. When Carson faced him, no trace of tears glinted in the morning light.

"I am at a standstill, Mr. Treadwell. The courier arrivin' yesterday brought bad news."

"How's that? We're not going in?" Treadwell got to his feet. He refused to be thwarted when they camped in the mouth of Cañon de Chelly.

"Major Abreu has been promoted away from my command. He's now lieutenant colonel, in command of the First Infantry in Santa Fé."

"There's no reason to hold back. You got well nigh four hundred men behind you. Some of the officers are right good at what they do." Treadwell wasn't sure if he put Carson in that group. Seldom had he seen a man better at tracking, but that wasn't a skill a colonel needed. When it came to command, Carson left much to be desired.

"Without Abreu, it'll be hell in there," Carson declared. "But you know the real reason I ain't intent on pushin' right in."

"Sena." With that single naming Treadwell condemned most of what was wrong with Carson's command. Two days earlier Sena had allowed a Navajo raiding party to run off forty-eight mules and seven oxen. This left Carson's supply wagons mired in the mud and snow. To invade Cañon de Chelly without the supplies carried by those wagons would be dangerous—maybe even suicidal.

"I sent a letter to the general tellin' him my problems. I want to pull back." Carson stood with his hands clasped behind his back. Treadwell heard him mutter "One entire hunnerd" again.

The scout did not badger Carson with the knowledge that he would never get his hundred prisoners for Carleton to parade around Santa Fé before sending them to Bosque Redondo. Not before Christmas. And without the mules and oxen, not before the new year.

"Have Captain Carey send more draft animals," suggested Treadwell. "There's no good reason to pull back, now that you've come this far. I don't see the sense in going into Cañon de Chelly only to capture starving Navajo, but to return to Fort Canby . . ."

"Colonel, a courier from the fort," called a sentry. For a moment, Carson looked upset, then he held up his hand to keep Treadwell from wandering away.

"A moment, Mr. Treadwell." Carson took the pouch from the messenger and opened it. He pawed through the contents, his eyes widening when he saw two letters. "My eyes betray me, Mr. Treadwell. Could you do me the favor of readin' these to me? 'Less I miss a guess, this here's from dear Jessie."

"Yes, sir, it is," Treadwell said, taking a letter from an elaborate envelope graced with floral patterns. "Jessie Frémont," he said, scanning down the beautifully written pages to the signature.

"John's wife," Carson said. "She is a fine woman. Please, do get on with the letter. There's another I need read, too."

Carson fingered the more official-looking one, turning it end-for-end as if it might burn his hands.

"Seems she's at an ebb," Treadwell said. "Or rather, she and the children are doing well, but General Frémont's fortunes are at a low point. She thanks your missus kindly for tending to General Frémont back in forty-nine." Treadwell glanced over. Carson sat with his eyes closed and fists clenched.

"I wish the general only the best, and he comes to such a point in his life that it makers a man wonder."

"Heard tell President Lincoln didn't much cotton to him trying to emancipate the slaves without telling anyone about it first."

"John Frémont has always been a progressive fella. Salt of the earth," Carson said. "He's too good for the posts the government assigns him."

"Mrs. Frémont goes on to congratulate you on your successes. She thinks a great deal of you, Colonel." Treadwell folded the letter and handed it back.

"Thank you, Mr. Treadwell. Now, please, read this one. I'm sure it's from General Carleton."

It took Treadwell only a few seconds to find that Carson was right. He started to read, then clamped his mouth closed.

"Read it straight out, sir. Do not dip the words in syrup for me. The general has a way of gettin' right to the point."

"Well, that surely seems the case, Colonel. He says that Sena ought to be flogged, and that any command unable to protect its own stock is not fit for his army. Then he goes on with how the Army of the Potomac carries eight days' rations in haversacks and marches everywhere in jig time. Unless fatigue and some privations are encountered by the troops, the Indians will get the best of your campaign into the cañon."

"What more?"

"He says your complaint about how Herrera Grande's emissaries were treated means little, now that Major Blakeney has been sent to Los Pinos. He thinks you're using this as an excuse to be a slacker." Treadwell saw the color rise in Carson's leathery cheeks. Whatever failings the colonel might show, being a slacker was not among them. He might do the wrong thing or have no idea how to deal with his fellow officers, but none could say Kit Carson shirked his duty.

"I want to talk with Herrera Grande, not fight him," Carson said angrily. "Killin' starvin' Navajo ain't as likely to benefit us as palaver now. I kin convince the lot of 'em to go to Bosque Redondo, as much as that rankles."

"Beats killing them," Treadwell said.

"Does it, now?" Carson began pacing. He came to a decision. "I shall accept the general's suggestion of remainin' in the field. However, I want you to enter the cañon immediately. Scout. Find Herrera Grande. Persuade him to surrender."

"Colonel—"

"I'll report to General Carleton that we're enterin' Cañon de Chelly from several directions. From the west, from the north, through this entrance. I kin send Sena back to Fort Canby for replacement animals. The general cannot object to a small shilly-shallying about if we're gettin' into position."

"If you're serious about this expedition, you might request that Captain Carey join us. I figure him to be about the best you have in your command."

"A good idea, Mr. Treadwell. I feel I kin trust Captain Pfeiffer, also. And Captain Berney. He's no stranger to this kind of patrol."

"You get your messengers sent, Colonel, and I'll get my cold hindquarters into the cañon." Treadwell stared up at the tall, imposing bluffs and shivered a little. The white snow clinging tenaciously to the sheer faces only made them seem more inhospitable.

As he prepared to go into the heart of Navajo power again, he vowed that he would not return without Gray Feather and his boys. Somehow, riding back into the cañon with this thought rattling about in his brain made the journey easier.

* * *

Two days, Treadwell grumbled. Two days of riding hard and fast into the cañon, and he had seen only a few traces of habitation. The first pass Carson had made through Cañon de Chelly had brought destruction to the rangeland and farms. Everywhere Treadwell explored he found only burned out hogans and the ashes of burned blankets, clothing, and other possessions.

He rode faster, the wind whipping hard across his face. Carson was playing a dangerous game with James Carleton if he delayed coming into the Navajo stronghold much longer. The weather might turn frigid again and trap the colonel's forces far from fort and fodder, or the Navajo might simply die of starvation. Treadwell shook his head remembering Manuelito's last raid against Fort Canby.

Ninety sheep. That had been the big attack. From the way the headman had portrayed his plans to the warriors around the bonfire, he would have pushed the entire U.S. Army from his homeland with a huge rush of screaming savages. Ninety sheep, and that had been viewed as a major victory for the Navajo.

Treadwell blinked when he saw the man standing in the middle of the trail ahead of him. A few seconds earlier he had seen only snow stretching from one red wall to the other a mile and more distant. Now a solitary man stood, naked to the waist in spite of the cold, arms crossed and staring hard.

"Good day," Treadwell greeted him, not sure what else to say. He might have whipped out his musket and let fly with a .50 slug, but the Navajo had obviously sought him out. If he had wanted, the brave might have remained invisible and simply let Treadwell ride past. An arrow in the back would have ended his scouting days forever.

"Do you come in peace?" came the question.

"There's an entire army nipping at my heels," Treadwell said. "Colonel Carson is bringing his troopers into your cañon right soon."

The Indian shivered a little and turned as if intending to walk away. Treadwell sat watching, unsure what to do. The Navajo warrior turned back.

"Do you have a blanket?"

"I need information," Treadwell said. "I don't care spit about Carson or what he's likely to do. I want to find Manuelito."

"I am of Herrera Grande's clan," the man said. "He will speak with you, if you come in peace."

"I seek only information."

The man turned and ran lightly, his moccasins making soft slipping, crunching sounds against the icy crust over the snow. He barely left footprints as he ran. Treadwell urged his horse forward, wishing he had his old mare back. This gelding was broken down the day he got it. Still, the horse sensed an end to the aimless searching and kept up with the Navajo.

Down a side cañon and then down still another they went. An hour later they came to a small gathering of people, twenty all told. Treadwell counted ten warriors, seven women and three small children. None was healthy or had the glow of someone with a well-fed belly.

"You are a scout?" asked Herrera Grande. Treadwell knew such abruptness was rude. Somehow, it mattered little to him what the Navajo thought.

"I scout for Colonel Carson."

"He comes," Herrera Grande said, a note of sorrow in his voice. "Again he comes to burn and pillage. Our fields and grain were stolen away. He killed our cattle and sheep. He ran off our horses and chopped down our peach trees. What more can he want?"

"General Carleton wants you to go to Bosque Redondo."

"With the Apache." Herrera Grande spat, then covered it with a kicked pile of dirt.

"We would no longer walk in beauty. We cannot leave our home." The warrior who had led Treadwell here spoke as an equal with the headman. Treadwell wondered if discipline had broken down among the Indians, or if this guide held a higher post than he had thought.

"It is the only way the bluecoats will leave you alone. Go to

the reservation prepared for you, and General Carleton will give
you food, blankets, all you need to live."

"We had those here!" The brave exploded in anger. Herrera
Grande silenced him with a small movement of his hand.

"We cannot trust the Biligáana," Herrera Grande said carefully, "after our two messengers were slaughtered in your fort."

"General Carleton regrets that. The officer responsible for the
killings has been . . . punished." Treadwell almost choked on
that. Blakeney had not been punished. If anything, his transfer
to Los Pinos might be viewed as a promotion."

"We sought peace, then. We seek it now," Herrera Grande
said. "We are tired. Cold. Hungry. We need rest."

"Even in Bosque Redondo?" Treadwell shot back.

Herrera Grande's slow nod surprised him. He thought the
headman would, like Manuelito, fight until his bones bleached
in the hot sun in the center of Cañon de Chelly.

"We die, either here or at the Biligáana reservation," Herrera
Grande said. "Why not try the reservation?"

"Is it better to die from an Apache knife in the back than to
fight for our homes?" The other warrior stormed about angrily,
his moccasins kicking up slush as he walked.

"Our hogans are destroyed, our herds run off. We have nothing here."

"Changing Woman promised us this land. We are not whole
unless—"

"Silence," cut in Herrera Grande, uncharacteristically interrupting. The rudeness shocked the warrior. He sank down and
glared hotly at Treadwell. It was the only heat in the camp.

"I need information," Treadwell said. "I would speak with
Manuelito."

Herrera Grande shook his head. "He is filled with boundless
hatred. Never will he surrender."

Treadwell glanced at the other warrior and saw that Herrera
Grande's submission pleased him less than mention of
Manuelito's continued ferocity.

"After I see Manuelito, I will speak to Colonel Carson. He

will gladly accept your surrender. If you can find eighty more to join you, he will be eternally grateful." Treadwell saw the puzzlement on Herrera Grande's face. He did not bother explaining white man's politics. For all that, Treadwell wasn't sure he understood them too well.

"So be it." Herrera Grande heaved a deep sigh and closed his eyes.

"There will be no repeat of the mistakes made dealing with your two ambassadors," Treadwell assured the aging headman. "Colonel Carson will see that you are given blankets and food and that your sick are tended properly."

Seeing that Herrera Grande had said his piece, Treadwell turned and mounted. The warrior who had brought him here trotted alongside until they were out of sight of the camp. The Navajo reached up and tugged at Treadwell's sleeve.

"You seek Manuelito? For a blanket I will tell you where he camps."

Treadwell silently pulled his spare blanket from his bedroll and handed it to the shivering Navajo.

Bones

December 24, 1863
Cañon de Chelly

It was a terrible Christmas present.

Just after sundown Treadwell found Manuelito's camp nestled between two towering red cliffs. He rode slowly, making no attempt to hide his approach. Everywhere he looked he saw only destruction brought earlier by Carson. Through the white drifts of snow poked burned tree stumps. And white through white shone the ribs of slaughtered cattle rising from the snow.

He had not been robbed, Treadwell saw right away. Dismounting, he found evidence of recent campfires. Within days. The warrior with the blanket in Herrera Grande's camp had not lied. Treadwell had simply been too slow in arriving.

Manuelito was gone—and with him his entire clan.

"Or what remains of it," Treadwell said, finding a hogan with walls still standing but a collapsed roof. He glanced inside and saw human skeletons. Feeling uneasy but knowing he had to do it, he slid through the tattered door hanging and studied the bones. One was cloaked in a shawl like those sold by Mexican traders.

"An old woman, maybe." He guessed in life she had been scarcely five feet tall. From the numerous ridges on the exposed bones, she had endured broken arms and legs throughout her life, then suffered with poor mending. "Not Gray Feather. Couldn't be."

The other skeleton turned him cold inside, though.

He dropped to one knee and rummaged through the belongings beside the body. He felt like a ghoul, a graverobber, some unclean fiend robbing the dead. Hand trembling uncontrollably, Treadwell picked up a shred of a blanket unlike anything the Navajo spun.

"Ute," he said, his voice choking as he recognized the blanket. He held in a cry of rage, of stark fear. He had come so far. His family had survived . . . until now. The skeleton was that of a boy, perhaps ten or twelve—the age of Shining Eyes.

And the blanket was one his mother had given the boy when he was hardly more than a toddler. Treadwell remembered watching Shining Eyes take his first steps, the blanket tied around his neck and dragging in the dirt as he explored his fine new world. As he grew, the blanket seemed to shrink. The last Treadwell had seen of the blanket, Shining Eyes had it slung around his thin shoulders.

Tugging, he pulled the rest of the shredded blanket from under the skeleton.

"You killed him, you filthy bastard," Treadwell grated out. "You might as well have stuck him in the belly with your knife." For a moment he was confused who he meant, who the object of his wrath was. Carson's destruction had brought nothing but suffering on the Navajo; if he hadn't destroyed their food, this boy might still live. But if Manuelito had not stolen away Gray Feather and Shining Eyes, his son would also be alive.

Why had they all intruded? Why couldn't they have left him and his family alone, to live in peace?

Treadwell reached out and touched the cold bone. How long the boy had been dead he could not say, but it had been some time. A week or more would not have dried out the flesh like this. Still, few among the Navajo showed any body fat these days. He searched the body for any other clue as to the identity.

He hoped to find a bracelet or trinket convincing him this was another boy.

He found nothing to dissolve the swirling dread that he had found one son.

Treadwell roamed the hogan, poking into the corners and hunting for anything that might give him a clue to Manuelito's destination after leaving this campsite. His heart almost exploded when he found a small doll, similar to the one Gray Feather had fashioned for Shining Eyes. Never had he seen one like it in a Navajo child's hands.

It even carried Ute decoration, though it had faded considerably. He glanced over his shoulder at the body. Shining Eyes would not have played with such a doll, but his brother might have. Goes to War.

"Gray Feather," Treadwell said, tears welling in his eyes. "I hope they all die. I hope they all burn in hell!"

He threw the doll across the hogan and sank down, crying. The hot tears turned frigid on his cheeks. Only then did Treadwell turn to the unpleasant chore of burying Shining Eyes.

Even as he rode away from the shallow grave in the frozen ground, Treadwell could not focus his anger. Carson. Carleton. Manuelito. The Navajo. Himself.

He hated all equally.

Surrender—or Die!

"We're comin' at 'em from three directions," Carson told Treadwell. "You've done good work, findin' where they're hidin' themselves."

Treadwell nodded absently. Everywhere he turned, he saw only a single destroyed hogan and the two skeletons within. The grave. His boy, alive and laughing in the warm sun. His son, buried in a grave dug too shallow because the ground was frozen and his fingers were too numb for proper shoveling.

"Herrera Grande's clan surrendering gives you some measure of bargaining power with General Carleton," Treadwell said. "Them and the others trickling into the camp. You might keep your troops in the field a month or more." Treadwell hoped Carson would lengthen his stay in spite of the inclement weather. He had failed repeatedly trying to track the elusive Manuelito. The man might have been made of smoke for all the trail he left behind.

Carson snorted at this. "Can't do that, Mr. Treadwell. Supplies. We lost some more, thanks to Major Sena. I swear, it makes me wonder which side he is on."

"Will Carleton send reinforcements to keep your troopers in the field?"

"That he will not. We are on our own. His orders were emphatic." Carson almost spat the last word. "The Navajo we find will either surrender or die. If they turn tail and run, we track 'em down and kill the lot of 'em."

"And the prisoners all go to Bosque Redondo," finished Treadwell.

"Compared to this place, it'll be a paradise. I used to think like General Canby, that they'd be better off in their own land. No more, not with the land burned to a crisp."

Treadwell glanced at Kit Carson, wondering if the man meant it. Eventually he had gone along with Ka-ni-ache and the other Ute taking Navajo slaves, not because it suited his beliefs about slavery, but because he thought any captives in Ute hands would be better off than being quartered at Bosque Redondo. This was a complete about-face.

"The general's convinced me of how right he is," Carson said. "He's a good godfearin' man. He wants only the best for the Navajo. And reports show the Navajo already at Bosque Redondo are prospering. They are takin' real quick to religion classes and adoptin' many of our civilized ways."

"Who wrote the reports?" asked Treadwell. Carson shot him a cold look, making Treadwell want to go even further and question who had read the reports to Carson, since the colonel did little enough of that on his own. He held his own counsel on this. Not being able to read or write was a sore point with the colonel. He wrote his own name passably well, but always at the bottom of a document someone else had prepared for him.

"They're scattering now. Before, they had small communities, if you can call them that," Treadwell said. "Some valleys held a dozen hogans and a hundred people, with their farms and sheep. Now—" He waved his hand over the dazzling white vastness of the cañons. New snow had obliterated old trails, but Treadwell found his way around the mazes of rock more easily now, getting a feel where the Navajo might have sought shelter.

"We will hunt 'em down one by one, if that's what it takes," Carson vowed.

"How close to a hundred are you?"

Carson chose not to answer. Treadwell saw how much it rankled that Carson had been unable to capture enough prisoners for Carleton to grant him Christmas leave to see his family. Treadwell closed his eyes and swayed a little. At least Carson *had* a family where he could visit.

"Major Sena's let our ammunition supply run perilously low, and the ordnance officer back in Santa Fé is draggin' his feet sendin' more. We are on short rations of ammo, Mr. Treadwell. Find us easy conquests till the ammo catches up with us."

"Not even Carleton can grease the track?" Treadwell marveled at the supply problems they endured. How they'd fought the Lords of New Mexico—and won—amazed him. Few battles had been fought. Tons of food and supplies had been destroyed, though, and in this attrition lay the winning strategy. Carson starved the Navajo into hiding, and he would starve them onto the reservation at Bosque Redondo.

Or into graves.

Like the one holding Shining Eyes.

"Split your forces again, Colonel," he said unexpectedly. "They won't fight you. Look strong. Ride strong. Bluff."

"Berney and Thompson jist brought in fourteen women and children," Carson mused. "Do you think it wise, sendin' them back out without proper rest?"

"Do it. Ride tall and spit in the eye of any warrior you find. Might use up some of the precious ammunition, but if you show weakness now, they'll eat you alive."

"Why not?" laughed Carson. "It's rumored they eat their own young."

Treadwell shivered. Carson had not witnessed utter deprivation, the way he had. He hoped that Gray Feather and Goes to War had not suffered such a fate. With Shining Eyes gone, he had little enough faith left.

"Colonel, lookee there! Up high!" came the cry from a sentry.

Treadwell squinted as he stared at the thousand-foot rim of the cañon wall. He made out four figures watching them.

"Get too close and they might drop rocks on our heads," cautioned Treadwell. "Want me to see what they want?"

"They're spyin' on us," said Carson.

"They could have done that without standing up and silhouetting themselves against the blue sky. They want more."

"Go ahead, Mr. Treadwell. And good luck."

He swung into the saddle and rode directly for the base of the distant cliff. Through some Indian magic, the four appeared at the base about the time he arrived. Sitting with one leg hooked over his pommel, Treadwell waited. The silence stretched as the four studied him as if he were a bug crawling along the desert floor. Treadwell had learned not to hurry them, though it wore on him now and then. Mostly he wanted to return to Carson's camp and sip another cup of hot coffee.

Finally deciding he meant them no real harm, the four stepped forward. One spoke in halting English.

"We surrender. No longer can we live. Our bellies." He rubbed his bare, bulging stomach. Treadwell saw decaying flesh under old wounds and wondered how the warrior had survived this long.

"Colonel Carson will accept your surrender and give you food."

"We have food," bragged another, holding up a leather pouch. "Piñon nuts."

"What else?"

The four exchanged glances as if they did not understand. Treadwell closed his eyes and tried to imagine these warriors living off nothing more than a handful of nuts gathered from trees left standing only because Carson's troops had not found them.

"We surrender to Red Clothes."

Treadwell motioned for them to follow. As they walked back

to the camp, Treadwell interrogated them about Manuelito and his whereabouts. The headman rode high in their regard, but they knew nothing that helped Treadwell find his family . . . what remained of it.

As they approached the camp, he saw the furor among the troopers. They hollered and carried on. As he and the four prisoners neared, Treadwell felt like losing what food rode in his own belly.

Cavalrymen rode into camp dragging bodies behind them. From the general shape of the carcasses, Treadwell had to guess they had once been human. Slipping along sharp shards of ice and the rocky ground had reduced the bodies to little more than butchered cadavers.

The four with Treadwell made as if to bolt, but he called them back.

"Food," he said. "Food." This overcame their fear of treachery long enough for Carson to greet them personally.

"Our doctor will tend your wounds," the colonel said, seeing how severely injured two of the men were. He watched as the four hobbled off, their weapons now taken by the troopers surrounding them.

"An unfortunate sight to see after you just surrendered," Treadwell observed.

"Indeed it is, but the men have their orders. Those eleven warriors fought."

"Do the orders include mutilation?"

Carson glared at him. "Mr. Treadwell, Captain Pfeiffer is leaving immediately to explore the Cañon del Muerto led by a half-dozen Dinéh Ana'aii. We have reason to believe a large group is hiding there."

"I see that Captain Carey's arrived."

"He brought with him a score of prisoners. We find ourselves overrun with captives all of a sudden."

"Have Sena take them back to Fort Canby," suggested Treadwell. Carson's grim expression told him this was not likely to happen. He knew better than to ask what more Sena might have done.

"Scout for Pfeiffer. His orders are to explore to the north rim, then circle 'round to the eastern entrance and rejoin our main body in two days."

"At your service, Colonel," Treadwell said. He joined Albert Pfeiffer's soldiers as they formed their column and began marching northward through the main valley of the cañon. For a spell he rode in silence, saying nothing. He figured if the taciturn officer wanted him to scout ahead, he would let him know.

From the corner of his eye Treadwell saw the officer lift out a flask and take a long pull. Like too many of Carson's officers, Pfeiffer could not control his thirst for firewater. But unlike the others, Treadwell knew some of the reasons behind the unquenchable thirst.

Pfeiffer was an old friend of Carson's and had requested this post after his wife and two children had been killed by the Apache. Treadwell suspected the Mescalero had done something to the officer, from the way he walked with a slight hitch in his step and the painful way he shifted in the saddle. Gossip had it they had skinned the man alive. Treadwell suspected something less atrocious. Bad sunburn might account for the patches of sickly skin and the way Pfeiffer favored certain parts of his body.

"A good idea, Mr. Treadwell," Pfeiffer said unexpectedly. "I believe Colonel Carson is too timid in his approach to the problem facing us."

"You want to charge flat out?"

"Absolutely."

Treadwell knew the captain's reputation of being an utterly ferocious solider. He seemed to know no fear when it came to battle. It had to wear on Pfeiffer that there had been so few open confrontations. The Navajo had learned to taunt and strike, an arrow here and a knife there, then slip into shadow, leaving no trace. This was no fit way to fight.

"You have been in this cañon before?"

"When I entered on my own, I rode along this track, but the snowfall changes the appearance."

"Three days," Pfeiffer said, more to himself than to Treadwell. "We shall sweep through, capture as many Navajo as possible, and still rendezvous with the colonel at the eastern entrance. We can do it because we must."

"You know the lay of the land?" Treadwell wished he had been more diligent about recording his wanderings in Cañon de Chelly. He knew many of the towering cliffs and buttes by sight after his earlier scouts, but the entrances to the jumble of rocky passages left him confused at times. "Are you sure we can leave to the north and get around the outside in only three days?"

"We are the best at Fort Canby. We will do it," Pfeiffer said, with such confidence that Treadwell almost believed him.

Resistance—and Surrender

January 10, 1864
Cañon del Muerto

Treadwell's rifle kicked hard against his shoulder. He wondered if he had tamped in too much powder, then realized the pain in his shoulder came from gnawing arthritis. He had healed after the knife slash from the Navajo when he had spied on Manuelito, but his entire body had reacted differently this time when it mended.

"Getting old," Treadwell said.

"You are indeed, Mr. Treadwell," came Captain Pfeiffer's steady voice. "You failed to hit the savage when you had a clean shot."

"Wanted to scare him," Treadwell lied. He had aimed smack dab in the center of the brave's body and had missed at a range of less than fifty yards. Now it was too late ever to hope to fire a second time. Like a mountain goat, the warrior had lit out and hit the cañon wall at a dead run. With incredible agility he had scaled the invisible path and was now halfway up the cliff, well out of range of any weapon save a cannon.

"He will not be the last we encounter," Pfeiffer said coldly. "Continue your scout, sir."

Treadwell nodded. He worked to reload his musket first, then went back to the center of the shallow, ice-locked stream they had followed for a full day. Walking on the frozen stream proved easier than making their way through the high drifts and treacherously hidden rocks on either side. Still, Treadwell wondered at the wisdom Pfeiffer showed in taking this route. They had been taunted by solitary Indians, and an occasional rock arced down from the high cañon rim to smash nearby.

They were exposed, but the real danger lay in the slippery footing. Even as this concern passed through Treadwell's mind again, he let out a shout. "Watch out! The mule!"

Treadwell grimaced as the pack animal ahead of him broke through the ice. The mule brayed its fear. With its feet plunging through the ice, the doomed mule opened a hole with jagged, icy edges that gutted it from neck to mid-belly. Loaded as it was, the animal had no chance to escape its fate.

Blood spilling over the shining ice, mule guts leaking onto the clean surface and into the freezing stream beneath, this spot showed what might happen to them all if they were not more careful. There was not a Navajo in the aptly named Cañon del Muerto who did not try to kill them.

"Get the pack off the poor beast," shouted Pfeiffer. "Do I have to tell you men everything?"

Two soldiers reluctantly set about rescuing what supplies they could from the back of the doomed animal. Treadwell grimaced again when he saw the mule was not dead—not completely. He rode over, leveled his rifle, and started to squeeze off a killing shot when Pfeiffer barked at him.

"Treadwell, stay your hand! Remember our predicament!"

He turned to the captain. He knew how low they ran on ammunition, thanks to Sena's ineptness. The mule also suffered. Treadwell's finger drew back and the mule gave one convulsive kick before dying.

"Mr. Treadwell, consider yourself on report for this."

"I don't let any animal suffer, Captain," Treadwell said,

matching Pfeiffer's tone. "And what are you going to do, put me in the stockade? Clap me in irons while we're on the trail?"

"There are the Enemy Navajo," the officer said. "They may not know this particular stretch of territory, but they are capable."

"The Enemy Navajo are good trackers, but they are walking on eggshells here, Captain, and you know it. If one of them fell into the hands of our friends yonder"—Treadwell indicated the high rims rising on either side of them—"they might last a week or more before they were allowed to die. I think you need my services. And I think the Dinéh Ana'aii agree." Treadwell did not bother pointing out that the Dinéh Ana'aii were traitors to their own people—and how could anyone truly trust such perfidy? The Dinéh Ana'aii might ride with the soldiers today. Where would their loyalty lie tomorrow?

Ahead rode three of the renegade Navajo. From their dour expressions, Treadwell knew he was right. Worse, so did Pfeiffer. The captain growled like a bee-stung grizzly and rode off without saying another word.

Treadwell skirted the spot where the mule had broken through the ice and rode on, his horse slipping and sliding over the icy surface. Alert for an ambush, Treadwell kept 100 yards in the vanguard. Too many days had passed without sighting a single Navajo, and now Pfeiffer had found a cañon filled to overflowing with them.

If only a few had chosen to surrender as had Herrera Grande, Treadwell might have ridden a mite easier. However, not a solitary Navajo had hailed them to surrender. The ones they found shot at them, pushed boulders off the tall cañon rims, and made life a dangerous hell.

"Ahead, Captain," called Treadwell. "I see one in a hollowed out snowdrift." Treadwell walked his horse over to where a squaw cowered. Her dark eyes blazed with hatred.

"We can give you food and a blanket," Treadwell said. He looked around for the Dinéh Ana'aii, but they had left the stream to scout the far cañon wall. The tall cliffs caused darkness to come quickly along the bottom of the cañon. Tenting in the open as they had the night before was a sure way to wake up with a slit throat.

The woman boiled from the snowy shelter and threw a rock at him. He ducked and his horse tried to shy. Treadwell drew back on the reins and quieted the horse.

He tried to make out what the woman yelled at him, but his command of Navajo curses was not good enough for him to decipher them all.

"Captain, you got yourself a spitfire here."

"Take her into custody," Pfeiffer ordered four troopers. "And watch your step. She might be dangerous."

"She's throwing rocks and sticks," Treadwell pointed out. But even as he spoke, he watched in a molasses-slow horror. The woman launched herself at the nearest trooper. The other three pointed their muskets at her, thinking this would deter the attack. Treadwell never knew which of the soldiers fired, nor did it matter.

The squaw jerked as a heavy slug ripped through her. Then she sank bonelessly to the snow.

Treadwell heard screaming, then realized the cries came from his own mouth. He slumped and stared at his saddle pommel when it became obvious the woman was dead, dead, dead.

"Corporal," Pfeiffer said angrily. "That was a waste of ordnance. You were told we are low on ammunition."

Treadwell stared at the tableau, then shook himself free as the captain dressed down the now-reduced-in-rank private. He slowly studied the surrounding terrain. His musket snapped to his shoulder, and he got off a shot an instant before the hidden warrior released his bowstring. Bullet and arrow crossed in the air; Treadwell's slug ripped through the warrior's chest, sending him backward to die in the snow. The arrow passed harmlessly over Pfeiffer's head. The captain hardly took notice.

"Ambush!" came the cry from farther back in the cañon. A ragged volley sounded, then died as a lieutenant got control of the men.

"Report!" bellowed Pfeiffer. "What's going on?"

"Two Navajo dead," came the quick reply from the company sergeant. "One Treadwell shot and another at the rear of the column."

"Curious," Pfeiffer said. "We ride for hours and never see one. Now we have three bodies to dispose of."

"Peach trees," spoke up one of the Dinéh Ana'aii who had returned from the head of the column. "An entire orchard there." He pointed down the cañon.

"Destroy the trees," Pfeiffer ordered. "Chop them to splinters. We are to leave nothing behind that gives aid or comfort to the enemy."

Treadwell stayed with the column as they made their way down the frozen stream to the edge of the peach orchard. Unlike white settlers, the Navajo cultivating these trees made no effort to place them in neat, straight rows. Scattered about, the trees not only provided fruit in season but gave a windbreak for strong gusts from the north and lent a certain beauty to an already gorgeous setting. Treadwell thought it would be right pleasant sitting under a tree in the summer sun, munching a peach and watching the leaves flutter as the stream passed by within a few yards.

His reverie died amid a flurry of arrows.

"In the orchard. A dozen or more braves. Take cover!" came Pfeiffer's order. Treadwell didn't need the urging to dismount and sink behind a large boulder. An arrow ricocheted off a rock inches above his head, feathered end flashing in the late-day sunlight. He worked to reload his musket, then bided his time. He waited for a single rifle report from the orchard, signaling the Indians had more firepower than they'd originally revealed.

"Captain, don't think of doing it," warned Treadwell, seeing that Pfeiffer was preparing for an all-out assault. To rush blindly into the clearing in front of the orchard spelled death—for the soldiers making the assault.

"We cannot let them keep their position," protested the captain. "I will not let them!"

"Look to the rim," urged Treadwell. Tiny black dots seeming more like crows than humans lined both edges. A hundred Navajo arrayed themselves above their heads.

"We're too exposed," Pfeiffer decided quickly. "We need to get away from the center of the cañon and find shelter along one wall."

"There are dwellings left by the Old Ones," a Dinéh Ana'aii said, crouching beside Pfeiffer.

"Dwellings?"

"In the face of the cliff," Treadwell said, craning his neck around. "Somebody's built a house into the mountainside. Never seen its like before, though I heard of similar dwellings in the oxbows along the Upper Colorado."

Pfeiffer sent orders to organize an orderly retreat. Slowly withdrawing, keeping the Navajo warriors pinned inside their orchard with methodical rifle fire, the troopers reached the cliff dwellings.

"Sergeant, post sentries," Pfeiffer ordered. "We camp here for the night. We move out at first light." He glared at the orchard across the cañon. Treadwell knew what thoughts tormented the officer. An entire orchard might supply hundreds of Navajo all summer long.

Still, their mission was to capture Navajo Indians as well as to destroy their supplies. Treadwell found a dusty corner in an old rock-fronted room and curled up. He was asleep before the last of the gunfire died.

"The orchard," complained Captain Pfeiffer. "We should have fought harder to burn it."

"There's no telling how many braves we were facing," Treadwell pointed out. "We haven't done so badly. We've collected a dozen prisoners since we left the orchard."

"A dozen is only a handful compared to all those we saw atop the mesa." Pfeiffer craned his neck to look above. The day before they had seen hundreds of Navajo there. Now only gray-cloud-heavy sky showed. A new storm brewed.

"You're carrying out the colonel's orders," Treadwell said. He had no stomach for killing old women, and he tired of having arrows shot at him from ambush only to find no one there when they stormed the position. The orchard had been an obvious spot to attack, had they more ammunition and troopers. Without the support, Pfeiffer had followed the sane path letting the trees go untouched.

"We need more prisoners." Pfeiffer pulled up the collar of his uniform jacket as the storm began howling in earnest. He kept the column moving, even after the snowstorm turned into a blizzard. Treadwell tried to scout but dared not get too far in advance of the column. He did not want to become separated. In this section of the Cañon del Muerto lay dozens of confusing branches.

Even the Dinéh Ana'aii seemed unsettled by the terrain and held back, refusing to leave Pfeiffer's side at the head of the column.

"This way," Treadwell reported. "We might get out of the cañon in this direction, even if we have to camp for another night to weather the storm."

Pfeiffer grumbled constantly but again showed his good sense as a commander. Although it was only early afternoon and they had traveled fewer than ten miles that day, he called a halt. The company pitched tents and settled in for the duration of the gale.

"How many sentries you want posted, Captain?" asked the company sergeant.

"Better consider several," spoke up Treadwell. He pointed to dark figures plowing through the thick curtains of snow. Four dark figures became six and ten and then twenty.

Pfeiffer's hand flashed to his sidearm, then dropped away when it became apparent the approaching Navajo had come to surrender.

"The expedition might be a success yet, Captain," said Treadwell. With the thirty new prisoners, Pfeiffer rejoined Carson's main force late the next afternoon boasting of forty-two captured.

That would have been exceptional, except that Carson had accepted the capitulation of more than 200.

Starvation and storm had surpassed force of arms in breaking Navajo resistance.

The Long Walk Begins

January 26, 1864
Fort Canby

Two Dinéh Ana'aii crouched beside the fire as Hastiin Biighaanii spoke eloquently of his plight. Joseph Treadwell followed much of what was said, and it gave him no pleasure to
hear of the headman's burden. Many in his clan had starved,
and none was well.

Treadwell had learned nothing of Gray Feather or Goes to
War. Those flocking to Fort Canby after Carson's winter campaign through the center of Cañon de Chelly were barely able
to stumble along in the cold. Their senses were befuddled and
none could even speak of where Manuelito might have gone
after leaving the camp Treadwell had found.

The camp where his son's bones lay in a grave.

"He's offering to bring in a passel of Navajo," Treadwell
translated quietly for Captain Carey.

"Herrera Grande and Soldado Surdo promised even more,"
Carey said uneasily. "We might find ourselves overrun in short
order. We have no facilities for so many."

"Reckon no one thought the Navajo would cave in so fast,"
Treadwell said. He had been out in the freezing winds and blind-
ing snow. Even if the Navajo had stored adequate supplies during the growing season, this would have been a harsh winter

for anyone to endure in Cañon de Chelly. That Carson had destroyed everything turned their plight from serious to hopeless.

"Things are at a fine point if even Sena can find over three hundred Navajo willing to surrender to him."

"That many?" Treadwell's eyebrows rose. He stamped his feet to keep the circulation flowing. "You might be right about developing real problems. The fort's not equipped to handle five or six hundred prisoners."

"Emigrés," Carey said. "That's what General Carleton has taken to calling them."

"They're not fleeing any political trouble," Treadwell said in disgust. "They're running to whoever can feed 'em."

"The supply train has yet to arrive," Carey worried. "And the colonel is preparing to leave later this afternoon."

"So the general granted him leave?" Treadwell was not surprised at this concession from Santa Fé. Carson's expedition had been required to bring in a hundred prisoners for eventual relocation to Bosque Redondo. Six times that now camped outside the fort with the promise of even more to arrive when Herrera Grande and Hastiin Biighaanii delivered their clansmen.

"For six weeks. I'll be in charge of the fort," Carey said. "I had not anticipated such difficulties." The captain chewed his lower lip as he scanned the rows of wagons, the stables where the mules and horses were quartered, and the more distant infirmary. "We have scant medical supplies and not one Navajo lacks a wound or disease sorely in need of attention."

"A full belly would go a ways in all their cases. You got the food?"

Carey did not answer, but Treadwell read the answer in the young officer's increasingly worried expression. Getting needed munitions from Santa Fé had been difficult, even in the middle of the recent campaign into Cañon de Chelly. Convincing the quartermaster of the need to feed former adversaries might prove impossible.

"Confab is over," Treadwell saw. Colonel Carson shook

hands with Hastiin Biighaanii, much to the headman's confusion. The headman pulled his hand back and stared at it as if he might be marked for life. Then he turned silently and left with two warriors trailing closely. The Dinéh Ana'aii spoke a few minutes longer with Carson, then left for their quarters behind the officers' barracks.

Carson strode over. Carey saluted smartly.

"Captain Carey, I'm handin' over Fort Canby to your command. I'll be back at the end of my leave."

"Off to Taos and the family?" asked Treadwell.

"Yes, Mr. Treadwell, finally." Carson smiled brightly, happy at the prospect of being with his family again. Somehow, the colonel's joy caused a huge void to form in Treadwell's gut. No leave would grant him time with his wife and son. He did not even know if they still lived, and that uncertainty burned as harshly as any doubt could at his mind.

"I'll take two hundred and forty of the captives to Los Pinos and leave them there for later transfer to Bosque Redondo."

"Are you sure you have enough supplies for them?" asked Carey.

"Barely. I'd be willin' to take more, 'cept there's not enough wagons to transport the sick and wounded. From there I'll report direct to General Carleton."

"He'll be pleased with your success, sir," said Carey.

"I'm sure he will, I'm sure he will." Carson saluted, did an about-face, then marched off to where the troopers accompanying him to Los Pinos formed their captives into a ragged line.

Treadwell watched as they left the fort, wondering what lay before them and all the other Navajo flowing toward Fort Canby. He shook off the idle speculation and went to mingle with those remaining in the camp, inquiring after Manuelito—and his family.

Capitulation

January 30, 1864
Fort Wingate

The day stretched forever. Blue skies with only a few white feathery ice clouds caused Delgadito to shield his eyes from the glare. Sun beat down and turned the land almost warm—almost. The chill running down his spine had little to do with the foot of snow he'd trudged through or the lack of decent moccasins on his feet. He tried to remember when these had worn out and could not. There had been so many more important matters to tend over the past months.

He walked unbowed, but inside, Delgadito knew only defeat. Face impassive, he slowly turned to see the line of his people stretching behind him. And ahead, across the fresh fall of glistening, pristine snow, outlined against the brightness and looking so solid, stood Fort Wingate. The gates were closed, as if this might hold out the cold and the depredations of the Dinéh.

It held back neither, and Delgadito knew it as surely as he knew it no longer mattered. Neither the fort nor its timorous soldiers inside had defeated him. The cold had. The cold and Christopher Carson.

"Do we camp here?" asked Oso Negro, hobbling badly. Most of his left foot was missing, causing some to call him Little Foot. "We are tired, and many of the women cannot go on."

Oso Negro coughed and spat. Dark blood stained the white snow.

Delgadito knew that Oso Negro could hardly continue. Turning, the headman studied the 680 Dinéh behind him. Once he had led war parties into battle. Now he led entire clans into slavery.

"We have no need to go farther. They know we are here." Delgadito pointed, using his finger to show contempt, hoping lightning would jump from his digit to the enemy. From the slowly opening gates rode an officer trailing a squad of cavalry troopers. They rode in a ragged line, their horses slipping on patches of ice. Delgadito felt only disgust at this acknowledgment of all he had done.

Surrendering in November had been difficult for him, but so many of his clan were ill that he had no choice. Death in Tseyi' or slaughter by Red Clothes and his men ranging through the cañon were his options to giving in to Carleton's demands. Delgadito did not like or trust Carleton and his fiery-eyed declarations, but where else lay any choice?

Death or slavery. Delgadito closed his eyes and took a deep breath. The land around Fort Wingate was different, sloping, with junipers and cedar and piñons everywhere. It reminded Delgadito of Tseyi'.

"What will it be like?" he muttered, knowing his brief stay at Hwééldi gave him a clouded view of his people's future.

"With Manuelito?" Oso Negro coughed again and sank to the ground, no longer able to stand. "He will fight until he dies. The Biligáana have promised food and peace."

Delgadito's face turned impassive as he heard such a fiery warrior speak of peace. He was an old man and entitled to think of peace where children might be raised without fear of starvation or death from exposure to the elements. Oso Negro had once been the clan's most outspoken against the Biligáana.

The lieutenant rode up and gave Delgadito a sloppy salute. "I see you've brought all your clan in. Good."

"More than just my clan travel with us," Delgadito said.

"Some preceded us by days. Colonel Carson accepted their surrender at Fort Canby."

"We heard all about that," the young officer said, slapping his gloved hand against his thigh to keep it warm. Delgadito eyed the glove and wondered if his own frostbitten fingers would ever again be warm. A hand-trembler had failed to cure the numbness. A Red Ant Sing would not be possible for some time. Did the Biligáana have medicines to prevent the flesh from falling off bone?

"We are hungry. Food was promised when we surrendered. And clothing, blankets, protection from the winter."

"We don't have any way to put you up in the fort," the officer said. "You folks stay right out here, and we'll get what supplies we can out to you." He rode back and forth for a moment, eyeing the long line of staggering, destitute, mostly naked Dinéh. "No weapons. You can't even carry your knives. Those are the orders I got to enforce."

"We need our knives to eat with," protested Oso Negro, showing a bit of his old fire. "We have already abandoned our muskets and bows and arrows."

"My men are ordered to shoot to kill at the first sign of weapons," the lieutenant said nervously. "I'm holding you responsible, old man."

Delgadito stiffened at this impertinence but did not reply. They were like the gah, the rabbit running here and there aimlessly. They knew no better, the Biligáana. It did not make his surrender any easier, knowing he had been bested by men who acted like small children.

"We need shelter. A new storm comes in from the west," Oso Negro said, shoving himself to his good foot and leaning heavily on a wooden crutch. "Before sundown there will be more snow." He turned and almost fell. Delgadito saw what troubled Oso Negro, and it bothered him, also. The sky darkened ominously. They had been lucky in their travel from Tseyi', missing the worst storms.

"I already said we'll do what we can. Blankets and maybe

tents. Colonel Carson gave orders to treat you good on your trip to Bosque Redondo," the officer said.

"Where is Red Clothes?" asked Delgadito. "I would speak to him."

"He's gone back to Santa Fé, or maybe Taos. The Injuns who surrendered to him at Fort Canby are camped at Los Pinos. We'll form up a caravan real quick and get you out of here. We got business to tend to, important business." Without another word, the lieutenant barked an order to his sergeant and trotted back to the fort. The sergeant fanned out the squad to form a skirmish line between Fort Wingate's gates and Delgadito's band.

The promised blankets and tents were never delivered. A few bags of flour and beans were dropped from the back of a wagon that quickly returned to Fort Wingate. That night the storm struck, raging for three days and dropping another foot of snow.

"What are we to do with their white dust?" Oso Negro asked, running his hand through the flour in the sack. "It is not corn. One soldier laughed and said it was wheat. It tastes terrible." The warrior dipped his finger in it and sampled. "The beans are worst of all. They give me the runs." Oso Negro shook his head sadly.

Delgadito replied. "Perhaps we have found why the Biligáana are so nervous. They eat the dark beans and must relieve themselves constantly."

Oso Negro laughed as he kicked at the bag of coffee beans. They did not cook up well and tasted worse.

"We need more than this." Oso Negro's humor turned to bleakness again. Delgadito understood the reason.

The old headman saw the snow kicked up by the approaching column of Dinéh. Zarcillos Largos's son, Soldado Surdo, brought in more. Delgadito sighed as he remembered his old friend Zarcillos Largos. They had joined Manuelito attacking

Fort Defiance. A thousand strong they had been then, and the fort had fallen.

Zarcillos Largos had emerged unscratched from the fight, only to die shortly after. Delgadito's chin firmed, and he fell into an impassive stare as his old friend's son brought in the newly defeated. Zarcillos Largos, also known as Becomes Chief Again, had gone to the Hopi with open hand and knife in sheath. Zuñi and Nakai marauders had found him on the trail near Oak Springs and fired at him. Delgadito remembered as if it were only yesterday when Zarcillos Largos, a man who shared Delgadito's passion for peace, had died behind his fallen horse, cut from under him by a fusillade of bullets. He killed four attackers before running out of ammunition and dying.

Such was the fate of those who sought only peace, Delgadito thought. His belly grumbled as he rose to greet Soldado Surdo, now headman of the Water's Edge People and doomed to lead his clan into captivity at Hwééldi.

The worst part for Delgadito lay in knowing the more than 1200 Dinéh cowering in the fresh snow outside the gates of Fort Wingate were only the first. So many more would come—or die.

Many Foes

"They pass below us soon. Then we strike," Manuelito said softly. His sharp eyes studied the path far below meandering along the bottom of the deep cañon. Shining Eyes moved closer to the verge so he could lend his strength pushing the rocks down on the unsuspecting Biligáana soldiers. They were so busy plundering the hogan they had forgotten to look above them. The walls of the cañon were steep, but evidence of recent passage ought to have alerted the troopers. Neither Manuelito nor Shining Eyes had taken the time to hide their trail.

"They are putting the torch to Stands Alone's hogan," whispered Shining Eyes in a tone matching Manuelito's, knowing how voices carried on the stillness. The last storm had left the ground covered with a thin sheet of ice and the air crystal clear and pure. Every breath he took drove a new knife into his throat and lungs, but triumph—at last, triumph!—burned fiercely in him. The soldiers had dogged their steps for more than a week. Now it was time to show them Manuelito's band had teeth and could use them.

"Stands Alone died there months ago," Manuelito said, nodding. "We should let them get ghost sickness."

"That takes too long," Shining Eyes insisted. He shivered.

The Moving Up Way chant had rid him of Follows Quickly's ghost, but it had been two long weeks before Manuelito had found a singer capable of performing the ceremony for him. So many of their singers had been killed or driven away. Shining Eyes closed his eyes and swallowed hard. Many had gone with Delgadito and Soldado Surdo to Fort Wingate, thinking their services could be put to better use there than in Dinetah. So many dead. Shining Eyes closed his eyes and saw Looking Arrow's mother die, and with her Looking Arrow's younger brother, cloaked in Shining Eyes's blanket. They had abandoned that hogan leaving behind many of their belongings to prevent ghost sickness. Even Goes to War's doll and Gray Feather's utensils had been left.

Such was the power of a wandering *chindi* to make them leave valuable blankets in the pit of winter.

"They will need the Evil Way chants," he muttered.

"What did you say?" Manuelito turned and put his shoulder to the large rock they had chosen.

"Nothing," Shining Eyes said, adding his strength to that of his father. With legs and arms almost devoid of muscle, the boy found it difficult to move the rock—but it did move, as if through sheer willpower on his part. He and Manuelito got it rolling and stepped back, watching as the large rock tumbled over the rim of the cañon and hurled downward amid a shower of snow, ice, and loose rock.

"Let's see how they catch this ball," Shining Eyes said with a cruel smile on his lips. Many times he had seen soldiers hitting at a cotton-stuffed leather ball with a stick and laughing, no matter if they struck it or missed. He did not understand the game, though it seemed similar to one played by young Dinéh children using sticks and stones. Shining Eyes preferred the intricate webs of string moved from one person's fingers to another's, always shifting into new and more complex patterns.

"I think they will catch it," Manuelito answered.

Shouts of fear rose from the hogan an instant before it was crushed under the small avalanche. Shining Eyes waited for a minute to be sure no one had been left alive in the hogan. Four shouting cavalry soldiers rode hard from the mouth of the cañon, but they were too late to help their comrades. Shining Eyes felt little jubilation at this victory. What was one death or a handful when the Biligáana replaced each dead soldier with a dozen more?

"Hurry, Angry Knife," urged Manuelito. "We must leave them behind, for they will follow us as surely as the sun rises in the east."

Shining Eyes knew the truth in this. Fearful though the soldiers would be, they would trail them until they lost the spoor or one side was eradicated completely. So it had been for long months, so many hungry mouths that Shining Eyes could no longer remember a life without bluecoats shooting at him.

"What of the others we saw?" Shining Eyes asked.

"The Zuñi war party moved south. We do not need fear them, but the others . . ." Manuelito's voice trailed off and his eyes glazed over in thought. Shining Eyes had seen this more and more of late. The headman drowned himself in the misery of his people and worried too much that they stood alone against their enemies.

The Zuñi and the Hopi sought them with rapacious glee, but they were not the worst. The bluecoats under Red Clothes might be—or the Nakai. Since Carson had begun destroying everything in his path, the Mexicans had ridden into Dinetah looking for stragglers, be they women or children, to take as slaves.

Shining Eyes's hand tightened around his knife hilt. Just after a fierce January storm, he had caught one small band of Nakai slavers with two small babies. He and another warrior—the name vanished in the fog clouding his mind—had followed for more than a day until the slavers had rested, thinking they were safe. Shining Eyes had slit one's throat as he'd slept. The other warrior had died valiantly, killing two of the slavers. By shouting crazily and acting as if all the Dinéh rode at his shoulder, Shining Eyes had chased off the two surviving Nakai.

He had taken the two babies back to Tseyi' for protection.

One died before reaching the towering red cliffs in the middle of Dinetah. Shining Eyes sighed deeply. The other had been taken to Fort Wingate with a small group of the Red-Streaked Earth People. As far as he was concerned, this young girl had died, also.

Hwééldi. Bosque Redondo. Fort Sumner. He cursed all the names for the same cattle pen. Manuelito had told him repeatedly that the Dinéh would die if they should ever dwell east of the Rio Grande. Shining Eyes didn't know where Hwééldi lay, but it was far to the east, among the treacherous Comanche and Apache.

"Angry Knife," Manuelito said, nudging him. "See?"

"A trail," Shining Eyes said, frowning as he dropped to one knee to study the spoor. The moccasin prints led away, but they were alone and the bluecoats fought to get up the steep cliff face to chase them. "Whose footprints?"

"Ute," Manuelito said, spitting.

Shining Eyes paused a moment, reflecting on his own heritage. Then he spat, too. The Pueblo tribes fought and ran away rather than face real challenge in battle. The Ute were more tenacious and fought like Dinéh. Worse, they took slaves.

"We must not let them roam freely," Shining Eyes said. He tugged at the blanket Looking Arrow had made for him to keep it around his shoulders. His thin arms were hardly more than bone, and he knew he did not look the part of a fierce warrior ready to die defending his land. But he was. He had proved himself too many times to back away from this trial.

"We must choose our fight carefully. Perhaps the soldiers are the better enemy this day," said Manuelito. "Perhaps it is best to ignore both and return to our hogan for rest. We have a little food." He patted the sack slung across his back. Manuelito had stolen provisions from a cavalry patrol, not much, but enough to feed Gray Feather, Goes to War, and Looking Arrow for a while longer.

"I am tired," Shining Eyes admitted, "but there are enemies to slay. We must—"

"We must live to fight another day," Manuelito insisted. "Here, take this and go to your mother, brother, and Looking Arrow." The headman split what he had in the pack in half and gave one section to Shining Eyes. "I must attend to Juanita. She is ill, also."

Shining Eyes blinked, realizing how Manuelito's concern was split in dozens of directions. He had a family before Gray Feather was captured, and the rest of his clan needed help, also. The winter had been brutal and fraught with starvation. Manuelito felt it greatly.

"When will you come to Gray Feather?" he asked.

"When I can. There is so much to do," Manuelito said.

"Are you going to surrender, as Delgadito has done? As Barboncito and the others have done?"

Manuelito paused, his face impassive. Shining Eyes saw the turmoil in the man's dark eyes, but no hint of what he thought surfaced.

"You cannot," Shining Eyes said angrily. "We would be slaves and nothing more. They cart our people off to Hwééldi and hold them among enemies."

"The Comanche and Apache mistreat them," Manuelito said carefully. "There have been reports from those who stayed for a while and then fled back to Dinetah."

Shining Eyes had not heard of these defectors from Hwééldi. He stayed silent to hear what Manuelito would reveal.

"Their lifeway is different along the Pecos at the foot of Fort Sumner, not of the Dinéh, not wreathed in beauty," Manuelito said. He lifted his eyes and stared into the distance, seeing nothing.

"You must not surrender. You are the leader of the Dinéh and all look to you for guidance." Shining Eyes saw this argument had no effect. "How will our children live? You say the lifeway is different at Hwééldi. Will Goes to War ever walk in beauty? Will any of the children?"

Manuelito's eyes snapped into focus and he laughed harshly. "You worry about the children? You, who are only twelve summers?" Manuelito shook his head sadly. "The fifth world is not for the Dinéh any longer, but where can we go? Do we leave our holy lands? To move east of the Rio Grande and lose all that has been given us by Changing Woman and the Hero Twins? Are the Monsters again walking amongst us?" Manuelito put his hand on Shining Eyes's shoulder and squeezed gently.

"I will not surrender," Manuelito said solemnly.

"Nor will I," Shining Eyes said loudly, his heart pounding. He clutched the small bundle of food intended for Gray Feather, Goes to War, and Looking Arrow and rushed away as determination burned hotly in his breast. He would follow Manuelito anywhere. Anywhere but to Hwééldi and slavery.

The Long Walk

Asa Carey pulled his cape closer to his body as the ripening storm chewed at him. His gaze fell on the pitiful Navajo assembled outside the entrance of the fort. Too few had adequate clothing. This bothered him greatly, but he knew staying at Fort Canby was no solution to their problems. Supplies ran perilously low because Santa Fé had refused to send support adequate to the task of feeding not only soldiers but those Navajo who surrendered in increasing numbers. Colonel Carson had been too successful, if the Dinéh Ana'aii were to be believed. Reports from the Enemy Navajo told Carey droves more approached Fort Canby, fleeing the cold and hunger of their red rock fortress.

Delgadito, Herrera Grande, and the other headmen had slowly come to the realization that they would not be slaughtered if they surrendered. This opened the floodgates of emigration to the promised fertile farmlands along the distant Pecos River.

Whatever their reason for coming to Fort Canby, the storm brewing promised even more suffering unless Asa Carey reduced the burden on his fort quickly by transferring large numbers of them to Bosque Redondo.

"Captain Berney," Carey called to the officer inspecting the mounted troopers. "Are you ready to move out?"

"Reckon so," Joseph Berney said, sauntering over, his horse following like an obedient dog. The cold seemed not to bother Berney one whit. His cheeks were rosy and his eyes clear and sharp. He tugged on his gloves and glanced in the direction of the fifty troopers preparing the Navajo for transport.

"I wish I could send more with you," Carey said. "There's no supplies, leastwise, no supplies to spare."

"They have enough to reach Fort Wingate," Berney assured Carey. "A pound of beef, a pound of flour, coffee beans for every last soul among them. What more could they want?"

"It's more than they've lived on over the past few months," Carey agreed. "Best get a'moving. The storm will freeze your feet to the ground if you linger much longer."

"True," Berney said. "With your permission, I'll get all hundred and sixty-five of them on the road." Berney waited for Carey to check the transit orders, verifying the numbers already exchanged verbally. Carey signed at the bottom of the sheet and handed the other captain the thick sheaf of papers. Berney tucked them into his jacket, smiled, and gave the post commander a quick, jaunty salute.

"We're off to Fort Wingate, Los Pinos, and then Bosque Redondo!"

Carey watched his fellow officer mount and move the column from the fort, glanced at the leaden sky dotted with white fluttering snowflakes, turned up his collar, and then headed for his office. He had work to do.

He had almost a thousand remaining Navajo to feed and shelter against a new storm.

"Another mile before we pitch camp," ordered Berney.

"Captain, them Injuns ain't keepin' up so good. They're falling behind. We cain't jist up and leave 'em along the trail."

"We'll never arrive at Fort Wingate if we maintain this snail's pace," Berney said peevishly. He pulled out his pocket watch, flipped open the case, and studied the face a few seconds. If he had not been burdened with so many civilians he could have pressed on for another hour. More.

"There's a stand of trees yonder, Captain," pointed out his sergeant. "We can take shelter there. We're sore in need of rest."

"Very well."

"You want me to post guards?"

Berney laughed. "Why bother? They come with us of their own accord. If they wish to leave, let them. They know in their hearts we shall civilize them and turn them into productive citizens once they arrive at Bosque Redondo."

"We had reports of a small band of men moving parallel to our track. I thought—"

"Don't hurt yourself too much trying to think, Sergeant Kincaid," Berney said in a joking fashion. "Take the chance to rest up. We have hard travel in front of us if we are to reach Fort Wingate speedily."

"Yes, sir. As you say." The sergeant rode off with the orders. Berney wiped the snow from his face and wondered if it would ever be spring again. Then he rode toward the refuge promised by the junipers, whistling "Tenting on the Old Camp Ground" as he rode. It was good to have his own command and to be away from that meddlesome Asa Carey.

That night four of the Navajo froze to death.

"You are sure you can continue, Captain Berney?" asked the commander of Fort Wingate.

"Major, I shall have no more trouble escorting fourteen hundred to Bosque Redondo than I had getting the one hundred sixty-one here from Fort Canby."

The officer glanced at the papers Berney had given him. "You're four shy, according to this manifest."

"The night was colder than anticipated, and blankets were in short supply," Berney said airily. "It is inescapable that a few might die. Their condition is perilous at best."

"I can see that, Captain. However, there is another aspect of the next leg of your journey you might not be aware of."

"Sir?" Berney's keen eyes fixed on the major. The man averted his eyes.

"Half your troopers must return to Fort Canby. There is growing need for them to aid in the emigration."

"I'm to oversee almost fifteen hundred savages with only twenty-five men?"

"Captain, I am sure you will perform your duty honorably and well." With this the major dismissed Berney.

Muttering to himself, Berney found his sergeant working to get his gear in order for the longer leg of their trip. Sergeant Kincaid shot to his feet.

"As you were, Sergeant," Berney said. He quickly outlined their orders. "I will not tolerate a force of fifteen hundred traveling armed whilst we can count on only twenty-five troopers with old-style muskets. Before we leave, disarm all the Navajo."

"They won't go along with that, not for 'ary a second, sir."

"Their chiefs do a fine job instilling respect in them. Have them say something about getting their weapons back when we arrive at Bosque Redondo. I will *not* permit so many armed antagonists around me on this pilgrimage. And be sure they have adequate food. I don't trust the post commander. He has the look of a man willing to keep some of the supplies to sell on the black market."

"Yes, sir," Sergeant Kincaid. "We can be on the trail within an hour."

Joseph Berney clucked his tongue and began to feel good about the trip again. With a proper disposition of the Navajo at Bosque Redondo, he might wrangle a promotion to General Carleton's personal staff.

* * *

"You poison us!" cried a Navajo woman. Berney stared at her in disbelief.

"Whatever are you doing, woman? You're *eating* the coffee beans! You boil them, then drink the liquid. Coffee! Have you never heard of coffee?"

"Sir," cut in Sergeant Kincaid. "I tried to tell you they don't ken too much of how to eat the food they—"

"They don't know how to eat? Balderdash!" Berney was outraged. They were five days out of Los Pinos and still had not reached Albuquerque and Tijeras Cañon. It might take two weeks of travel to get to the Pecos if they maintained this slow pace.

"Our food's different from theirs. I had some of the boys show 'em how to use the flour. They've taken to making a paste of it, then cooking it in their fires. And not many of them have taken to the bacon. They eat beef and mutton, they say."

"They'll eat what they are given, the ingrates! My own men are not as well provisioned!"

"Our men are used to the food, sir. We don't get the dysentery the way they seem to. Makes 'em weak and puts a terrible strain on keepin' up with the column."

"The Lords of New Mexico," scoffed Berney. "They do this to make me look bad in General Carleton's eyes. How dare they! I must keep to the schedule. The general expects nothing less of me." Berney stamped about, splashing freezing mud as he moved. He spun away from his sergeant and glared southeast, in the direction of the distant Manzano Mountains. The peaks seemed close in the cold, sharp air, but he knew they were two days distant. It was not fair to be burdened with such shirkers. They had started with only fifteen days of supplies, calculated for the barest rations each day. Stretching those stores would be impossible.

There had to be some way of changing the equation. More supplies? Impossible. That left the need for fewer Navajo.

Sergeant Kincaid shrugged off his commander's wrath. He

had seen it before many times when events did not turn out exactly the way Berney anticipated.

"They are doing better with the food, sir," Kincaid said, "but we lost another two last night."

"Disease? They are a poxy lot."

"Frozen, the pair of them. We need more blankets. Some are walking along these roads barefoot. Bloody stumps slow their pace."

"Have them ride in the wagons, then. Do I have to tell you every detail?"

"Sir, the wagons are broken down, overcrowded the five of 'em. 'Less we get rid of supplies, there's no way the mules can pull with a heavier load."

Berney clasped his hands behind his back and began pacing. His mind raced to find a solution. He saw no easy course ahead.

"Did any more catch up with the caravan?"

Sergeant Kincaid shook his head. He did not know if more Navajo had joined them.

"We might have lost a few, but we have gained more. That will look good in the report," Berney said. He smiled broadly, almost happy at the idea of arriving with more Navajo than he had left Los Pinos with. "We might not even have to report any deaths en route. This will provide good training for the Indians, this forced march. Good, good. Carry on, Sergeant."

"Sir." Kincaid saluted and hurried off. He had too much to oversee and so little time before they moved out at first light.

That night the Mexican slavers who had followed them from Fort Wingate kidnapped three young boys.

"Fort Sumner," sighed Captain Berney, stretching tall in the saddle. "At last."

"Where shall I have them camp, sir?" asked Kincaid. "And what of the, uh, the ones who died last night?"

"Damned shame, getting so close to Bosque Redondo and then dying like that." Berney had lost twelve to disease and the biting New Mexico winter, while another three had been spirited away by bold slavers. It had been difficult not giving in to the Navajo demand for the return of their weapons, but he had parleyed long with the headmen and convinced them the slavers would not trouble them further.

With only twenty-five troopers, Berney had played a daring hand and won. The slavers had been content with their paltry prizes. And now they had reached Bosque Redondo. He was happy with his success, even if he had been forced to leave some behind to ensure the survival of the rest.

"Assemble them on yonder flats," Berney ordered. "They are trained well enough in the ways of issuing rations. Let us dispense what we have left to them as soon as they are seated and quiet."

"It's little enough we have remainin', sir. Even the headmen are complainin'."

Berney had given the headmen their rations first, counting on them to make their fine speeches how they were walking to the Promised Lands along the Pecos. Interpreters had assured him the headmen were telling their people that fighting the white man was futile and that their only salvation lay in the new reservation.

"Captain Berney?" A tall, well-built officer riding from Fort Sumner reined back a few yards distant.

"Sir!" Berney snapped to attention as the major dismounted and walked over. "I am to turn my charges over to Major Wallen. Are you he?"

"I'm Henry Wallen. You are a few days late in arrival. We had expected you earlier."

"There were some small problems along the trail," Berney said, considering how to shape his report. Honesty would be the best, he quickly decided. Major Wallen had the look of a man used to ferreting out the truth, no matter what dirt he might kick high getting to it. "Slavers stole away three boys, and ten died of the elements. Further, two walked away soon after we left a camp last night along the Rio Pecos."

Wallen heaved a sigh. "This will be a significant addition to those already here."

"More follow, sir," Berney said, hoping he would be promoted away from being a shepherd to another flock of poxy Indians. "In truth, we added fourteen from our initial number, joining up as we marched."

"You seem to have them well in hand."

"They sit quietly until we dispense their rations. We always give the headmen an extra sheep or sugar, to keep them firmly on our side. It has worked well enough on the journey."

"When they are fed, we'll get them situated in houses along the *acequia* we are building," Wallen said.

"It will be good for them to reunite with brothers and sisters. A touching sight it will be, Major. I am sure joyful tears will flow as they find mothers and fathers among those already present."

Wallen grunted. Berney hesitated, then made his final request.

"Sir, may I address them one last time?"

This took Wallen by surprise. He silently acknowledged Captain Berney's right.

Berney cleared his throat and stepped forward. He spoke in a loud, clear voice.

"Headmen, leaders of your people, I salute you for your deportment these past trying weeks. Your lives now change for the better. No longer do you have to starve and be killed for naught. Your white father will teach you to farm these lands. If you do as directed, you will become a good and prosperous people."

Berney snapped a salute in the direction of the gathered Navajo, executed an about-face, and marched off, satisfied that he had done his job well and had served not only his own people but the Navajo as well.

Enemies

March 1864
Bosque Redondo

"This is the greatest humanitarian effort of our time," James Carleton declared. He put his hands on his hips, then sucked in a deep breath of the cold air as he looked around appreciatively. "I envision another City Upon the Hill, as the Pilgrims established so long ago, to serve as a shining example for all Indians." Carleton began walking and the men with him hastened to follow, not sure where the military commander headed.

"There are real problems with your vision, General," spoke up Michael Steck, refusing to acknowledge Carleton's dream. The new Superintendent of Indian Affairs looked to Kit Carson for support. The small mountain man shifted uneasily, not wanting to get embroiled in the argument.

"There ain't—isn't enough food to go 'round, General," Carson said carefully. "I think that's what Doctor Steck is commentin' on. We can always use more food and supplies."

"The winter is about gone from the land," Carleton said, lengthening his stride and forcing the others to run to keep up. "The *acequias* will run deep with pure water diverted from the Pecos and make these lands blossom. The Navajo will have food, God willing, and with our help, find their way to true civilization."

"You can't do this, Carleton," Steck said, at the end of his patience with the general's vision of utopia for the Navajo. "They're prisoners of war and *must* be treated as such. I am ordering Agent Labadie to refuse to have anything more to do with them. No more supplies, no more money to support them. They are wards of the War Department, not the Interior."

"Doctor Steck," Carleton said coldly, "you neither share my view of how to deal with the Navajo nor have one grain of common sense. They are happy here, away from the war. They are fed sufficiently well, they—"

"Begging your pardon, General," cut in Carson, "but they ain't got enough food. The Mescalero steal it. Without horses, without weapons, the Navajo have nothing to protect themselves with."

"Give them horses and they run off," scoffed Carleton. "And weapons? That captain—what was his name?"

"Berney," supplied Steck. He almost spat the name.

"Yes, Captain Berney. A fine officer and a true gentleman. He knows his duty and does it without shirking. He realized how difficult the journey here would have been should they retain their weapons."

"We cain't defend them from the Apache," Carson said, his legs pumping to match Carleton's longer pace. "The two tribes are eternal enemies."

"We need to convince them to adopt our ways and live in harmony with the land and with each other." Carleton didn't listen; he was too lost in his vision of what might be.

"They did a fine job in Cañon de Chelly, until Carson destroyed their flocks and farms," Steck said.

Carson drew back, even less willing to get involved in the battle between the two men. He had been feeling anxious and poorly at the same time, ever since his leave had ended. Some anxiety plagued him because Josefa was due to deliver a new member of the family any day now. Beyond that, he never quite regained his full strength. Long rides wore him to a frazzle and even sitting at a desk exhausted him unduly.

And now this feud between the general and Doctor Steck.

"As much as I admire General Canby and his notions," Carson said, carefully picking his words, "General Carleton's right. It'd be a grave mistake to let the Navajo stay on their land. Here on the reservation, well, there ain't any better place for 'em."

"The Interior Department has no money to feed both the Apache and the Navajo," Steck said, anger rising. "As you say, I favor General Canby's plan to allow the Navajo to remain on their land, on a new reservation along the Gray Colorado. We would not need to—"

"Doctor Steck," Carleton said, paying no attention to the superintendent, "you must accede to an expert's advice. Colonel Carson has lent his good name and efforts to making the dream of Bosque Redondo a reality."

"They're starving!" shouted Steck, temper lost. "They are freezing out there. And does this bother you? No! You have them digging irrigation ditches—your precious *acequias!* You—" Steck began to sputter from the rush of his anger.

"Doctor," chided Carleton. "Often it is necessary to endure the walk through the parched desert before reaching the promise of the oasis."

"How many of them died getting to your damned oasis? Captain Thompson lost almost two hundred out of twenty-four hundred Navajo on the forced march from Fort Canby. And he did well! Dysentery, death by freezing—the list is endless on how many died before Thompson. Berney lost twelve, leaving some behind to starve and freeze when they couldn't match his pace."

"It is true there were losses," Carleton admitted. "Hardly an outrageous number considering the intemperate weather and the distances covered. What would you say, Colonel? No more than a hundred and fifty were lost prior to Captain Thompson's journey?"

"Listen to yourself, General," Steck pleaded. "Perhaps five hundred have died simply getting to Bosque Redondo after surrendering, thinking you would give them the supplies you promised. And after they got here, you cut their rations in half."

"They must learn to farm."

"They *know* how to farm. They can't do it here. Not easily. No one can. The land isn't right. The bugs eat every sprout poking above the ground. They freeze in their hogans because all the wood has been taken for firewood long since. There is no game—unless you count the Navajo as prey for the Comanche and Apache."

"I am not a little astonished, Doctor Steck, that yer ignorance of this country and the Indians inhabitin' it is so great," Carson said, working the words over and over in his head before speaking them. "The general has lived and fought in this land. He knows what is best for those pitiful wights."

Carson was warmed by the smile given him by Carleton.

The general cut off any further protest Steck might have with the wave of a hand.

"We can feed six thousand Navajo on this reservation."

"There are more coming," warned Steck. "You know the numbers better than I. Ask Captain Carey at Fort Canby. Or check with your scouts at Fort Wingate and Los Pinos. There will be mass starvation in your paradise."

"Every care will be taken that we do not overrun six thousand quartered here," Carleton promised.

"How? There are at least that many more still loose in Dinetah."

"Doctor Steck, those wantin' to surrender already have. There is no problem with them remainin' at the western end of the territory," Carson said. He ached all over and wondered if he was coming down with a case of the grippe. The trip from Santa Fé had been hard on him, harder than any journey ever had been, and he did not know why. Perhaps it was the pain of separation from his family wearing on him.

"Let me put your mind to rest, Doctor. The greatest care will be taken to make every ounce of food count at Bosque Redondo. Colonel Carson has my full confidence he will be able to tend our wards until they learn to lead productive lives without our daily supervision."

"They were doing a fine job before you burned them out of their homes." Steck went to a rock, sat on it, and stared at the ragged fields already plowed by the Navajo. It required four men or five boys to drag the heavy plows; mules were nonexistent for the work, and Carleton refused to allow them horses yet, fearing they would escape.

"I'm recommendin' that Fort Canby be closed and the garrison at Fort Wingate reduced," Carson said. "By closin' down those outposts, we can give more supplies and attention to Fort Sumner and Bosque Redondo."

"Why bother?"

"Doctor Steck, I *want* the Indians to have enough food. I don't want them droppin' like flies in front of me. The general's—and my—solution to the problem of them keepin' on raidin' just don't match yours, that's all."

"A treaty. Get a treaty signed and we—"

"History tells us they've never been great ones for obeyin' the treaties they've signed. That's part of General Carleton's dream. Teach them to follow the treaties they sign."

"Dream? It's a nightmare. So many have died," Steck said. "Between you, Berney, Thompson, and who knows how many other soldiers, you've broken their spirit and killed *thousands*. And do not be the first to cast a stone, Colonel. We have not done too well following the spirit of the treaties we have signed."

"Cain't rightly say how many of them died, Doctor Steck," Carson said, turning the matter away from treaties, "but a thousand seems way too high. And not a single officer did anything to kill a single Navajo entrusted to them gettin' to Bosque Redondo."

"Kill them outright? No one's accusing your men of that, Colonel. But they were abandoned to die if they could not keep up. Mothers left their babies unburied because of the rigorous march schedule. But once they got here, tell me soldiers haven't rounded up Navajo and shot them on the spot."

"They tried to escape," Carleton said. "Doctor Steck, this

discussion is turning tedious to me, as I am sure it is to Colonel Carson, also."

"Carleton, Carson, you are both—never mind. I know when I'm wasting my breath. I'll file my protest in Washington. The Navajo will not remain wards of the Department of the Interior. They are prisoners of war and thereby the responsibility of the War Department. Further, I swear I will do everything possible to have these starving unfortunates removed back to their homelands."

"Your ignorance of our objectives and methods are appalling, sir," Carleton said. "Those Dinéh Ana'aii from Sandoval's band are peaceably settled from Cebolleta and have been here for more than two years. They are a shining example of what can be done."

"Traitors, damned traitors to their own people," grumbled Steck. "They sold their souls long ago to the Mexicans."

Carleton did not hear. "Their misery is passing, soon to be gone after they learn what we can teach them. Our policy is both righteous and humane, and its execution is in Colonel Carson's capable hands. He knows the Indians of the territory far better than you ever will, sir—or anyone from Washington. Now, let us return to the fort and have lunch. I need to return to Santa Fé soon."

Steck stormed off, ignoring his two adversaries. Carson stood on the bank of the irrigation ditch the Navajo had dug, following the *acequia* toward the stony fields. Carleton was right. This was best for the Navajo. He was a learned, wise man and knew what was right. This land would turn into productive farmland before they knew it. And the Navajo would come to love this new land given them.

Kit Carson turned wearily after the general, trudging along and wondering why every footstep he took weighed like lead.

Promise of Parley

April 11, 1864
Fort Canby

"Did Carson find anything on his scout?" Joseph Treadwell asked of Asa Carey. The young captain's face screwed into what might have been a grimace. He did not answer Treadwell's question any other way. Since Kit Carson had returned to assume command of the post in mid-March, no one had been too talkative. The rumors of Fort Canby being closed threatened them all with a rapid transfer to less pleasant duty.

"Heard tell he didn't get too far this time out, Joe," shouted one of the troopers. "Wore down right quick, I heard. I even heard he was wobblin' about in the saddle, as if he was took sick. He—"

"Corporal, shut your mouth," snapped Carey. "You will not speak ill of your officers."

"Sorry, Captain," the trooper said. From his tone, he didn't have a whit of apology in him. The corporal touched the brim of his cap in Treadwell's direction and headed off to tend to his chores.

So it had gone ever since Carson returned from his furlough. Treadwell had heard Carson and Carleton held a meeting at Bosque Redondo that did not set well with any of the men. The scout could only wonder what the Navajo went to from the hell of their existence in their traditional homelands. An even worse hell?

A steady stream of refugees still flowed from the bowels of Cañon de Chelly. Each wave of them seemed weaker and less well equipped than the one before. It struck him as a hard fact that the Navajo who surrendered early on had a better life of it than the ones who had remained on their land, refusing to buckle under to the Army's commands. Worst of all for Treadwell, each Navajo he questioned only stared blankly at him when he asked after his wife and child.

"Need to find them," Treadwell mumbled to himself. "They need my help more than ever." He spoke the words to quell the rising fear that they, like Shining Eyes, were dead. Treadwell was never quite able to face the notion that they were buried in unmarked graves, but the lack of news about them preyed on his mind.

Sitting and speaking with a small knot of nearly naked men and women produced no information he could use. Treadwell considered finding one of the Dinéh Ana'aii and using him as interpreter to be absolutely sure. He turned from the pathetic walking skeletons and started for the barracks when a hush fell over the fort. Such silence drew his immediate attention.

The drilling soldiers stopped. Their sergeants did not yell at them for this sudden halt of all movement. They, too, stood and stared at the gates.

Kit Carson hurried from his office, Captain Carey matching his pace. A solitary Navajo translator trailed them. Treadwell forgot his intention of locating a translator and turned toward the gate to see what the fuss might be. His heart almost stopped when he recognized the man he had hunted for so many years.

Manuelito rode slowly into Fort Canby, weapons gone and completely alone.

The man ought to have presented a sorry picture, like the other Navajo straggling into the post. Somehow he sat ramrod straight on his scrawny horse, unbroken by the war of attrition.

It flashed through Treadwell's mind that Manuelito would die, but never would his spirit be shattered.

Fingers tightening around the knife at his belt, Treadwell found himself walking faster and faster to where Carson and his officers gathered in front of the Navajo headman. They might have been peasants begging an audience with a king for all the deference they showed.

"Are you seeking to petition for surrender?" Carey asked.

"I do not surrender. I want only for my people to live in peace."

"You stole my family!" shouted Treadwell. He surged forward, but strong hands held him back. Trying to draw his knife proved impossible. Someone plucked the knife from his belt and tossed it aside. It did not matter to Treadwell. He would throttle Manuelito and choke the words from the man's throat.

"Get Mr. Treadwell to his quarters," Carson ordered.

"No, wait, no. I'll not try to give him what he deserves. But I want to know about my family."

"Your family?" Manuelito's face was impassive. "What do a few matter when so many suffer at your hand?"

"I wasn't the one taking them as slaves. You stole them away. You took them!"

"Mr. Treadwell," cautioned Carson. The post commander seemed tired, almost dejected. "The war is over. There ain't none of them out there worth fightin' anymore."

"We will accept your surrender gladly. We do not want to continue hostilities," Captain Carey said. Treadwell saw the power at Fort Canby had shifted. Rumors that Carson had requested transfer to Santa Fé must be true, that Asa Carey would be the new commander—or was he already in charge? The Army did little to keep its men informed.

"We will peacefully live on our land and make war no more," Manuelito said.

"No!" Carey's denial was abrupt. "That is not acceptable. You must take your band to Bosque Redondo and settle with the rest of your people."

"Bosque Redondo?" Manuelito's words carried a steel edge. "We will never leave Dinetah. This is *our* land. It is holy land."

"You will go to Bosque Redondo," insisted Carey.

"We will settle outside your gates," Manuelito countered. "Your guns will be trained on us day and night. Our flocks will graze and we will grow corn and—"

"No. Not even on the land surrounding the fort," Carey said. "General Carleton demands you lead your clan to the reservation."

Treadwell's heart almost stopped when he read the determination to die rather than go to Bosque Redondo on Manuelito's face.

"My family. Tell me what you've done with them. Where are—" Treadwell was hauled away by a half dozen soldiers.

"We will not go to the reservation," Manuelito said.

"We must parley further," said Carey. "We can work out a peace that will satisfy us all."

"We do not go to Bosque Redondo. Ever." Manuelito wheeled his horse, then stopped and looked from Carson to Carey. "Consider the peace I offer. Again, later, we will talk. In one month." With that the headman rode off.

Treadwell watched with great fear that he might never find Manuelito again. The Navajo knew what had happened to Gray Feather, and Treadwell was unable to get that information from him.

"Mr. Treadwell, do not think to track him. He would not take kindly to it in his mood," ordered Captain Carey. "Be content with the knowledge he will return to parley."

"Waiting is hard enough, but—"

"You will wait, Mr. Treadwell, or suffer the consequences, which will be extreme," Carey said firmly. "I know your impatience. More than your wife hangs in the balance. If Manuelito surrenders, the hostilities will be over for good. Peace means more than any single life." Captain Carey looked at Kit Carson for approval of his order. The old mountain man nodded slowly before speaking.

"The Navajo War is at an end. Never thought to see Manuelito come ridin' in like this," Carson said tiredly. "You make a good commander, Asa. Wait till he's settled down and accepts the notion of defeat. In a month's time, he's gonna get powerful hungry—hungrier than he is right now. Talk again with him then and convince him to go to the reservation."

"Yes, sir." Carey saluted Carson as the colonel went back to his quarters.

Joseph Treadwell stared after Manuelito. His hands clenched into fists, then relaxed. He had done nothing but wait for over three years. The next month would prove harder than all the months since Gray Feather had been taken away from him.

Parley

Manuelito rode slowly toward the tight knot of bluecoats gathered a hundred yards outside the gate to Fort Canby. The horse limped slightly; Manuelito knew it would pull up lame soon, but it was the best in his string. The other horses showed ribs through their flanks, almost starved in spite of the lush spring grasses. It took so long for them to recover from the bitter winter months.

The Dinéh headman rubbed his left shoulder. It took ever longer for him to heal. His shoulder bothered him every time the wind blew and the rains came. But he would feel better after these talks concluded. He had spoken with Captain Carey a month ago and would learn General Carleton's answer now. Over the last month there had been few Dinéh raids to show their desire for peace.

"Welcome, Chief Manuelito," greeted the officer. Asa Carey was Carson's most trusted officer and in charge while Red Clothes whiled away his life in Taos with his family. Manuelito was glad to see Carson removed from the field; Carey had shown himself to be a more reasonable man, willing to negotiate. All Carson wanted was to destroy and drive the Dinéh across New Mexico to Hwééldi.

"Captain Carey," Manuelito replied. He jumped lightly from his pony and walked forward. He came alone today, an insult to the Biligáana, but they hardly took note of his lack of advisers. "You do me honor in parleying again."

Carey snorted and shook his head. "The last time was not good, Chief," the young officer said. "I thought you would surrender. I notified General Carleton that you had finally relented. He was not pleased to find you had no intention of giving up."

Manuelito held his tongue at this rebuke. He had come to Fort Canby a month ago trying to remain in Dinetah. The intervening time had shown the Biligáana hostilities need not continue, though in truth, Manuelito knew the temporary truce had worked as much in favor of the Dinéh as for the soldiers. Sings had healed many sorely wounded warriors and driven away sickness from women and children. Corn grew slowly, but it grew again after being destroyed by Carson and his soldiers. But the flocks were gone, all run off or destroyed, and not even Ganado Mucho had any cattle left. Manuelito closed his eyes for a moment.

Like a Ute, he had eaten the last of his dogs in the coldest days of February. But spring had brought milder weather and the opportunity to fight more effectively. Starvation no longer rode at his shoulder as a constant companion, though Manuelito had to look sideways now and then to be sure.

"Surrender is not negotiation," Manuelito pointed out. "You have spoken with your general. How does he answer my offer?"

"What offer is that?" Carey said, running his hand nervously up and down on the hilt of his sheathed sword. He took a step one way, then reversed, as if he would explode into flight at any instant. Watching him made Manuelito uneasy. He might be watching a lizard trying to walk across a hot rock.

"The Dinéh—the Navajo—must remain on our land."

"Navajoland is ill-defined," Carey said. "General Carleton will never relent on this point. You must abandon your homeland and move to the Bosque."

Manuelito's eyes widened in surprise at such arrogance and affront.

"The Dinéh remain on our lands, and in return we will honor a peace treaty. The past month has been free of raiding."

"It has not," contradicted Carey. The young officer's nervous gestures increased and a tic appeared at the corner of his left eye. "There have been numerous raids."

"I cannot control the Pueblos, the Hopi, the Ute. All continue to raid, as do the Apache to the south. If any Dinéh warrior has stolen from you, he will be punished as a token of our honoring a new treaty."

"General Carleton has been specific and clear on this matter," Captain Carey said. "There can be only one peace for you, and that is to go to the Bosque. Anything less than your immediate departure will constitute continued aggression and be treated as such." Carey heaved a deep sigh, as if he finally had gotten a distasteful message out of his mouth. Manuelito thought the young officer's lips must burn with such venom. And there was little indication any of it was his.

"I should talk directly with your general. Carleton must see the benefits to allowing us to grow our crops and live in peace."

"The general has a view of the territory that many share," Carey said, choosing his words carefully. "Colonel Carson agrees, and most of the other officers do. You'll be better off at Bosque Redondo. Fair Carletonia, they are calling it. You cannot—will not—be allowed to remain in Cañon de Chelly and other parts of Navajoland."

"No," Manuelito said forcefully.

"Why not?" Carey sounded at wit's end. "Do you want to continue your suffering? I know what the winter campaign cost you. I've seen your peach orchards chopped down, your fields burned, your hogans destroyed. Your people suffered horribly because you would not accept our offer to move to Bosque Redondo. Tell me why you resist so."

"You would move my people to Hwééldi to slaughter them."

"What?" Carey shook his head. He took off his cap and ran

his hand through sandy hair, then put it back on before answering. "I don't understand why you think this. Resist and die. Go to Fort Sumner and you will be taken care of for the rest of your days. You will be fed and clothed and given fine adobe houses. You cannot stay in Navajoland. You cannot."

"I remember Fort Fauntleroy," Manuelito said, "1861, the massacre."

"Men died then," Carey said, "but this will not happen at Bosque Redondo. We seek only to teach and help, to Christianize you, to let you live lives of peace and prosperity."

"But not on our own lands."

"Bosque Redondo will be yours, if you make it a home. There is water from the Pecos River and plenty of land for farming. Better dirt for growing than anything I've seen in this godforsaken land."

Manuelito fell silent and his eyes looked past Carey to Fort Canby without really seeing it. He thought of the past and the suffering he and the others of his people had endured. Carleton's soldiers would never permit the Dinéh to again walk in beauty. There would be more and more invasions into Cañon de Chelly and more destruction.

Another winter would wipe out the Dinéh.

Yet the Biligáana had not dealt fairly before. What was he to do?

"I would speak to another, one already at Hwééldi," Manuelito said. "Herrera Grande is an honorable man."

"He is your principal chief there," Carey said, nodding. A small smile moved to lift the corners of his lips. "I am sure a meeting can be arranged to allay your doubts."

"My suspicions," Manuelito corrected.

"Herrera Grande is a wise leader and one who has worked with those at Fort Sumner and Bosque Redondo."

"If I am not permitted to see him, we will simply vanish into the cañons and mountains."

"Tracking you is well nigh impossible," Carey admitted with a laugh. "Heaven knows how I have tried. Sometimes, not even

Colonel Carson was able to find your tracks. It's as if you become part of the land. But even the rocks can be worn down."

Manuelito remained impassive when Captain Carey said this. The Dinéh had launched no raids on Biligáana forts or soldiers because they had needed time to heal. They had also been harassed by the large numbers of Hispanos seeking slaves. Too many bands had barely survived the winter and now fell easy prey to the slavers. Manuelito did not understand the Biligáana war that had raged so long far from the Rio Grande, but it had had to do with slaves.

How the bluecoats could fight those who would enslave and yet allow it under their noses confused Manuelito. It was only a part of the contradictions he saw.

"I will speak with Herrera Grande soon?"

"Colonel Carson will arrange it. He returns to command in a few weeks. Letters must be sent to General Carleton, but the meeting will take place. I would prepare for the trip to Bosque Redondo, though. I am sure your chief will give nothing but glowing reports of life along the Pecos. The sooner you get there, the sooner you can begin to enjoy your life again." Carey sounded confident, but Manuelito had no good feelings. The young officer had done nothing to persuade him the Biligáana gathered the Dinéh only to murder them in the reservation.

Manuelito had nothing more to say. Although he had misgivings, he would speak with Herrera Grande. Herrera Grande was a decent and honorable man and would tell the truth about conditions at Hwééldi.

Nodding to indicate the meeting was at an end, Manuelito turned and mounted his weak pony. He walked the animal for a half mile, then urged it to a canter. If it stumbled here the soldiers would be less likely to note that the famed war chief of the Navajo rode a broken down horse.

Gray Feather

May 9, 1864
Fort Canby

"We could have caught him by now," fumed Treadwell. The mountain man honed his knife for the hundredth time in a month. The keen edge caught the bright spring sun and split it cleanly. He kicked at the shadow on the ground, then spat. That is what he would do to Manuelito when he captured the Navajo.

"Waitin' ain't never easy," opined a sergeant from Captain Pfeiffer's company. "Always better gettin' saddle sores, livin' off tubers and piñon nuts and bein' a target for every Injun between here and the Pacific."

Treadwell turned a deaf ear to such sarcasm. The schism between those troopers serving in California and the natives in the First New Mexico Volunteers had never narrowed, even after Blakeney had been transferred. Now that Kit Carson was in charge of Bosque Redondo, criticism of his days in command at Fort Canby reached epic proportions. Treadwell was no supporter of Carson's, but the tales being spun made the man out to be a bloodthirsty ogre.

Treadwell would show them blood thirstiness, given the chance, but Captain Carey had restricted patrols to the immediate area around Fort Canby, not wanting to damage the delicate negotiations being conducted with Manuelito and other important Navajo headmen still refusing to go to the reservation. Herrera Grande had returned from Bosque Redondo and made many forays alone into Cañon de Chelly to parley with the others, but Treadwell saw no progress. A steady stream of those surrendering poured through the post, but Manuelito and his band were not among them.

Every chance he had to ask after his wife and young son, he took. He was about broke from paying the Dinéh Ana'aii to translate for him, but money and tobacco meant nothing without Gray Feather.

And Goes to War.

Treadwell bit his lip, worrying over the young boy's chances for survival. If Shining Eyes had died, how could a baby survive?

"We been burnin' and lootin', but not findin' a whole lot, of late," the sergeant rambled on. "With all the Injuns we sent to the reservation, you'd think they'd want us to put a cork in the bottle now."

"Yeah, put a cork in it," Treadwell said, standing and walking away. His restlessness knew no bounds. Two companies of soldiers had been transferred to Fort Wingate, preparatory to closing Fort Canby entirely. Carson had promised that closure to save money, to funnel more supplies toward Bosque Redondo. Treadwell saw this as another betrayal. With their post nearest Cañon de Chelly closing, how could they continue to wage any kind of war against the stubborn Navajo?

How could he find Gray Feather?

"Mr. Treadwell, a moment of your time." Treadwell glanced over his shoulder and saw Asa Carey hurrying from the officer's mess hall. The expression on the young commander's face was a curious mixture of dread and anticipation.

"What can I do for you, Captain?"

"Get on over to the barracks and find Herrera Grande."

"Why?"

"We need him at the powwow."

"Manuelito's come back to give up?" Treadwell's heart raced at the news.

"Can't rightly say, not yet, but a scout saw him and a handful of other warriors coming this way. They weren't trying to hide their tracks, so it must mean he's thinking on quitting his war."

"I want to be there," Treadwell said.

"I know, Joe, I know. And so you shall. Now, find Herrera Grande and fetch him. We'll meet Manuelito a hundred yards outside the post gates." Carey strode off, his expression still a mixture of torment and hope.

By the time Treadwell roused the sleeping Navajo headman in his quarters behind the married officers' barracks, Carey and a small knot of soldiers had ridden from the fort. Treadwell and the Navajo recently arrived from another foray into Cañon de Chelly galloped after them.

By the time they reached the bonfire where the conference had already started, Treadwell was out of breath. It might have come from the rush getting here—but he knew it was the nearness of success. For three and a half years he had sought his family. Now the man responsible for stealing them away promised to surrender. Treadwell hoped against hope that Gray Feather and Goes to War had not died, that Manuelito had kept them safe.

Still, a part of his mind cried in agony over the suspense. So many Navajo had died from exposure, of starvation, of U.S. Army bullets.

The instant Manuelito saw Herrera Grande he lifted his chin and motioned the elderly headman to one side. Treadwell started to protest, but Captain Carey stopped him.

"Let them talk a spell," he told Treadwell. "Manuelito is being bullheaded about going to Bosque Redondo. I'm sure Herrera Grande can convince him that is the only way he and his people will survive even another month."

"My wife and son," Treadwell said, straining to get closer to Manuelito. "He knows where they are." He swallowed hard and fought the flood of angry tears as he amended, "He knows what happened to them."

"He might not remember. Look at him, Joe," urged Captain Carey. "He's one of their most powerful chiefs, and he rides here on a skeleton of a horse. His clothing is tattered and his moccasins have holes in them."

"He'll give up," Treadwell said, relaxing a mite. "He has no choice."

"He has no choice," Carey agreed. "We've burned him out of his home and destroyed anything of use. He has to accept our generosity at the reservation."

Treadwell shot the captain a quick look, wondering if Carey was being sarcastic. Treadwell had heard the stories about Bosque Redondo. The Army did not supply enough food or blankets, and every crop proved a failure either from insects or poor soil. The Apache and Comanche raided the Navajo, taking some as slaves and killing others. Worst of all, those surviving the forced march to the reservation had not been given sufficient time or food to recuperate fully. They were as emaciated as the men riding with Manuelito.

"No!" bellowed Manuelito, stepping way from Herrera Grande. The sudden outburst in English brought all the officers about. Treadwell strained to hear what Herrera Grande told the other headman but could not. The soft words were meant to soothe; they failed. Manuelito grew angrier by the moment.

"He's not surrendering," Treadwell observed aloud. "He won't go to the reservation."

"Nonsense," said Carey. "He wants conditions. We can give in on a few points, but—"

Manuelito twisted away and mounted his horse. He glared at Carey and the others. "Never will my people be boxed in at this horrible place you call Bosque Redondo to cringe under the bluecoats' guns. Better to die free in Dinetah!"

Manuelito put his heels to his horse's flanks and raced off. Treadwell reached for his knife, then froze, knowing he needed more than the blade now. He should have brought his musket.

Even at this range he could have winged the Navajo warrior. And then it was too late for any action. Manuelito darted behind a low ridge and was hidden by hill and tree.

"He refuses to leave our land," Herrera Grande explained slowly. "No matter what I could tell him of the reservation, he refused to listen."

"He will die," Carey said carefully.

"He will die proudly, in beauty," Herrera Grande said. "He is a bullheaded one and can never recognize futility." The aged Indian swung onto the back of his pony and returned slowly to Fort Canby. Treadwell stared after him, then spun and tried to make out Manuelito's retreating form. Not even a cloud of dust marked the headman's departure.

"What now?" he demanded of Carey.

To his surprise, the officer was already giving commands. Captain McCabe trotted back to the post for his detachment.

"Want to go on a quick scouting trip, Mr. Treadwell?" asked Carey. "You will ride with Captain McCabe and bring Manuelito back."

"Yes, sir," Treadwell said. He knew this was as close as the captain could come to giving him his head. "Are we at full war with Manuelito?"

"We have never ceased," Carey said. With that he mounted and rode back into the fort.

Joseph Treadwell could hardly restrain his impatience waiting for McCabe's company to get their gear and come riding out in their long column behind a standard bearer.

"Three dead," Treadwell reported. "Just over that rise."

"How did they die, Mr. Treadwell?" McCabe moved with nervous gestures evident in his every action." He might have been a spring coiled and ready to explode—in all the wrong directions.

"Scalped. My guess is that some of the Hispanos roving the

countryside got to them. Word is that they've been marauding between here and the Chuska Valley."

"Why were the Navajo here?" mused McCabe.

"My guess is that they were coming in to surrender," Treadwell said. "That's the only reason I can see for them to be here rather than in Cañon de Chelly with Manuelito."

"He's not there, no. That one's a wily fox. He would lead us a merry chase except we know he is raiding, that he has to raid to stay alive."

"Well, Captain, there's nothing we can do for these three. I say we push on and swing about along yonder ridge to see if we can find Manuelito's camp."

"You found traces of the man?"

Treadwell nodded slowly. He might be mistaken, yet in his heart he did not think so. They had been after Manuelito for almost a week after his refusal to go to the reservation. This was the first time Treadwell felt *right* about finding him soon.

"Very well. We can march through the night, if necessary," McCabe declared. "The moon will be bright and the stars free of clouds."

Treadwell mounted his tired horse and headed back for the ridge where he had found the dead Navajo. Much of the story unraveling here he had guessed at. A silver concho like those favored by the Hispanos lay half submerged in the blood and dirt in the camp. And the tracks of shod horses told him the Navajo had not been attacked by another Indian tribe.

They might have fallen prey to some Colorado volunteers intent on wiping out the Navajo menace in this part of the country, but Treadwell did not think so. It didn't feel right.

The dark provided clear and cold cover as they made their way along a tree-littered ridge. Here and there the white trunks of aspen rose like ghosts quaking in the night. Mostly the juniper and piñon proved difficult to get around, so thickly were they clumped. But through the forest scent of pine and juniper came another distinctive smell.

"Let me scout on foot," Treadwell asked McCabe. "Keep your men well back."

"They can rest," Mccabe said. "They have been marching since dawn."

"Let them sleep all they want. If that's Manuelito's camp ahead, we can get into position and attack at sunrise."

Treadwell moved through the forest like a shadow, his feet never making even a whispering sound against the carpet of fragrant pine needles. The smell of burning wood grew stronger. He went to his belly and wiggled forward, even more careful not to make any sound. As he topped the rise, he caught sight of both campfire and camp.

Manuelito!

Treadwell spent the better part of a half hour fixing the terrain in his mind and determining that the headman had women and children with him.

Gray Feather might be down there, or she might be dead. Treadwell wished he knew. If only he knew, he could advise McCabe how best to attack the camp. He finally slid back into the forest and retraced his steps. For a moment Treadwell thought he had missed the soldiers' camp, but an alert sentry stepped into view, musket leveled.

"You alone, Mr. Treadwell?"

"I've got the information we need, Corporal Furlan," he said, recognizing the sentry immediately. "Where's Captain McCabe bedded down?"

"Yon lump next to the log is him," the corporal said, swinging the rifle around to indicate his commander.

Treadwell wasted no time locating the captain. He dropped to one knee and shook the sleeping man. McCabe came awake instantly, revolver in his hand. He relaxed when he recognized Treadwell.

"Report, sir," he ordered.

"If we start now, we can circle them and catch them unawares at first light. There might be as many as thirty or forty in the camp, mostly women and children by my count. Not more than ten are full-blooded warriors."

"But it *is* Manuelito?"

"No question," Treadwell assured him. "I saw him outside a lean-to. I'd recognize him anywhere."

With that assurance, McCabe pushed out of his bedroll and began rousing his men. They moved out an hour later, making hardly any more noise than Treadwell had earlier. At dawn they were ready for their attack.

"Shall I give the order, Mr. Treadwell?" asked Captain McCabe.

"I don't see Manuelito or several of the others with him. We want them all," muttered Treadwell. "We should wait."

"We cannot tarry too long. If we try, someone will give away our position by a careless action."

"Attack," Treadwell decided. Better to lose Manuelito and find Gray Feather than to risk missing them all.

A ragged volley rang out, the bullets ripping through the tents and lean-tos below. This flushed out those bearing weapons. A second volley tore though those wanting to fight. From all sides came the cry for those remaining in the camp to surrender.

"There, there's Manuelito's campsite," Treadwell said to McCabe, cutting and running down the hillside. He stumbled and fell, rolled a few times, and came to his feet. Paying no attention to the slow firing of soldiers above him, he darted through the camp and came to a halt in front of the lean-to. A young woman, barely fifteen, confronted him with a drawn knife and hatred in her dark eyes.

"Manuelito," Treadwell shouted. "Where is he?" The young girl lowered the knife point, showing she was a deadly fighter and Treadwell risked being gutted if he moved too close.

"Is he inside? Let him come out and fight."

The girl moved with the speed of a striking snake. Treadwell caught her slender wrist and easily tossed her to one side. She was half-starved and weak from exposure.

"If Manuelito's not in there, where is Gray Feather?"

The girl's eyes widened at the mention of Gray Feather. Treadwell's pulse drummed in his temples as he pushed aside a hanging curtain of tattered blanket and saw the litter.

Gray Feather lay on the pallet, pale as death. Her eyelids flickered weakly, and she saw his face for the first time in three and a half years. A tiny smile curled her lips and then her eyes closed again.

No Exceptions

May 12, 1864
Cañon de Chelly

"Take her to Fort Canby," Treadwell demanded. "You can't force her to go to Los Pinos." The mountain man's fingers tightened around his musket, lying across his saddle pommel.

"Los Pinos is closer, Treadwell," came Major Blakeney's mocking reply. "We do things by the book. General Carleton ordered all captured Navajo taken immediately to the reservation."

"She's sick," protested Treadwell. "I carried her out of the cañon myself. She's hacking and coughing—it might be pneumonia. You know how deadly it can be."

"Especially when you're as scrawny as she is." Blakeney enjoyed the taunt and seeing Treadwell's rising fury.

"Carson cut off all their food," Treadwell said, struggling to contain his emotions. "There's no way for her to be fat."

"I did my part. You did, too, 'less my memory's playing tricks on me," Blakeney said. He motioned to his troopers to hoist Gray Feather into the bed of a supply wagon. The handful of others Treadwell had brought with him out of Cañon de Chelly was in equally bad condition.

"Major," spoke up Captain McCabe, "we can take the prisoners back to Fort Canby. We were sent out to bring these particular renegades back after Manuelito refused to give himself up."

"I appreciate your attention to duty, *Captain*," Blakeney said, accenting McCabe's rank to put the officer in his place. "I reckon it is a good thing we happened to spot you riding along the way you were. It would take an extra day for you to reach Fort Canby. Los Pinos is just around the corner."

"About equal distance," Treadwell said, fighting to keep Gray Feather from the major's custody. Blakeney blamed everyone at Fort Canby for his transfer and had done nothing to mend his ways. Treadwell saw Blakeney hit the bottle, taking a deep draught of liquor before hiding it away in his saddlebags.

"The way's easier to Los Pinos. Since I outrank you, Captain McCabe, I'll assume charge of these Navajo. You saunter on back to Fort Canby. Colonel Carson will get my report when I get around to it."

"Captain Carey's in charge now," McCabe said. Blakeney's eyebrows rose in surprise.

"Hadn't heard. Then I won't bother with a report. Carey ought to be reporting to me." Major Blakeney puffed up like a rooster about ready to assert his dictatorship of the chicken yard.

Treadwell considered stealing Gray Feather from the major and getting back into Cañon de Chelly. He knew the turns and windings of the red rock cañon well now. He could hide from the cavalry officer long enough to tire him and force an eventual retreat.

"What's this squaw to you, Treadwell?" asked Blakeney, seeing how distant Treadwell's thoughts had become.

"She's my wife."

"Wife? She's a damned Navajo!"

"She's Ute," Treadwell said, feeling cold rage mount within him. He had sought his wife for three and a half years and wasn't about to let her go now.

"One red nigger is like any other," Blakeney said, his bloodshot eyes boring into Treadwell.

"Joe, go with her to Los Pinos and take care of her," urged McCabe. "I'll explain to Captain Carey what happened."

"Explain that I'm doing my duty and this *scout* isn't," Blakeney said. "And I don't need any Ute-loving civilian riding with my company, slowing us down as we do our honor-bound duty to keep the peace. Sergeant!"

"Sir!" A grizzled bear of a man rode up, his swaybacked horse struggling under his weight.

"This here is Joseph Treadwell. You recognize his ugly face?"

"Sir, yes, I've seen him before. He's a scout with Colonel Carson's unit."

"If you ever see him again, under any circumstances, shoot him. That is a direct order."

"Yes, sir," the sergeant said slowly. His brow furrowed, and he made a sour face, as if sucking in alkali water.

"A reward will go to the sharpshooter who takes him off his feet and puts him in a grave. Fifty dollars."

"Major, this is outrageous. You can't—" McCabe quieted when Blakeney glared at him.

"I can and will, Captain," Blakeney snapped. "I am obeying General Carleton's orders to the letter. I have reason to believe you would not take this *Navajo* squaw to Bosque Redondo. She will be sent there immediately—under heavy guard. General Carleton said there would be no exceptions, under any circumstance."

"Let me go with her. She's sick, Major. I can help hunt, find food, do things around camp." Treadwell began to choke on a rising desperation. Letting Blakeney see it was a mistake, but Treadwell could not keep it bottled inside. He was losing his wife again.

"My order stands, Sergeant. If you see one hair on this man's filthy, lice-ridden head inside of five minutes, you and all the troopers are ordered to kill him."

"Yes, sir." The sergeant's frown told Treadwell two things. The sergeant thought little of his commanding officer—and that he would carry out the orders given him, anyway. The non-com was a conscientious soldier.

"Come along, Treadwell. We can get this sorted out once we get back to the post." McCabe tugged on Treadwell's sleeve.

"Blakeney, I—"

"If he threatens me, execute my order immediately," Blakeney said.

"Come on, Joe. Come *on*." McCabe forced Treadwell to turn and ride off, leaving Gray Feather behind in the wagon. She moaned softly but did not regain her senses. After they had gone a few hundred yards, McCabe said, "There's a hate burning in him brighter than the sun. Arguing with him only feeds his need for revenge."

"I don't care what he thinks of Carson or Carey or any of the others. Even me. That's my wife!" Treadwell guided his horse over to the wagon and stared at her gaunt, pale face.

"I love you," he said softly. She did not stir, and he could only hope she understood. "I won't let you stay at Bosque Redondo. I won't let you remain in Blakeney's grip, either. If I have to, I'll track him down and kill him."

"Sergeant! Weapons at the ready!" Blakeney lifted his arm as if ordering a firing squad. Treadwell got one last look at his wife before McCabe pulled him away.

"I understand, Joe," McCabe said. "Really I do, but you can't fight him directly. It's too damned bad we ran into his column on our way out of the cañon."

Treadwell knew McCabe was right. Blakeney had more than a hundred men riding behind him. McCabe had fewer than twenty. Worst of all, Blakeney was right that Los Pinos was closer than Fort Canby. The only hope Treadwell had was that the post doctor at Los Pinos would help Gray Feather before sending her to Bosque Redondo.

The Reservation

May 28, 1864
Bosque Redondo

"Why wouldn't he help me?" Treadwell asked, though he knew the answer. He had ridden straight through to Santa Fé to petition the governor to release Gray Feather. Leaving her in Blakeney's hands rankled worse than anything else he had ever done.

"Governor Connelly is something of a coward," answered Michael Steck. "I have never known him to oppose Carleton in any matter, however small. Even if he is not willing to lock horns with Carleton, he was the proper route for you to take. Situations such as these must be brought to his attention. Perhaps moral suasion will wear him down into doing the right thing." Treadwell heard the consoling tone Steck used, but this did nothing to ease his heavy heart. He had fought through miles of bureaucracy to even reach the governor's assistant. The few seconds he had spent with the territorial governor had not been enough to convince him of the need of freeing Gray Feather.

"I knew better than to ask Carleton. The man is crazy."

"No, not that," Steck said. "His affliction is something worse. He is a man with a vision, an unshakable vision to change people in ways they can never be altered."

"I appreciate all you're doing for me, Doctor, but you might

have to do the asking when we reach Bosque Redondo. If I see
Kit Carson, I might try to strangle him."

"You're too hard on Colonel Carson, also," Steck said. "He's
not a bad man, just a sick one."

"What do you mean?"

"You must not have seen him in a spell. Pale, gaunt, worn
down by duty that is too much for him. Carson looks to be a
broken man, for all his victories."

"What's he doing at Bosque Redondo?"

"He went out to Fort Canby on April tenth, turned over command to Captain Carey, and then reported as acting military
superintendent of Bosque Redondo."

"He's not the source of my problems any more than Blakeney
is," Treadwell said. "Manuelito stole her away and started all
this. But I can forget vengeance on the Navajo if I can only get
her back."

"And your son," pointed out Steck. "You don't know where
he might be."

"Probably with Manuelito," Treadwell said. "With Gray
Feather's help, I'm sure we can get him away from Manuelito."

"So many problems, and many of them trace back to Carleton
and his intransigent view of the Navajo. Since arriving at
Bosque Redondo they have worked hard to fit the mold he has
cast for them, and to no avail."

Treadwell listened with half an ear to Steck's appraisal of the
obstacles faced by the transplanted Navajo. He had no love for the
Navajo; his only concern was his family. To have come so close
to getting Gray Feather back and then losing her again to a fool
like Thomas Blakeney was a burr under his saddle. Every move
he made worried it a bit deeper into his flesh.

"Up ahead. There's Fort Sumner." Steck pointed into the distance. A dust cloud rose near the fort, barely visible through
the shimmer of summer heat.

Treadwell fought to concentrate on his goal: find Gray
Feather and get her away from Carson's clutches.

"Do we have to report to Carson first? I want to find Gray Feather and—"

"Joseph, we've been through this before. There's no way we can sneak anyone out of Bosque Redondo without the cavalry knowing and coming after us. The Navajo have tried to escape repeatedly. This keeps the soldiers on duty alert and ready to shoot."

"If it's such a paradise on earth, why would they want to escape?"

"You know the answer," Steck said angrily. "Carleton's promised supplies never arrived. They live a tedious life, a precarious one balanced on the brink of starvation. I have done all I can to increase their rations, to no avail. The Department of the Interior has no surplus to send them."

Doctor Steck started listing all the methods that might possibly change the Navajo's sorry situation at the reservation. Treadwell ignored him and focused on the slowly growing brown dot ahead that was Fort Sumner. This was only the next battle to be fought, Treadwell knew. Gray Feather would require long days of tender care before she recuperated fully.

Then there was Goes to War, still with Manuelito's band.

"Hey, Joe, you comin' in to sign up with the colonel ag'in?" came the loud cry from a soldier walking sentry duty.

"No way," Treadwell said, remembering the soldier from duty at Fort Canby. "I'm here with Doctor Steck for something else."

"Go on in. I'm sure the colonel will be glad to see you ag'in. He needs some cheerin' up. Garrison duty ain't his cup of tea."

"You seem well liked by the troopers," Steck observed.

"Riding with them for months—even years—puts you in touch with a lot of people. That guard? I saved his life. He probably saved mine, too, but I don't rightly remember. That's the way it was."

"With the Navajo capitulation, that's all changed," Steck said.

"Manuelito's still out there. It can never end until he's brought down."

"A matter of time, that's all," Steck said.

Standing in the center of the parade ground was a short,

stocky man Treadwell recognized immediately. Kit Carson's braid gleamed in the summer sun, but somehow Carson appeared even shorter than before, diminished, crushed by the weight of his responsibilities at Fort Sumner.

"What brings you here, Mr. Treadwell?" Carson asked. "I can imagine what brings *him* out in the hot sun." Carson looked squarely at Doctor Steck and said, "We ain't changin' one thing here. We can't, unless General Carleton orders it."

"I'm here with Mr. Treadwell on a mission of mercy. One of the Navajo isn't—"

"She's not Navajo. She's Ute," cut in Treadwell.

"Your wife?" Carson's eyebrows rose in surprise. "You are a lucky man, Mr. Treadwell. I congratulate you on your success in findin' her. I know how difficult the hunt has been for you and all the troubles you've endured."

"She ought to have arrived by now. Three weeks back I brought her out of Cañon de Chelly."

"Why did you not stay with her?" asked Carson.

"Major Blakeney took her before I could get her back to Fort Canby," Treadwell said, not trying to hide his bitterness. "He said there would be no changing Carleton's standing order to send all the Navajo to Bosque Redondo."

"Why did you go to him for help?" Carson jerked his thumb in Steck's direction. "Didn't you think I would help a loyal, worthy scout?"

"You're Carleton's lackey," said Steck. "Mr. Treadwell tried to petition Governor Connelly for Gray Feather's release."

"Connelly?" Carson shook his head sadly. "There's no help to be found there. I oughta know. I've tried often enough. But come on in out of the sun. Let me find the lists of those brung in over the past week or so. I'm only actin' superintendent. General Carleton promised to make it official sometime in July."

"I rode hard and killed two horses under me, Colonel," Treadwell said. "It's almost a two-week trip from Los Pinos. I wanted to be here as soon as I could to claim her."

"I don't know of any recent caravan from Los Pinos. Haven't heard of one, at least." Carson climbed the four steps to his office tiredly, as if the effort wore him to a nubbin. He flopped heavily into the chair behind his simple desk, closing his eyes for a moment.

Treadwell exchanged looks with Steck. He knew what the Indian agent meant now. Carson looked to have one foot in the grave.

Carson's pale eyes opened, and he leaned forward. A few seconds of shuffling papers brought out a long list of names. He pushed it across the desk to Treadwell.

"Take a gander at that and tell me if your wife's listed."

Treadwell impatiently read each and every name, to be sure he did not miss Gray Feather's. When he reached the bottom of the second page, he went back and reread the names.

"She's not here, Colonel."

"Then she might be with the next group from Los Pinos. Blakeney has been sending us as many as a hunnerd at a crack. A minute, gentlemen." Carson pushed out of his chair and went to the door where he yelled, "Sergeant Need. Is there a new batch of residents for the Bosque due soon?"

Treadwell did not hear the reply, but his pulse hammered when he saw the expression on Carson's face.

"You're in luck, Mr. Treadwell. Sergeant Need says there's one a'comin' soon. Why don't you ride on out to the reservation and wait there?"

"Right away, Colonel." Treadwell shot from the office. Steck trailed more slowly.

"Have you reconsidered your position, Colonel?" asked Steck.

"I have, Doctor, I have indeed. I reckon I'm too wore out to keep on here much longer. I'll be resignin' as soon as I can convince General Carleton. Is that what you wanted to hear?"

"Not really. I wanted you to make Carleton see the error of his ways."

"Don't know he's wrong." Carson paused a moment, infinitely tired. "Don't know he's right, either."

Steck grunted with disdain and rushed after Treadwell, catching the mountain man already in the saddle.

"Where do we go? I want to be there when she arrives. We can ride along the trail toward Albuquerque and—"

"Rein back, Joseph," cautioned Steck "The caravans take anywhere up to two weeks. The desert heat might slow them considerably. You rode like the wind to get to Santa Fé. They will travel far slower, in deference to the sick and injured."

"Gray Feather," Treadwell said. "I want to see her again. I need to hold her."

They rode from Fort Sumner and turned south along the Pecos. When they crossed the *acequias* built by the Navajo for irrigation, Treadwell knew they were close.

"There are the buildings constructed for them," Steck said, pointing out one-story adobe houses. "They look enough like the hogan so the Navajo will use them. It is hard to believe we are spending $50,000 a month to feed them."

"Their crops. Where are they growing food?" asked Treadwell. He studied the sterile streets laid out in straight lines so unlike anything he had seen in Cañon de Chelly. There the Navajo blended in with the countryside rather than challenging it with imposed order.

"Carleton wants his noble experiment to succeed," Steck said. "The Hopi like the Navajo being sent here."

"They would," said Treadwell. "The Moqui have always hated the Navajo."

"Carleton wants to allocate huge amounts of money so the Navajo will have no reason to return to Dinetah. I have opposed Carleton at every step, but he is too strong politically for me to resist much longer. I am returning to Washington to try to change the minds of those in Congress."

"Who's that? The officer over there?" Treadwell squinted when he saw an army officer directing a group of Navajo. "It looks like one of the Navajo has a ball and chain fastened to his leg!"

"That's Captain Calloway. He's in charge of seeing that the fields get cleared. The prisoner must have tried to escape. Carleton's standing orders include preventing anyone from leaving the reservation, no matter the reason."

"A prison, that's what this is. And it's too late to start growing crops for this year, unless winter takes its sweet time a'coming," declared Treadwell.

"So it is," Steck said. "And there is no support if they fail to get the crops in before first frost. Carleton has ninety civilians stealing from the till."

"What do you mean?"

"Joseph, I've made no bones about my opposition to Carleton's plan for Bosque Redondo. As I feared, the Navajo are continually receiving less than their allocated portions because of fraud and outright theft. Captain Garrison is the district commissary officer. He reported theft to the Commissary General, going over Carleton's head."

"Doubt General Carleton liked that too much," Treadwell said. He stood in his stirrups looking past the toiling Navajo in the field to the horizon as he tried to make out the cause of a distant dust cloud. A caravan from Los Pinos might kick up dust like that. It was the right direction and moving, he saw—moving toward him.

"With the Navajo entirely dependent on largesse from the government, every stolen nickel takes away food and medicine from them." Steck coughed and spat. "This damned New Mexico dust. It gets into everything. And the heat!"

"Could that be a wagon train coming?" Treadwell could not restrain his eagerness. "I'll ride out and see."

"Watch for Mescalero, if you do," cautioned Steck. This caused Treadwell to hesitate.

"Are you afraid I'll be attacked by them?"

"They have long memories, and not even Carson has been able to keep them on the reservation. They prey on lone riders

and any Navajo they can find. The more Navajo at Bosque Redondo, the bolder the Apache become. They are not suitable
co-residents."

"I'll take my chances," Treadwell declared. He urged his
horse forward, over a wooden bridge crossing the *acequia ma-
dre* providing irrigation water to the fields where Captain Calloway and the Navajo labored. As he rode through the
reservation, Treadwell was struck by how barren the place
seemed. The flatness of the land, uninterrupted save by gently
rolling hills, was completely alien when he compared it to the
rocky vastness of Cañon de Chelly. The Chuska Mountains had
a majesty about them lacking here. Worst of all, he saw not a
single smile among the Navajo who watched listlessly as he
rode past their dwellings.

"Gray Feather," he said, reminding himself why he had rid-
den so hard for Santa Fé and Fort Sumner. First he would nurse
Gray Feather back to health, then he would find Goes to War.
And Manuelito.

Less than an hour riding brought him to the wagon train's
scout.

"You headed for Bosque Redondo?" he called to the Dinéh
Ana'aii.

A single nod was all the answer he got.

"I'm looking for one of the women riding with you. Gray
Feather. I rescued her from Manuelito."

The mention of the headman produced an animal-like growl
deep in the Indian's throat. Treadwell didn't have to be told the
Dinéh Ana'aii had no fondness for Manuelito or his clan.

"Who's the officer in charge?" He feared Blakeney might
have ridden out with Gray Feather. To his relief, the Dinéh
Ana'aii named a lieutenant as leading this small expedition.

He rode back, hunting for any officer wearing a lieutenant's
bars. He found Lieutenant Edgar riding alongside a wagon filled
with unmoving Navajo.

"Who be you?" called the lieutenant.

"Joseph Treadwell. My wife's with them. She got taken by

accident. She's Ute, not Navajo. She was captured by Manuelito and I rescued her, but Major Blakeney insisted she be sent here."

"All the Indians are going to Bosque Redondo," the lieutenant said, puzzled. "The major didn't say anything about a Ute being with the others."

"Doctor Steck is waiting at Bosque Redondo to square things. If there's any problem turning her over to me, Colonel Carson will vouch."

"Don't know who this Doctor Steck is, but everyone's heard of Kit Carson. He's 'bout the greatest Indian fighter ever."

"Gray Feather is her name. She had a bad cough. Might have been pneumonia."

"Ride on back and look to your heart's content. If she's as bad off as you say, you'll want the doctor at Fort Sumner to look at her."

"Thank you, Lieutenant. Thank you."

Treadwell examined all the Navajo in the three wagons with great anticipation that turned into dread when he could not find his wife. He trotted back to the head of the column.

"Lieutenant, she's not here. Has another caravan left Los Pinos recently? Ahead of this one? Or maybe is one leaving later?"

"Nope, we're about it. The Navajo aren't surrendering the way they were even a month back. We've shipped well nigh six thousand to the reservation."

"But she wouldn't have been kept at Los Pinos. Blakeney insisted she had to be sent to Bosque Redondo."

"I've got a list of those accompanying us," Lieutenant Edgar volunteered. "There's a couple who died before we even left." He held out the sheet of white paper in the bright New Mexico sun. The glare almost blinded Treadwell as he took the sheet.

Tears did blind him when he read Gray Feather's name on the list as having died before the wagons had left Los Pinos.

Small Victories

August 20, 1864
Cañon Bonito

"Captain Thompson," came the scout's terse report, "we're two miles from the last sighting of the enemy."

Thompson nodded brusquely. For days they had been chasing shadows. The Navajo appeared for an instant along the rim of this damnable cañon and then vanished by the time even a nimble scout could reach the spot. He shuddered and pulled his hat brim down over his eyes to shield his eyes from sun reflecting off the red cliffs. He had nightmares of those tall cliffs, edging closer to crush him in his dreams. Thompson was not an imaginative man, but he thought Navajo savages lurked behind every soaring needle of rock, in every niche, everywhere.

Sometimes he was right. And then he always sustained casualties. On this scout he had done well enough. Carey would not congratulate him for taking no casualties, but it was better than the last incursion into Cañon de Chelly, when he had lost his sergeant and had had four troopers severely wounded in two different ambuscades.

"What of their strength?" he asked the Ute scout. "How many are there?"

The Ute shrugged, as if it didn't matter to him how many Navajo he killed. After sucking on his teeth for a moment, the

Indian finally answered. "Not many. Six men, a woman, and a child."

"More fleeing for cover," Thompson said. Still, finding a band this small with six men in it constituted a war party. Or so his report would read.

"We can kill them and move on. You know Carleton's orders."

"Don't preach to me," Thompson snapped. He put up with the scouts because they were better than any of the others stationed at Fort Canby. But he saw little difference in killing Navajo or Ute. "I know the general ordered us to find some of their chiefs."

"Headmen," corrected the Ute. "They do not have chiefs. Headmen."

"Carleton wants us to capture Manuelito or Barboncito or one of their principal *chiefs*." He bore down on the word to put the scout in his place. The Indian's face turned impassive, telling him he had succeeded in showing who commanded this detachment.

"Kill all six and tell Carleton one is Manuelito," suggested the scout.

Thompson looked past the Ute to his company of men. They had roamed through Cañon de Chelly for the better part of two weeks and had not found anything worth burning, much less two of the men responsible for fighting so tenaciously in this awful country. Thompson longed for greener pastures, cooler climes. He wished he could be fighting real battles instead of chasing shadows.

"Even if Carleton wouldn't know the difference, Colonel Carson would. So would Captain Carey. They are not fools."

With over a hundred men at his disposal, Thompson had to decide how best to capture those six. Even a handful of captives showed his competence to the colonel. He signaled for two squads to ride forward.

"Lieutenant," he said to the officer in command, "we shall go directly down the cañon floor. You will take one squad and swing around, cutting off retreat. I will go in directly and capture the enemy, accepting their surrender or engaging them if they prove hostile. If shots are fired, you will attack immediately. Give no quarter."

"Yes, sir," the lieutenant replied, giving him a snappy salute. Thompson's return salute was more lackadaisical. This young snot wanted to get promoted fast and would do everything he could to make his captain look foolish. Thompson knew it and had to guard against making any foolish mistakes.

Six captives were nothing, but then few patrols returned with any since the Navajo had begun surrendering in March. With thousands already at Bosque Redondo, why did Carleton persist in his war? Thompson didn't know, but he followed orders. The few remaining Navajo gave only spotty resistance, even if their raids did cost the cavalry many horses and not a little embarrassment.

"For'ard!" He lifted his saber and got his squad moving. From the corner of his eye he saw the shavetail getting his squad moving in ragged order. Thompson walked his horse slowly to give the lieutenant time to get into position. The scout rode silently at his side, offering no suggestions. That suited Thompson fine. He didn't need any ignorant savage to tell him how to conduct a skirmish, even one of no consequence.

"Ahead," the scout finally said. "Up in the rocks. I saw them there."

"Starved and willing to give up, I would say," Thompson said, hardly listening. He saw nothing of the lieutenant but knew the officer would be in position now. He stood in his stirrups and gave the command.

"Attack!"

The squad rode forward, rifles firing. The first volley took the small band of Navajo by surprise. One sank to his knees, clutching his thigh. A lucky shot, Thompson thought. None of his men was a marksman. There hadn't been ammunition enough for practice in more than three years. What didn't get routed back East to the real battles was hogged by Carson and his men, not given to those needing it in the field.

The first blush of surprise faded from the attack, and the Navajo began to fire back. A musket ball whizzed past Thompson's head, turning his hat to one side. He reached up and saw a bullet hole in the brim. The nearness of the slug infuriated him. The Navajo all used stolen muskets, weapons stolen from his comrades.

"For'ard! Attack on foot!" Thompson jumped off his horse and started up the steep slope, finding cover as he went. His squad followed gamely. The only shots fired now came from his men, but arrows began singing through the air telling him the Navajo had run out of ammunition.

"That way. Flank them. Move up the slope and get them in a crossfire." Although the fight was of no importance, blood pounded in his temples and he came alive. This was better than having his men picked out of the saddle, shot from behind and then finding no assailant after long searching.

Horses' hooves told him the lieutenant had remembered his orders and came to support them.

"Surrender, damn your eyes," called Thompson. "Surrender and we will let you live!"

Two warriors tried to escape. Both were cut down, though neither was killed. Somehow, this took all the fight from the remaining braves.

"We would parley," came a tired voice. "Do not shoot."

An old Navajo rose with his musket held above his head. He came from the rock defenses and moved arthritically down the slope. Only when he stood a few feet from Thompson did the captain order him to halt.

"You surrender unconditionally?" Thompson demanded. "We will kill the lot of you if you do not."

The grizzled warrior nodded sadly. "I surrender. All my people surrender." The Navajo chattered in his infernal language for a few seconds, and the others began their way down the side of the mountain. Thompson waited to be sure this wasn't a ruse before sending four of his men to fetch those wounded and unable to walk.

"Not too bad," he said, putting his pistol into his holster. "You were right. A woman and her child and six men. Six warriors. Not a bad day's work."

The Ute scout stood and stared at the old man still holding the musket above his head in a gesture of submission. He spat.

"You have captured five warriors," the scout said. "Five warriors and Barboncito, headman of the Coyote Pass People."

Captain Thompson simply stared. He had caught one of the men Carleton wanted so badly—and it had been done with hardly a fight.

Treadwell and Manuelito

January 2, 1865
Cañon Bonito

"What a crazy notion," Treadwell said, reading the report Captain Carey had given him. "Who is this Ethan Eaton? He doesn't know squat about the Navajo, if he says Manuelito is the only headman left and that his band numbers less than fifty."

"The fight between Steck and Carleton is reaching a breaking point," Carey said. "Major Eaton conducted his survey, going only along the eastern edge of Navajoland. He didn't try entering Cañon de Chelly."

"Good advice. The whole cañon is still dangerous territory if you don't have a couple companies of soldiers backing you up." Treadwell folded the paper and tucked it away. He was fed up with the constant bickering between Carleton and Steck. Steck's heart was in the right place, trying to get the Navajo off Bosque Redondo, but Treadwell favored Carleton's approach of forcing Manuelito to surrender.

Gray Feather and Shining Eyes might be dead, but Treadwell still had some faint hope of finding his only son. Goes to War was out in Dinetah with his foster father.

"Carleton denies Steck's claim there are thousands of Navajo still roaming free. Ethan's report only stirred up Carleton to bring in Manuelito and put an end to all speculation." Carey shook his head. "They've stripped me of most troopers. There's no way I can launch a new campaign against Manuelito, not if he stays in Cañon de Chelly."

"Carleton won't risk losing any soldiers," Treadwell said, thinking hard on the subject. "He'll try to persuade Manuelito to surrender, as he did before." Treadwell straightened when he saw Carey's face harden. "He's already tried, hasn't he?"

"He ordered several Dinéh Ana'aii sent to Manuelito out in Cañon Bonito. Manuelito's answer was the same. He would farm the land in defiance of Carleton's orders and would never go to Bosque Redondo."

"What now?"

"I want you to go with Herrera Grande."

Treadwell spat and tried to hide his contempt. Carleton had used Herrera Grande as a stalking-horse before, with no result. Treadwell had come to despise Herrera Grande for the lies he'd told about Bosque Redondo. Treadwell had seen firsthand how badly the Navajo Indians there lived. He had no love toward them, but that did not stop him from realizing Carleton's dream of civilizing the Navajo had failed. They would all die first rather than abandon their traditional ways.

"Lifeway," Treadwell muttered. "Carleton doesn't understand the Navajo lifeway."

Carey stared at him curiously. "You will go with Herrera Grande? Manuelito has agreed to a parley at Deer Springs."

"Near the Zuñi pueblo?" Treadwell's eyebrows rose. It was strange Manuelito wanted to meet so close to his enemies. Or perhaps not. It was his way of showing contempt for both the white man and the ancestral enemies of the Navajo.

"This time, there's no reason for you to hurry back. Herrera Grande and his guides can find us." Carey smiled at Treadwell's reaction.

"Thanks, Captain. It isn't much, but maybe I can find my boy this time."

"We haven't had any luck tracking Manuelito. Now that we know where he'll be, and when—well, use your conscience as a guide, Joe."

"Thanks, Asa. Thank you." Treadwell pumped the captain's hand and rushed off to prepare for a scout. A long one, if necessary.

The snowy ground had been churned by dozens of ponies. Treadwell wanted to circle and find the direction Manuelito had approached the Zuñi pueblo from but knew there was no time. The parley had to start on time or Manuelito might fade back into the rocky maze of Cañon de Chelly, never to be found again until he desired another conference.

Herrera Grande dismounted and walked slowly through the frozen mud, bent with age, every step looking as if it might be his last. How the old headman might convince a warrior with fire in his belly, Treadwell did not know. Still, there was a chance he might succeed. The winter had been harsh and Manuelito had nothing to eat, save for hibernating prairie dogs and the odd tubers found growing in his cañon.

Kit Carson had made good his objective of destroying the center of Navajo power with his excursions through Cañon de Chelly.

Treadwell sat ramrod straight in the saddle when he saw Manuelito and a half dozen braves flanking him. They were gaunt to the point of emaciation, but they carried themselves with dignity—and arrogance. They would never be beaten, only killed, Treadwell realized.

Even in death they would remain unconquerable.

"It is good to see my brother again after so many months," Herrera Grande began. "Come, let us sit by a fire and warm ourselves. The winter chews these old bones."

"If it weren't for the north wind, you would not have any breath left," Manuelito said. Treadwell tried to decide if

Manuelito mocked Herrera Grande and could not. The old headman took no offense, if Manuelito had meant to set a barb.

Treadwell remained in the background, listening to the rapid
discussion with only half an ear. The first words from
Manuelito's mouth set the tone for the meeting. No matter how
Herrera Grande sang the praises of the reservation, Manuelito
would have none of it.

"You have no hope left," Herrera Grande said. "Life is not
so bad at Hwééldi, at Bosque Redondo. Leave your pitiful life
behind and join us. It is the only way the Biligáana will ever
stop this fight. You must surrender to save what remains of your
clan. There is no other way."

"My god and my mother lived in Dinetah," Manuelito said
stiffly, "and I will not leave them. The Biligáana prison you
call Bosque Redondo is not for us. To go to Hwééldi is a death
sentence."

Treadwell slipped from the circle of warmth cast by the fire
and went to his horse. Tracking in the twilight would be difficult, but his skills would serve him well. He might never get
another chance to find Manuelito's camp—and Goes to War.

The confab broke up, Manuelito refusing to leave his home
and Herrera Grande pleading with him to reconsider. The
pounding of hooves told Treadwell to get on his way. He rode
in a wide circle, intent on finding Manuelito's tracks away from
the Zuñi pueblo.

Manuelito headed away from Deer Springs, then angled to
the north and east. Treadwell had to drop from horseback several
times to be certain he followed the proper spoor. When the stars
came out and lit the snowy landscape almost as if a new sun
had risen, he made faster time. He wanted to rush along after
Manuelito but knew better. Manuelito had survived thus far
because of a combination of daring and caution. Few of the
other Navajo headmen mixed the two with as much success as
Hastiin Ch'ilhaajinii, Man of the Black Plants Place. After all
this time, Treadwell knew him better than he'd ever known his
own family.

Wary of Manuelito doubling back to see if any trailed him, Treadwell continued his tracking until dawn, when he saw Manuelito had stopped to rest. Wearily, Treadwell tumbled from the saddle and fixed himself a spartan breakfast of jerky and trail biscuits. A scoop of snow melted to water finished the meal for him in time to start after Manuelito again.

Treadwell saw that Manuelito rode directly for Cañon de Chelly, never veering from a direct route. He worried the headman knew he was being followed and led his pursuer into a trap. Then Treadwell realized it did not matter to Manuelito. He knew whoever might follow did not have a company of soldiers with him. The brutal winter forced most of the troopers to stay close to their posts.

Joseph Treadwell rode once more into the rocky redoubt, alone and determined.

"Will you ever stop, you red-skinned bastard?" Treadwell shivered and hugged himself. How Manuelito with only a blanket draped around his shoulders held back the cold, Treadwell did not know. He had followed Manuelito for almost a week through the twists and turns of the cañon, with no end of travel in sight. He needed to light a fire but found little firewood—and dared not do so for fear of alerting the Navajo of his presence.

Treadwell used every trick he had ever learned to stay hidden from prying eyes. Even then, he worried a sentry along the three-hundred-foot cañon rim might have spotted him as an intruder and signaled Manuelito. The cunning war chief might be leading him on a wild goose chase before lifting his scalp.

Past caring about himself, Treadwell wanted only for the chase to end so he could see his son. Gray Feather had died, following Shining Eyes to a better land. He wanted his only flesh and blood with him and would do anything to achieve that end.

Finishing a simple meal, Treadwell buried the airtight the peaches had come in and mounted for another few hours of tracking through the boundless cañon of red rock. To his surprise, Manuelito had ridden only a mile beyond. Four hogans showed puffs of smoke billowing from their chimneys. A small flock of sheep nibbled at grass long since overgrazed. A few horses stood in a simple log corral and two dozen head of cattle lowed against the indignity of having to nose through a crust of snow to find their own fodder.

"Which is your hogan, Manuelito?" Treadwell asked himself through chapped lips. He pulled his jacket tighter around his shoulders and rubbed his hands to warm them. He could never fight his way free; subterfuge had to rule this day. But Treadwell was not going to leave without Goes to War, and if he had to fire his musket he wanted supple fingers on the stock and trigger.

He rode to the shelter of a copse of juniper and dismounted, knowing he had to study the narrow valley carefully to identify Manuelito's hogan before proceeding. When it darkened, he could slip down and steal away with his son, if he could identify him. A tear formed and turned icy on Treadwell's cheek when he realized he did not even know what Goes to War looked like.

"I'll find you, Son. I promise on your mother's grave, I will find you." Treadwell's fists clenched again as he made the solemn promise. He had never been able to discover where Gray Feather had been buried. At every turn Blakeney had thwarted him, even on such a small detail. Those dying on the trip to Bosque Redondo had been buried with no marker on their graves. Those dying before the caravan left were buried in a mass unmarked grave.

Twilight came soon and gave Treadwell the chance to move into the Navajo village. The first hogan was abandoned and he moved past it on feet as light as falling snow. The second had a small thread of white smoke rising from the chimney—Manuelito's. He had seen the headman enter and leave this hogan several times before nightfall.

Treadwell froze when a small child came running from the hogan, followed by a boy of perhaps thirteen. At first Treadwell could not see the youth's face because of deep shadow. Then the boy turned and looked squarely at Treadwell.

"Shining Eyes!" Treadwell cried. "You're alive!"

The boy's hand flashed to the knife at his belt. He drew the wicked blade and grabbed the small boy, pushing him to one side.

"Shining Eyes, it's me, your father. Joe Treadwell." Treadwell walked forward in a daze. The shock of seeing the son he thought to be dead addled his brain.

"Get back," Shining Eyes snarled. His knife slashed the air in front of him in a practiced way that would gut anyone foolish enough to come too close.

"You don't recognize me," Treadwell said in horror. "I'm your father. You were stolen away four years ago. I—"

"Back!" Shining Eyes advanced, ready to fight. He put himself between Treadwell and the young boy. This move shook Treadwell into another realization.

"Goes to War. That's Goes to War, your brother. My son. My *sons!* Don't you know me?"

A quiet voice shook Treadwell to the core of his being. Manuelito emerged from the hogan and said, "He knows you. He has seen you before, since he became Navajo."

Treadwell lifted his musket, then lowered it when he saw that Shining Eyes moved to protect not only Goes to War but Manuelito with his own gaunt body. He lowered his rifle, not sure what to do. He could not fight his own son.

"I thought you were dead. I found a body wrapped in your blanket, with a Ute doll."

"That was another who died—my brother-in-law," Shining Eyes said.

Treadwell found himself at a loss for words.

"He is no longer a boy. He is a man, a warrior." Manuelito spoke with the mixture of pride and regret that any father might use to describe a son moving through life.

"You stole him away. Him and Gray Feather." Treadwell fell back on the hot emotions that had driven him so long.

"The way you speak tells me Gray Feather is gone." Manuelito towered above Treadwell. "I feel new sorrow. I feared she might have died when Herrera Grande could not remember her arrival at Hwééldi—at Bosque Redondo. She was so sick even our best singer could not drive away the evil inhabiting her."

Treadwell said nothing. Manuelito fixed him with a pair of eyes welling over with unshed tears.

"I hoped—futilely, it seems—that your medicine men might allow her again to walk in beauty."

"She died of pneumonia before reaching Bosque Redondo," Treadwell said. He could not put into words his hatred of the man consigning her to such a death. But surprise grew in Treadwell's breast when he realized that man was Major Blakeney and not Manuelito.

"Many did not survive the Long Walk," Manuelito said.

"The Long Walk," parroted Treadwell. It seemed appropriate of the relocation from their homeland to the reservation. *The Long Walk*. The name rang in his ears like an echo that refused to die.

"Come into my wife's hogan," offered Manuelito. "We have much in common."

Treadwell glanced at Shining Eyes. Tears did flow now when the boy did not relax. He swiped the air with his knife. Treadwell wondered how many lives had been taken by that keen-edged blade, then decided he was better not knowing.

"My son, he is to be our guest."

"He tried to kill us! I heard him at the campfire that night!" Shining Eyes's anger boiled over.

"He is your father, as I am your father," said Manuelito.

"No! You are my father! My *only* father!" This denunciation cut Treadwell deeper than the boy's knife ever could. He almost wished Shining Eyes would step forward and drive the blade to the hilt in his chest. The end would be less painful than losing his son forever to the Navajo.

"Join us in our meal," urged Manuelito. "You need not fear us."

Treadwell laughed scornfully at that. Then his laughter died, and he followed Manuelito into the hogan, followed by his two sons. Or were they his lost sons?

A young girl placed food in front of him. Treadwell ate mechanically, his eyes on the two boys who kept their eyes averted in Navajo fashion. Treadwell noted how close Shining Eyes sat to the young girl—his wife? It was not polite to stare, yet Treadwell could not help himself. Goes to War looked so much like his mother! And Shining Eyes was grown into a fine young man, whip-thin, but otherwise healthy enough. He had so much to tell them, and yet he sat as a guest—a stranger—as he ate with them.

"I loved Gray Feather," Manuelito said simply. Treadwell started to protest, then held his tongue. "I married her in proper ceremony, and I mourn her leaving. If it had been possible, she would have gone with us as we fled. It was not." Manuelito ate a few mouthfuls and continued. "I knew better but hoped she might find strong medicines with your people."

"I did all I could to save her. I thought she was being sent to Bosque Redondo, but she died." Treadwell was drained as he relived every moment of his search for her. "I loved her, too. I wish you had never stolen her away."

"The Ute enslaved many of my people," Manuelito answered after a long silence. "The Dinéh accepted Gray Feather and Shining Eyes as if they had been born into my clan, the Folded Arms People. They were never treated harshly, as slaves, as anything other than equals."

Treadwell read the truth of Manuelito's words in Shining Eyes's face.

"It is not good to hate so fiercely," Treadwell said, his words directed toward his son.

"You slaughter us, you destroy our farms and flocks. You starve us and freeze us to death!" Shining Eyes's hand went to his knife, then he subsided, seething with rage. The girl whispered to him. This settled him a mite.

"If you come to add to Herrera Grande's words, I will not listen. We will not go to Hwééldi," Manuelito said. "My son's anger is righteous and matches my own."

"I came for my sons. I buried a boy I thought was Shining Eyes, and only after did I learn of Goes to War." Treadwell smiled in the young boy's direction. The four-year-old boldly stared at him, then averted his eyes. Already he learned Navajo ways.

Treadwell sighed. And why not? Goes to War had been born among the Navajo and knew nothing else.

"You would give your life to see your sons again?"

"Yes, I would. I hoped to take them back with me, to save them from starvation and cold. General Carleton will never stop his war against the Navajo until you are all at Bosque Redondo. I want them safe from any new expedition into Cañon de Chelly."

"And I will never walk the banks of the Rio Pecos, calling Hwééldi my home. This is my home. These cañons will once again ring with the joyous sings of the Blessing Way, the frolicking and fun of racing fine horses, the laughter of fat children walking in harmony. No one will force me from my holy homelands."

Treadwell sat for a spell, his mind turning over everything Manuelito had said. Deep down, he knew the Ute had caused the raid Manuelito had led four years back. If they had not sent their warriors south to find slaves, Manuelito would never have come north to try to rescue those of his clan stolen away. That did nothing to ease the pain of losing Gray Feather and Shining Eyes—his wife permanently to the cold ground in an unmarked and unsanctified grave.

"I want only to be with my sons," Treadwell said, his words filling the silence. The crackle of the fire and soft whistle of wind through chinks in the mud walls vied for his attention. But he saw that Manuelito hung on his every word. "They will surely die if they stay with you. Let them return with me where they can be fed and clothed, where they will be safe."

"No! I would die first!" Shining Eyes jumped to his feet. His knife again slid from its sheath. "I will not abandon you, Father. I would rather die at your side than to be imprisoned like a slave at Hwééldi! Looking Arrow and I will die first!"

"They won't go to Bosque Redondo," Treadwell promised Manuelito. "Carleton will never know they've come with me. We can go back north, to be with their mother's people."

"Nota-a!" Shining Eyes spat the word as if it were a curse. "I was born among them, but I became a man with the Dinéh! I am Dinéh now, and will die Dinéh!"

"If they come with me, they will never go to Bosque Redondo. I swear on Gray Feather's blessed soul," promised Treadwell. "We need not live with the Ute, either. There are any number of places we could go. Santa Fé, or perhaps to the west." Treadwell fell silent when he saw a curtain of worry draw over Manuelito's face. He let the headman take all the time he needed to consider the fate of his adoptive sons.

"Is your word good?" asked Manuelito. "You will never permit them to go to Hwééldi?"

"I've seen the place. It's a hellhole," Treadwell replied. "They are my sons. Never will they be sent there unless it is over my dying body."

"No, I—" Shining Eyes was silenced by Manuelito's chopping hand gesture.

"Long have I known the Great White Father will never stop sending his droves of bluecoats to kill us. Red Clothes burned our trees and crops and blankets. Many suffered and froze. Others died going to Hwééldi. We suffer now. It will only get worse."

"It will. I can do nothing to stop General Carleton and his fever dream for your people." Treadwell felt almost sorry for the fate of the Navajo.

Goes to War began coughing. The boy wiped his nose, but the coughing refused to stop. Manuelito placed a hand on the boy's back. Treadwell saw determination push back the curtain of contemplation that had held Manuelito for the past few minutes.

"My sons—our sons—will go with you. It will mean your blood if you send them to the reservation," Manuelito warned.

"I will die before they go there."

"No, no, Father. You cannot send me with him. He has killed many of our clan. His heart is filled with hatred and he does not walk in beauty. I am a man, a blooded warrior. I will not be sent away like a child!" Shining Eyes backed away, pushing Looking Arrow behind.

"He is known as Angry Knife because of his temper and resolute behavior," Manuelito said with some pride. "He is right. I can no longer decide for him. He is a man, an equal in our clan, and wed to Looking Arrow. If he wishes to go with you, so be it. If he decides to stay, not even your entire army of soldiers can prevent it."

Treadwell's eyes welled with tears again. He had thought Shining Eyes was dead and had worked to accept it. Seeing him alive rekindled old emotions. But he could not force his son—this man—to a path not agreeable with him and the girl—so young—Shining Eyes's wife.

"Goes to War will come with me?" Treadwell asked.

"Father, you send my brother to live with the enemy!"

"He weakens daily. He has fallen ill, and our singers cannot cure him," Manuelito said. "We cannot even feed him properly."

"I can care for him!" Looking Arrow spoke for the first time.

"Better to die Dinéh than to become Biligáana!" This from Shining Eyes.

"Shining Eyes is a fierce warrior," Manuelito declared. "Looking Arrow is a devoted wife and daughter-in-law. It is his will that he stay, with his wife beside him. So be it. Goes to War is my son, and it is my will that he go with you."

"Goes to War is my son, and I will protect him with my life," Treadwell said. "What can I do for you, for Shining Eyes and his wife?"

"Nothing."

There seemed nothing more to say. He had found and lost one son, and had gained another he had never before set eyes on. Mixed with his joy came fear that he might never again see Shining Eyes, a youth who hated him and refused to acknowledge him as his father, or Looking Arrow, his daughter-in-law. It was not entirely satisfactory, but Joseph Treadwell knew half a loaf was better than none at all. He had found Goes to War but not Shining Eyes.

If only things had been different . . .

Adamantine

The skeleton danced closer, taunting him. A fleshless white finger pointed at him and accused him of terrible crimes, of murder, of arson and worse. Treadwell struggled, fighting to keep the bones away. *Chindi* threatened him with ghost sickness and other graves behind the cavorting skeleton opened cavernous mouths. He tried to scream, to run or fight. He could not move a single muscle. His body paralyzed, Treadwell could only scream.

He sat bolt upright in bed, his heart racing, sweat drenching him. Treadwell wiped his face and tried to push the image of Shining Eyes's body rising from the dead out of his mind.

"He's alive, he didn't die. He's with Manuelito," he told himself over and over until his fright passed. The nightmares increased, the longer he stayed in Santa Fé. Treadwell took this as a message of what he had to do.

Pushing from the bed, his bare feet touched the cold Spanish tile floor. Shivering, he pulled a blanket around his shoulders and padded softly to the next room. Goes to War slept peacefully in his trundle bed. Since arriving in Santa Fé and finding a nurse, the boy had filled out and looked positively angelic. His cough had diminished and the doctors Treadwell had paraded through the house to examine the boy had all pronounced him fit as a fiddle.

He would have been dead if Manuelito had not allowed him to return with Treadwell. And the mountain man could only wonder how Shining Eyes fared—how Shining Eyes and his wife fared. Treadwell had great difficulty thinking of his boy as being married. Reports of the Navajo Campaign were sketchy since Treadwell had abandoned his position as scout at Fort Canby. All he read in the newspaper had James Carleton's stamp on it with glowing words of repeated, stunning victories against the Navajo.

Try as he might, Treadwell found no word of Manuelito's capture in any newspaper. Only with the capture of the headman of the Folded Arms People would victory be assured. Nothing less would mark Carleton's triumph.

Treadwell went to the small bed and laid his hand on Goes to War's head. The boy stirred, murmured quietly, and clutched at a Two Gray Hills blanket for comfort, pulling it tightly to his cheek. Treadwell pulled the covers up over him and silently left the room to sit by the embers of the fire in his own bedroom. Closing his eyes, he wished life had taken different turns. If only Gray Feather were here to see how her son grew!

If only Shining Eyes were here. Who was Looking Arrow? Treadwell wanted to know who had married his son. A pain came to Treadwell's chest, and he pushed himself to a full sitting position. He had spent too much time chasing Manuelito and the other guerrillas fighting against Carleton's settlement plans. He reached for the *Las Vegas Optic* and held the paper up to better illuminate the general's words:

In their appointed time He wills that one race of men—as in the races of lower animals—shall disappear off the face of the earth and give place to another race, and so on in the Great Cycle traced out by Himself, which may be seen, but has reasons too deep to be fathomed by us. The races of the mammoths and Mastodons, and great Sloths, came and passed away: the Red Man of America is passing away!

Treadwell folded the paper over his lap and leaned back to consider Carleton's progress in removing the Indian from his homeland and civilizing him. Sleep crept up on him before he worked over the ideas in his head.

"Look after him real good now," Treadwell cautioned the nurse. The Mexican woman bobbed her head.

"He is a good boy."

"You keep on with his lessons while I'm gone. I want to be back soon, but this might take a day or more. Teach him all the Spanish and English you can."

"*Sí*, I will."

"Good, good," Treadwell said, already distracted by his ride into town. He left nurse and son and rode slowly toward Santa Fé and General Carleton. He had petitioned the territorial military commander for an audience weeks ago, immediately after recovering Goes to War, but the gears turned slowly at Carleton's headquarters.

Just off the plaza, Treadwell dismounted and went into the adobe building where Carleton held court. This was the only way Treadwell could describe it. Carleton never talked, he preached. He struck a pose and launched into long-winded speeches. Treadwell had decided the time was over for such high-flown words; actions counted more now.

"Joseph Treadwell to see the general," he told the orderly in Carleton's outer office.

"General Carleton will see you in a few minutes," the lieutenant said. "He's almost finished talking to the reporters."

Treadwell looked around for a chair and found none. He stood to one side of the room so he could look into the courtyard, where a half dozen men vied with each other to capture the general's words for their newspapers. Treadwell tried to make out what was being said, but failed. He shuffled his feet with increasing impatience after the reporters filed out, mumbling to themselves or trying to catch a quick look at another's notes.

"Think he's ready for me now?" Treadwell asked, after ten minutes had passed.

"When he's ready, he will see you."

"To hell with that," declared Treadwell. He got past the lieutenant before the officer could stop him. Marching purposefully, he stopped in front of Carleton's huge desk. The general looked up, startled. For a moment Treadwell wondered if the man even recognized him.

"Mr. Treadwell, what a pleasure. I was not aware you had returned from Fort Canby."

"Glad you remember me, General. That makes matters a bit easier."

"What matter might this be, sir?" Carleton motioned to his aide to leave. Treadwell saw that there wasn't a chair in front of the general's desk, either. Any visitor had to stand in Carleton's august presence.

"Reckon you might have figured that out," Treadwell said. "I spent the better part of four years wanting Manuelito's scalp."

"A worthy pursuit. He is a red devil."

"He's nothing more than a man trying to hang on to his own land, General. He's no devil. He's no saint, either."

"Are you pleading his case? You need only accept his surrender and repatriation to Bosque Redondo and all his crimes will be forgotten. I will put that in writing."

Treadwell blinked. Visions of dead Navajo, frozen and starved and diseased, flashed in front of his eyes. Nowhere in that fleeting glimpse of the past did he see Manuelito responsible for such vile crimes against the white man.

"Colonel Carson, on your orders, burned his orchards, destroyed his crops, slaughtered his sheep and cattle. He's out there starving in the cold."

"All the more reason to stop being pigheaded and come to the reservation."

"There's no opportunity at the Bosque," Treadwell said. "You've started issuing ration cards because the men in charge of the commissary are stealing from the supplies promised the Navajo. The Indians are as hungry on your reservation as they would be out in Cañon de Chelly, their holy ground."

"I dispute that claim, sir. What is it you want?" Carleton drew himself up ramrod stiff and glared at Treadwell.

"General, I thought I buried my son out there. You can't know what that felt like, me digging a shallow grave with my bare hands in the cold ground. Turns out he's still alive, but his mother died on the way to Bosque Redondo along with who knows how many others."

"A few might have died, but they were ill when they began the trek."

"The Long Walk, General, that's what the Navajo call it. The Long Walk."

"How colorful, but then, they are a colorful people. Not a single soldier killed a ward on those trips."

"Maybe not, but none did squat to help any Navajo falling behind. The sick and the weak died by the hundreds getting to Bosque Redondo. And now that they're there, you're still starving them into submission."

"I repeat, Mr. Treadwell, what do you want from me? To abandon the noble experiment? I will not. The Indians are being assimilated into civilized society. They are being taught how to farm and get along with their fellow man. It is Manuelito who resists change and causes dispute."

"I know you and Carson think this is a good idea, but you turned them into sitting ducks. I even heard the colonel say he can't help but pity them because they'll be wiped out soon enough."

"You are referring to the Comanche and Apache raids. Our soldiers have been instructed to take appropriate measures to protect the Navajo. As with any new venture, it takes a while to settle the details."

"The deadly details," Treadwell said, seeing he was getting nowhere. He wondered why he had bothered.

"You and Doctor Steck share similar sentiments. However, those sentiments are wrongheaded. No, let me say only that they are misplaced. The Indians are being swept away by the tide of our civilization, and it is our duty to help them in whatever way we can. We know what is best for them. We are the standard bearers of culture and Christianity."

"My wife's been swept away in that tide, General I've lost one son and his wife to it and danged near lost the other. Change your policy. Let them go home."

"Never!"

The general's adamant reply told Treadwell he was never going to batter down the barricades of faith, He had marshalled the best arguments he could and now realized they were frail against Carleton's vision. Treadwell was right, but that didn't matter. He left the office, hoping only that he could figure out a path that would reunite him with Shining Eyes and give him a chance to know a daughter-in-law.

Somehow, it didn't seem likely, and that burned as fiercely in him as a flaming arrow.

Defeat

"They cannot find us," Shining Eyes said with satisfaction. "We have kept them from finding us for more than two weeks." The thirteen-year-old sat straight on the pony's back. The horse pranced under him, a good horse stolen from the Biligáana. Shining Eyes had crept into Fort Wingate and then walked boldly to the corral. He had chosen carefully, thrown a blanket over the horse, and then ridden away without a single sentry noticing. His only regret was not bringing out more horses.

They were so lazy and oblivious, the Biligáana.

But how did they continue to wear down Manuelito's band? Shining Eyes tried to remember spending more than a few days at any camp. The traditional ranges within Cañon de Chelly were continually burned, and any animal was slaughtered. Even the most secure reaches of the cañon occasionally trembled under the fire of the bluecoats' powerful new repeating rifles. Only constant vigilance kept more of the Dinéh from being caught.

A smile danced on Shining Eyes's lips when he reflected on how successful they had been. Manuelito's band had not suffered a single casualty to the Biligáana soldiers over the past four months from hunger and exposure. He was a master at anticipating troop movement. The smile faded when Shining Eyes remembered how many had died during those cruel months. Winter never got easier to endure with no crops grown during the spring and summer and no flocks of any size grazing in Dinetah.

And then there were the other enemies. The Biligáana fought shadows. The Pueblos and the Ute killed shadows.

"We should take a few of their mules," Manuelito said, rubbing his chin stubble. "They do not treat them properly, and we can use them to pull the supply wagons." He inclined his head in the direction of two horseless wagons they had found and loaded with captured supplies. More than fifty of the Folded Arms People gathered.

"The roads are muddy," Shining Eyes said. "The sun melts the snow. We ought to find rockier country."

"The wagons are of no importance," Manuelito decided. "Still, having pack animals would be a boon. The women tire, moving so often."

Shining Eyes said nothing. Looking Arrow's health remained fragile, and a steady diet of little more than piñon nuts and mountain potatoes did little to strengthen her. He jerked up when he heard a yelp and saw a scout running toward him, slipping and sliding on the snowy ground.

"Ahead," he panted. "Do we attack now?"

Capturing supplies was the easiest way of attracting notice. The thought made Shining Eyes fall silent. He had not done well recently, scouting long distances for Manuelito and finding nothing. Looking Arrow had traveled deeper into Tseyi' with her clan. Shining Eyes wished he had a gift for her, a real one and not simply tidbits left over from battle. He turned covetous eyes to one wagon. An entire wagon of supplies for Looking Arrow and her relatives would be a gift both needed and appreciated greatly.

Shining Eyes would rise even more in her estimation.

He let out a sigh and shook his head. They had foraged for almost a week and found barely enough to keep them all alive. The supplies Manuelito had secreted around Dinetah years ago were exhausted. Shining Eyes puffed out his chest and vowed to do better.

"We will find great riches," he told Manuelito. The man nodded solemnly.

"Go to Looking Arrow and see how she is feeling," Manuelito said. "The Biligáana are far away from here." He moved restlessly on his horse. Shining Eyes saw the motion and wondered.

"What is wrong?"

"A feeling, not even a vision, but a feeling," Manuelito said. "When you have spoken with your wife, go on a scout to the north."

"What is north?" asked Shining Eyes. "There is no way for the Biligáana to come upon us."

"Not the Biligáana," Manuelito said. "Never mind now. Go to Looking Arrow and comfort her. I will ride in that direction. Join me when you can."

"Be careful, Father," said Shining Eyes, unsure of himself. "I *did* have a vision."

"What was it?"

"Fire. Everywhere was fire. All around us." Shining Eyes sat on the cold ground and made his pronouncements as an old headman might.

"I will look for fire," Manuelito said, not gainsaying his son.

"And arrows. From places you do not see." Shining Eyes gaped at this, as if the words slipped from his mouth and they horrified him.

"Go to your wife," urged Manuelito. Shining Eyes grabbed the reins trailing from his horse. Manuelito rode away slowly to the north, summoning others to join his scouting mission. Shining Eyes chafed at the delay, but he knew he had to be sure his wife was comfortable before all else. She might be with child.

An hour's ride brought Shining Eyes to the tent strung into a lean-to from a low piñon branch. Looking Arrow lay on a stack of Army blankets Manuelito had stolen from a supply

train early in October. They had meant the difference between
life and death throughout the winter.

"I worried," Looking Arrow said, sitting up. She wobbled
slightly as dizziness seized her.

"Manuelito has gone on a scout to the north and wanted me
to be sure you had enough food."

"There is enough," Looking Arrow said. Shining Eyes tried
to remember hearing her complain and could not. She was
Dinéh, enduring hardship and striving to walk in beauty.

"Something bothers you," Shining Eyes said. "Are you ill
again?"

"No, no," she denied. "I had another vision. We should be
ready to travel fast and far. Soon," she added, her young face
etched with the endless pain of suffering.

"You worry too much," Shining Eyes said, trying to brighten
his wife's spirits. "Settle down, and I will be back in time for
a meal at sunset." He saw that the small packet of food would
be ample for them and Manuelito, should the headman choose
to join them. Shining Eyes was not sure where Juanita camped.
Possibly with another twenty of the clan down the rim of the
mesa.

Shining Eyes spun when he heard the hard pounding of
hooves. He touched the hilt of his knife, then grabbed for his
bow and arrows.

"What is it?" Looking Arrow demanded. "Manuelito!"

"I see him," Shining Eyes said, swinging onto horseback.
"Do not worry. Get ready to move camp. I'll be back when I
can." Shining Eyes put things into a sack, spilling as many as
he stuck in. He put his heels to his mount and raced through
the camp. Manuelito would never return like this unless some
danger presented itself.

"Ute!" went up the cry, an instant before arrows arched down
into the camp. Shining Eyes bent low and kept his horse galloping
until he reached a small area of tumbled lava rocks where
Manuelito and four others made their stand. Manuelito's musket

barked. Shining Eyes thought he saw a Ute warrior sink back into the underbrush but could not be sure.

"They laid a trap for us," Manuelito said, working to reload. Shining Eyes remembered how the headman had once chided Follows Quickly for use of the musket. Now he preferred it to his own bow and arrow.

"How many?" asked Shining Eyes, studying the silent terrain dotted with patches of white snow. The rocky areas between might conceal a clever warrior. As the thought crossed his mind, Shining Eyes drew back the bowstring and let the arrow fly. It drove deeply into the thigh of a Ute covered with mud and working his way to a tumble of rocks fifty feet away.

"Enough," Manuelito said. "Too many. They closed their trap too soon. They might have worried that we led a larger band and thought to snare only us." Manuelito fired again. And again Shining Eyes wondered if the bullet hit anything as it tore through the sparse underbrush of a stand of pines fifty yards away.

He slipped away and circled, only to find the Ute had the same idea. Shining Eyes fired almost point-blank into the chest of a man twice his size. The Ute's eyes went wide in surprise and pain, then he let out a screech that shattered the silence. Shining Eyes rushed forward, knife slashing, but the keen edge found only dead flesh as he raked it over the fallen man's throat.

Looking up, Shining Eyes tried to count the attackers. He retrieved his bow and let fly another arrow into the thicket where Manuelito concentrated his musket fire. The arrow caused a sharp outcry—but of incredulity, not pain. The Ute had not expected to be attacked from this direction.

As he nocked another arrow, Shining Eyes noticed the ground wavering and retreating. He lowered his sights and drove a steel-headed arrow into another Ute as he tried to slip out of the mud and back to cover. Others rose and ran, drawing fire from Manuelito and the others. Within minutes horses' hooves pounded.

"They have gone to find easier prey," Manuelito said, as he stood beside the warrior Shining Eyes had killed. "Times are hard.

The Ute don't steal much for us to take off their dead bodies."
He kicked at the fallen man and rolled him over. Shining Eyes
stared at the corpse without emotion: Capote Ute, to judge by
the war paint, a distant relative—but no longer. An enemy to
be plundered in death. Shining Eyes claimed the beaded belt
and pouch, throwing out the useless religious articles. His own
pouch carried corn pollen and a piece of turquoise. He balanced
a knife and decided to keep it.

"I don't want anything more," Shining Eyes said, disdaining
the moccasins and blanket drawn tightly around the Ute's well-
muscled body. This one had no trouble finding food, Shining
Eyes thought bitterly.

Now he would be food for the ants and worms.

"Let the coyotes dine on him," Manuelito said, as if reading
his son's thoughts.

They made a quick search of the area to be sure the Ute had
retreated. Then they went into the camp and found Looking
Arrow already packed and ready to travel.

"We drove them off," Manuelito said, "but you do well to
prepare as you do. We should join the others at the base of the
mesa. The Ute would never attack a band of seventy or more."

"We're ready," Looking Arrow said, no hint of tiredness in
her voice.

"We can be down the trail two miles before sundown,"
Manuelito said, helping get their horses ready. Looking Arrow
rode with supplies slung behind.

"That way," Manuelito said, picking a way through the trees
and down a trail so faint Shining Eyes had to blink twice to see
it. He rode behind his wife while Manuelito led. All around the
others struck camp and walked and rode down. Shining Eyes
was loath to leave them behind, but they could not spare horses
to pull the bulky, balky wagons.

Shining Eyes coursed from one side to the other to be sure the
Ute left them alone. He no longer thought of such a forced movement as retreat, merely as a moving on. It had been too long since

he had slept in a hogan not to consider the stars more a roof than one caulked with mud and covered with tree branches.

Falling into a stupor, Shining Eyes rode along. Lulled by the gentle sway of his horse, Shining Eyes failed to see the first flash from a musket. A second, third, and tenth sounded. By now he saw the foot-long tongues of flame leaping from both sides. And accompanying the harsh roar of the rifles came the familiar swish of arrows.

"Hopi!" called Manuelito from ahead. "Hopi!"

"That way," urged Shining Eyes, getting Looking Arrow moving to the left. If Manuelito drew fire from both sides, they might slip around the ambush and continue down the steep trail off the mesa. He did not stay to see if they were safe. He let out a yell of outrage and fear when he saw Manuelito tumble from his horse.

"No!" shrieked Shining Eyes, putting heels to his horse's flanks. "No!" Hopi arrows flew around him as he dashed through the middle of the fight. A lance flew. Shining Eyes threw up his arm and deflected it even as it knocked him from his horse. He hit the ground hard and lay stunned. More flashes blazed through the twilight and confused him as he gasped for breath.

Rolling onto his side on the fragrant pine needle carpet, he saw Manuelito a dozen paces away.

"Father!" he called. Shining Eyes forced his knees under him, only to be bowled over as a Hopi swung the butt of his musket and caught him on the side of the head. Shining Eyes rolled and lay still. From half closed eyes he saw moccasined feet approaching. Summoning all his strength, he rocketed upward, his arms going around exposed legs.

His insignificant weight was overshadowed by the force of his attack. He knocked the Hopi warrior back and sent him toppling to the ground. The instant of surprise in his foe let Shining Eyes whip out his knife and drive it into an exposed chest. For the second time today he killed. The first had been a relative. Now he killed a Hopi.

Shining Eyes whipped around, droplets of blood flying off

his knife blade. The fight had moved through the stand of trees, going downhill as the Dinéh fled. Shining Eyes heard sounds of flight in all directions. The ambush had taken everyone by surprise and scattered the clan.

On hands and knees, Shining Eyes made his way to Manuelito's side.

"Father!" Shining Eyes touched the arrow that had gone entirely through Manuelito's left arm and into his body. "Father, tell me what to do!"

Shining Eyes held the still body in his slight arms. Manuelito gave no answer to the frantic importuning.

Again, a father had abandoned Shining Eyes.

The Long Walk Continues

September 1, 1866
Fort Wingate

"They send out patrols to flank us," Shining Eyes said nervously. He watched as the soldiers swung wide in a pincer that could cut off any retreat. He closed his eyes as he hobbled along, his leg throbbing painfully. The deep cut sustained when he fell from his horse, the pony cut out from under him by a Nakai slaving party, had not healed in two months. Only continual application of ground herbs had kept the leg from swelling beyond endurance. As it was, every step sent waves of misery into his thigh and hip.

Or was it his leg that hurt at all? Shining Eyes closed his eyes again, counting those around him. Twenty-two others. All that remained after so many years of dodging the Biligáana bluecoats. His pain came from the soul as much as from his leg.

The thudding of hooves caused him to open his eyes. Four soldiers approached cautiously, hands resting on their pistols but leaving them undrawn . . . for the moment. Shining Eyes saw the officers' tenseness. Any movement on their part and a heavy cavalry pistol would swing out and fire a single shot that would bring soldiers galloping in from both flanks. No one would survive.

Just as no one could survive in Dinetah. Autumn brought silver to the aspens. Caught in sunlight, the leaves shimmered like rivers of silver high above his head. But with such whispering, sighing beauty came a chill that refused to go away. Autumn would eventually turn to winter—and death.

"You comin' in to give up?" bellowed the officer, from what he thought was a safe distance. Shining Eyes gauged the land, noted how the puffs of wind might deflect an arrow, and knew the officer should die with one of his arrows buried in his chest.

He would have, too, if Shining Eyes had any arrows left. The last two had been spent trying to bring down a doe. One arrow broke against a tree trunk; the doe had leaped away with the other arrow stuck in its hindquarters. Shining Eyes had been unable to run the deer down and retrieve either arrow or meat. From the spoor, the doe had been only slightly wounded and might have put up a fight if he had caught it.

All history. All past. His belly grumbled and his hands shook badly now. Only his vision remained clear.

"We would parley," came a weak voice from Shining Eyes's right. "Are you in command?"

"Reckon so." The officer allowed his horse a few crow hops closer. "Who be you?"

"Manuelito," came the weak voice. Shining Eyes heard the attempt to put defiance in that simple reply. The once strong, commanding voice quavered and broke. Shining Eyes dropped to one knee and helped Manuelito sit up on the litter borne by the only horse in their possession. His left arm had turned to raw meat in spite of the application of the same herbs that helped Shining Eyes's leg.

"Don't go lyin' to me. Manuelito's dead. Has been for six months."

"I am Manuelito," the Dinéh headman said, struggling with his injured left arm. It hung limp at his side, bulky from the rags around the wound.

The officer—Shining Eyes saw the golden bars of a lieutenant—rode closer and peered into the sun to get a better view of the man surrendering to him.

"I'll be switched," the cavalry officer said. "You look the world like him. Heard tell you'd died. Hell, your death was reported to General Carleton months ago."

"There was some dancing in the streets of Santa Fé," piped up the soldier right behind the officer. "We all got an extra ration of coffee that day."

Shining Eyes noted the sarcasm in the trooper's voice but said nothing. He had learned to remain impassive and let the waves of emotion wash over him and leave him behind, unscathed.

"Where are your weapons?"

"Gone," Manuelito answered, struggling to get to his feet. Shining Eyes and another warrior had to help support him. "They are gone, with our blankets and horses and other belongings."

"Most of you are buck naked," the lieutenant allowed. "You bucks are buck naked." This produced a small laugh. Shining Eyes did not understand the joke.

"We surrender. All of us, including the warriors," Manuelito said. He stood taller now. "Six warriors and eighteen women and children. We ask only for food and shelter."

"You'll get that—at Bosque Redondo."

Manuelito's head sagged. At the officer's beckoning, Manuelito, Shining Eyes, Looking Arrow, and the others began shuffling toward Fort Wingate. And from there to Fair Carletonia.

Bosque Redondo.

The General's Promise

May 30, 1868
Bosque Redondo

Shining Eyes tried to shift his weight off his stiff leg and failed. He stared straight ahead of him at the dull brown adobe wall, eyes unfocused and mind ranging widely. The pain in his young body slipped away and his thoughts again roamed free.

The rattle of sabers and the clicking of bootheels brought him back to the dingy interior where Manuelito, Barboncito, and twenty-seven other headmen gathered. Most stood or sat cross-legged on the dirt floor. A short table with a half dozen empty chairs dominated the center of the room.

Shining Eyes squinted as Lieutenant General William T. Sherman entered, sunlight flashing off his highly polished sword. Behind him came his assistant, Colonel Samuel Tappan. For two days they had ridden from one side of Hwééldi to another, studying, badgering with their questions and making notes. Shining Eyes had heard the shaggy-haired general's sharp orders and increasing anger. At whom this anger was directed was not obvious, but he had dutifully reported all he had heard to Manuelito and the other headmen.

"Gentleman," Sherman said without hesitation. "I wish to discuss a matter of great importance."

Manuelito nodded slightly. Lips hardly moving, he whispered

to Shining Eyes, "The Coyote Ceremony last night. Its prediction comes true."

"Home?" Shining Eyes hardly believed this. He had not been at the sing, after following the blustery general on his investigations of the reservation. He hardly believed such a prognostication, after being so long imprisoned on these miserable lands, starving from poor crops and getting nothing but curses and occasional gunfire from the soldiers at Fort Sumner. Dinetah? Shining Eyes could not believe it.

Too many times Treadwell had visited and promised it, but Shining Eyes had steeled himself never to believe. His white father had tried and failed to gain his son's release, but Shining Eyes had always refused unless Looking Arrow accompanied him. That had never been possible, due to James Carleton.

But now? Now his will weakened. Shining Eyes wanted to believe.

"I wish to make an offer," Sherman said, eyes raking the gathered headmen. "If you agree to relocation in Indian Territory—"

"No!" Such vehemence rode in Barboncito's reply that the general rocked back, his eyes going wide in surprise. In spite of the impolite outburst, Barboncito continued. "We will never agree to go anywhere but our home."

"Yes, well, I understand that you consider Navajoland to be holy and that it is intertwined with your personal and religious beliefs," said Sherman. "Commissioner Steck has made the point eloquently, although General Carleton has other feelings on this matter."

Barboncito slumped back, his face showing no emotion. They had agreed. Either they returned to Dinetah or they died at Hwééldi. There would be no more Long Walks. The Comanche and Apache reduced their numbers with occasional raids. The crops failed. They had no sheep or cattle. The Lords of New Mexico were no more.

If they could not live in Dinetah, they would die on this reservation.

"I have examined Bosque Redondo for two days and find myself appalled at the conditions," Sherman went on. "Going over reports, I find that Canby might have been correct."

"What of Canby?" asked Barboncito. He, like the others, did not understand the path taken by the general's words.

"He recommended your people be allowed to remain in Navajoland, that this be your reservation." Sherman cleared his throat and accepted a thick sheaf of papers from his aide. "We, Colonel Tappan and I, have been appointed peace commissioners with full authority and responsibility to negotiate this treaty. You will agree never again to engage in war against the United States of America or any of its territories or peoples. In exchange, you will be moved to a new reservation."

Shining Eyes heard Manuelito catch his breath. The headman rubbed his useless left arm in a habitual gesture acquired over long months of pain.

"This new reservation, following the recommendations of General Canby, will comprise what you call Dinetah. Further, after inventory of your possessions, Colonel Tappan and I have determined you would be unable to survive off Bosque Redondo."

The colonel opened a folded sheet and glanced at it. When Sherman nodded, Tappan said, "I have found only 1550 horses, 20 mules, 950 sheep and 1025 goats on this reservation."

"Once we boasted of sixty thousand horses and half a million sheep," Manuelito said softly. "We have lost so much, so very much."

"Once there were more than thirty thousand Dinéh," Shining Eyes said. "There are fewer than seven thousand now."

"We find such provisions unacceptable once you return to Navajoland," Sherman went on. "Accordingly, after discussion with your agent, Colonel Dodd, we have agreed that the United States shall render to you the sum of $150,000 for rehabilitation, an additional fifteen thousand sheep and goats, with five hundred head of cattle supplied as soon as possible. Further, every member of your tribe shall receive the annual payment of five dollars."

"And," went on Tappan, "should any of your tribesmen turn to cultivation of crops in Navajoland, an additional five dollars shall be applied."

"The Gopher argues well for us," Manuelito said, a hint of humor in his voice. "Ten dollars a year! We shall be wealthy men!"

Shining Eyes had never liked Theodore Dodd and had eagerly used the nickname of "Gopher" applied to him by the others. The squinting man bustled about, hiding in his burrow of papers, seldom coming out in the bright light of day. He preferred to remain in his quarters and only appeared after sundown. Still, he argued with the bluecoats at Fort Sumner for them when disputes arose and even carried their requests directly to Santa Fé and General Carleton. Gopher had accomplished for them what their own efforts could not.

"We will return to Dinetah?" asked Barboncito.

"That is our intent and recommendation. Since we have been given far-ranging powers in this matter, there is no question it will be agreed upon in Congress," said Sherman.

"When do we return to Dinetah?"

Sherman exchanged a quick glance with his aide, then turned to Barboncito and in a clear voice said, "There is no reason you cannot return to your new reservation—to Dinetah—within two weeks of signing the treaty."

The Long Walk Home

June 18, 1868
Bosque Redondo

Dawn slid silently like warm honey over the plains to the east. Shining Eyes stared at it, knowing this would be the last sunrise he would ever watch from the accursed Hwééldi. No more disease, no more bluecoats or raids from their enemies. Again the Dinéh would live proudly.

Again they could walk in beauty.

"That's a powerful lot of wagons. Haven't seen that many since me and the the colonel fought at Valverde," Joseph Treadwell said. Beside him stood Goes to War. Shining Eyes bit his lip. That was no longer his brother's name. Joseph Manuel Treadwell. Shining Eyes had not liked it when told, but he recognized the sacrifice his other father had made to rename the boy.

"Only fifty," Shining Eyes said to Treadwell. "They need four companies of cavalry to escort us."

"Maybe they think you might make a break for Dinetah," Treadwell said, trying to keep the words light. He pulled his six-year-old son closer even as Goes to War—Joseph Manuel—tried to run to his brother.

"General Sherman promised us protection from the Ute and Pueblos. And from the Nakai."

"And the Biligáana," Treadwell finished for him. "Son, you have no idea how happy I am to see you returning to y-your land." The small stutter betrayed him. His head might be happy for the Dinéh, but not his heart.

"I miss your mother," Treadwell went on. "I'm worry about all that's happened."

"I am sorry Carson did not live to see this moment," Shining Eyes said. "We return to the land he destroyed."

"He was a good man, Son. His only fault was in lookin' up to the wrong men." Treadwell spat and muttered something about Carleton "Don't think too harshly of us. Any of us."

Shining Eyes squarely faced Treadwell, his thoughts chaotic. This man had done what he could to save Goes to War. The boy had meat on his bones and looked healthy. But Gray Feather was gone. So many others were dead because of him. Shining Eyes took a deep breath and tried to understand Treadwell, tried to understand what lay in his own heart.

"You'd better get goin', Son. There's your wife."

Looking Arrow approached, their two-year-old daughter cradled in her arms. She looked hesitantly at Treadwell, then flashed a small smile. Treadwell had been good to her and the baby, giving them medicine and what food he could. And always he had tried to get them freed from the reservation, only to get the same answer again and again.

Shining Eyes could go; his wife and daughter had to remain behind. Treadwell felt some small pride in his son for remaining with his family. He knew what was real in the world.

Treadwell had done what he could, but nothing could make up for the years of killing and destruction. He hoped Shining Eyes did not judge him too harshly.

"Good luck," Treadwell said, thrusting out his hand. It hung in midair for a moment before Shining Eyes gripped it firmly, then pulled Treadwell to him in a strong embrace. They pushed back, Treadwell hiked Joseph Manuel to his shoulder and it was time to go.

Manuelito and the other headmen rode at the head of the ten-mile column. Each day saw only ten or twelve miles covered, but they did not stop. On July Fourth, they reached Tijeras Cañon. The next day they went through Albuquerque, forded the shallow Rio Grande, and by the end of July reached Fort Wingate. From there it was a short trip to their holy land.

The Dinéh finally returned home.

SMOKE JENSEN
IS
THE MOUNTAIN MAN!

THE MOUNTAIN MAN SERIES
BY WILLIAM W. JOHNSTONE